PRAISE FOR STEPHEN McCAULEY'S

The Easy Way Out

"I have a theory: Stephen McCauley is really the secret love child of Edith Wharton and Woody Allen. How else to explain *THE EASY WAY OUT*, Mr. McCauley's superb second novel? . . . Few writers of either sex can write about women with the same kind of shrewd empathy and insight that seem to come naturally to Mr. McCauley. . . . McCauley's knack for detail, and the way it's applied to the self-delusion of an engaging cast of characters, is what makes *THE EASY WAY OUT* so satisfying. . . . The hugely talented Stephen McCauley has made it look easy."

—*The New York Times Book Review*

"*THE EASY WAY OUT* is the best kind of contemporary fiction. Stephen McCauley captures not only how we live, but how we love, and even how we get through the day. *THE EASY WAY OUT* manages to be miraculously both a joyous and important book."

—*Wendy Wasserstein*

"Delightfully eccentric characters. . . . A gentle, quirky, and very funny novel. . . ."

—*Houston Chronicle*

"McCauley has a good time with his settings, describing them with great visual and psychological accuracy. . . . Droll and astute. . . . Stephen McCauley casts an astute eye on relationships. . . . How easy to take for granted the tremendous technical accomplishment of Stephen McCauley's sparkling fiction."

—*Boston Globe*

A Book-of-the-Month Club Alternate Selection

"McCauley is a writer with near perfect balance; he is as funny as he is smart. He manages to deliver every joke that comes within shouting distance of his characters while never once ignoring or trivializing the complexity of their inner lives."

—*Mirabella*

"McCauley's witty, frequently epigrammatic style . . . is redolent of Oscar Wilde. . . . *THE EASY WAY OUT* is engaging, satisfying . . . appealing."

—*Cleveland Plain Dealer*

"A sweet, sad, and funny novel. . . . full of McCauley's characteristic sly charm and gentle humor."

—*San Francisco Chronicle*

"A daffy, often sage, touchingly wistful tale. . . ."

—*Boston Sunday Herald*

"This beautifully written, heartbreaking book . . . is an eloquent depiction of the compromises lovers and families make to keep relationships alive. . . . Its considerable drama arises from the clever, revealing dialogue and the reader's intense involvement with the sharply drawn characters."

—*Publishers Weekly*

"Funny and painful. . . . *THE EASY WAY OUT* is an engaging novel."

—*Houston Post*

"What a joy it was to curl up with the new McCauley and find it every bit as beguiling as his first. *THE EASY WAY OUT* weaves its way deftly through the tangled web of modern allegiances, heaping irony upon irony, yet never once losing its remarkable generosity of spirit. The people we meet here are as exasperatingly human as our own friends and families. No one tells truths of the heart quite like Stephen McCauley."

—Armistead Maupin

Also by Stephen McCauley

The Object of My Affection

Published by WASHINGTON SQUARE PRESS

The Easy Way Out

Stephen McCauley

WASHINGTON SQUARE PRESS
PUBLISHED BY POCKET BOOKS

New York   London   Toronto   Sydney   Tokyo   Singapore

For Luppus

This book is a work of fiction. Names, characters, places and incidents are either products of the author's imagination or are used fictitiously. Any resemblance to actual events or locales or persons, living or dead, is entirely coincidental.

A Washington Square Press Publication of
POCKET BOOKS, a division of Simon & Schuster Inc.
1230 Avenue of the Americas, New York, NY 10020

Copyright © 1992 by Stephen McCauley
Cover design by John Gall
Front cover illustration by Terry Widener

Published by arrangement with Simon & Schuster Inc.

McCauley, Stephen.
   The easy way out / by Stephen McCauley.
      p.   cm.
   ISBN 0-671-78738-1
   I. Title.
[PS3563.C33757E27   1992b]
813'.54—dc20   92-42590
                                                            CIP

First Washington Square Press trade paperback printing July 1993

10   9   8   7   6   5   4   3   2

WASHINGTON SQUARE PRESS and colophon are
registered trademarks of Simon & Schuster Inc.

Printed in the U.S.A.

Part
1

One

Four and a half months before his wedding, my younger brother called me from Chicago at one in the morning. I'd been having a nagging problem with insomnia for about five years, so I was always thrilled to hear the phone ring, the smoke alarm sound, a picture fall from the wall, or anything that gave me an excuse to get out of bed. On that particular night, I'd been thrashing under the covers since the end of the late news, scratching my armpits and bouncing my legs, all quietly enough to leave my lover Arthur's sleep undisturbed. At the sound of the phone I leapt up, ran into the living room, tripped over a pile of clothes and picked up the receiver. As soon as I heard Tony's voice, I mumbled something about having been asleep. With my younger brother, I try to grab the advantage immediately.

"I'm sorry, Patrick," he said. "Do you want me to hang up?"

I pretended to think it over for a few seconds and then, always magnanimous, said, "Don't bother, I'm awake now."

I was actually delighted to hear from Tony. He almost never called me anymore, and when he did, I was just dumb enough to be flattered by the attention. Tony is exactly the kind of loud, right-wing bully I feel obliged to take a stand against on principle but from whom I secretly crave approval. He's taller than me, broad-shouldered, and at the time of the call, he was living a thousand miles from home. He's never been quiet about the fact that he views my life with mild disdain; I'm not as handsome as he is, I'd gone from teaching school to being a travel agent ("an even bigger loser profession"), I hadn't supported a single winning candidate since the day I registered to vote, and my sex life was considered reprehensible by every candidate who did win. For my part, I consider myself smarter than Tony, but I suspect he has more common sense. In any case, he only called when he had a problem he wanted to discuss (usually something profoundly meaningful, like a lost airline ticket or a hotel reservation botched by his secretary), and I loved feeling like an older brother, with age and experience and some advice worth listening to.

He didn't say anything for a minute, and then, irritably, he asked, "So what's been going on?"

"Don't expect me to supply the news," I told him. "You're the one who dialed the phone."

"I guess that's true," he said and then lapsed into silence.

Since late January, my mother had been calling me with unusual and disturbing frequency and feeding me a lot of unfinished sentences that had something to do with Tony. "That brother of yours," she'd say dolefully.

"What's wrong with Tony?" I'd ask. It had to be Tony. Ryan, my older brother and only other sibling, was generally referred to as either "the saint" or "that poor slob."

"Who said there was anything 'wrong'? Why does there always have to be something 'wrong'? My God, Patrick. I was just wondering if Tony . . . Oh, never mind; you wouldn't understand."

Whether I'd understand or not, I was eager to fill in some of the blanks for myself, but I knew I'd have to play along with that brother of mine if I wanted to get any information out of him. Like my father, Tony could be astonishingly circumspect, a trait I admired as a sign of masculinity and lack completely. I reveal my most intimate secrets to any innocent bystander who'll listen.

I told Tony I was planning a trip to Egypt in May, a travel agent's junket, and that I was thinking about buying a new car. Both intimate secrets were lies, but Tony loves to give advice on automotives, and I always try to make him think I live a glamorous, globe-hopping life.

He made a disparaging comment about the Egyptian military and launched into a nonsensical tirade against all foreign cars.

I was lying on the antique sofa in the living room, naked under a scratchy afghan. It was early in March, and winter, which had been regrettably mild that year, was doing me the favor of lingering on in the form of chilly nights. The air felt icy and sharp, and the living room was filled with faint blue light from either the moon or the streetlamp below. Through the tangle of hideous Swedish ivy leaves blocking the front windows, I could see the lights of Boston off in the distance, and I let myself sink into a kind of romantic lassitude. I reached behind me and turned on the late-night jazz station to heighten the effect. A tortured saxophone rendition of "Ill Wind" came on. Quickly, I lost track of Tony's political rant and imagined myself in some far-off, suffocatingly polluted city. Maybe it was Cairo. I was dragged back to reality by the sound of my brother shouting at me for seeking out consumer magazines, in which American-made products often ranked poorly.

"All right, all right," I said. It was a ridiculous charge. I shop the same way I choose lovers—impulsively and with a sense of desperation. Then, hoping to get to a more interesting topic, I told him I'd been hearing some rumors about him from Rita, our mother.

"You and your gossip," he said. Tony liked to gossip more than anyone I knew, but he considered it effeminate and only felt safe doing it with me. "What rumors?"

Arthur had been awakened by the phone, and he looked in on me to make sure it wasn't someone calling about a friend's hospitalization or plunging T cell count. He was wearing his pervert outfit: a boyish blue-plaid bathrobe and a pair of black socks pulled up almost to his knees. He gave me one of his worried, compassionate looks, the kind that always makes me want to knock his block off. Not that I would ever have knocked Arthur's block off. For one thing, he's over six feet tall and outweighs me by a good fifty pounds.

"Everything's fine," I barked. "Go back to sleep." And then, instantly regretting my tone, I added gently, "It's Tony." He nodded and lumbered on to the bathroom.

"That Arthur?" Tony asked.

"Yes," I said. "Unfortunately."

"Honest to God, Patrick, I don't know how that poor guy puts up with you, I really don't."

Every member of my family showed his reluctant acceptance of my homosexuality by constantly pointing out to me that I was unworthy of my lover.

"Listen, pal," I said. "I've been hearing some rumors from your mother that you're having doubts about this wedding."

She hadn't told me anything of the kind, but I knew all the sighing over Tony had to have something to do with the wedding. I had my

own theories about Tony's pending marriage, and most of them revolved around the word "doubts." Among other things, I thought
Tony was unworthy of his fiancée, she was unworthy of him, he
wasn't in love with her, and neither one of them was ready for
marriage.

"Sure I'm having doubts. Who doesn't have doubts? I'll probably
have doubts ten years after we're married. Are you telling me you
don't have any doubts about Arthur?"

"None," I said. I heard the toilet flush and watched as Arthur
padded back to the bedroom. "And if you give me a gun, I'll prove
it."

He sighed wearily.

"Anyway, I'm not the one getting married in July," I said.

"That's obvious, Patrick."

A tiny bell sounded in the background in Chicago, and I heard
my brother rustling paper. I could picture Tony sitting in his sterile
apartment, pulling a frozen dinner out of the microwave at midnight,
and I felt sorry I'd used the flippant tone that had marked our relationship for at least a decade, especially since I sensed he was calling
in some distress. It often happens that people in my family call me
when they're at the end of their ropes. I'm the family stand-in for a
priest, since they all know I'll never marry.

For the past three years, Tony had been living in Chicago and
working for a consulting firm that advises mid-sized companies on
the best ways to replace employees with complicated computer systems. He spent a substantial amount of time racking up miles on his
frequent flier programs, traveling to cities in different corners of the
country. He'd once confessed to me that although he liked living out
of a suitcase in the cheerless hotel rooms he admired for being "spotless," he often woke up mornings with no clear idea of where he was.

From what I could gather, Tony's job consisted largely of ingra-
tiating himself with a staff of low-level employees, convincing them
to confide in him about the work they did, and then figuring out the
best way to drop them from the payroll. His job struck me as morally
objectionable, but it suited his personality perfectly. He could be
effortlessly charming and had always had a mania for efficiency. Tony
had never been keen on dealing with the emotional complexity and
unpredictability of human beings. He liked things neat and tidy.

According to my mother, and the hints he himself dropped from
time to time, Tony was doing quite well financially, certainly better

than either Ryan or me. I'd always imagined that Tony would end up working for the CIA, but I suppose they don't pay enough. Immediately after graduating from a small college outside Boston, Tony had enrolled in one of the many business schools that sprang up in the area shortly after Ronald Reagan began his eight-year nap in the White House. He set up an apartment in the basement of my parents' house and made a few desultory attempts at helping out in O'Neil's Men's Shop, the clothing store my parents owned and had been pushing into bankruptcy for thirty years.

The day he graduated from business school, he announced that he'd found a job in Chicago, and was gone within a week. My parents were too stunned to raise any objections about his leaving the family store, which was probably why he slipped out of town with so little effort.

He'd driven west with all his belongings loaded into the trunk of his American-made car. Left behind were his weight set, his Heather Locklear posters, his motorcycle, and his girlfriend of several years, Loreen Davis. He was twenty-five then, and for all his bluster, it was his first real brush with independence. I could only imagine his re- action to the freedom and loneliness that confronted him when he moved into his own place, and I imagined all that had at least as much to do with his decision to get engaged as any genuine feelings he had for Loreen.

The problem wasn't that he and Loreen were a mismatched cou- ple; in my opinion, the problem was that they weren't a couple at all. As far as I could tell, their only shared interest was Tony.

Arthur and I had visited Tony in Chicago during a mercilessly ill-advised cross-country train trip. His tenth-floor apartment was one of those depressing cinder-block boxes done up like a showroom in a furniture warehouse: all characterless couches, thick beige wall- to-wall carpeting, and closets with folding louvered aluminum doors. Tony had always been a fanatic about cleanliness, so the place didn't even have the advantage of being dirty. The bathroom had a liquid soap dispenser, matching towels, and some weird contraption shaped like a mushroom, which kept the air smelling, in theory, of new- mown grass. Put a strip of paper around the toilet seat, and you'd swear you were a paying guest in one of the nicer Best Western motels off the Jersey Turnpike. The final note of desperation was the artwork, photographs of dandelions gone to seed, snow-covered trees, and sailboats on Lake Michigan, which Tony had taken himself and had mounted in pastel mats and metal frames. From my observations, no hobby attracts more lonely single men than landscape photography.

By the time I'd taken in the microwave, the sectional sofa, the hayfield bathroom, the collection of New Age CDs (which Tony referred to as "classical music"), and those perfectly focused, unpeopled photographs, I'd decided that if I ever wanted to do myself in and couldn't find a suitably dreary motel room in Boston, I'd head out to Chicago and end it all in Tony's pale-blue living room.

But underneath my lack of respect for my brother's taste in furniture and despite his condescending attitude toward me, I liked him, and for as long as I could remember, I'd felt compelled to try and save him—from what I'm not sure. Probably the very things I admired about him.

Now I shifted the phone to my other ear and listened to him rustling paper and clanging silverware as he set out his solitary midnight microwaved dinner. I admitted to him that I'd been lying about our mother's "rumors" and apologized for my joke about killing Arthur. There was a hole in the afghan, through which I'd distractedly stuck my penis. I wrapped the blanket around me more modestly and tried a different tone of voice. "So you're wondering if you should go through with the wedding," I said. "Is that it?"

"Something like that."

"We don't have to talk about it if you don't want to."

"I want to," he shouted.

"Okay, well, how do you feel about Loreen?"

"Don't give me that 'how do you feel' nonsense, Patrick. What difference does it make how I feel? I got engaged, didn't I? Draw your own conclusions."

I was at my parents' house when Tony presented Loreen with an engagement ring, and it wasn't a pretty sight. I thought back to that night as I listened to him shoveling food into his mouth and rambling on about the dangers of confusing facts with feelings.

It was a rainy Sunday evening in November, more than a year earlier. Loreen's birthday was in three days, and Tony had flown to Boston to surprise her with a diamond. Arthur and I drove out to my parents' house in the suburbs, at my mother's insistence. "Surprises are such fun," Rita had said. "Even you might enjoy yourself, Patrick."

I knew something was up as soon as we walked into the house. My mother was standing in the kitchen, nervously wringing a dry dish towel over the sink and humming something that sounded a lot like "Put the Blame on Mame." She had on a severe dark-blue pleated skirt, a starched white shirt, and penny loafers. Her face was heavily made up, and her red hair was even stiffer than usual. She looked a lot like a brilliant, troubled lesbian math teacher I'd had in junior high. She started complimenting Arthur the minute we walked in the door. From the enthusiastic way she hugged him and completely ignored me, I knew she was hiding something. Then I heard my father, Ryan, and Tony shouting at each other in the basement.

Arthur looked at me over Rita's shoulder and rolled his eyes. I hadn't yet taken him for a visit when there wasn't a battle or a scene of some sort.

"What's going on?" I asked.

"Nothing's going on, Patrick. Why does there always have to be something 'going on'? A little political discussion, that's all. You know how your father loves to shoot off his big mouth."

My mother grabbed Arthur's hand, dragged him into the family room, and incoherently started to tell him that she'd rented *Yentl* the night before and still couldn't get over the beauty of Barbra Streisand's Semitic profile. The last time he'd visited, Arthur had been regaled with tales of a wonderful bar mitzvah she'd been to forty years earlier.

I left them and wandered downstairs.

Not long after Tony had moved out of his subterranean apartment, Ryan and his wife had separated and my older brother had moved in. The one finished room, next to the garage, was strewn with Tony's rejects from his basement bachelor-pad days and odds and ends from Ryan's childhood bedroom. Tony's round king-sized bed with built-in stereo was covered with twin-bed-sized sheets imprinted with racing cars and tugboats.

My father, Ryan, and Tony were furiously pacing around in concentric circles, shouting back and forth. Ryan was guzzling from a massive can of Australian ale, and my father, dressed in a powder-blue suit that was too outdated for even O'Neil's Men's Shop to think of selling, was sucking on a cigarette.

I made eye contact with my father, opened my mouth, and was instantly cut off.

"The last thing we need around here is more input, Patrick, so don't even ask what's going on. Where's that tall friend of yours?"

My parents, my brothers, and I are all short. The closest we ever come to functioning successfully as a family is in discussing someone else's height in disparaging tones. "Arthur's upstairs," I said. "He and Rita are debating the Old Testament."

"You treat that guy like dirt," my father said, "leaving him up there with your mother. She could go on for hours, chewing his ear off."

Tony turned to me. "I'll tell you what's going on, Patrick. What's going on is they already told her."

"You're kidding!" I said, appalled. I didn't know what he was talking about, but I was so happy to be taken into someone's confidence, I jumped at the chance to side with him. "Told who what, by the way?"

"They told her," he repeated, his palms pleading to the ceiling. "These two and the one upstairs invited Loreen over here for dinner two weeks ago and told her I was going to propose to her."

My father and Ryan began shouting in unison, insisting that it had slipped out, that it had been an accident. "He talks as if we planned it," my father said to me. He turned to Ryan. "Tell your brother what happened. I'm too upset to get into it."

Since Ryan had moved back into my parents' house, he'd gained forty pounds and lost a considerable amount of hair on the top of his head. He was spilling out of a gray jogging suit with a peculiar hooded jacket and matching pants with red stripes down the legs. Ryan had always been a lovable teddy bear of a person, with one of the kindliest dispositions I'd ever run into. Unfortunately, he'd fallen in with a bad crowd about thirty-five years ago—my parents—and all his good intentions were merely paving his private road to hell.

He looked at me warmly and said, "I'm sorry about the turmoil, Pat. But you're going to love the dinner we're having. I bought a huge ham, one of those smoked things you send away for in the mail? They sent it special delivery. It just got here yesterday morning." He took a swallow from his beer, and then his face crumpled. "Oh, Jesus Christ. Arthur isn't going to be upset about having ham, is he?"

"I seriously doubt it."

"Well, that's a relief."

"Could we get to the story here?" Tony asked.

"All right already," Ryan said, clearly offended. "Reenie was over here for dinner two weeks ago. Nothing special; the poor kid needs a good meal every once in a while. Anyway, I went into the kitchen to check on the roast beef, and apparently your father let the whole thing slip."

"Him?" Tony asked. "I thought you said it was your mother who let it slip."

Tony dressed exclusively in navy-blue pin-striped suits, which made him look especially broad-shouldered and authoritative, almost as if there were a gun tucked under his arm. He appeared particularly dashing that day, in a dangerous way, and I felt like telling him he had nothing to worry about. Whether Loreen knew or didn't know, he was a shoo-in.

"It was your mother," my father said. "She's got that big mouth, and she never pays attention to what she's saying. In the store the other day, she tells this customer—"

"Snap out of it," Tony said, "and get back on track."

My father glared at him but obeyed. "Loreen was talking something about rings, rings—I don't know—some story about a ring. I adore that girl, but I can't follow her conversation half the time. But your mother, who probably wasn't listening, thought she was talking about *this* ring, and she said, 'Oh, did Tony go and tell you about the engagement ring and spoil the surprise?' We never did figure out what the hell Loreen was talking about."

"You know, I'll bet she was talking about Ring-Dings," Ryan said, "because when I came back from the kitchen she was finishing a story about one of her diet people going on a chocolate binge. Come to think of it, she didn't even look surprised."

Loreen was a nutritionist at a weight-loss clinic in a shopping mall in a neighboring suburb. The whole incident sounded highly implausible. "Well," I said, "there's not much you can do to change it, Tony. The surprise is spoiled, but so what?"

"The surprise isn't the only thing that's spoiled," Tony bellowed.

There was another bout of shouting, which was brought to a dead stop by the sound of the doorbell. "That must be Reenie," Ryan said, tilting back his head to finish off his beer. "Reenie" was a diminutive Ryan had invented for Loreen. Tony called his girlfriend by her full name, when he called her anything at all.

My brothers and my father looked at one another in a conspiratorial way, and I felt as though I was missing a crucial element of the plot. Ryan put down his beer can, my father stubbed out his cigarette, and Tony shrugged himself into his suit jacket.

"Ryan's going to be my best man," Tony told me. He put his hand on my shoulder. "I thought I'd tell you now, Pat, just so there's no hard feelings later. Don't forget, I was his. If I could have two, you'd be the other one."

The three of them walked upstairs, mumbling and gesturing, and I was left standing in the basement, thoroughly confused. I hadn't heard another word about the ring or the Ring-Dings or much of anything to do with the engagement itself until Tony's midnight call.

"I don't know why," I said to him now, "but I don't think the fact of your engagement says a whole lot."

"Maybe not, but it's what we're stuck with, isn't it? We have to deal with reality here."

"Tony, come on," I said. "Are you in love with Loreen, or aren't you? That's all that matters." Even as the words were leaving my mouth, I saw a band of other considerations and obligations marching my brother down the aisle to the altar. Surely no one in the real world ever bases his decisions on intangible concepts like love.

"I love Loreen, of course I do." From the sound of his voice, I'd have guessed his chin was resting despondently on his chest. "And let's face it, Patrick, it's much easier to go through with the thing."

"Easier to go through with it? I'm sorry, but I don't understand you." Of course I did understand him, only too well. The fact that I stayed with Arthur was not entirely unrelated to the fact that it was the easy thing to do.

Then it dawned on me. I tossed off the afghan and sat up on the edge of the sofa. The ancient springs groaned. In the blue light, my skin looked morbidly pale, and I shivered with cold and excitement and the promise of some really absorbing gossip. "You're seeing someone else," I said. I tried to keep my voice level, but I must have let a bit of enthusiasm slip in.

"For Christ's sake," Tony shouted, "why do you always have to think the worst of people? I'm out here miserable and lonely, eating a frozen chicken dinner that's probably going to kill me, if I'm lucky. I call you for a little talk, and you have to assume the worst. I don't think you like people very much. You know that? You didn't use to be this way. You used to have a more generous view of humanity. Now you want to believe that everyone runs on lust and greed and hunger for power."

It was a fair assessment of his own philosophy, but I apologized. "It was a passing thought," I said.

"And is that so terrible, even if it is true? Is that such a terrible thing?"

"Who said terrible?"

"You implied it. It isn't as if I was looking for trouble, you know.

It isn't as if I was hunting someone down in a singles bar. I was at a training seminar in New York four months ago. She was staying at the same hotel for a business meeting. The elevator stopped at the twenty-sixth floor, and she got on. What can I tell you? We were in the wrong place at the wrong time."

"What does she do?"

"Lawyer. Big shot, too. She has an office in the Sears Tower. I wouldn't tell this to just anyone, Pat, but she makes about five times what I do." He let out a huge sigh. I heard him scraping food off a plastic plate and then the sound of a garbage disposal crunching bones. "If you want to know the truth," he said, "the worst of it is I think I'm in love with Vivian."

There's something about names with a lot of *v*'s in them that has always grated on my nerves. But he'd said it so slowly, with so much care and suppressed feeling, I felt my chest swell with love for my poor, handsome brother. Nothing warms my heart more than a heterosexual man struggling to show emotion. His declaration of love and the tone of his voice made me feel as if the ground had shifted beneath the house or the wind had suddenly blown in from another part of the world. Something, I knew, was about to happen, though I couldn't have said what. I looked around the living room, at all the worn, cozy furniture Arthur had inherited from his folks and the watercolor landscapes his mother had painted, almost as if I were seeing it all for the first time. Or possibly the last. One thing I had to say about living with Arthur: even if I didn't have a life of my own, I did have furniture.

A plane taking off from Logan flew over the house. The windows rattled, but then it was miles away and the room was once again filled with the sound of saxophones. I was tempted to rush into the bedroom to make sure Arthur was still there. I sometimes worried that he might suddenly disappear, especially when I'd been spending a lot of time fantasizing about leaving him.

"Frankly, Tony," I said, "I envy you. I really do."

"Envy? What's there to envy? I'm ready to jump out the window."

"You're in love." I was desperately envious of people who could throw back their heads and say, without equivocating, that they were in love, that hopeless, helpless state of being.

"Love, sure, but what's the point? I'm engaged. Next thing you know, I'll be married. I can't call off the wedding. There's absolutely no way I can do that. Your parents would have me assassinated.

That's for starters. Don't torture me by talking about love. Vivian and I have a lame-duck relationship. There's nothing I can do about it." He turned on a faucet and, over the sound of rushing water, asked, "Is there?"

There was such a pleading tone in his voice, I knew he was really desperate. He was at the end of his rope.

Half an hour later, I crept back into the bedroom. Arthur was asleep, snoring lightly with his hands folded on his chest. I lay down on the air mattress on the floor beside our king-sized bed and pulled the blankets up over my face. I'd been sleeping on an air mattress for over a year now because the bed had been giving me backaches. Arthur, a confirmed hypochondriac himself, never questioned a health complaint.

"Everything okay?" Arthur slurred.

"Fine," I said.

"What did he want at this hour?"

"Just gossip."

Arthur prized a good night's sleep more than anything in life. It was the one thing I never tried to deprive him of. Besides, Arthur was above gossip. Tony's news would be of passing interest at most.

"That family," he mumbled. "Poor Patrick. Good night, sweetheart. I'm crazy about you, you know." He made a loud kissing noise and began to snore again.

My family was quite right; I wasn't worthy of Arthur, not for a second. That wasn't the reason I spent half my waking time thinking about leaving him, but I figured it might do as a convenient excuse sometime in the future. I sat up and reached for a T-shirt. Light was coming through the venetian blinds in blue bands, casting shadows all across the room. I leaned over and gazed at Arthur's face. He was thirty-nine years old and had an unwrinkled complexion that looked almost childlike. I was eight years younger, but my face looked like a scrotum by comparison. His youthful appearance could only be explained by the sweetness of his nature. He was handsome in a solid, shapeless way and had brown eyes that wouldn't have looked out of place on a golden retriever. I felt a rush of tenderness for him and looked down at him fondly, something I often did when he was asleep.

Then he stopped snoring, gave a snort, and became still. With his mouth open and his hands folded on his chest, he looked suddenly like a corpse. I stared at him for a moment and got up to close the blinds more tightly. The room went dark. I shuddered as I flopped back onto my mattress. Not, I'm sorry to say, at the thought of Arthur being a corpse, but at the thought of my choosing to sleep in the room beside someone who looked like one.

T W O

Over the next few days, Tony called me several times. His second midnight call came as less of a surprise than his first, and he sounded a good deal more relaxed, almost as if he'd spent a few hours getting sentimental with a bottle of Jack Daniel's. He'd recently become a fan of New Age music, possibly to make the transition from blank hotel rooms and elevators to his blank apartment even smoother. I could hear the numbing tinkling of "MoonSlide," one of his favorites, tinkling in the background. A little drunk, he was probably sprawled out on the sectional sofa in his living room.

"You know, I've been thinking about this all day," he said, "and it seems to me I didn't tell you very much about Vivian last night."

"No," I said. "I suppose you didn't."

"I should have told you more, Pat. I want you to get the right idea about her. She's not some flighty kid who's interested in me because she knows I'm not available. She's a hell of a lot smarter than I am. She's got brains, in addition to everything else." He paused long enough to sigh and then said, "You believe me, don't you?"

I thought it over and told him honestly that I didn't have any reason not to believe him. Actually, Vivian's personality was of considerably less interest to me than the fact that my younger brother cared so much that I approve of her. It was the first sign I'd had from him in a long time that he cared about my opinion on much of anything.

Of all the members of my family, Tony had responded most negatively to the fact of my homosexuality. When I broke the news to him, almost ten years earlier, he told me that he was gravely disappointed. Up to that point, we'd been fairly good friends.

"It's not that I care how you throw your life away," he'd said then, "but I'm in trouble with a couple of girls I've been seeing, and I was planning to introduce you to one of them and have you get her off my back. Now that you tell me this nonsense, I have to figure some other way out."

Our relationship fell off into a more or less polite acquaintance in which we traded a lot of harmless, but freighted, insults. I tried to convince myself that if he was so narrow-minded, it didn't really matter to me. But seeking his approval was a challenge I hadn't been able to give up entirely. His apparent fondness for Arthur was paltry, unwelcome compensation.

I settled back, basking in the flattery of his sudden respect for me, and listened to him ramble on about Vivian's virtues, most of which seemed to revolve around her toughness and her ability to see through his macho defenses. My brother had always gone out with frail, submissive women he could hold in thrall. Judging from the way he was talking about Vivian now, he'd obviously figured out that he, like most aggressive men and all dogs, wanted nothing so much as to be put in his place by a strong and unyielding master.

"If she told me to go out right now and swim across Lake Michigan, I'd do it, Pat. I'd chop through the ice and swim."

"Sounds like love to me," I said, a little put off by the quaver in his voice. "How about if she asked you to cancel your wedding plans? Has that possibility come up?"

"No," he said. "It hasn't. Do you think that's a bad sign? You don't think it means she's not really interested in me, do you?"

"Really, Tony, I wouldn't know."

Tony had, since adolescence, affected the deep, hypermasculine voice of a lubricious radio announcer and spoke mostly in staccato sentence fragments: "Big deal!" "So what?" "My ass"—that kind of thing. On the subject of Vivian he spoke in a lovesick whisper that involved a lot of swooning. Of course I'd always rather hear about someone's miseries than about their happy love affairs—nothing kills a person's sense of humor faster than a good marriage or a satisfying sex life—but I couldn't get around the pleasure of having him choose me as the earpiece for his oozy confessions of adoration.

I became obsessed with his dilemma. I suppose it appealed to both the cynic and the romantic in me (not that there was much difference between the two), because it involved both a new, tempestuous love and an old, failed one. I'd come up with a number of ideas to help him get out of marrying Loreen. Most, however, were overdone scenarios involving sudden trips to the other side of the planet, the kind I sometimes concocted for myself when I fantasized about leaving Arthur. I tried mentioning a few of them to him, but I could tell he wasn't taking my ideas seriously.

"Why the hell would I want to move to Australia?" he asked.

"I guess you wouldn't," I said. "I just think you'd feel a lot better if you came to some kind of decision."

"I came to a decision. Unfortunately, the cord on the electric radio won't reach to the bathtub."

It occurred to me after I'd hung up that my sensitivity to the subject of decisions probably had as much to do with my own situation as it had to do with Tony's. Arthur and I lived on the top floor of a three-family house that had recently been put up for sale, and Arthur, who'd inherited a small but not insignificant sum of money when his father died, was adamant about buying a place of our own. The closer he came to his fortieth birthday, the harder it was for him to write a rent check. In the course of my working life, I'd amassed a fortune of four thousand dollars, which I was contributing to the down payment. It was a fairly minimal contribution, but at least it gave me veto power I'd thus far managed to exercise over every potential purchase.

When I first moved into Arthur's apartment, the idea of living with him hadn't seemed all that threatening. It's true, I did begin having an affair with someone the night before I dragged my few belongings to his place, but that was an error in judgment I don't like to dwell on, especially since the affair lasted only two weeks. Arthur and I were tenants at will in a rented apartment, and his name was the one on the lease. I lived with the reassuring illusion that I could pack up and sneak out any old midnight I chose. No matter how often I'd thought about moving to Brisbane, it wasn't until the subject of buying a house came up that the walls had really started to close in on me.

Not that I didn't love Arthur; for all I knew, I did. I might not have been willing to swim across Lake Michigan for him, but we'd been living together for six years, and despite my joke with Tony about the gun, I rarely thought about murdering him. Our relationship had developed into the kind of benign domestic dependency that takes love for granted and accepts as inevitable a certain level of boredom, discontent, and suppressed rage.

At its worst moments, my relationship with Arthur reminded me of a particularly annoying toothache I'd had a few years back. The pain had been so minor and sporadic it didn't seem worth a trip to the dentist, despite the fact that something was clearly wrong with one of my molars. I'd almost wished for one night of blinding pain that would justify having the thing pulled, just as I sometimes wished Arthur would turn grossly malicious, violent, or psychotic, making a break in our relations inevitable.

As it was, though, I worried that sneaking out in the middle of the night was the only way I'd be able to leave Arthur, assuming that was what I really wanted to do. He was the most aggressively kind man I'd ever met. When I dared to criticize him for an offense as minor as putting too much vinegar in the salad dressing, he'd pout for hours. Discussing dissatisfaction with our relationship would probably send me into such a frenzy of guilt I'd end up pledging lifelong commitment. It was much easier to think of ways to help my brother reach a decision than it was to come up with my own.

Tony's third call was more of the loopy, sentimental same, with the addition of an embarrassing bit of rhapsodizing about the charming way Vivian lined up the shoes in her closet. But during his fourth, he nonchalantly told me something about his engagement to Loreen that convinced me he couldn't go through with the wedding and that I had to help him get out of it.

"And the irony of the whole thing," he said, "is I knew I shouldn't be marrying Loreen, even before I met Vivian, even before I gave her the ring."

"That doesn't make any sense, Tony," I reminded him, eager to be the voice of logic. "If you felt that way, why did you do it?"

"Because I couldn't get out of it. Don't tell me you don't know what was going on the night I proposed."

I confessed I didn't. He let out one of his mammoth sighs and proceeded to tell me, as if it was something of little consequence he was tired of repeating, that to begin with, my father had been the one to suggest he give Loreen a ring for her birthday.

"To tell you the truth, Pat, I didn't think it was such a hot idea right from the start, but I was desperate to try and come up with a present. You know how bad I've always been at buying gifts. I figured I might as well. Anyway, shopping for a ring was less humiliating than trying to pick out a dress for her. I spent a fortune on the thing, my first mistake."

According to the running tab I was keeping, it was far from his first, but I made an encouraging grunt, and he went on:

"Even before I had the box in my hand, I was terrified someone was going to steal it. I was convinced of it. I started having trouble at work, sleeping, you name it. It got worse as soon as I picked the damned thing up from the jeweler. It became an obsession. I'd go from carrying it with me all the time to keeping it under the mattress to trying to rig up a hiding place in the tank of the toilet."

Tony's apartment was such a tight, solid cell, it was hard to figure out how oxygen could get in, never mind a thief.

"The funny thing was, all that worrying made me think I was doing the right thing by proposing. I figured I must have really cared about her to care so much if the ring got stolen. And then, on the plane to Boston, I started talking to this woman sitting next to me and she ruined my life."

"That's what you get for flirting the night you're going to propose."

"It wasn't flirting. She was one of those types you used to hang out with in high school: know-it-all genius with a face like a horse. I told her why I was going to Boston and said something about how relieved I'd be to deliver the ring and get it out of my hands since I was living in constant fear that someone was going to steal it. She was sitting there with a calculator, and without even looking up, she said, 'Maybe you're *hoping* someone will steal it.' And that was it, Pat, that was all she said, but I looked over at her and I knew she was absolutely right. I wanted that ring out of my life. If the window on the plane had opened up, I would have chucked it out. By the time we landed in Boston, I'd decided to put off the engagement. I went to one of those airport shops and bought Loreen an expensive clock radio for a birthday present. I told your parents I planned to postpone the whole thing, that I just wasn't sure. The two of them went completely nuts, locked themselves in the bathroom and started fighting. Half an hour later, they told me they'd already spilled the beans. So what was I supposed to do? Loreen arrives all dolled up, Ryan has this fancy meal prepared, your father has on a suit, for Christ's sake. . . ."

Tony's call waiting clicked. A few minutes later, he came back on and said, "It's her," and cut me off. I had no idea which "her" it was, and the uncertainty left me reeling. I settled down on my air mattress and spent the better part of the night grinding my teeth, doing scissor kicks, and trying to find exactly the right position for my head on the pillow. For years, I'd been convinced that my parents had played a major role in disrupting Ryan's happy marriage, and now it seemed they were engineering an unhappy one for Tony. Fortunately for me, there was no sign of homosexual marriages becoming legal in the near future.

The top sheet of my bed had had a hole near the foot when I'd crawled under the covers, and by the next morning the thing looked like the Shroud of Turin. I peeled it off my body and quietly stole out of the bedroom. Arthur wasn't awake and wouldn't be for at least another hour. He required a good deal more sleep than I did, largely because he was so much more productive. Arthur was a lawyer for the Immigration Rights Project. He spent his days helping the tired, the sick, the hungry, the poor, the politically oppressed secure legal access to the land of opportunity. Russian Jews, Salvadoran rebels, Cuban queers, Romanians, Albanians, and tax-poor Irishmen. Not an easy job by anyone's standards, and even I wasn't about to grudge him a good night's sleep. I found my job as a travel agent exhausting, too, but in an entirely different way.

I went into the living room. Some twisted, proprietary impulse led me to scatter my belongings, clothes and books and magazines, all over the house, particularly in those rooms where Arthur spent a lot of time. I found it almost impossible to look at his favorite reading chair without feeling compelled to strip off some article of clothing and drape it over the seat. Arthur is tidy, though not compulsively so. We'd squabbled about clutter until Arthur's ex-wife, a psychologist, had come up with the endearing suggestion that I could be as messy as I wanted from 8:00 P.M. on, as long as the house was clean when Arthur got up in the morning. Of course it was a ridiculous idea, but I went along with it because I was fond of Beatrice and I like being told what to do by people who have no real power over me. I'm not a slob by nature. I'd taken up being sloppy in my early twenties, thinking it gave me personality, the way some people take up macramé or cocaine. Now that I was stuck with it, I realized it was an inconvenient and time-consuming personality disorder, about as appealing as psoriasis.

Sunlight was streaming through the bay of dirty windows, flooding the living room with hazy yellow light. The place looked wonderfully inviting, as it had ever since I'd heard the building was up for sale. When Arthur's father died two years earlier, his mother, who'd been bitten by the Georgia O'Keeffe bug, had given up their apartment in Brooklyn Heights and moved to New Mexico to paint. Arthur was an only child, and he'd inherited all the family furniture. Our place was filled with it. The living room was decorated with glass-fronted bookcases, mahogany chests, several overstuffed chairs complete with antimacassars and footstools, lamps with rosy silk shades, and the excessively heavy brown velvet sofa on which I spent a good deal of my free time. The place looked like a hybrid of a library in a men's club and a Victorian bordello. The chairs and the sofa had been worn down to a comfortable sheen by the indeterminable hours Arthur and his parents had spent in them reading weighty books—the kind of thing they did to amuse themselves on a Sunday afternoon. Most of the springs in the seats were shot and the arms broken down. I suppose none of the furniture was worth anything, but every time I walked into the room I was struck by the fact that I, who'd grown up in a house where JFK memorial plates were the only artwork, actually lived in what looked to me like antique splendor. What I hadn't taken into account was how depressing antique splendor can be. There were days when the overstuffed chairs seemed to be puffing themselves up. More than once, when I'd fallen asleep reading on the sofa, I'd dreamed about those brown velvet cushions falling on my face and snuffing out my life.

I fought my way through the hideous Swedish ivy plants—Arthur has a fondness for houseplants and pets—and opened one of the front windows a crack. A cold, damp breeze blew in, bringing with it a faint smell of the Charles River. The apartment was in Cambridgeport, a few short blocks from the river and about half a mile from Harvard Square. I stood in front of the open window and shivered happily. I was convinced the planet was about to expire from heat exhaustion, and I couldn't get enough cold weather. I'd been trying to store it up all winter to keep in reserve against the coming spring and summer, those two seasons I'd recently grown to detest.

Conveniently located though it was, the building we lived in was badly in need of paint and had never been properly insulated. But Arthur had been a tenant for over ten years, so the rent we paid was stupendously low. The building had been owned by a ninety-year-old woman, one of those squat Sicilian widows with more stamina than a Latin American soccer team. She'd lived in the suburbs with her daughter and took the bus to Cambridge once a week to do little projects around the house: chop down trees, shovel snow, pour a new cement walk, shore up the foundation. She'd worshiped the ground stalwart Arthur trod and hated everyone else who lived in the building. Out of deference to her favorite, she pretended I didn't exist. But shortly before Christmas, she'd had a stroke while doing some rewiring in the basement, and the suburban daughter and her husband had nailed a For Sale sign onto the front of the house before her corpse was loaded into the ambulance. Arthur had immediately contacted a real estate agent, and we'd been house hunting since.

I took the pants, sneakers, gym shorts, and several pairs of woolen socks I'd draped over the backs of chairs and flung onto the bookcases and heaped them up in the middle of the floor with the newspapers and the latest issue of *Weatherwise* magazine. I got a trash bag from the kitchen, loaded it with the refuse, and dragged it to the room behind the kitchen, which Arthur had designated as mine when I moved in. It was a tiny room with a narrow, drafty window that looked out to the back porch and the yards of the houses that surrounded us. I had a daybed with about a dozen pillows, a small desk, and a telephone. There were piles of books scattered around—the true-crime thrillers I read on the sly, my collection of books longer than eight hundred pages, which I kept for times of extreme anxiety—and the grotesque religious knickknacks that Arthur had quietly suggested I might like to store "out back" to make the room feel more homey. I can't see a glow-in-the-dark plastic religious icon without buying it. All those crass little figures strike me as funny and comforting. Arthur had informed me the statues were my way of dismissing the church as laughable while covering my tracks in case I was wrong. I found this, like many of Arthur's insights into my personality, condescending and accurate.

It wasn't an especially attractive room, but it was as close to a life of my own as I'd had in the six years Arthur and I had been sharing quarters. There was access to a stairway in the back hall, and if I'd been that kind of snake, I could have carried out all kinds of indiscretions right there behind the kitchen. I, however, was the kind of snake who preferred to carry out his indiscretions elsewhere.

I arranged my clothes in neat piles on the floor, paid off a couple of overdue insurance bills, stripped off my underwear, threw myself onto the daybed, and dialed my friend Jeffrey in New York. His machine answered, so I went to take a shower.

Three

An hour later, I told Arthur about the content of Tony's several calls. He was standing at the stove scrambling four eggs for our breakfast, waiting for the toast to pop up. Arthur has a completely healthy, wholesome attitude toward food. He knows what he likes and what he needs to keep himself fit and functioning efficiently. He rarely indulges in empty calories or packaged foods with a shelf life of more than two years. I've never known him to go without three solid meals a day. He has one cup of coffee with breakfast and one at 11:15 A.M., doesn't eat between meals or snack before bed. Unfortunately, his attitude toward sex is similarly well balanced.

He listened to my story with mild, lawyerly interest, asked an occasional question to clarify the sequence of events, and did a good deal of nodding and throat-clearing. I was sitting at the kitchen table, clipping my fingernails over a wastebasket, and I knew his main interest was in making sure the clippings didn't end up on the floor. When I finished relating the details, he put the plates down on the table, cleared away the wastebasket, and sighed. "That family. I don't know how you turned out so normal, Patrick. It must be my influence. Just joking, sweetheart. Well, there's only one thing that matters here: does Tony love Loreen or doesn't he?"

"Oh, please, Arthur, life isn't like that. There are too many complicating factors, too many variables and obligations to consider."

"Such as?"

"My parents."

He picked up the newspaper and sank his fork into his eggs. "What do they have to do with it?"

"They want him to marry Loreen. They seem to like her."

"Well, don't hold that against them. They like me, too. Now, here's a house that sounds interesting. In Cambridge. Two bedrooms, a fireplace, and hardwood floors throughout. Wood stove. I wonder if Eben has a listing for it."

"What about central air conditioning? That's what we should be looking for. Wood stoves are obsolete. A few more greenhouse years, and fireplaces will be, also. And anyway, I feel bad for Tony. It sounds as if he was roped into this thing."

Arthur put down the paper and his fork and looked at me critically. He had on a gray suit and a white shirt, and he looked particularly wise and formidable. In a business suit, Arthur's large, oddly shapeless body took on broad and imposing definition. Arthur has a soft, rather plain face, distinguished mainly by his deep-set eyes, a chin with a cleft so deep you could hide a dime in it, and fascinatingly large ears. His head is almost completely bald, except for a monkish ring of hair, which he keeps stylishly trimmed and which makes him look a little like Thomas Merton. In many ways, the most striking of Arthur's features is a bulging prolapsed vein that runs down his forehead to his right temple and throbs when he's considering something seriously.

All in all, his impressive cranium makes you think there must be a preternaturally large brain inside, just dying to get out and take over the world. It's hard to look at Arthur and not feel intellectually inferior, an advantage for his clients and a real problem for his lover. Once, years earlier, I'd made some vague hints that I might like to get my own apartment. He'd responded by saying, "You can't do that." I was so accustomed to believing everything he said, I took his words as literal truth and dropped the subject.

"I hope you're not planning to get involved in this, Patrick. It's exactly the kind of intervention that's going to make you unhappy, and it won't accomplish a thing."

"Don't forget, he's my baby brother."

"Your baby brother is almost thirty. He can solve his own problems. And between you and me, sweetheart, how much can it matter? Tony's a Republican."

"You wouldn't understand," I said. "You're an only child." Relevant or not, it always helps to pull an irrefutable fact out of nowhere when you're losing an argument. I picked up the salt shaker and started to slide it back and forth between my hands across the slick surface of the table. The kitchen table was one of the few contributions I'd made to the apartment, a chrome-and-Formica greasy-diner special I'd bought at a junk sale years earlier.

"Maybe you should get a little more involved in our situation with the house instead of your brother's life." He looked over at me, his vein throbbing, and I could tell he was making a mental calculation. "The other day," he said, "Eben asked me if I thought you were really serious about buying a house. You've found something wrong with everything he's shown us for the past two months."

"True," I said. "And it's lucky for you I have, or we'd be stuck with a loser now and we'd both be broke. Anyway, I'm not sure I trust Eben or Evan or whatever his name is."

"Let's not start."

"Those perfect teeth of his make me nervous."

He frowned at my plate. "Aren't you finishing your eggs?"

"I've lost my appetite. Do you want them?"

"No, but I'd like you to stop playing with that salt shaker and finish them. You had a cold for a week last month. You don't eat enough; you don't take care of yourself."

No matter how old I got, Arthur would always be eight years older, a fact he took as license to use a parental tone whenever he got frustrated. I usually countered by acting like an adolescent. I began tossing the salt shaker with a lot more enthusiasm. "Don't get like that with me, Arthur. You know that tone won't get you anywhere."

He cut me off by asking if I wanted to go to a movie that night. Arthur knew I could always be stopped dead in my tracks by the suggestion of going to a movie with him. There wasn't much I liked better than sitting beside Arthur in a dark theater, sharing a vat of popcorn and disagreeing about everything related to the film. I'd tried to cure myself of the pleasure I took in it, but nothing seemed to help. If every major film studio in the world suddenly went bankrupt, I might, finally, be able to leave Arthur.

"What did you have in mind?" I asked. Arthur, whose idea of a light read is *The Ordeal of Richard Feverel* and who claims to have never once turned on a TV set, has a real fondness for insipid, life-affirming comedies. The flabbiest, most badly acted of these could send him into storms of hilarity. I prefer something with a lot of action and corpses.

"Your choice," he offered.

"Forget it," I said, getting hold of myself. "I have to go to the gym after work."

"You can skip your routine for one night."

"Impossible." It was one thing to be stuck in a passionless domestic relationship and quite another to be out of shape and stuck in a passionless domestic relationship. Arthur kept himself fit with a brisk daily walk, fifty push-ups, and one hundred perfectly executed sit-ups.

"We could go to a late show," he said.

"That wouldn't work, either. You wouldn't get your eight and a half hours of sleep and your whole day tomorrow would be ruined and dozens of people would get deported and it would all be my fault because I wouldn't finish my eggs."

"No connection," he said and opened up the paper again.

I knew better, so I started eating.

"And something else," Arthur finally said from behind his paper. "You shouldn't criticize Eben because he has perfect teeth."

"It's not just the teeth," I said. "It's what they represent: the prep school, the sailing lessons, the boxer shorts, the whole package. Didn't he say he plays tennis?" Except in the case of lesbians, playing tennis is usually little more than a crass display of social ambition.

"I wouldn't know," Arthur said, obviously determined not to play along. He was charmed by our real estate agent, a tennis player with a wife and a family and the kind of legally binding security that Arthur longed for. "And you'd better eat more slowly, Patrick, or you might find yourself at work on time this morning."

Four

My office was in Harvard Square, and I bicycled there most mornings, even in winter. Bicycling through bad weather and driving a pre-1975 Volvo are two particularly Cantabrigian affectations. I liked to pedal a circuitous route to the office, winding in and out of the back streets of Cambridgeport, studying the triple-decker houses and brick apartment buildings, trying to imagine how different my life would be if I lived alone in one of them. Happier, I tended to think, although I was never able to come up with any concrete images of what my happiness might look like.

The neighborhood, wedged between Harvard and MIT, was surprisingly untouched by either towering institution. The old working-class Irish families who'd lived there for a couple of generations mixed peacefully with recently emigrated Haitians and Jamaicans and an increasing number of young professional couples who drifted across the river from Boston in search of a backyard. Most of the buildings were reasonably small, most of the streets were tree-lined, and in summer, cool breezes blew up from the river. Although I'm loath to wax rhapsodic about anyone or anything, I sometimes laughed aloud at my good luck in living there.

On a mild, cloudless morning a few days after Tony's distressing fourth call, I bicycled to work in a light cotton sweater. In the short time it took me to make the trip, I broke out in a sweat, another clear indication that the planet was rapidly reaching the boiling point. Arthur analyzed my greenhouse-effect obsession as a displacement of my anxiety about AIDS, which might have been true but didn't explain why we'd had a heat wave at Thanksgiving. Given the opportunity, I'll always believe the worst-case scenario. I'm not an especially optimistic person. I wasn't brought up on optimism. The closest thing to optimism I heard as a child was my father's reassuring statement in times of crisis that the situation could be worse. "And don't forget," he'd usually add, "you can always kill yourself."

When I arrived at the office, I hoisted my bicycle to my shoulder and carried it into the building. The owner encouraged employees to bring bicycles and pets to work, to give the agency a more relaxed, collegiate atmosphere.

The travel agency was located in a small house in a back alley several blocks from Harvard. It was a dusty, ramshackle building with paint peeling off the walls and plaster chipping from the ceiling. Drafty without being well ventilated and old without any antique charm, the agency had an established reputation among the Cambridge intellectual crowd: Harvard professors, hippies who'd become civil rights lawyers and therapists, and New Age birdbrains of all sorts. I think the shabby conditions of the place somewhat mitigated the trivial, bourgeois nature of travel in our clients' minds. And then there was our name, Only Connect Travel,. a reminder that the owner, who had a Ph.D. in philosophy, had read *Howards End*. The staff was made up of a bunch of overqualified individuals with advanced degrees and, in more than one case, a substantial private income. Everyone in our office either had done something more substantive or at least gave the impression of being capable of doing something more substantive. The travel industry is a real haven for burned-out teachers and social workers and est trainers. I was one of the burned-out teachers. Technically, I suppose I was one of the burned-out travel agents, too, but I couldn't afford to quit.

Fredrick, the receptionist, handed me a stack of pink call-back slips and looked at his watch. "Late again," he said wearily. "Always, always late."

"I'm sorry," I said. "But at least I'm earlier than I was yesterday."

"Please don't apologize, Patrick. I couldn't care less. I was just making a casual observation."

Fredrick—it never occurred to me or anyone else in the office to call him Fred—was a recent Harvard graduate, a stout, pleasantly bored young man with a passion for Charlotte Brontë and French pastry. His hair color varied wildly from week to week, and his eyelids were remarkably heavy and oily. There was much discussion around the office about whether or not he wore mascara. He was far from the most efficient receptionist we'd ever had, but apparently the boss felt that having someone at the front desk reading *Villette* compensated for the fact that he often neglected to answer the phone.

I liked Fredrick, mostly because he never bothered me about my own inefficiency and was the only person I'd ever met who could wear pedal pushers and a bow tie at the same time and somehow look dashing. I was fascinated by his sexual interests, which were as varied as his wardrobe and his hair color. I'd once asked him if he considered himself a bisexual. "Basically," he'd said confidentially, "I fall in love with anyone who'll stay in the room after I've taken my clothes off."

I apologized once again for being late. He shrugged, adjusted his bow tie, and remembered that there was a client waiting to see me in my office. "He got here a while ago," he said.

"Oh?" I had a list a mile long of clients I had no desire to see.

"Fifteen minutes ago. Tall, long arms. Talks so soft you can't hear a thing he says."

Worse news than I'd feared. Dr. Fields, a Harvard professor, had come in months earlier to plan a trip I still hadn't done any work on. I lifted my bike to my shoulder and carried it into my office grudgingly.

My desk was in a small, narrow room at the rear of the house, probably part of the pantry when the place was lived in by a single family. I loved my office, mainly because it was so aesthetically unappealing that I was left in relative peace. I had a sagging bookcase laden with heavy rate tariffs and hotel books, and a rack of outdated brochures was nailed to the wall. Fields was sitting in front of my desk, studying a hotel guide and jotting in a tiny notebook.

"Sorry I'm late, Professor," I said as I dumped my bike against a wall. "I have a sick dog at home, and I didn't want to leave him." Fields was a zoology professor, so I thought he'd take to an animal excuse.

I swept a stack of papers off my chair and sat down. I love to sit behind my desk and at least appear as if I have all the answers.

"I was just in the neighborhood," Fields whispered, "and I thought I'd drop by and see how the reservations are coming."

Fields was a pathological passive-aggressive type. His particular act of hostility was to talk so softly I had to sit on the edge of my seat and strain my ears to hear what he was saying. I'd tried asking him directly to speak up, told him I was hard of hearing, and forced him to repeat every sentence he uttered. Finally, I'd discovered a solution that worked.

"Oh, thank you," I said loudly. "I got it on sale at Filene's. I wasn't sure about the fit, but twenty-five dollars for an all-cotton sweater, how can you go wrong?"

Fields smiled condescendingly. He had a long, craggy face and one of those unkempt, stained beards so popular among fifty-year-old Harvard professors with marital problems. "Very nice," he said softly. "But I asked about the reservations."

Better, but not good enough. "That's what *I* thought," I said, "but in fact, it doesn't show the dirt at all. And it's one-hundred-percent washable." I shrugged and folded my hands on my desk. "What brings you in this morning?"

"Did you get the hotel reservations?" he asked in a normal tone of voice.

"Yes," I said. "They haven't sent in the confirmation slip yet, but I'm expecting it any day."

"I'm beginning to get worried, Patrick. You're sure it's all confirmed?"

"Quite sure," I said. "I can't imagine why they haven't sent the slip."

He looked at me suspiciously, but I knew he wouldn't call my bluff. We had an understanding.

Fields had come in in January to book a trip to Bermuda for Memorial Day weekend. He told me he was taking his niece, Zayna Carmine, out of obligation to his sister, whose husband had just divorced her. I thought nothing of it at first, and then he told me, in his moronic whisper, that I wasn't to cross-reference the plane reservations in any way, that Zayna's ticket was to be paid in cash, and that I was to assign seats for them on different parts of the plane, "in case of a crash." I wasn't to call him at home or office, and I wasn't to send any information on the trip through the mail. Whenever he did call me, it was from a phone booth, with traffic noise in the background. I imagined him standing in a rest stop on the Mass Pike in a long coat and sunglasses. To confirm my suspicions, I called Harvard student information and asked if they had a listing for Zayna Carmine. I was promptly given a telephone number, which I didn't write down.

I honestly wouldn't have cared if he was traveling with a donkey he planned to sodomize on the lawn of the Houses of Parliament. But I resented his effort to hide the obvious, as if I couldn't read the signs, would care, or was likely to be indiscreet. Half the leisure-travel industry has something to do with illicit sex—what made him think he was so special? I'd managed to get him seats on the plane, but the hotel was another story. He wanted to stay at an exclusive resort— basically a pink stucco drinking club for wealthy anti-Semites—and each time I called the place, I thought about Fields boozily chasing Zayna around a king-sized bed, lost heart, and hung up. If the trip came together at this point, it would be a miracle.

"Now, I really could try to get a child's fare for Zayna," I said, "if you think your niece could pass for under twelve."

"Doubtful." He laughed. "She's very mature for her age."

Equally doubtful, I'd have guessed. Mature college students are the ones who know their place. Zayna's place was not with a married zoology professor in any case, and certainly not under a moon-gate arch in Bermuda.

I looked at the call-back slips Fredrick had handed me. There were three from a divorced man who was trying to give meaning to his life by planning a trip to swim with dolphins, two from Tony's fiancée (I was booking their honeymoon at a health spa in California), and one from my friend Jeffrey in New York. I crumpled up the first five and tossed them into the wastebasket. Jeffrey's I impaled on my message stick.

"Is there something else I can help you with?" I asked, hoping to make him think I'd helped him with anything at all so I could get rid of him and call Jeffrey.

"Yes, as a matter of fact," he said quietly. "I'm thinking of taking my wife on a little trip after Bermuda." He pulled on his nasty beard and flipped through his notebook. "I wanted the name of an inn less than an hour from Boston. I wrote down some places while I was sitting here waiting for you for the past forty-five minutes. Maybe you could tell me if any of them is particularly nice?"

Not surprisingly, his handwriting was so minuscule it looked as if it had been written with a strand of hair. I squinted. From a business standpoint, the advantage of booking a tryst trip is that it's usually preceded or followed by a guilt-induced vacation with a spouse. Fields's suggestion was one of the more token efforts I'd encountered in a while.

I handed the notebook back to him and leaned my forearms on

my cluttered desk. I like to keep the top of my desk a mess so I can shuffle through papers as a stall tactic when pressed for information. "Those places you've written down," I said, "are what we in the business call 'cheap motels.' You might spend a weekend there, but not with your wife."

"No?"

"Trust me."

He looked at his list with new interest. I hadn't met his wife, but I imagined her to be one of those well-meaning, hopelessly drab Cambridge academic wives. You saw them walking around the Square dressed in crocheted shawls, peasant skirts, and knee socks, with mandalas on leather cords around their necks. I took down a book of classy New England inns and lovingly picked out the most attractive and expensive of the bunch. Mrs. Fields would be comfortable there. She'd fit right in with the dried-flower arrangements in the bathrooms and the white tufted bedspreads.

"This is your place, Professor," I said. "Very quiet. Romantic, but in a tasteful way, if you know what I mean."

What I meant was, the place was so suffocatingly cozy, he'd have the perfect excuse for falling asleep on the far side of the canopy bed at nine-thirty without touching his wife. Sex was about as appropriate in one of those places as it was in a telephone booth.

"A little pricey, isn't it?"

Needless to say, the hotel he'd picked out in Bermuda was one of the most expensive on the island. "Think of it this way: it's half the price of the place in Bermuda, and this includes breakfast. A huge meal a wild animal couldn't finish."

"I suppose you're right."

I told him I'd make reservations and, just to let him know I wasn't as dumb as he thought, said I would mail a confirmation for this one to his home.

He gathered up his briefcase and his tweed sport coat and stood up. He was staggeringly tall. His arms seemed to hang down unusually low, as if he'd been observing the behavior of gorillas for too long. Perhaps Zayna was attracted to his mind. "And you'll check on the other reservation?" he whispered.

"No problem," I mouthed silently.

Five

As soon as Fields was safely out of the office, I dialed New York. Jeffrey was an old college chum, with whom I'd been especially chummy for the past year and a half. We were having an affair, though that term suggests something too established and committed for either one of us. "Fooling around" was more the way I'd describe what he and I did, even though I got nervous sometimes thinking that maybe what I really wanted was to fall madly in love with him.

Or at least with someone.

I was planning to visit him that weekend, and since he rarely called me at work, I assumed something had come up and he wanted to cancel. We had a loose arrangement in which neither of us could complain of disappointment at anything the other did.

"So let me guess," I said as soon as he picked up the phone. "You've fallen for someone, and you'd like me to vaporize, at least for this weekend." Jeffrey was a painter, who made a meager living doing illustrations for medical textbooks. He worked at home, always with loud jazz blasting on his stereo and his window shades drawn tight. I figured I could afford to joke with him about having met someone else, since he rarely left his apartment.

He groaned, an exaggerated, unconvincing attempt at sounding contrite. An essential part of being a good liar, one of my few talents, is being able to spot a bad one. "Don't make me feel worse than I do," he said. "It's just that I haven't accomplished anything all week and I have a deadline on Monday. I wouldn't be any fun to be with, Patrick, I swear. You don't mind, do you?"

It wasn't within my rights to mind, so I told him I didn't. "I can spend the weekend house hunting with Arthur, which is probably what I should be doing anyway. I think he's beginning to suspect I have a mean case of cold feet."

"We wouldn't want him to think that."

"No," I said, "we wouldn't." I couldn't tell if his tone had been sarcastic, meaning he was unacceptably jealous of Arthur, or serious, meaning (unacceptably) that he wasn't. "I can come down in two weeks, if that sounds all right."

"That's fine. I mean, it's a long way off, but I guess we'll both survive. Give my best to Arthur."

"Sure," I said. He and Arthur were always sending messages of goodwill back and forth, even though they didn't much care for each other. As far as Arthur knew, Jeffrey was just my good friend. Arthur and I had a strictly monogamous relationship, which I interpreted somewhat loosely as meaning I could do whatever I wanted as long as it was in the realm of "safe" sex and Arthur never found out about any of it. Sharon Driscoll, my best friend and mentor at the travel agency, had been influential in making me believe that telling the truth and lying convincingly are more or less the same thing.

I went back to trying to find a room for Professor Fields. I felt fatigued. It really is exhausting to spend eight hours doing a job with no redeeming political or social value. Arthur often tried to make me feel better about my profession by telling me there was something noble in having one of those jobs about which it could be said, "Well, someone has to do it," but the way I looked at it, the world would be better off if no one dirtied his hands in the travel industry. Tourism is destroying the environment and culture of entire continents, not to mention the perspectives of a lot of silly people who honestly believe they're gaining an understanding of the world by sitting in an air-conditioned bus for six days, speeding through China.

I certainly didn't plan to spend the rest of my life booking reservations, but it wasn't as if I had a wealth of other options to choose from. Unlike my younger brother, I was born a bit too soon to be genuinely comfortable with computers or to admit that there are real advantages to having an MBA. I'm pretty much grounded on the wasteland between capitalism and idealism, incapable of either changing the world or making money. I had expected to spend my life teaching school, but that had lasted only three years. One thing I learned from the experience is that it's dangerous to tempt vengeful fate by making long-term plans. Tony's wedding was an obvious example of the pitfalls of that practice.

In my early twenties, I sincerely believed the world would be a better place if teenagers could only learn to love literature. It really was an audacious notion, since, it occurs to me now, I didn't love literature all that much myself in those days. I read in a steady, random fashion, choosing whatever books I happened to find at stoop sales or on top of friends' coffee tables. It was Arthur who gave some direction to my reading and made me realize it was all right for me to admit that, despite my upbringing, I'd read and enjoyed (even if I hadn't entirely understood) a certain three-thousand-page French novel about cookies. In his married life, Arthur had earned a doctorate in English literature. His field was Restoration comedy, just the thing—along with a passion for Gilbert and Sullivan—for his repressed-homosexual incarnation.

I'd inherited my love of reading from my father. He was constantly moving his eyes from left to right across a page of print, although he made little distinction between, say, *The Naked and the Dead* and the label on a soup can; both served the purpose of blocking out my mother and the rest of his surroundings.

My mother viewed reading with suspicion and often tried to discourage it, possibly because my father did so much of it. During adolescence, the only way I was able to read in peace was to lock myself in the bathroom and pretend I was masturbating.

As soon as I graduated from an overrated college isolated in the woods of New York State, I moved to Cambridge to look for a teaching job. Jeffrey and I, who were just pals at the time, had talked about moving to Manhattan together, but I decided I'd rather live in a city where my accent was easily understood. Half my time at college had been spent dodging words with the letter *r* in them so I wouldn't have to repeat or translate, as if I were speaking a foreign language. I figured I'd have enough trouble in the classroom without the added problem of a language barrier.

It took me a long time to find a teaching position. For one thing, I was underqualified (I had no teaching certificate and little experience), and for another, I have red hair. People tend to regard redheads with a fair degree of suspicion, especially when it comes to working with children.

What I had going for me was principally a handsome, if slightly outdated, suit I'd snatched from the racks of my parents' store. I think it was the suit that finally secured me a part-time teaching position at a snazzy private day school near the city. I taught two classes of ninth-grade English for several months, and then, thanks to the unexpected suicide of a staff member, I was offered a full-time position.

At the time I thought I was Socrates, but when I analyze the situation, I realize I was a mediocre teacher. I often lost patience with my students, and there were days when I was so fantastically bored, I'd blank out or fly into a rage just to keep myself awake. I wasn't very good with discipline, either. I was probably too close to my students' age to command their respect and not tall enough to inspire fear. And despite my vague idealism about teaching, I didn't much care for the profession as a whole. Every time I walked into the teachers' room, I'd choke on the clouds of cigarette smoke and the overwhelming stench of unacknowledged countertransference.

In looking back, however, I think it was probably none of these factors that made me leave teaching so much as it was a feeling of grave social inferiority to most of my students. Late in my third year of teaching, I finally realized what my students had obviously known all along: no matter how much I thought I had to teach them, no matter how much they did or didn't learn under my tutelage, no matter how many homework assignments they missed or how many books they didn't read, they would very probably, thanks to nothing more than family connections and social standing, end up doing something with their lives a lot more satisfying and financially rewarding than teaching the likes of them. The curiously sympathetic condescension with which the students had been treating me since the day I arrived began to make sense to me.

Once I'd accepted this reality, I lost almost all my interest in teaching and gave my notice. The fact that I, never a serious athlete, was waist deep in the humiliation of having to co-coach the soccer team was unrelated.

Arthur thought my action precipitate, but my friend Sharon, a burned-out teacher herself, approved. She'd left her job at a similar school but a lot more spectacularly. She ended up screaming and swearing at her students and walked out of the classroom, coatless and into a blizzard. Sharon was the one who got me the job at Only Connect. She had me hired as her personal assistant. Later, when our friendship was jeopardized by our work, she talked the owner into promoting me to my own, well-hidden desk.

I was thrilled with the travel job for a long time, and I wasn't all that bad at it. Coming from a family of salesmen had taught me a thing or two. After teaching, I felt a relief in doing something that seemed irresponsible. I felt more adult than I'd ever felt as a teacher; I could gossip openly with my co-workers, flirt with the customers, wear tight pants to work, drink at lunch, and swear on the phone. There was nothing about the actual day-to-day grind of teaching that I missed.

Gradually, however, I did come to miss the notion, however foolish, that by going to your job and putting in your time, you could make a tiny fraction of the world a better place. I didn't miss the Friday-afternoon headaches endemic to the teaching profession, but I did miss hanging on to the idea that I was contributing. Or at least trying to contribute. At the agency, the most I did was send people off to various parts of the world to hasten their chances of skin cancer and amoebic dysentery.

Sharon, my mentor in the field, saw things very differently. She thought of herself as a foot soldier in a people's revolution against big business. She was extraordinarily good at what she did, and mostly what she did, sometimes for twelve or more hours a day, was try to figure out creative ways for people to get around the rules and regulations of the airlines and hotel chains so they could afford to take the vacations they wanted. She once told me that her original plan after leaving teaching was to move to San Diego and help Mexicans enter the country illegally. When those plans fell through, she vowed that she'd turn any job into an equally antiestablishment venture. She always impressed me as being deliriously happy with her career—if ridiculously overworked—and so were her devoted clients. She had a cult following and brought so much business into the office that the owner let her do whatever she wanted, even though her compulsive bending of the rules set a bad example for everyone else who worked there.

Six

Sharon came into my office shortly after noon. The two of us ate lunch together whenever she had a break in her schedule, which wasn't all that often. Most days she stayed at her desk, plotting, without going out. I was still searching through hotel books, desperately trying to come up with something resembling a bed for Fields. I'd called more than a dozen hotels and guesthouses, but they were all booked to capacity for Memorial Day weekend. Sharon put her feet up on my desk and started to poke at a callus on her big toe. She wore Roman-style leather sandals twelve months of the year, no matter what the weather. They drew a lot of attention during a snowstorm, not that Sharon needed them to stand out in a crowd. She was close to six feet tall and had straight dark hair so long she could sit on it if she lifted her delicate chin to the ceiling.

"Get those hams out of my sight," I said, looking down at her feet.

She pulled a piece of skin off her toe and tossed it into the waste-basket. "Bad morning?"

"Disastrous. I botched a hotel reservation for Memorial Day. Bermuda. Harvard professor. No rooms available, two hundred and four people on the hotel wait list, he came in three months ago to book it. I've had it. I really should kill myself now so I don't have to face the consequences."

She gave me one of her disapproving looks, a sort of disgusted, impatient frown. Sharon had an unusually animated face. She was an avid cardplayer and had taught herself to use her expressive eyes and the corners of her mouth to her advantage. "You really didn't learn anything working with me, did you, Patrick? All those months, and you didn't learn a thing. What would I do in this situation?"

"I don't know. I suppose you'd lie."

"I wouldn't say I'd lie; I'd say I'd try a tactic. Everything's a tactic when you get down to it. You tell the truth, it's a tactic; you don't tell the truth, another tactic. In this case, all you have to do is type up a fake hotel voucher with the words 'Confirmed' and 'Guaranteed' printed in red and underlined about fifty times. Five minutes' work at the most. He'll probably get a room anyway, and if he doesn't, you just make up a story."

"What kind of story?"

She opened the huge straw bag she always carried slung over her shoulder and pulled out a pack of Luckies. "You tell me," she said, banging the pack against her wrist. "Go ahead, just off the top of your head."

I hated being quizzed by Sharon and having my basically honest nature judged as lack of imagination. "I'm not sure. I suppose I could always tell him the computer ate his reservation. Something like that."

"No good. No one believes that story anymore. And I hope you're not still using computer excuses. Computer excuses went out in 1985." She had an unlit cigarette dangling from her lips and was fiddling with an orange disposable lighter that wasn't working. I could tell she was getting irritated. Impatience was one of Sharon's virtues. "I stopped using computer excuses years ago. They're too common. Human error is a much safer option, but you have to be specific. Tell him there was some kind of convention or big group booked into the hotel, a planeload of models doing a shoot for Ralph Lauren, something like that. Harvard professors are unbelievably impressed with vacuous, pop-culture glamour. Tell him the hotel was in the middle of a corporate takeover and the new management inherited this group from the old management and no one was sure exactly how many rooms they needed. Tell him they intentionally overbooked by fifty rooms."

"Better say forty-seven," I told her. "It sounds more convincing."

"Good idea." She tossed the lighter into the wastebasket and snapped her fingers at me. I reached into my desk and passed her a book of matches.

"Thanks," she said. "Tell him we had three other people confirmed at the hotel that night and they all got turned away. It always helps if they don't feel like the only one who got shut out. Tell him we're filing a class action suit in small claims court for breach of contract, something like that. Throw around a lot of litigation-sounding words. He isn't a law professor, is he?"

"Zoology."

"Zoology? Is this the jackass with the teenage girlfriend he's trying to pass off as his niece?"

I nodded.

She blew a stream of smoke up to the ceiling. "Oh, come on, Patrick, you're wasting my time. Someone in his situation is never going to complain, no matter what happens. Don't even bother with the fake voucher. You can stick him anywhere. I know a great motel down there no one books. One of the few murders in Bermuda's history was committed in a room at this dump. It's always available." She reached across the desk, grabbed the hotel book out of my hand, and slammed it shut. "Let's get out and get some lunch. I've got a hell of an afternoon ahead of me, and I need to store up some energy."

It was after one o'clock by the time we left the office. The sky had turned a foreboding shade of gray, and the air felt seasonally cooler. Both were signs that delighted me.

"This feels about the right temperature," I said, checking out the cloud cover. "The normal average for today is forty degrees. If it cools off tonight, we should just about hit it, maybe a few degrees below."

"Listen to yourself," Sharon said. " 'Normal,' 'average.' Is that what you aspire to? I hate 'normal.' I hate 'average.' I wish it was twenty below. I wish it was ninety-eight in the shade. Let's break a few records here," she shouted, flinging back her head.

I caught the alarmed glance of a young woman walking past with a loaf of French bread tucked under her arm. "I wish I had your outlook," I said softly.

Sharon was wearing a billowing green plaid poncho and a pair of khaki stretch pants that didn't quite cover her ankles. Despite her height, her wide shoulders and large hands, Sharon had very thin ankles, a feature I found almost unbearably touching. She walked with a delicate, halting step that was quite unexpected, given all her other extravagant gestures and great, expansive movements.

When I worked as Sharon's assistant, most of my time was spent falsifying documents to prove the outlandish stories she invented, either to save money for her clients or to prevent them from discovering her mistakes. I typed medical excuses from phony doctors; letters from invented hotel managers apologizing for not honoring reservations that she, in fact, had never made; even death certificates. Sharon had a typesetter friend in the Square who would print up counterfeit obituaries for particularly sticky refund situations. I became an expert at erasing the dates and fares on plane tickets into illegible smudges and, short of supplying a written script, making sure every passenger had his story straight.

Sharon would sit tilted back in her chair, chain-smoking and eating egg salad sandwiches, instructing some confused and enthralled couple who'd come in intending to buy a simple ticket. "Okay, now," she'd say. "If they stop you at the gate and question you, just tell them your mother died and you have to get on this flight even though you don't have a reservation. Can you cry on cue? No? That could be a problem. How about this: You're terrified of flying and you had a bad flight west, so you went to a fortune-teller in Bolinas and she told you you had to take this flight and none other. Come to think of it, I know a great palm reader in Bolinas, if you're interested. You can act nervous, can't you? Just bite your lips and tug at your hair a lot. We haven't used this excuse this month, have we, Patrick?"

I was responsible for taking notes on what she was telling people, to make sure we didn't have passengers with the same story on the same flight.

"Now, I'm counting on you to pull this off," she'd tell her clients. "If you get caught with this ticket, I'm out of business. Just so you'll know the kind of risk I'm taking for you."

Miraculously, no one ever did get caught. Sharon's charisma made people feel they were acting in an important piece of guerrilla street theater. She was the director and the star, and none of the bit players wanted to let her down. So many people benefited from her creative maneuvering, it would have been churlish to point out the role self-aggrandizement played in her practices.

I'd met Sharon eight years earlier, shortly after moving to Cam-

bridge, on a snowy day in late January. I was driving a dilapidated
Chevy Nova through an intersection on Mount Auburn Street, when
Sharon ran a stop sign and plowed into the car's rear end. The Nova
spun around, jumped the curb, and hit a tree. It wasn't as spectacular
an accident as it sounds—it was a small tree—but it did attract a
crowd. Sharon rushed from her car with a lit cigarette in her hand.
Once she'd established that I was unharmed, she began telling me
how I could collect from my insurance company, Chevrolet, and the
city of Cambridge—and then sell the wreck to a junkyard. I was still
strapped into my seat, slightly dazed. I remember looking out the
window through the falling snow at Sharon, dressed in sandals and
bell-bottoms that were too short, rummaging in her bag for her
business card. "Boy," she said sincerely, "you're lucky I'm the one
who hit you instead of some jerk."

I didn't think to question the logic of her comment until much
later, and by that time we were good friends. I was living on the top
floor of her house when I met Arthur. She was indirectly responsible
for our meeting, a fact for which she's never entirely forgiven herself.

As we made our way through the lunchtime crowd in Harvard
Square, I told Sharon I needed her advice. When it came to relationships or life management, Sharon was one of the most perceptive
people I knew—mostly, I suspect, because she was rarely in a relationship herself and paid no attention at all to managing her own life.

"You know my advice," she said. "Leave him and take the rug in
the living room."

"It's not about Arthur." Unlike most of my friends, Sharon did
not feel that I was lucky to have reliable Arthur as my lover. "It's a
family crisis."

"Oh, good. Did Ryan shoot them both or just your father?"

"It's about the other one."

I insisted we walk out of Harvard Square to a greasy pizza and
submarine sandwich shop on Broadway, across from the public library. It was pointless to try and talk to Sharon in a restaurant in the
Square itself; she was always running into clients who'd demand
advice on their travel plans, or friends, like me, who had some personal problem they wanted to discuss with her. We cut through
Harvard Yard, past all the depressing libraries of Sharon's alma mater.

Like both my parents and neither of my brothers, I often give the
false impression of being emaciated. (For years I was buoyed up by
a one-night stand's comment that I looked better out of clothes than
in. Later, I realized it was intended as an insult to my wardrobe, not

a compliment to my body.) Side by side, Sharon and I exaggerated each other's physical extremes. We once went on a travel agent's junket to Brazil and shared a room. Everyone else on the trip thought we were lovers. We took great pleasure in sitting around the hotel pool in our respective bikinis, keeping our companions horrified.

As we slowly traversed the paths through the campus, I told Sharon about my phone conversation with Tony. She'd met my younger brother once, at a dinner she and I gave when we were roommates. Upon hearing that Tony was planning to attend a business school, she went into a vituperative rant against MBAs and then suggested to him that if he wanted to really make money he should move to northern California and grow marijuana. Every few hundred yards, Sharon would stop, lean against my shoulder, and adjust the straps on her sandals.

"I have to take these in to be repaired," she'd say. "Go ahead with your story; I'm listening."

Sharon was the one person I knew who could carry around extra weight as if it were a luxurious fur coat she had draped over her shoulders. She was probably more than ten pounds outside the "ideal" range on even the most generous weight-to-height charts, but it was all smoothly and evenly distributed and perfectly proportioned. She never made any excuses for her size and often took delight in flaunting it by wearing tight-fitting slacks or skimpy sundresses with pinched waistlines. The result was oddly, almost disconcertingly sensual, as if she were the manifestation of natural appetites and others the product of self-denial and some puritanical persecution of the flesh. Still, she smoked far too much and often seemed winded when, as now, she walked too far too quickly. It was obvious she was stopping to catch her breath, not adjust the straps on her beloved sandals.

When we got to the sandwich shop, I held the door open for her, and she swept into the place in the loud way she had of entering rooms. She was barely inside before she was pulling her poncho over her head, shaking out her curtain of dark hair, and dramatically proclaiming that she was about to pass out from hunger. There were no other customers, but the owners, a couple of swarthy, quarrelsome brothers, looked up from their newspapers as if they'd been simultaneously jabbed with pins. The younger of the two, an astonishingly handsome man in a rugged, potbellied sort of way, immediately began to make eyes at Sharon. There were two types of men who were particularly drawn to Sharon: wiry, energetic hippies with tangled hair who wanted to be mothered by her, and dark Mediterranean men with piercing eyes who had something else entirely in mind.

The shop was a filthy little place, with fluorescent lights and dreary blue walls encrusted with layers of grease and cigarette smoke. I often had lunch there; the food was acceptable and the prices were amazingly low. Neither of the brothers had ever acknowledged me, but now, seconds after we walked in the door, they were fighting over the privilege of making Sharon's sandwich, advising her on whether to have french fries or onion rings, and calling her "babe" and "angel." Both terms struck me as inappropriate.

"Don't listen to him, angel," the younger, handsome one said. "He'll help your friend. I'll tell you what you want."

"Believe me," Sharon told him, "I never have any trouble figuring out what I want."

"I like the sound of that. What did you have in mind?"

"Lunch," she said, flirtatiously bored.

"Lunch is a great place to start. I'll tell you what you want to have."

"How about this: I'll tell you what I want, and you tell me if you know how to make it. After I've tasted it, I'll tell you if you were right or not."

The younger one jabbed his brother with his elbow. "You see," he said. "I like this. She knows what she wants. That's good."

"Don't get carried away," Sharon said. "I know what you want, too, so let's just get to the meal."

We took our food to a table by the storefront window, and I watched as Sharon bit into her sandwich. Her sparring with the handsome brother had resulted in a grilled meat special. The grease from the steak and the cheese was soaking through the bread in an appealing stain. I had a dry tuna sandwich that looked anemic by comparison.

"Oh, God, this is good," she said, shaking her fingers out as if she couldn't contain her pleasure. Sharon's enthusiasm for the things she liked—good food, all travel, poker, and *Jeopardy*—was one of her most endearing qualities. I tend to withhold enthusiasm, for fear of having the things I really care about taken from me.

"I think he'd be happy to cook for you anytime."

"Sure, as long as his wife's out of town. I know the type, and I'm not impressed. Believe me, Patrick, I am not impressed at all." She took a great swallow of orange soda. "So you want me to tell you what I think about this garbage with that fascist brother of yours? I'll tell you, but remember you asked. Stay away from it."

Sharon was not known for her laissez-faire attitudes toward others, and I was disappointed by her response. "But, Sharon," I said, "he got roped into the engagement. Don't forget that."

"People his age don't get roped into relationships, Patrick. They make it look as if they do, so they don't have to accept responsibility for them, that's all. And in any case, it's none of your business."

"Well, there's a consensus on that point. Arthur said the same thing." Sharon considered Arthur stuffy, pedantic, and suffocatingly boring, even though she shared his point of view on almost every imaginable subject.

"He did? Oh. He did, really? That's too bad. I hate to agree with him on anything. But let me tell you something else: the only reason you want to help your brother is because you can't seem to help yourself. You can't leave Arthur, so you have to save your brother from getting stuck in some dead marriage. If you'd leave Arthur and move back in with me, none of this Tony business would matter to you in the slightest."

"You're forgetting," I said, "that Arthur and I have been so happy together lately, we're about to buy a house. So let's not get on that topic."

"Fine with me. By the way, are you still sleeping on the floor?"

I nodded, and she raised her eyebrows and took a huge bite of her sandwich. She gave a thumbs-up to the handsome brother and returned to her lunch, ignoring me.

"It's my back," I said. "Conventional mattresses give me backaches, so I sleep on the floor." When Arthur and I first lived together, we shared a double bed. Arthur liked to wind his big body around mine, and I always felt protected and warmed by him. Then, after a couple of years, warm turned to hot, and we got a bigger mattress. Then I developed an allergic reaction to our sheets and started sleeping in a mummy-style sleeping bag. Unfortunately, I was always rolling off the far side of the bed. Then my back problems began, and now I was on the floor. "It's actually a very common problem."

"Absolutely. I know lots of people who live with someone who sleeps on the floor beside their bed. In most cases, though, the someone is named Fido. By the way, still having trouble with insomnia?"

I wrapped up the uneaten portion of my sandwich and tossed it into the dented metal trash can by the door. It landed with a thud that sounded as if a piece of the ceiling had fallen in. The conversation was not going the way I'd hoped. For once, I'd wanted to talk with Sharon about a troubled relationship other than my own. I felt cheated, foolish, and disloyal. I had a sudden urge to call Arthur and try to make plans to go to a movie with him. There was no way to win with Arthur. Every time someone told me how wonderful he was, I felt compelled to point out his many faults, and every time Sharon ventured to say a word against him, I wanted to cradle him in my arms. I was angry that she had the effrontery to insult Arthur and question the sense of our buying a house together; only I was allowed to do that.

I snapped open a can of diet soda. "I happen to have a lot on my mind," I said. "That's why I have trouble sleeping. I'm in way over my head at work, for example."

She mopped at her mouth with a wad of napkins and then started to scrub at the grease on her hands. "And you think I'm not? I've got a lot on my mind, but that doesn't mean I don't sleep. Actually, I had trouble dragging my body out of bed on Sunday. I didn't get up until four in the afternoon. I suppose I needed the rest."

Behind the counter, a small yellow plastic radio sat on a shelf against the wall. The handsome brother was standing on a chair and spinning the dial from one crackling station to the next. He finally settled on a Muzak station playing an upbeat version of "The Shadow of Your Smile." I looked over at Sharon, swamped with regret. We hadn't spent any time together in over two weeks, and I hadn't bothered to ask her a single question about herself. Even in my most self-absorbed moments, I try to take a genuine interest in my friends; but with Sharon, one of my best friends, I often lapsed. It's easy to ignore a person's frailties when they're manifested only in her ankles. Besides, there was a part of me that was frightened by the thought of being around when the fortress of Sharon's defenses came crashing down.

She tossed her napkin on top of the uneaten portion of her sandwich.

"It wasn't so delicious after all?" I asked.

"After the fourth bite, it was all downhill. The fifth bite is the real test of food. Remember that. The fifth bite, the third date, the fourth fuck, and the sixth year of marriage. Everything else is inconsequential." She gathered her hair together and hooked it behind her ears with her fingers, a gesture that reminded me of a girl who'd sat in front of me in third grade. Sharon was thirty-seven, but in certain of her facial expressions, and in much of her loud bravado, the ten-year-old in her was very close to the surface. I asked her how things were going with her new housemate, and she shrugged.

"Roberta? She's driving me insane. I don't know why I let her move in."

"Well, why did you?"

"I felt bad for her. She's a friend of some friend's husband's friend, and she was desperate."

"Divorced?"

"Separated. She'll never get divorced. All she talks about is how much she hates her husband, a sure sign she'll be with him for life. She keeps telling me how lucky I am to be alone, and how I obviously did the right thing in deciding to never get married, as if I spent the past ten years turning down proposals. You should meet her. It's an exquisite experience."

In the eight years I'd known Sharon, she hadn't been involved in a single romantic relationship that had lasted more than two months. There were an ample number of men who expressed an interest, and an equal number who became obsessed with her and ended up calling the house at three in the morning or sitting out in front of her house in their cars. She always tossed them off (after the third date or fourth fuck, I suppose) with a ludicrous objection: "He uses deodorant." "He wears earmuffs." "He's used the word 'lifestyle' four times since we met." "He said I have nice feet." She had passionate love affairs on her travels, but those lasted only for the duration of the trips. Her severe single status had been a social liability for most of her late twenties and early thirties; she was always attending weddings and baby showers, anniversary parties and housewarmings, for a whole cast of close friends who liked to assure her that she was "next." Now, however, everyone she knew was breaking off a relationship, settling a divorce, haggling over custody of a child, a house, or a dog. Her bachelorhood, once a slight embarrassment to her friends, had become, in their eyes, a sign of emotional stability and strength of character. The fact that it might also be lonely was usually skipped over.

Sharon owned a Victorian house in Cambridge, an enormous wreck of a place she'd bought before the real estate boom, with money she claimed to have won playing poker. She was always hosting one or two relationship runaways in her extra bedrooms. She was the Jane Addams of the Cambridge divorce court crowd.

"What happened to the salesman?" I asked. The month before, the owner of a furniture showroom in Newton had been in hot pursuit.

"Boring," she said, and tossed him off with a flick of her hand. "You meet a man who's past a certain age, and all he wants to talk about is his bitch ex-wife and his needy widowed mother. I spent an entire evening with him a couple weeks ago, and he didn't ask a single question about me. Not one. Just an endless gush about himself. And his 'needs.' I managed to get a scrap of information about my life into the conversation, but I practically had to use dynamite. Finally, I just held up my hands and said, 'This has been one of the most boring nights of my life.' "

"You did?"

"Of course I did. You think I was afraid of hurting his feelings? He wouldn't have noticed if I'd dropped dead over dinner. I was so crazy from listening to him, I swear if I'd had a gun I would have opened fire in the restaurant. The only thing he said about me was that I had nice eyes."

Sharon's eyes were an astonishing shade of green, almost the color of the flesh of a kiwi fruit. She usually deflected compliments about them by saying they were given to her to draw attention away from her large nose.

"Maybe you should set him up with Roberta."

She frowned and rummaged through her huge straw bag. A deck of cards fell onto the table. "They'd last two minutes with each other. No one to listen. And if I forgot my cigarettes, I'll collapse. Did you notice if I put them in here back at the office?" She took out several more decks of cards, a paperback book on how to manage time, three tubes of lipstick (even though, to my knowledge, she never wore any), a damp bathing suit, and a bottle of sunscreen. Sharon had a pale, flawless complexion that was highly susceptible to sunburn. She once explained to me that she couldn't stand having a burn because it made her look too vulnerable. At last she came to the Luckies and sighed gratefully. She lit up and inhaled with such voracious relief, my mouth watered.

"Have you ever thought of switching brands?" I asked tentatively. "In the scheme of things, unfiltered Luckies are pretty high up there in the danger zone."

She daintily peeled a flake of tobacco off the tip of her tongue. "Please, Patrick. Next you'll suggest imitation mayonnaise. I'm not about to waste the good time of my life denying myself pleasure in hopes that I can add on a few years at the end when I'm old, poor, and bedridden. Some things are worth dying for."

"The brother who's so crazy for you, for example." He was standing on the chair adjusting the radio again, a stained white apron around his waist. His hips looked wonderfully narrow. "He has a nice behind," I said.

She sighed longingly. "I suppose he does. But he can keep it. Anyway, I have to get back to the office and make another few dozen people happy. We should get going." She dropped her cigarette into my soda can and swirled the dregs around until the sizzling stopped. Then she stood up and slipped on her poncho, making a great show of adjusting her hair. "Since you paid for my lunch, Patrick, I'll give you a piece of advice on your brother's wedding; try to stall the shower. Once they have the shower, he has to go through with it. But I still think you should keep out of it. If you'd leave Arthur and move in with me, I wouldn't have to put up with jerks like Roberta, and you could have your own life and wouldn't have to fly to New York for sex. But that's just my opinion."

As we were leaving, the handsome brother asked how everything was.

"Heavy on the grease," Sharon said. "Too much cheese, too many hot peppers, and the bread wasn't fresh. You guys are never going to make a go unless you serve fresh bread. And wash the windows every once in a while. It might help if people could see into the place. Well, then again, maybe not. Maybe better if they don't see it."

The brother beamed, as if she'd made some outrageously flirtatious comment.

Seven

}

Arthur and I had a Sunday-morning routine that varied little from week to week. No matter what the season, Arthur prepared an elaborate cholesterol-and-calorie-busting breakfast of pan-fried potatoes, a meat carefully chosen for its high fat content, fruit, and pancakes or waffles. In Arthur's book, it didn't count as an indulgent meal, because it was figured into his weekly food plan. Bloated from the binge, we'd crawl into the living room and read the Sunday papers as a team. Arthur summarized all the local and international political news, economic indicators, and op-ed pieces. I kept us both up-to-date on environmental disasters, plane crashes, train wrecks, earthquakes, and the latest murders. When we were finished with the papers, Arthur put on a Gilbert and Sullivan operetta, and we listened to it straight through, usually following the libretto.

Initially, I'd recoiled from the ritual, finding it too depressingly predictable. But Arthur had convinced me to keep at it, and now I had to admit it I took a certain degree of comfort from the boredom of the routine. Going along with this one weekly event assuaged a tremendous amount of anxiety I had about minor indiscretions like discussing my home life with Sharon and fooling around with Jeffrey.

The Sunday after my lunch with Sharon, Arthur and I were in the middle of listening to *Ruddigore* when Tony called. He called almost daily now, and although I'd tried to take Sharon's and Arthur's advice to stay uninvolved, I wasn't finding it easy. I think there was something in going against their advice that made me feel especially close to my brother, as if he and I were involved in secret negotiations. It reminded me of the time Tony, at age twelve, had a particularly fierce fight with my father and decided to run away from home. He and I stayed up late every night for a week, planning his escape, stockpiling supplies, stealing money from Ryan's bureau drawers. Tony left one day at noon and returned in time for dinner, explaining to me that he didn't want to hurt my mother's feelings by missing the meal.

"What do you think, Patrick?" he asked that Sunday morning. "Do you think that your parents suspect I might be seeing someone else?"

"I doubt it," I told him. "I'm sure your father imagines you spend every free minute in bed with a woman you picked up at the grocery store, but as for a real person, with a name and a face, I doubt either of them suspects a thing." My father had been obsessed with Tony's sex life ever since my younger brother reached puberty. The problem, as far as I could tell, was jealousy. "I'm sure you'd know it if they did."

"You're probably right. Want to hear something pathetic?"

"Absolutely."

"I actually feel bad for those two."

I asked him what he meant, although I understood perfectly. The only person I knew who was more unhappy than my parents was me when I thought about how unhappy my parents were.

"The store's about to fold," he said, "they hate each other, they ruined Ryan's marriage and now they have to live with that, and every time I turn around, your father's in the hospital having another organ removed. Look at their lives."

"I'd rather not, if you don't mind." I could feel my chest beginning to cave in and a peculiarly hollow feeling developing in the pit of my stomach. I conjured up a few bland phrases I remembered from listening to a call-in radio shrink and told him that he wasn't to blame for our parents' problems and couldn't solve them if he tried.

"That's true, but I don't want to make them worse, either. What's all that racket in the background?"

"Gilbert and Sullivan," I told him. "Arthur's specialty."

"Opera, isn't it? Vivian and I went to the opera the other night."

"You did? My little brother at the opera? What's become of you?"

"Vivian's into that kind of thing. At least I stayed awake. Half the men around me were actually snoring. And so loud I couldn't have nodded off even if I'd wanted to. It wasn't too bad, considering they could have cut two thirds of the thing and the acting was a joke. A two-hundred-pound lady in bed singing so hard her eyes are popping out of her skull, and you're supposed to believe she's dying of consumption. They should have cast someone like Julia Roberts and then dubbed in the voice. It's the second one she took me to. They're all pretty much about the same thing—star-crossed lovers like me and her. I even shed a couple of tears at the end."

"Tears?" At age seven, Tony fell off the roof of the house and broke his leg. That was the only time I could recall seeing him cry.

"Who wouldn't cry, with all that singing and dying?"

I wouldn't. I'd leap over the balcony before I'd let myself cry in public. Or in private. "Have you talked with Loreen yet?"

"Last night."

"And?"

"And nothing. I told her it was raining, I talked about work, she gave me an update on the honeymoon plans, and we hung up. Listen, Pat, don't try to make me feel bad. I'm such a wreck, I've lost five pounds in the past two weeks. Maybe I should stop calling her for a while."

"What does Vivian make of all this?"

"She's not putting any pressure on me, like I told you. I almost wish she would. It's too bad you can't meet her. She understands everything."

I could hear him gearing up for another hymn of praise, something I was not dying to sit through.

"I don't know why, but I tell her things I've never told anyone else. Things about when I was a kid, your parents, school. Even about you. You'd approve of her attitude on that score, by the way. She doesn't see anything wrong with the whole gay thing."

"Imagine."

"Vivian thinks I took such a hard line against you because I was threatened."

"Tell her to hang out a shingle. Those shrinks make big bucks."

Arthur was sitting on the brown sofa in the living room, with the newspapers stacked up at his feet. The Gilbert and Sullivan had reached its happy ending, and he was motioning for me to finish my conversation, pretending to slit his throat.

"I'm sorry, Tony," I said, "but Arthur's telling me to get off the phone. A real estate agent's coming over to show us a house."

"A house? You two are buying a house?"

"We're looking," I said. I was delighted to hear the surprise in his voice; I took it as confirmation that the whole venture was out of character for me.

"Finally settling down. Good for you, Pat. Do your parents know about this?"

"I don't think so."

"They'll be thrilled. They like the idea of us all settling down. As long as we're not too happy about it. You're not too happy about it, are you?"

"Not too. Anyway, I don't want to hear your parents' opinion, so let's leave them out of it."

"Fine with me. If I add a couple more subjects to the taboo list, I'll never have to talk with them again. Maybe I'll call you later tonight," he said and slammed down the phone.

Our real estate agent had called earlier that morning and was due to arrive at any minute to show us what he'd described to Arthur as our "dream house." I couldn't imagine it would be my dream house, as that mythical dwelling was located somewhere in another hemisphere. I'd already worked up a battery of objections before even looking at the place—the systems this, the gutters that, the roof, the basement, the kitchen, the bath—but I still had to get dressed in something that made me look credible as a potential home owner.

Arthur followed me into the bedroom and watched as I changed my clothes. "How about a white shirt?" he suggested. "People are always impressed with a white shirt."

"You're wearing a white shirt," I reminded him. "We don't want to look like twins."

"Not possible, Patrick. I'm too tall and you're too handsome. When Beatrice and I had lunch the other day, she went on and on about how handsome you are, how lucky I am to have met you." The opinions of Arthur's ex-wife counted for a lot in our relationship, mostly because Arthur was still so attached to her. "All of our friends are always telling me that."

I looked at him doubtfully and changed the subject. Along with every member of my family, the friends Arthur and I had in common were always reminding me of how wonderful Arthur was. Half of them had named one of their kids after him, and the other half had made him godfather to their firstborn.

"Tony's new girlfriend started taking him to the opera," I said. I wanted Arthur to approve of Vivian, but so far he'd shown only a mild interest in the subject of my brother's wedding. "She's turning him into a fan. They went last night."

"*Traviata*, I'll bet."

"Sounds that way. How'd you guess?"

"It's about a doomed woman who can't have the man she loves because of his familial obligations. She dies tragically and the man has about ten minutes of happiness before facing a lifetime of regret. Sound familiar? And speaking of regret, Patrick, Eben was especially positive about this house, so I hope you're going to keep an open mind when we look at it. I don't want to regret turning down the perfect place for the next year and a half."

"I'll see what I can do." Arthur and I saw time differently. When he planned for our future, he talked about what we'd be doing in the next five or ten years. I tended to see the future in terms of fifteen-minute blocks. "Should I wear a tie?"

"Better not. We don't want to make it look as if we're trying too hard."

He stood behind me, reached his long arms around me, and squeezed tight. I had a sudden need to scratch the top of my head where his chin was resting, but I couldn't move my arms.

"Try to think of this house the way you think of me, sweetheart. Maybe not perfect, but with enough good to make up for the bad. When you add it all up, I'm worth putting up with, aren't I?"

I tried to answer, but he was cutting off my oxygen. Fortunately, he decided he had to floss his teeth, so he let go of me before I passed out and before he had time to start getting amorous.

The only thing that depressed me more than the ecological breakdown of the planet and my parents' unhappiness was my sex life with Arthur. There's no point in going into it in detail. In the end, all unhappy sex lives are alike. I don't blame Arthur. The problem was as much my fault as his. Whenever I thought about our sex life, I thought about two bald tires, spinning and spinning and spinning on a patch of ice. Once you've tried pushing, pulling, putting chains on the wheels and sand on the snow, there's not much you can do but turn off the engine, take the key out of the ignition, and start walking.

*   *   *

Our real estate agent ushered us into his spotless, mint-condition 1974 silver Volvo that Sunday morning, all smiles and goodwill. "Now this is an incredible morning!" he said, shaking his head in amazement. He could even make an observation about the weather sound like a compliment, and I felt embarrassed, as I usually do when confronted with optimism.

Arthur claimed our real estate agent's name was Eben, and I insisted it was Evan. Because E. had treated us like best friends five minutes after we met, and because he was too assiduously casual to give out business cards, it always seemed rude to ask for clarification. We avoided using his name. When it was necessary, we referred to him in a garbled slur that came out sounding like Eh'en.

E. was the kind of hale and hearty, extremely tall and lean man New England was famous for producing. Glowing good health oozed from his every Congregational pore. He had piercing blue eyes, a full head of prematurely gray hair, which he wore tied back in a stylish ponytail, and the kind of bright-white, perfectly formed teeth that can't help but make a person look a little shallow. I never felt more like an escapee from some holding tank on Ellis Island than I did in the presence of this captain of the *Mayflower*.

He slapped me on the back as I got into the rear seat of the car. "Ready to change your life, Patrick?" he asked, grinning.

I told him I'd been ready for that for years.

"Is there really an orchard of fruit trees in the backyard?" Arthur asked.

"Not exactly an orchard, but you have to see it to believe it, guys." E. always referred to Arthur and me as "guys" or "men," possibly to reassure us that he didn't doubt our masculinity.

I strapped myself into the back seat, delighted to see that Max, E.'s basset hound, was along for the ride. I reached out to pat his head, and as usual, he looked over at me with his bored, bloodshot eyes and bared his teeth. What he really wanted was for Arthur, the one true love of his life, to turn around and smile at him. This was enough to set his tail wagging for hours.

Arthur loved dogs. Dogs loved him. Strays were always coming up to him on the street and nuzzling against him lovingly. I've never had much rapport with animals, even as a child. My parents once announced to my brothers and me that they were going to buy us a dog, but we had to decide on a breed. Ryan wanted "some friendly old mutt" rescued from the gas chambers of an animal shelter, Tony wanted "the biggest, meanest, ugliest German shepherd" we could find, and I wanted a turtle. We compromised on an aloof, elderly cat Tony named Rover. Rover ran away one week after we got her, and the subject of pets was never mentioned again.

As E. pulled away from the curb, he said, "You know what, guys? This place is so perfect, I don't think even you'll be able to find anything objectionable in it, Pat."

"Are you a gambling man?" I asked.

"He's joking," Arthur said. "I can't believe it has so much space. Anyway, I trust your taste. Patrick does, too."

"He does," I said. "Don't I, Max? Max is looking particularly bright-eyed this morning, Eh'en. He isn't pregnant, is he?"

"To tell you the truth," E. said, "Mona and I were even thinking about trying to get our hands on this place ourselves." Mona was E.'s wife, a pediatrician. E. mentioned her name once every ten minutes, an unnecessary reminder of his heterosexuality. "We decided it wasn't big enough for the family. But she agreed you guys would love it."

In addition to E., Mona, and Max, "the family" comprised a three-year-old son named either Nathan or Ethan and an in-utero daughter named Regina, due in four months. Arthur and I had once been invited to dinner to meet "the family."

"Let's hope she's right," Arthur said. "We can have you all over for a celebration as soon as we move in."

I rolled my eyes at Max. While our dinner with "the family" hadn't been the most riotously good time I'd ever had, it had been pleasant enough. Still, I wasn't thrilled at the thought of adding yet another crazy-in-love couple to our list of friends. Almost all of the people Arthur socialized with were married couples who at least appeared to be content, secure, and monogamous. On the whole, they set a bad example for Arthur. My friends were a group of singles, disappointed in love, in despair at being alone, petrified at the thought that they actually might meet someone and have to make a commitment. Arthur hadn't taken to many of them.

Although our dream house was close to the noise and traffic of Mount Auburn Street, it was set off in a tiny, tranquil neighborhood that seemed removed from the rest of the city. E. turned off the main street and onto a narrow road so rutted with potholes he had to slow to a crawl. We crossed an abandoned railroad track, wound around a complex of three or four Victorian brick buildings used by the

maintenance crew of the Mount Auburn Cemetery, and entered a
dead-end lane lined with a half-dozen shabby, asphalt-shingled
houses. At the end of the lane, off to one side and surrounded by a
stand of scruffy fir trees, was a clapboard Greek Revival cottage with
a bracketed canopy over the front door and a For Sale sign hanging
on the picket fence. It was painted a wonderfully garish shade of
yellow and stuck out from the houses around it like a daffodil in a
junkyard. It appealed to me so immediately, looking so secluded and
cozy, my spirits sank in defeat.

E., who obviously sensed that something was up, turned around
in his seat and said, "Nice, isn't it?"

"Loud," I said.

"Patrick loves loud," Arthur revealed.

E. led us through the rooms on the first floor, all low-ceilinged
and sunny, with cheerful white walls. Arthur was walking more and
more slowly, mesmerized by the charm of the place. Max slobbered
around after him, sitting at his feet and looking up with adoration
every time he stopped to admire some particularly appealing feature—
the rough planking on the floors, the polished woodwork around the
windows, the obsolete fireplace.

There were three small bedrooms on the second floor, the largest
of which looked out across the rolling backyard to a twelve-foot
stucco wall that divided the property from the cemetery. The wall
was covered with ancient, ropy vines, and the branches of the trees in
the cemetery hung over into the yard.

"Now, there's a view that isn't going to change anytime soon," E.
commented, his arms draped over our shoulders as we stared out the
window. "And that cemetery is a bird sanctuary. In the spring and
summer they have bird-watching walks every morning at sunrise."

"Sign me up," I said. I tried to make the idea sound loathsome,
but I was up at dawn anyway, and it crossed my mind that it might
be nice to learn a thing or two about birds before they were all killed
off by heat and pollution.

The owners had left a note saying they'd gone out for a few hours
and advising us to stay as long as we liked. They'd drawn up a plan
of the backyard, detailing the beds of perennials and the genera of the
numerous trees. I wandered down from the second floor and sat at
the kitchen table, gazing out the windows to the peaceful yard, trying
to keep my promise to Arthur and look at things with an open mind.

I hated to admit that E. had been right, but I hadn't yet seen anything I could reasonably object to. Unfortunately, our real estate agent knew his business.

When Arthur and E. came down to the kitchen, I was carefully slicing a pear from the bowl in the center of the table.

"I like this place a lot," Arthur said. "And you know what, Eh'en, I think Patrick likes it, too."

"He does," I said. "But let's get down to the systems here."

"All brand-new. New furnace, new plumbing, new wiring throughout. Gas heat. Even a burglar alarm system."

"There's the rub," I said. "Arthur isn't good with those kinds of things. He'd have the police out here every time he opened the door."

"I'll learn," Arthur said. He was fiddling with a panel of switches against one wall, flicking the lights on and off. Max was at his feet, gazing up, transformed by love, oblivious of the light show.

All the electricity went off and then back on. "You'd better be careful," I told Arthur. "You break it, you buy it."

He hit another switch, and an icy breeze came pouring out of a vent over my head.

I reached up my hand. "What's that?"

"Must be the central air conditioning," E. said. "Did I forget to mention they put in central air, too?"

Arthur sat down at the table opposite me. "Think you could stand to live here, Patrick?" he asked.

"It isn't unimaginable," I said, and in truth, it wasn't. Optimally, I'd be living there alone, but that hadn't been the question. I cut up the rest of the pear and passed the slices around. It was then I noticed that Arthur and E. were both trying to suppress narrow, self-satisfied grins of victory.

Eight

}

I called my parents' store the following week to try and get some information about the wedding. Ryan answered the phone, sounding typically distressed and addled. My older brother has the vocal inflections of a man suffering from chronic stomach cramps.

"O'Neil's Men's Shop, may I . . . It's under the counter, Rita. May I . . . In the drawer, in the drawer under the counter, with all the other receipts. Well, where else would I put it? I'm sorry, can I help you with something? Well, it's definitely under there. Just look around. Hello?"

I said, "I'm trying to find a pair of leather pants with a sixty-two-inch waist."

"Patrick. She's driving me crazy today. She's got some lunatic idea about reorganizing the filing system, and the whole place is in an uproar. You don't know how lucky you are you stayed out of this business. How's it going?"

"Better than ever." Complaining to Ryan was definitely a case of carrying coals to Newcastle.

"Oh, good, good. I'm glad to hear it. How's my buddy Arthur?"

"Breathing, last time I checked."

"Great," he said, in his earnest, vague way. Most often, Ryan paid little attention to what was being said to him or going on around him. Ever since he and his wife had split up, he'd retreated more and more into his own world, the boundaries of which seemed to be closing in on him. Ryan's life was beginning to look to me like something out of a TV movie, one of those stories in which an adult kidnapping victim gets chained up in someone's basement and is forced to serve dinner to his captors.

My suspicion was that my older brother was scarred by his name, not that it was anyone's fault. Ryan is my mother's maiden name, and she named my brother in honor of her dying father. Ryan O'Neil is a perfectly solid name, and no one had any reason to suspect that just when our Ryan was coming of age, a handsome young actor named Ryan O'Neal would be the hottest thing in Hollywood. Every time my brother was introduced to a roomful of people, there was a flurry of amusement and interest, which usually evolved into a discussion of how talented and good-looking the other Ryan O'Neal was, and left a trace of disappointment that it was only my well-meaning brother who'd joined the company.

"How's business today?" I asked.

"Pathetic," he whispered. "Not a customer since ten o'clock this morning."

"Maybe it's the season."

"You're right about that," he said loudly, with a forced gaiety that was obviously intended for my parents. "We're having that big spring sale soon, and we'll be bouncing off the walls."

O'Neil's Men's Shop had never exactly been a threat to Filene's, but when I was growing up, my parents had done a fairly booming business in the thriving downtown section of the suburb where we lived. About ten years earlier, a shopping mall was built in a neighboring town, and O'Neil's, along with the other downtown shops, had begun sliding downhill. When Tony was still living in the basement of my parents' house, he'd help out at the store from time to time, especially when my father was in the hospital. As soon as he moved to Chicago, my parents, for reasons that defy comprehension, had convinced Ryan to give up his modestly successful sales job with an athletic-shoe company. They lured him into O'Neil's by playing up my father's bad health and the amount of work that was left in my mother's lap during his frequent hospitalizations. Now they always talked about the store in glowing terms when Ryan was within earshot. He thought their optimism was genuine and was unflappably upbeat around them so he wouldn't be the one to let on that their business was dying.

I said, "I'm calling to try and get some info on this wedding shower for Loreen and your brother."

"Oh, we're counting down the days," he said.

"Me, too. What is the countdown, by the way?"

"To tell you the truth, Pat, I don't know. Hold on while I get the boss."

He called out to my mother and began arguing with her about some misplaced order forms. I heard Rita say, "Stop acting like a child, Ryan; you're thirty-six years old." She grabbed the phone. "What is it now, Patrick?"

"Just calling to say hello," I told her. "I'm at work, so I really can't gossip for too long." I began to tap at the keys of my computer to intimidate her. O'Neil's had not entered the computer age. "How's business?"

"Terrible," she whispered. "I'm pretending to organize some nonexistent filing system just to look busy. Your father doesn't do a thing but read the paper. If you'd come here to work, Ryan wouldn't feel so isolated. He keeps telling me he wishes you'd come work with us."

It was one of her standard comments. My mother and I were always knocking heads about the store. She'd designated me as the son who could or should have made something of himself, preferably—who knows why?—an anesthesiologist. At the same time, she was convinced that I refused to work at the store because I thought I was better than my brothers. By becoming a teacher and then a travel agent, I was a disappointment because I hadn't lived up to what she saw as my potential and a threat because someday I might. Trying to figure out the logic of wanting yet another person working in a store that did no business made me feel as if my brain was going to explode, but I was fishing for information, so I held my tongue. "Listen, I had a dream about Tony and Loreen last night, and I woke up and realized I didn't even know when the shower was going to be."

"Well, I wouldn't lose too much sleep over it, dear. You're not invited anyway."

"I know. I just wanted to make sure I buy a present on time. And before you send out the wedding invitations and everything."

"Wedding invitations? My God! What's the sudden interest, Patrick? You haven't had any curiosity about this wedding for the past twelve months, and now you're asking me about wedding invitations. Why do I get the feeling there's something you're not telling me?"

"Because you have a suspicious nature, that's why."

"That must be it, then." She sighed and scolded Ryan loudly, accusing him of acting like a three-year-old. Nonchalantly, she asked me if I'd heard from that brother of mine lately.

"Tony? I haven't heard from him in months. He never calls anymore. My phone bills are so high, I can't afford to call him. Is he still living in Chicago?"

"This is odd," she said. "I talked to him a couple of days ago, and he told me the two of you had had a nice conversation within the past week. One of you must be confused."

Tony had sworn me to secrecy about his phone calls. "Come to think of it," I said, "you're right. I guess it slipped my mind."

"Slipped your mind? He said you talked for over an hour. Why the secrecy?"

"Well, why did you ask, if you knew the answer?"

"I asked a question, you lied."

"When you come right down to it, Rita, the question was a lie, too." My family was held together by a network of intricately woven deceptions. It meant very little to be caught in a lie, because, as in this case, the exposure usually revealed someone else's lie. "I'd say we've reached an impasse."

"We have indeed. How's Arthur?" she accused.

"Managing."

"If you mean he's managing to put up with your treatment of him, I wouldn't make it sound so casual. It can't be an easy job."

"All right, all right, let's call a truce. I'm having a lot of trouble at work today."

"I'm sorry, Patrick. I got carried away. I'm cracking under the pressure of trying to keep all my sinking ships afloat—the store, your father, Ryan. It's not an easy job. I'm beginning to feel like I'm sinking myself. I didn't mean to snap at you." She suddenly sounded so weary and sad, I regretted calling and even bringing up the subject of the wedding. "Anyway," she said, "I've been meaning to ask you out here for dinner. We haven't talked in a while. We can go out to a restaurant and have a friendly chat."

"Just the two of us?"

"Don't sound so surprised, dear. Why not?"

"It's not the norm, you have to admit."

My parents were now, and always had been, inseparable. They only spent time apart when my father was in the hospital, which probably explains why he had so much surgery. The mystery of why two people who clearly disliked each other as intensely as they did would choose to spend so much time in tandem had plagued my brothers and me. Finally, Tony came up with the theory that they couldn't be apart for long because each was afraid the other might be having a good time. As long as they were together, each could make sure the other was miserable.

"I didn't know you were so concerned with norms, dear. Just plan on Thursday night after work. And bring along the information you've got on the honeymoon. I want to go over the details with you."

"Loreen's taking care of the honeymoon," I said. And there isn't going to be one, I thought.

"I know. But there are a few little extras I'd like to spring for."

Loreen had planned a trip to a health spa near Palm Springs. She'd told me she could use it as a tax write-off, since she'd be learning new menu ideas and exercise techniques for her diet clients. In addition to being attractive and soft-spoken, Loreen was extremely practical. I'd never heard of anything that sounded more unbearable than a week in the desert in July, eating eggless omelets and taking aerobics classes around the clock. If I were Tony, I'd have canceled the wedding just to get out of the trip. I agreed to bring the information to dinner and let Rita take a look at it.

"Thank you," she said. "Now we're friends again. The answer to your inquiry is that the shower isn't until June. You've got plenty of time to buy a teacup or something. And you'll know about the wedding invitations when you get one in the mail. What are you and Arthur doing for fun these days? Or aren't you planning to tell me about the house?"

"House?" Obviously Tony had been in a particularly talkative mood during their phone conversation.

"I don't see why you'd want to keep something like that a secret, dear. I hope you were at least planning to send me your new address."

"The house is a possibility," I said. "Nothing definite."

"Your father and I were delighted to hear about it. I hate to say it, but that Arthur is the best thing that ever happened to you. You should be thankful for the day you met him. You're not planning to jinx the deal, are you?"

"The thought had crossed my mind."

"Well, just remember, it isn't every day someone buys you a house."

"I'm putting up some of the down payment, Rita. He's not buying it for me; we're buying it together."

"Good. As long as you admit that someone's buying it. Tony is all excited about it. I kept asking him about the wedding, but all he wanted to talk about was this house."

"That Tony," I said. "Always thinking of someone else."

Nine

}

Arthur and I had words on the way to the movies that night. Arthur and I always had words when he was driving. Years earlier, we'd had a couple of friends who lived in a house out in the suburbs. We'd had to give them up over the driving issue. If I drove the fifteen miles, Arthur accused me of being overly controlling. If he drove, we fought so much about his driving, the evening invariably turned into a nightmare. It was part of Arthur's fear of being criticized. He wanted to be accepted by me, and everyone else, one hundred percent, even if that meant my sitting quietly in the passenger seat and watching him plow head-on into a sixteen-wheeler.

Arthur is the single worst driver I've ever met. When I cornered him with accusations that he was a menace on the road, he reminded me that he'd never had an accident. My theory was that when people saw Arthur coming, big body hunched over the steering wheel, face practically pressed against the windshield, vein in his forehead throbbing, bald head gleaming, they got out of the way fast. Arthur braked at green lights. He alternated between running stop signs and coming to a dead halt in the middle of intersections. He had a mortal fear of passing anyone, and he slowed nearly to a stop when anyone passed him. His driving was so indecisive, I was sometimes amazed he could summon up the will to push his foot down on the accelerator with enough force to move the car forward.

"You're in the wrong lane," I told him as we crawled down Memorial Drive, far to the left. "We have to make a right turn there at the bridge, and if we miss it, we end up miles out of the way."

Arthur said nothing. He had on the pair of black-framed glasses he used only for driving and was peering out the window as if trying to see through a sandstorm. He was still wearing the suit he'd worn to work that day, and he looked impressive. No one would ever accuse Arthur of being handsome in a traditional way, although he did have his physical assets. Personally, I've never understood my friends' mania for attaching themselves to handsome men and beautiful women. After a month and a half of any relationship, you get so accustomed to your lover's face, you don't really see it anyway—handsome, hideous, or anything in between. Long after you've stopped being able to appreciate your lover's looks, people on the streets are turning somersaults, making outrageous passes at him, and hating you for being the lucky toad who ended up with Adonis. An ordinary-looking Joe (or Arthur) is a much more sensible choice.

I had my elbow stuck out the window and was leaning my head in my hand, looking at the lights of Boston across the expanse of the Charles River. "You should start pulling over now," I said.

"I'm driving, Patrick," he said calmly. "You can drive when you're driving, but I'm driving now. Not to mention that this is my car. I think I'm capable of driving my own car by my own self. Check to see if there's anyone on my right, so I can inch over, will you?"

I craned my neck. There was a steady stream of cars passing us on the right, at twice our speed. "Don't try it," I said. "You should have been in that lane for miles now. You should have switched lanes back at the Hyatt. Before the Hyatt."

"No lectures, thank you."

He tried to edge into the right lane by giving the wheel random little jerks. The cars whizzing past honked and swerved. "You're going to kill us!" I shouted.

We missed the turn.

"Damn," he said under his breath. He relaxed into his seat, brushed back his nonexistent hair, and adjusted his glasses. "Oh, well, how was work today, sweetheart?"

"Arthur," I said, "we're going to have to go miles out of our way.

We're late already because it took you so long to get out of the driveway back home. We're not going to get a space anywhere near the theater, and we'll miss the beginning of the movie. Let's not even bother to try."

"Maybe you're right. But I'll tell you something, Patrick: someone at my office saw this movie and said it was lousy. We're probably better off missing it." He rolled down his window and stuck out his hand. "It's nice and cool tonight," he said, "just the way you like it. Maybe we should be buying a house in northern Minnesota."

The truth was, I hadn't wanted to see the movie anyway. It was one of those tiresome thrillers about a psychopathic killer whose reign of terror over a big, polluted city is ultimately brought to an end by a team of two mismatched cops who become buddies and end up saving each other's lives in a scene heavily laden with homoerotic overtones. Lots of cars rolling over and bursting into flames and tough-guy dialogue about assholes. But when Arthur and I were discussing what movie to see that night, I'd tried to use it as a bargaining chip so we wouldn't end up at a festival of early Burt Reynolds comedies.

The breeze blowing in through the windows was cool and damp. A thin, late-winter fog hovered over the city, which looked far away. The thought of crossing the river and entering the traffic and noise of downtown Boston was exhausting, and I was suddenly delighted the trip had been canceled. I pushed the recline button on my seat and shut my eyes. Arthur slipped one of his homemade tapes into the player, and an ancient recording of Richard Tauber singing selections from German operettas came on.

Arthur and I had distinctly different musical tastes. My idea of auditory heaven would be living in a smoky cocktail lounge where Ben Webster was forever playing lush ballads. Arthur didn't care much for jazz. Spontaneity and improvisation of any sort made him nervous. The only music he ever listened to was reassuring light opera and Mozart symphonies, those models of absolute perfection. Out of deference to Arthur's feelings, I listened to my tapes long after he was asleep, and to my great surprise, I'd grown to appreciate his ancient recordings of operettas. All those warbling sopranos and tenors fighting to be heard over the crackling of surface noise struck me as terribly poignant. There was a purity and innocence about the sound, which I loved and identified with those parts of Arthur I most admired—Arthur the gentle, loving soul fighting to be heard above the rumbling injustice of fascist dictatorships and the INS.

Now that the movie had been ruled out as a possibility, I relaxed back into my seat and concentrated on Tauber singing a waltz aria from *The Merry Widow*. Arthur began to tell me about one of his clients. He was working on the case of a student from Singapore whose visa had run out; he was about to be sent back home. The complicating factor was that he'd tested positive for HIV. If sent back, he faced being ostracized by family and friends and finding health care that was, for his particular problems, vastly inferior to what he was likely to find in Boston. "And as if all that isn't bad enough," Arthur said, "the poor guy gets separated from his American lover for an indefinite period of time. The case is breaking my heart."

Most of the cases Arthur related to me were heartbreaking. The recurring subplot in many of them was the threatened breakup of familial or lover relationships. This theme was so pervasive, I sometimes had to remind myself that Arthur was a lawyer and not a family therapist.

In one way or another, Arthur was always trying to keep people together.

Somewhere in the middle of this story, I realized he'd probably planned the whole evening right from the start. He'd never intended to see any movie, which was why he'd agreed to my choice so swiftly. Knowing how much I distrusted his driving, he'd used it to achieve his end.

I sat up in my seat with a familiar panic gripping me and lowered the volume on the tape player. Arthur was behind the wheel, and I was the passenger. When you're the passenger, there's nothing you can do but go along for the ride. Wherever Arthur wanted to go, I would be taken, which was very likely no place any more exotic than home.

Arthur turned the car around and we headed back, west along the river, with a full moon above us and the stunted skyline of Boston to one side. Once again I let myself be lulled by the night. Perhaps it didn't matter so much who was driving, as long as Arthur didn't get us killed. All that lilting, graceful music issuing from the speakers was beginning to put me into a trance.

We passed the turn to our street.

"Where are we going?" I asked.

"I want to take another look at our house." Arthur had been referring to the house near the cemetery as "ours" for the past few days, an attempt at subliminal manipulation, which, however unsubtle, was perhaps having some effect on me. I'd begun to think of the place as the Yellow Fever, but I'd begun to think of it often. "Beatrice said we should get an idea of the house and the neighborhood at different hours of the day."

Arthur's dragging Beatrice into the negotiations was not a good sign. He always used her as the voice of professional sanity and rationality, although I sometimes suspected he made up half her quotes himself. "In other words," I said, "you had it all planned that we'd miss the movie and come out here instead."

"Oh, sweetheart, don't be so suspicious. Life isn't a constant battle. We're out driving anyway, we missed the movie, and it seemed like it might be a nice thing to do."

He reached over and put his hand on my knee and looked at me sweetly through the lenses of the black-framed glasses, glinting now with the light of passing traffic. With his big body and bald head, Arthur had never really looked young, but he had that smooth complexion and those kind eyes, which gave his face an ageless, angelic quality. I couldn't decide if Arthur had manipulated this trip or if I was merely being churlish. No one could make me doubt my own perceptions more effectively than Arthur.

The house was dark except for a light in the living room window, shining through the branches of one of the fir trees. In a few months, virtually every window would be shaded in leafy privacy. Even at night, the yellow was so bright, the walls of the house seemed to be glowing.

I tried to imagine what it would be like sitting in there now, sleepy and secure, the house filled with music, but the fantasy quickly became confused with an image of Tony and Vivian curled up on a sectional sofa, listening to *La Traviata*.

"Remember the summer we went to Nova Scotia, Patrick? Remember the house we rented?"

"Of course I do," I said.

"Doesn't this house remind you a little of that one?"

"A little," I told him. The similarity had crossed my mind a few times already and contributed to a vague sense of peacefulness that overtook me when I thought about the place.

Early on in our relationship, Arthur and I had taken a ferry to Nova Scotia. We drove along the Canadian coast with no clear destination for several days and ended up in a tiny fishing village. There, we rented a cottage on the edge of a cliff perched out over the ocean.

It was a weatherbeaten, faded-yellow place with sloping floors and warped paneling and sulfurous drinking water that was pumped up from a well and was either poisonous or wonderfully healthy. We spent three weeks in the house, reading our way through a huge stack of books and listening to Arthur's tapes. The mornings were foggy and the days clear and mild, always with a salty breeze blowing the curtains into the house. We rarely left the porch, which stuck out, almost treacherously, over the water. In the afternoon, when the wind shifted, we'd wrap ourselves in blankets and read until the late, orange twilight. All night long, we could hear the sound of distant foghorns and the rushing of the tide, and sometimes the moonlight was so bright and so blue, I found it frightening.

I suppose it was on that trip that a slight, almost imperceptible shift in our relationship occurred. Some bond between us was cemented, and I began to think of Arthur, along with my need for an income, my family, and the mole on my right shoulder, as a part of my life. We often talked about how happy we'd been during those three quiet weeks. Increasingly, though, it had all begun to sound to me like my longing for a cooler, greener world, one that no longer existed and could never be wished back into existence.

As we sat in the car in front of the house, we discussed a particularly lovely morning we'd spent in that other house, over a thousand miles away, and when Arthur asked if I didn't agree that this city house was a deal too good to pass up, I agreed that it was, thinking about Nova Scotia and that trip we'd been on years before, my brother's passionate relationship with a woman I'd never met, and Rita's cautionary words about my jinxing the deal on the house.

"If we're going to make an offer, we should make it soon."

"Probably the sooner the better," I said.

"Tomorrow," Arthur said.

"At the latest."

Arthur was beaming. "I don't think you'll regret this, Patrick. I really don't."

I did regret it, the minute I realized what I'd said. We drove off down the narrow street, and as soon as the house was out of sight, I turned up the volume on the tape player and concentrated on the fact that in a little more than a week I'd be on the shuttle headed to New York.

Part
2

Ten

The day before our dinner date, I called my mother to confirm our plans. Rita told me that she'd invited my father, and Ryan, who otherwise would have been stuck home alone, had decided to come, too. I should have known the dinner would evolve into a group project, but I was disappointed anyway. I'd imagined that my mother and I would have an easier time of discussing Tony's wedding without the rest of the crowd. To get revenge, I lied and told her I'd invited Sharon.

"Sharon?"

"You remember Sharon. You and your husband came for dinner once when I lived at her house."

"Believe me, I haven't forgotten Sharon. That would be like forgetting the Statue of Liberty. She was wearing sandals and a sundress in February. Five minutes after we walked in the door, she cornered me and asked if I'd ever regretted marrying your father. As if it isn't obvious. Why would you invite her?"

"Well, why would you invite Ryan and Dad?"

"I hope you're not comparing them to that woman, Patrick. Please. If you have to invite someone, why don't you invite Arthur? At least he doesn't talk as much."

"Unfortunately," I said, "she decided not to come."

"I'm sorry the idea of having dinner with us was so unappealing to her. Just make sure you're on time. If Ryan doesn't eat by eight, his blood sugar goes crazy, the poor slob. He inherited your father's health. Have you signed any papers about this house deal?"

"Nearly," I said.

"Nearly? What are you waiting for, dear?"

I told her I was having trouble finding a pen and quickly hung up. Arthur had already made an offer on the house, and we were waiting to hear if it was accepted. Arthur and I were both nervous about the outcome, although for different reasons.

The next evening, I was held up at the office by an emergency involving one of the other agents.

Grace was an ex-nurse, a frail, somewhat timid woman in her late thirties, who seemed to be constitutionally incapable of contradicting anyone. No matter what ridiculous vacation scheme a person came in with, Grace would cheerfully say, "I think that sounds wonderful. I'm sure you're going to have a wonderful time," and send them off. She refused to warn people about food poisoning, political unrest, or potential health and safety hazards, theorizing that it wasn't fair to upset them and ruin their vacations. "Oh, don't worry about the water," I'd heard her say countless times. "I'm sure it's fine. Why worry about water? Just enjoy yourself."

It was hard to imagine Grace enjoying herself under any circumstances. She had absolutely no personal experience with travel, because she was terrified of every form of transportation except the swan boats that glided across the pond on Boston Common. She enrolled frequently in fear-of-flying seminars, but never dredged up the courage to take the flight to Hartford that constituted graduation. I loved being around her; she made me feel adventurous.

This particular crisis concerned the plight of a fifty-three-year-old, recently divorced woman who'd come in looking for a trip to a warm island where she could relax in the sun, be completely safe and unchallenged, and forget the rest of the world and all her personal traumas. Bermuda would have been the most obvious choice, but Grace, inexplicably, had sent her to a small resort town in Jamaica known primarily for its liberal attitudes toward nude sunbathing and drug use. The client had called around four-thirty that afternoon, demanding that she be put on the next plane back to civilization so she could file a lawsuit against Only Connect. She'd arrived in the town on a broken-down school bus, and as soon as her feet hit the dirt road, she was accosted by a mob of men trying to sell her ganja, nose candy, LSD, magic mushrooms, and aloe vera massages. Accompanied by a team of Rastafarians, she landed at her hotel—a glorified campground—in time to see "a bunch of filthy drug addicts" washing off in an outdoor communal shower. Once she'd closed the door to the wobbly shack that Grace had described as a "private villa," she heard a scrambling noise from above. She looked up and saw a mongoose chasing a rat across the beams near the ceiling.

After lambasting her with insults and accusations for a full five minutes, the customer told Grace she'd call back in an hour, expecting arrangements to have been made for her immediate departure from the island.

Now Grace was sitting at her desk awaiting the second call, pale and prim, mumbling something that sounded vaguely like an affirmation. She had her hair pulled back in a bun and was wearing a tidy blue dress with a white lace collar. Very possibly, Jane Eyre would have ended up looking like Grace if she'd gone off to work at Bitternutt Lodge in Ireland instead of marrying Rochester. There was no way Grace could fly the woman out of Jamaica in the next forty-eight hours. There were several large resort hotels not too far away, but they were all booked to capacity. Even if the customer did agree to stay for a week, she'd have to spend at least two nights in the shack. Between sobs, Grace was blaming Sharon for the situation. Sharon had a special affection for this particular town and recommended it often. She herself spent at least two weeks there every year and had had two of the most passionate love affairs of her life at that very campground. She was perched on the edge of Grace's desk, smoking and frowning, listening to her accuser with no visible remorse.

"I send people there all the time," she finally said, "and they love it. But I don't suggest it for everyone. I wouldn't suggest you go there, for example. Don't blame the place, blame your own bad judgment, Grace. The whole thing doesn't make sense to me; how can these people she's complaining about be 'dirty drug addicts' and be taking a shower? And I'd like to know how she managed to find the only working telephone in the whole town."

The boss had gotten word of the threatened lawsuit. He was pacing around, chewing his lips. Tim was a lean, nervous wreck of a human being. He had his Ph.D. in philosophy from Harvard, and he clearly wasn't cut out for the frantic pace of the business world. There were always rumors circulating around the office that he was being treated for some nervous disorder or other, but I doubt any of them was true. Still, he dashed around the little rooms that made up the agency, sweating through his shirts, tugging on his lips, desperately trying to keep everyone happy and in line. He was intimidated by Sharon, which was probably for the best, as she had much better business instincts than he did.

Grace had asked me to stand by her until she finished with the second call, so I felt obliged to hang around. It was after six and the office was closed by the time the call came. Grace answered with a barely audible hello. "We're all deeply sorry about this, Ruth," she began, "but the fact is, you're going to have to spend tonight in the villa. Yes, just tonight, that's all. One night. And maybe tomorrow night, too."

Tim looked to Sharon for help, and she grabbed the phone.

"Is this Ruth? Ruth, this is Sharon Driscoll. I'm Grace's supervisor here. It sounds like you're having some trouble adjusting." She winked at me. "Put them on the defensive" was one of Sharon's mottoes. "Who? Ruth Bourne? You're kidding. I didn't know it was that Ruth. How was that hotel in Seattle? Sure, I send everyone there; they all love it. If it wasn't for me, that hotel would have gone out of business years ago. Did you mention my name? And did you get treated like royalty? Good. What was in the fruit basket? Why didn't you come to me for this trip? Yeah, but I wouldn't have been too busy for you. So what's going on down there?" She motioned us all out of the office and told us to shut the door on the way.

Grace, Tim, and I went to the reception desk and listened to Fredrick yawn his way through a tale of a torrid love affair he was having with a sixty-three-year-old Catholic priest. Ten minutes later, Sharon emerged, calm and smoking. "You should have told me who it was. Ruth's completely insane, but if you know how to talk to her, she's fine."

"Did she say anything about the lawsuit?" Tim asked.

"Grow up, Tim. There's not going to be any lawsuit. She's staying. I gave her the name of this guy I know pretty well. I told her to look him up and tell him I sent her. He'll introduce her around, and I guarantee she won't set foot on American soil until June."

Eleven

I was close to an hour late in leaving the office, and the traffic out to the suburbs was predictably heavy. I was driving my Yugo, a red piece of rusting metal I'd bought two years earlier against the strong objections of Tony, Arthur, Sharon, and two friends who owned one. My theory is that all cars are worthless junk, a danger to your well-being and the health of the entire planet, so it's best to spend as little money on them as possible. I thought it was a brilliant purchase. The Yugo hadn't given me any trouble at all, and I loved cutting off the old Volvos that dominate the streets of Cambridge in such a small, ugly, cheap red car. It made me feel powerful.

It was one of those early evenings in late March that inspire deep longing. The trees along the side of the highway were mostly bare, and the air was fragrant with the smells of approaching spring—some combination of mud and rotting leaves. I loved knowing that, at least for the next month or so, the northern hemisphere was still tipped comfortably away from the sun. I kept the windows rolled down so I could stick my hand out from time to time to make sure there wasn't a sudden surge in temperature. Late days in spring often make me yearn for baseball games and high school days. The yearning makes no sense at all, since I've never watched even a single baseball game, and all through high school I was friendless and miserable. I spent most of my youth and adolescence sitting in movie theaters and reading true-crime books about parents killing their children or children killing their parents. I had a passing interest in a variety of solitary athletic pursuits—biking, running, swimming, and calisthenics—mostly, I suspect, because they suppressed hormonal urges I found confusing.

Ryan, Tony, and I are close in age, but we never spent much time together once we got to high school. Ryan had a thoroughly undistinguished career as a left fielder on the intramural baseball team and played drums in a rock band that never made it out of the bass player's garage. Sometimes, when distracted, Ryan still drummed on tabletops or on the dashboard of a car. I don't think he ever entirely gave up his dreams of being a rock star, although it was hard to tell what Ryan dreamed about. I had trouble believing he dreamed at all.

Tony, of course, had the most active social life of the three of us; starting in junior high, he had a steady stream of girlfriends calling the house and cruising the neighborhood in hopes of catching sight of him. At the dinner table, he and my father would have long, explicit battles about Tony's involvement with his latest "slut," whom my father, in fishing for details, would invariably accuse of being pregnant or having a venereal disease. Tony would accuse my father of taking his frustrations out on him, knock back his chair, and leave the table in a melodramatic huff. My mother would worry over Tony's unfinished meal and chastise my father for talking about sex in front of her, while Ryan complimented the food and reached for thirds. I usually took solace in the basement, where I'd smoke pot and assume some ersatz yoga position that quickly degenerated into masturbation.

However miserable I'd felt in high school, I at least hadn't felt responsible for causing anyone else's misery, a definite advantage to being without friends or lovers. Perhaps that was why I was secretly hoping that the offer Arthur and I had made on the yellow house would be turned down: we wouldn't be stuck owning the place, and no one would be to blame for Arthur's disappointment except the greedy owners.

My parents' store was on the ground floor of a two-story brick building that they owned. The top floor held the dusty offices of a grotesquely fat divorce lawyer and the dentist my brothers and I had been sent to as children. (The latter had recently been indicted on charges of a Medicare scam that involved treating people for nonexistent gum diseases.) On one side of O'Neil's was a jewelry store, which, according to my father, had not made a sale since the day the nearby shopping mall opened, and on the other was a barbershop that had been converted into something called Samurai Death Martial Arts Institute. Samurai Death was one of four martial arts institutes that had opened up in town in the past decade. They heightened my feeling of being in strange, hostile territory, where everyone was capable of smashing blocks of concrete with their bare hands.

The window display at O'Neil's hadn't changed significantly in almost a decade. Two androgynous mannequins wearing unconvincing wigs and ill-fitting green suits were standing in limp-wristed parody of a fashion model pose. Surrounding this hapless couple were stacks of sun-bleached work clothes, underwear from another generation, and clunky black shoes. Occasionally, my mother would haphazardly toss a pile of new gym uniforms or socks into the stew. A Boston TV station had recently done a special on the demise of the downtown areas of suburbs. Repeated shots of O'Neil's windows flashed across the screen. I was heartbroken, but my parents claimed to be thrilled (at least in front of Ryan) with what they considered free publicity.

I locked the Yugo against the roving bands of Samurai Death squads and rapped on the glass door. Ryan came forth, grinning and apologizing, a ring of keys in his hands. He ushered me in with a warm hug. He was spilling out of a white dress shirt and a pair of gray flannel trousers. "Nice material," he said, fingering the lapels of my black sport jacket. "You obviously don't shop here." He forced out a laugh and tossed a limp hank of hair out of his eyes by snapping back his head.

Ryan had inherited my father's dark, handsome coloring and my mother's strong chin and jawline. Feature for feature, he was a lot more striking than either Tony or I, but in the last few years he'd taken on the neglected look of a person who had long since given up on the idea of having a sex life. His black hair had receded unevenly from his temples and brow. A good haircut would have done wonders for him, but out of loyalty, he insisted on going to a local barber who snipped away artlessly and left an archipelago of hair clumps scattered across his skull.

I straightened out his tie and tucked in his shirttails. "If you don't mind me saying so, Ryan, this outfit doesn't do you any favors. Couldn't you find anything more attractive on the racks around here?"

"I don't need favors, Pat, I need miracles, something this store doesn't specialize in."

"Any business today?"

He shrugged. "We always get some. It's a big week for socks. How's Arthur? You should have invited him to this dinner to liven things up a little. I better go dig out your parents. They're probably in back, fighting."

He wandered down the center aisle, tugging at his shirt until he'd disarranged it.

The store was long and narrow, cluttered to an almost incomprehensible degree from the linoleum floor to the high, pressed-tin ceiling. There were tables on either side of the center aisle, stacked with shirts and sweaters and pants in no particular order. Customers generally had to stand by helplessly while Ryan sifted through the piles in search of their size. The racks of suits against the wall were hidden behind racks of sport jackets that were hidden behind racks of winter coats, making almost everything more or less inaccessible. Ryan worked up front, while my mother kept to her station behind a glass display case at the rear. Rita's counter contained the more expensive dress shirts, tie clasps, cuff links, handkerchiefs, a few bulky watches, and a selection of striped ties of a medium width that was never exactly out of fashion and certainly never in. Because Rita was so eager to look busy, she spent most of her time polishing and shining the glass. She'd amassed a collection of cleaners that included virtually every product put out by Amway, Procter & Gamble, and Dow Chemical.

My father generally stayed out of the front of the store altogether. Eight years earlier, he'd cleared a space behind the dressing rooms, from which he rented formal wear. I think it was the only money-making square footage in the place, although my mother claimed he'd opened it up simply to get away from her.

My parents still had a loyal following of customers, but most of them were getting on in years and had less and less need for new clothes as they retired, got sick, shrunk down a size, and returned to clothes they'd worn in the 1940s. Someone under the age of sixty-five did occasionally come in, but it was rarely to buy anything more expensive than a gym uniform or a package of briefs.

Each time I entered the store, I was swept away by nostalgia and dread. The smell of all that denim and polyester and accumulated dust hit me in the face the way a blast of heat from the engine of an idling car hits you on a hot summer day. The truth is, I loved my parents' store and had since I was a child. I loved to go there after school and play in the piles of clothes stacked in the dark storeroom. On Saturdays, the busiest days in that era when the earth was cooler and my parents ran a thriving business, I was allowed to help out in front, talk to customers, and operate the cash register. Now the image of myself as the eager, helpful little boy in tie and jacket—a miniature mock-up of my father—made me cringe. But then I had loved being a dutiful son. Neither Ryan nor Tony had had the slightest bit of interest in the store, yet they were the ones who ended up working there. Sometimes I worried that what would make me happiest would be to step into Ryan's arch-supported shoes and take over the family business. During slow periods at the travel agency, I often fantasized about going into O'Neil's with a work crew, cleaning it from top to bottom, chucking out all the old merchandise, and snazzing things up.

My mother came out from the back room, her head tilted to one side as she screwed in an earring. "Late again, Patrick," she said without looking at me.

"Problems at work," I told her.

She took her position behind the glass case and looked at me doubtfully. "I've never known anyone who has as many problems as you do. How do I look, dear?"

She had on a white blouse and a gray flannel skirt, a feminized version of Ryan's outfit, and she looked particularly short and uncharacteristically defenseless. Rita dressed for work in sedate, slightly mannish outfits that complemented the severe and rigid sides of her personality, those I liked the least. Her hair, which had been a dark and glamorous red, was now tinted some shade dangerously close to orange. She'd worn it in the same style forever—shoulder-length, brushed off her face, and held in place with a plastic headband.

Age and worry over my father, the store, and her three sons had deepened the lines in her face and given her the tough look of the hardworking and slightly contemptuous.

"You look very nice," I said.

"Oh, good. I don't know why I trust your opinion, but I do. Listen, Patrick, I have a favor to ask. I can count on you, can't I?"

"It depends on the favor."

She sighed, disappointed. "The whole point of a favor is that you do it, you don't question it."

"I'm not going to agree to just anything, Rita."

She frowned. I was standing in front of her counter, trying to organize the ties according to color. "Don't mess that up," she scolded. "I won't be able to find anything. All I want you to do is go along with the suggestions I make for the honeymoon. No matter what I say, your father will disagree with me, but you might carry some weight, since you're the travel professional."

"I promise to listen to your plans; how's that?"

"Thanks for nothing."

Ryan came out of the back room, snapping open a beer can. My father trailed behind.

"You're going to drink that now and spoil your dinner?" my father asked. "What sense does that make?"

"Stop bossing him around, Jimmy. You treat him like a child."

Ryan winked at me and took a swallow from the can.

"Where's the funeral, Patrick?" my father asked.

"Black is fashionable," Ryan said.

"Well, it just goes to show. And I thought we were on the cutting edge here. Get rid of the plaids, Rita; black is the big color for spring."

Twelve

〜

I drove to the restaurant—an eatery in the lobby of the hotel beside the shopping mall—with my mother in the passenger seat, nervously clutching the dashboard, and Ryan and my father packed into the miniature back seat. My father is thin and short, but, particularly in cars, he tends to sit with his arms stretched over the back of the seat and his knees spread, thus taking up twice as much space as his body requires. In the past five years he'd been operated on for bleeding ulcers, kidney stones, and gallstones. ("Marry a man," my mother liked to say, "and end up with a rock quarry.") He'd spent almost as much time in the hospital as he had at home. He'd developed emphysema the year before and supposedly given up cigarettes, though he occasionally lit up.

"What the hell," he'd say optimistically, "I can always kill myself if it gets too bad." He was almost seventy. Despite the weariness brought on by his bad health, he'd retained a certain dashing appearance. His sunken cheeks and the lines around his eyes added more drama to his face. Only his neck, which was terribly thin, showed the ravages of his various illnesses.

He was still attractive enough to make mildly suggestive comments to comely relatives and waitresses without looking completely ridiculous. But when he did flirt, he did so with the hostility of an aging handsome man who's bitter for not having taken full advantage of his looks in his youth.

"Jesus Christ, Patrick," he said as I drove through a tangle of prefab housing projects and condo villages, "it's so cramped back here, it's like riding in a coffin."

"Please," my mother said.

"I think this is perfect for Patrick," Ryan said, still knocking back his beer. "It's bohemian."

I tried to change the subject by mentioning that I'd been giving some thought to the store lately.

"And you're coming to give your brother a hand," my mother stated flatly.

"No."

"We could use the help, Pat."

"You see, your brother is asking you to come work with him. I'm glad you're speaking up for yourself, Ryan."

"I've been thinking the way to increase business might be to specialize. Target a particular customer, one who doesn't get what he needs at the mall. I thought it might be a good idea to try specializing in large sizes."

"Clothes for fat people?" my father asked me, appalled.

"James!" My mother's backward glance clearly indicated she was offended on Ryan's behalf.

"Well, heavy, also tall and broad-shouldered. Big-boned people."

"For Christ's sake, Patrick, the store is crowded enough as it is. The last thing we need in there is a lot of fat people pushing through the racks."

"Well, maybe we should critique your body next, James." She turned toward me. "For someone who claims to have no interest in the store, you certainly have a lot of ideas."

"I've never said I have no interest in the store."

"No, you don't say it, you just refuse to work there, you refuse to offer your brother a little support. It isn't as if that travel nonsense is getting you anywhere. Click, click, click on the computer all day. You just think you're better than Ryan, that's all."

Ryan objected, and my mother apologized to both of us, though the cutting tone in her voice hung in the air. There was a tremendous amount of anger between my mother and me, although usually we kept it just under the surface. In addition to everything else, I don't think she ever completely forgave me for being homosexual. She took

"I'll have what she's having," my father said, folding up the gigantic menu.

"I guess I should have the same thing," Ryan said, unconvincingly.

"Don't be a martyr," my mother said. "He'll have the shrimp scampi."

The waiter was in his early twenties, one of those pumped-up suburban men with wide shoulders and no waistline and a thin, pointless mustache. He reminded me of Tony at that age. He looked to Ryan and cocked his head.

"I'll just have the chicken breast like them."

"Give him the scampi," my father said.

"Oh, all right, I'll have the scampi. What are you having, Pat?"

I quietly ordered a plain broiled breast of chicken. The waiter was obviously having trouble hearing what I said, and I felt like Professor Fields.

When Ryan was off perusing the hors d'oeuvres bar, I took out the file on Tony's honeymoon and set it on the table in front of me. I folded my hands over it and looked at my parents.

"What's with the look?" my father asked.

"Before we talk about the honeymoon," I said, "I have a few blunt questions I'd like to ask you about the wedding."

"Oh, good. I love blunt questions," my mother said. "All you have to do is pretend you're offended, and you're off the hook."

My father, on automatic pilot, picked up a plastic card from the center of the table and began reading about the exotic cocktails the restaurant served.

"If at all possible," I said, "I'd like you to be completely honest with me."

"Unfortunately, dear, I left the lie detector at home, so you'll just have to trust me."

"I'd like to know what you think about this marriage. Honestly."

"What we think?" my mother asked.

I nodded.

"Well, I'll tell you what *I* think," my father said. "I think Loreen is the sweetest, kindest, prettiest girl I've met in a hell of a long time. And she's got brains, too. If I was given the chance to handpick a daughter-in-law, I doubt I could do better than Loreen. She's too good for that brother of yours, but that's not her fault. Does that answer your question?"

"Not really. I asked about the marriage, not Loreen."

"Oh, I forgot," my mother said. "Loreen has nothing to do with the marriage. She's just an innocent bystander. Of course, I know you've never liked her, Patrick."

"Not true. I've always liked her a great deal."

"If you did, I don't think you'd be asking questions in that accusing tone of voice. Jimmy, would you put that card down and listen here? He makes his speech and then goes back to that cocktail list. He knows he can't drink anyway, but he wastes everyone's time with that nonsense."

"Meanwhile, she's solving the world's problems over there. I thought Patrick might like one of these drinks. I was trying to be considerate. And I don't know why you decided to get that chicken, Rita. You know I'm sick of chicken."

I looked across the restaurant, trying to figure out where the conversation would head after their skirmish. Ryan, ever affable, was at the salad bar, laughing it up with one of the businessmen. My original plan had been to talk quietly with my mother and get her to acknowledge that Tony probably wasn't in love with Loreen and that he'd been tricked into giving her the ring. I figured that was one small thing I could do for my younger brother. I didn't believe for a minute he actually intended to go through with the wedding, and I saw myself as opening the exit door for him. I don't know why, but I felt it was up to me to secure Tony's freedom. No one else cared. Even Vivian wasn't pressing hard enough. But I felt oddly outnumbered, overwhelmed just as Tony had probably felt when he tried to put off the engagement.

"Let me put it this way," I said, cutting through the flak. "Do you think Tony's in love with Loreen?"

"Does this have something to do with that long, secret phone conversation you two had?"

Ryan sat down and began to eat from a plate heaped with scallops wrapped in bacon.

"For Christ's sake, Ryan," I said, "is that what you call watching your cholesterol?"

"It's what I call watching my cholesterol skyrocket." He chuckled to himself.

"Leave your brother alone, Patrick," my mother said. "I never heard of anyone dropping dead from a scallop. Where did you get your medical degree? What's *your* theory on Loreen?"

"I think Tony isn't in love with her, that's my theory."

"The only thing that brother of yours has ever cared about is a certain part of his body," my father said, "and he wouldn't know love if it came and bit that off, which is probably the best thing that could happen to him and the rest of us."

"That's lovely talk in a restaurant," my mother whispered, "not to mention in front of me. He always has to reduce everything to its lowest level."

"As if I didn't try to control Tony all alone," my father said, slumped over his glass of water. "As if I wasn't the only one who did."

My mother waved his words off. "I'd like to know why you're bringing this up now, Patrick."

"Because," I said, "Tony told me on the phone the other night that he wanted to put off giving Loreen the ring, but he couldn't because you'd already told her he was going to propose."

"Oh, that," my mother said, obviously relieved. "That was so long ago, who even remembers."

"Listen, Patrick," Ryan said calmly, "no one is in love when they get married. You get married, you settle down, you ease into it. After a while, you don't know whether you're in love, out of love, here, there, where you are. You get up, you go to bed, you're in love, you're not in love, that's the way it is."

"Those scallops have gone to your head, Ryan."

My father said, "He's making perfect sense to me, Patrick, and I think he knows a little more about marriage than you do."

"Come on, Ryan. You were in love when you got married, weren't you?"

"Sure, but that's different. Elaine was the first girl I'd really dated, so of course I was in love with her. I probably still am, for all I know. But Tony's another story."

"You can say that again," my father said.

Our dinners were brought. I noticed my mother observing me, as she usually did in restaurants, to see if I was trying to make eye contact with the waiter. When he'd arranged the plates in front of everyone, he asked if there was anything else we needed.

"Doesn't that come with a bib?" my mother asked nervously, pointing to Ryan's plate.

"A bib? No, that's only for the lobster, not the shrimp."

"Well, this looks thoroughly unappetizing," my father said once we were alone.

My mother took a pair of half-glasses out of her handbag and examined her chicken as if she expected it to fly off the plate. "Overdone," she declared, looking around first to make sure no one could hear.

"Anyway," I said, "I really don't understand how you could have told Loreen about the ring. I've given this a lot of thought, and it seems cruel. I don't include you in this, Ryan."

"Listen, Pat, let's just try to enjoy the food here."

"Typical of you, Patrick, to think you know so much more than the rest of us, you and that brother of yours," my mother said. She still had on her glasses and was slicing into the chicken, apparently trying to find an edible mouthful. "It just goes to show you don't know everything, because we never did tell Loreen Tony was going to give her a ring."

"Excuse me?"

Ryan looked up at me and shrugged.

My mother took off her glasses, slipped them into her handbag, and snapped it shut with an efficient click. "We never told Loreen a thing. It would have been cruel to spoil Tony's surprise like that. When he came home and tried to back out of the engagement, we just made that story up, that's all."

When Tony and I were kids, we often engaged in heated wrestling matches, while Ryan stood by and tried to pry us apart. Once, Tony ended up sitting on my chest, with a pillow over my face, and just before Ryan managed to pull him off, I passed out. It left me with a phobia of being trapped in closets and elevators and relationships. That panicky feeling of imminent asphyxiation clutched at me as I looked around the table at my parents' faces, ghoulishly lit from above by the fake Tiffany lamp.

My father had his knife in one hand and his fork in the other, and he put them down noisily against the sides of his plate. "Don't make a big deal of this, Patrick. It was my idea, and I don't think it was cruel, and I'd do it again tomorrow if it came up again tomorrow. If you want to talk about cruel, I'll tell you about cruel. That brother of yours led on that poor Loreen for years. Then, at the last minute, he decides to back out of his duty and not propose. I suppose you think that's fair? Tony decides to dump her so he can go prowling around Chicago like he was back in junior high? No way. That's not my style."

"Your style? What does it have to do with you?"

"Anyway, dear, someone had to do something if Tony was going to move out to Chicago and ignore her after dating her all that time. How's that chicken?"

"Lousy," I said.

"Mine, too. This place is a disaster. This spotlight is giving me a headache."

"I feel like an exhibit at a wax museum," my father said. "We should have let Ryan cook."

"Don't look at me. The scampi's great. The rest of you should have had it."

A plate shattered against the floor on the other side of the room, and a hush fell over the restaurant. We all looked in the same direction. One of the pasty businessmen had dropped his salad and was standing with a look of utter horror and contrition on his face. The front of his pants was covered with salad dressing. Ryan tried unsuccessfully to stifle a laugh. "The poor bastard. I just had a nice talk with him, too. His consulting business is going broke."

My father said, "He sure didn't waste any money on that toupee. The things you see when you don't have a gun."

For a moment, I forgot about Tony. I forgot why I was at the restaurant in the first place, and why I'd been so angry. For a moment, I forgot to be angry at all. The four of us nearly collapsed with laughter at the unfortunate businessman's unfortunate clumsiness, and I felt welcomed back into my family. In that passing moment of hilarity and familial acceptance, Tony's situation was no concern of mine.

Then the moment passed.

"And I'll tell you something else, Patrick," my mother said. "That brother of yours is going to be very happy. Loreen adores him, and he loves her—as much as he's capable of loving anyone other than himself."

"Of course they'll be happy," my father said. "Not that Tony deserves to be happy."

"Now, now. Everyone deserves to be happy, Jimmy."

The bad food had given me a stomachache and the laughing had made me dizzy, and I could feel myself floating off, the way I sometimes float off when the dentist injects too much Novocain. I opened the folder for the honeymoon plans and explained the health-spa trip. My mother made notes on a napkin about changing around the flights and the hotel arrangements and adding a side trip to San Jose so the happiest couple in America could visit some elderly cousin of hers. I sat and listened to it all complacently, lacking the energy even to be outraged. When my father began to object, I backed up my mother's ideas. The waiter cleared off the plates and asked if anyone wanted dessert. Ryan said he wanted a piece of baked Alaska but he wasn't going to have it. One piece, my mother assured him, wasn't going to kill him. Ryan resisted. My father ordered the baked Alaska for himself but told the waiter to put the plate in front of Ryan. My father gave some signal to my mother, and she took a pack of cigarettes out of her purse and coyly handed one over. "I hope you realize," she said, "that this is it for the rest of the week." The dessert came, and Ryan spooned it down, talking about the World Series and his plans to take his daughter to Disney World the following fall. The hair on the front of his head kept slipping down and falling into his eyes. My father put on my mother's half-glasses and started to total up the bill. "Lousy and expensive," he said. "My favorite combination."

"I wish Arthur had come," my mother said, applying lipstick. "Why didn't you invite him, Patrick?"

"I didn't want to, that's why."

"Well, don't take that tone. You don't know how lucky you are to have someone like Arthur."

"Oh? How lucky is that?" I could feel myself choking again: my father in my mother's glasses, my mother with my father's cigarettes, Ryan up to his neck in baked Alaska.

"Look around you, Patrick. I'd say you're pretty lucky. Now he's even buying this house."

"We're buying it together."

"You know what I mean. And to be perfectly frank, dear, it isn't only the house. There are other reasons I'd stay close, if I were you."

"What's-their-name's son," my father said, as if he'd picked up a coded message from her.

"They've been our neighbors for the past thirty years, and he doesn't even know their names. Callahan. Bill and Frances Callahan. Their son is in the hospital again. Pneumonia," Rita said significantly.

"AIDS?" I asked.

My mother looked around to make sure no one had heard me and then closed her eyes and shrugged.

"The poor bastard," Ryan said.

"The point I'm trying to make," my mother said, "is that it's a scary world out there. Wouldn't you agree?"

"I would."

"And in a scary world, you'd better hang on to what you've got," my father said. When they weren't fighting, they had an eerie way of finishing each other's sentences.

Their voices had softened, and I was touched at this hesitant attempt to express genuine concern. Clearly, they'd discussed the plight of their neighbors' son and its possible relevance to my life. They'd never mentioned AIDS to me or asked any direct questions. Since they never discussed anything of importance directly, it wasn't surprising. From time to time, one or the other would pointedly ask if I'd seen *Nightline* or read "that article" in the *Boston Globe* Sunday magazine, usually an indication that the topic had been AIDS. If I had been more responsible and mature, I suppose I would have brought the topic up with them myself and made some reassuring comments about the fact that I take vitamins, exercise, and practice safe sex. But I'm not better at honest discourse than either of them.

My mother took a little mirror out of her purse and pulled the conversation in another direction. "Not everyone manages to stay with someone for as long as you two have remained friends." She inclined her head meaningfully in Ryan's direction.

Ryan's face seemed to have dropped, and I wondered if he'd caught the significance of my mother's comment. I gazed across the horrid dining room and felt the kind of hopelessness I sometimes feel when the temperature soars over ninety and there's no hint of relief in the weather report. My mother asked me something about the Yellow Fever house, while my father complained that the coffee was giving him indigestion.

"There's one last thing I'd like to say," I blurted out, ignoring them both.

My parents stopped talking, and Ryan smiled hesitantly and expectantly.

"There isn't going to be any honeymoon to rearrange or marriage to meddle with or anything else. There isn't going to be any wedding this July. Tony's in love with someone other than Loreen, someone other than himself."

My father looked at me skeptically, and Ryan gave me a disapproving glance. The traffic was rushing past the huge windows across the room in a blur of lights. A drop of sweat fell from my armpit and rolled down the side of my body. I felt stranded on the island of our wide, round table. "Her name," I said, "is Vivian."

Then, thinking I was making a stand for my two brothers and myself, I told them the rest of what I knew.

My mother dropped her napkin onto her plate, my father shook his head in disgust, and Ryan excused himself and left the table.

"We all know who's to blame for this, Rita, don't we?"

"Oh, sure, let's hear it," my mother said. "Let's begin."

I could tell by the way they were sitting up in their chairs they were indeed about to begin. I got up to go to the bathroom, thinking I could wash my hands of the whole messy affair.

Thirteen

〜

In the men's room, I turned on the tap full force and splashed my face with cold water. It was a cavernous bathroom, with gold faucets shaped like sea serpents, scalloped sink bowls, marbled mirrors, and floor-to-ceiling gray tiles, all gleaming in the bright light. There was an unpleasantly strong chemical smell in the air, reassuring the clientele, I suppose, that we wouldn't catch anything from the toilet seats. Over the sound of the rushing water and the piped-in Muzak, I heard a magnificently loud sigh emerge from one of the stalls. I turned off the taps, looked into the mirror over the sink, and called out into the void. "Ryan? Is that you?"

There was no response, but the sighing stopped. I went over to one of the stalls and knocked on the metal door. "Are you all right?" I asked.

"I'm fine, Pat, I'm fine. I've just had a rough week, that's all. I'll see you back at the table."

"Come out and talk to me, will you?"

"Is there anyone else out there?"

I assured him the coast was clear, and when he emerged, his face pale and puffy, I put my arm around his shoulder. "What is it?"

"It's nothing, Pat. Nothing. One Big Nothing."

Ryan was such an unlikely candidate for an existential crisis, I knew he had to be referring to something specific. "I hope you don't feel responsible for this Tony situation."

He pulled away from me. "Tony? That's none of my business. It's Elaine. I might as well tell you, since you're going to find out sooner or later anyway. She's seeing some new guy, someone she's getting serious about."

I felt my shoulders drop. "I'm sorry," I said.

"I first heard about it from Stacy, but I didn't pay much attention. The poor kid even told me the bastard's name. Not that I know he's a bastard; he's probably a nice person."

He went to the sink and washed his face. "Christ, will you look at me," he said, water rolling down his cheeks. "Fat, homely. Look at the bags under these eyes. I guess it's time I joined one of those goddamned gyms. That'd be a laugh, wouldn't it?" He wiped his face with a handful of stiff paper towels, straightened his jacket, and turned to me, shaking his head wearily. "She wants a divorce."

I leaned against the wall for support and tried to think of some consoling words. My mind felt emptied out, and all those gleaming tiles were beginning to make my vision blur. "Let's go for a walk," I finally suggested. "These tiles are corroding my soul."

"What about them?" he asked, motioning toward the dining room with his head.

"They'll be fine," I said. "They're fighting."

Elaine Moody was the first real love of Ryan's life. She was a plump, pixieish legal secretary, with a voice that could easily have belonged to an eight-year-old. Her face was so open, round, and plain, her features sometimes looked as if they'd been drawn on the bottom of a paper plate with a thin crayon. Her mother had died when she was fourteen, and her father, when last seen, was drinking himself to death in a furnished room in Portland, Maine. Elaine was the youngest of seven children and determined to be the survivor of a bad lot. She'd put herself through college by working long shifts at a variety of thankless jobs, and eventually she'd secured a position as the indispensable secretary to the head of a small law firm in downtown Boston.

She and Ryan had glowed in each other's presence. My brother couldn't keep his shy hands off her. No one didn't get misty at their wedding. Even Tony, who considered Elaine too bossy and ambitious, admitted that he'd felt a sentimental ache as the two walked down the aisle.

The whole time Ryan was dating Elaine, Rita and James would smugly say of her, "She's no dope, you know," mostly because they felt reasonably assured, despite evidence to the contrary, that she was. Her voice and her pink cheeks had misled them. But after the marriage, Elaine proved that she really was no dope, especially when it came to my parents. She wasn't interested in playing the dutiful daughter-in-law and wasn't interested in watching her husband devote his life to filial obligations. Ryan had confided to me on several occasions that he'd felt torn between Elaine and my parents. When it became obvious that Tony was leaving town, Elaine lobbied strenuously and wisely for Ryan to stay out of the business, hang on to his job with the athletic-shoe company, and not take on my father's illnesses as his own problems. Ryan wasn't able to follow her advice. The birth of Stacy was the final blow. Elaine, my parents argued, was trying to keep them from seeing their grandchild. That she was continuing to work after the baby's birth was proof that she wasn't devoted to her own child and was just trying to make Ryan feel inadequate as a provider. "But what can you expect," they'd say, "coming from that kind of family. It's not that she wants to be like this; she just can't help it."

Ryan began making secret visits to my parents with Stacy and got increasingly haggard and unhappy. Then, three years after he got married, one year after Stacy was born, six months after Tony packed off to Chicago, "the saint" moved into the recently vacated basement of my parents' house.

We walked out of the bathroom and across the hotel lobby and into the cool night. What little snow there had been that winter had melted from the ground, but there were still patches of filthy ice in the corners of the parking lot. Ryan wrapped his sport coat around himself more tightly. "What a life," he sighed.

"I don't want to criticize, Ry, but didn't you think something like this might happen? It's been almost three years you two haven't been together."

"I'd say it's obvious I wasn't thinking at all, Pat. I've been coasting for three years. Let's go stand over there by the highway and watch the lights."

The parking lot was up on a bluff, looking over Route 128. Benches arranged carefully around the edge provided, like the dining room, a glorious view of the cars whizzing by and the gargantuan shopping mall glowing in the distance like a newly landed alien spacecraft. We sat down on a bench and watched the light show for a while. I had to admit there was something exciting about all that speed and noise almost within reach.

"I've been living in a dream," Ryan said. "The only time I ever see Elaine is when I go to pick up Stacy, and I guess I read the signals wrong. I must have thought as long as we shared Stacy, it would all work out. What a joke. You know how much I love Stacy, Pat, don't you? You don't think I was using her, do you?"

"I think you're a good father."

"Time got away from me, that's what happened. Three days, three years, who knew? I guess I was pretending we were still a couple. I certainly haven't had any interest in anyone else. I knew Lainie went out on dates sometimes, but I never worried about it. I thought of her the same way I always had, so I figured she felt the same way about me. Living in a dream. I always have been a sap." He paused and caught his breath. "The lights are nice, aren't they? Kind of like Christmas."

"All those cars," I said. "All that pollution."

"Oh, come on, try to look on the bright side. It's good about this house you're getting. You know I always liked that Arthur. Tony's life sounds all fucked up, mine too, but you're doing all right now. Try to enjoy it a little, Pat. You don't know when everything might change."

I wanted to tell him I was desperately, eagerly waiting for anything to change, but I was afraid it might make him more unhappy.

"Poor Loreen," he said. "She's a sweet kid. She doesn't deserve this. I guess that's the whole point—no one deserves what they get in life, and no one gets what they deserve. Everybody's barreling along in the passing lane, except for the saps like me, driving at the speed limit."

It sounded to me more as if he'd been in reverse for three years. "Do you plan to fight this divorce?" I asked.

He slipped his hands into the pockets of his jacket and shrugged. "Who knows? If she wants out she wants out. To tell you the truth, I've been in that basement so long, I don't have a whole lot to offer her anymore."

"Don't be such a defeatist," I said, even though I could see his point. The fact that he'd lasted in the basement as long as he had made Elaine's request for a divorce seem entirely justified. "You could at least tell her how you feel about her."

I had a sad feeling that even if Elaine wasn't exactly the right person for Ryan, she was his only chance before he sank too deeply into his subterranean life.

He got up from the bench wearily. "I don't know, Pat. I've still got some pride, you know. We better go inside," he said, "and make sure Romeo and Juliet haven't killed each other."

Fourteen

⌇

"You see," Sharon said, rolling a cigarette between her thumb and index finger, "that's what I've been telling you all along. Ryan is afraid your parents will literally kill each other if he's not around to protect them from themselves. That's why he's stuck in that dungeon."

"Let's not go overboard here."

"Frightening," she said. "Imagine a man of thirty-six . . ." Her voice trailed off, and she blew a column of smoke rings up to the ceiling. "Really frightening."

Sharon was stretched out on the nubby blue sofa in her living room, her bare feet against one armrest, her head against the other, her dark hair hanging down to the floor. I was sitting behind her in a rocking chair—a piece of rusting metal porch furniture that had no business being indoors—and although I could see Sharon's face and she couldn't see mine, I felt like the patient in our exchange. I often felt like a patient in my discussions with Sharon. The living room had twelve-foot ceilings and was barely furnished. The walls and the tall, elegant windows were completely bare. Sharon found the idea of curtains laughable. "Let 'em look" was another of her mottoes.

It was early evening, almost a week after the family dinner. I'd taken Sharon to see the yellow house, hoping she'd soften her strong objections once she saw the place. She'd conceded that from a purely architectural point of view it was appealing, but she'd stuck to her advice to forget buying and to move back in with her. Only after we'd returned to her house did I dare confess that Arthur and I had made an offer and put down a thousand dollars two days before. She'd merely frowned her disapproval, almost as if I was too hopeless to bother with.

We'd gone into the kitchen to get drinks, and I started to tell her about the dinner at the restaurant. As soon as Sharon opened the refrigerator, her housemate, Roberta, had clomped down from the second floor.

Sharon looked at me and groaned, rather blatantly, I thought, and Roberta immediately took center stage. She was dressed in a worn turquoise satin nightgown with lace shoulder straps and a pair of green flip-flops held together with duct tape. Her hair was done in a Bride of Frankenstein frizz and tied back with a filmy scarf. As she bustled around the kitchen, talking frantically and preparing a brew of thick coffee, she gave off the scent of some heavy and expensive perfume.

After a second of penetrating eye contact, she said, "You must be the famous Daniel. I'm delighted to meet you."

Sharon raised a single eyebrow. "This is Patrick," she said. "I don't know any Daniels. My entire life, I've never known anyone named Daniel, Berta."

"Oh?" She contemplated this for a moment. "My mistake," she said, as if there had been some doubt. "I'm sure Sharon's told you all about me, Patrick."

"I haven't," Sharon said.

"Please don't believe a word of what she's said. Ben's worse than she could possibly describe." Her laugh was desperate but good-humored and added to her air of faded glamour. "Did she tell you what I said to him as I was leaving him? Well, it's a classic. I was walking out the door, this was a month and a half ago, the night I found out I could move in here, thanks to Sharon, my guardian angel. So, I was walking out the door with my huge suitcase, and Ben said to me, 'Berta, you've turned me off women for the rest of my life.' So I just looked at him and I said, 'Well, Ben' "—here she clutched at her throat and swallowed hard as if to control an incipient fit of hilarity—" 'well,' I said, 'I figured that was the least I could do for my sex.' " She held up her hand: No applause, please. "And then

I just strolled out." This said, she doubled over laughing, as Sharon and I watched in silence. She composed herself and filled a tall thermos with her coffee.

"What do you do for a living, Daniel? Patrick!" She stomped her foot and repeated my name three times. "Now I'll never forget it again for as long as I live. You were saying?"

"I work with Sharon."

"How nice. Married?"

"Homosexual."

"Oh, good. I'd love you to meet Ben sometime and see if you think he's gay. You and Sharon have the right idea. Stay single and you'll never be lonely."

"I'm not single," I told her.

"I am lonely," Sharon said flatly.

I was taken aback by this sudden confession, but Roberta ignored it. "Believe me, kiddo, you don't know lonely until you've tried living with Ben. You live with someone, and you get weak. You're strong. I envy you, I really do." She stepped up behind Sharon and gave her a hug, a sort of consolation prize.

Roberta supervised a lab at a biochemical firm in Waltham. According to Sharon, she made a huge salary and was much sought after in her field. I imagined that every person working under her had heard the famous exit line at least several times.

A few minutes later, the phone rang and Roberta grabbed for it. "What do you want?" she said. She winked at Sharon and me as if we were finally about to see the performance we'd bought tickets for. One of the lace straps had slid off her shoulder and lay slack against her thin, freckled arm. "I can't, Ben, it's out of the question. Because I have plans. Plans! You've heard the word before, haven't you? Well, I've got them. I'm dressed and about to go out the door. That's none of your business. And what if it was a date? As a matter of fact, it is. Absolutely not. He's standing right here. I will. I intend to. Same to you." She slammed down the phone. "See what I mean?" she asked no one in particular. She slid the strap over her shoulder and smiled at me warmly. "Fortunately, Ben's a very small word in my vocabulary these days." She gathered up her thermos and headed off to her bedroom.

"Now tell me you'd want to live with that," Sharon said as we listened to Roberta's flip-flops clacking against the stairs.

It was the first time I'd ever seen Sharon upstaged, and I found it worrisome. I counted on Sharon to stand out in any crowd. "I'm not sure. There's something appealing about her, I suppose. Have you met Ben?"

"Met him? He practically lives here. He's one of those handsome liberated men; nice chest, no brains. Some kind of crackpot shrink: Heal the Inner Child—that level of sophistication. So understanding about everything, he bleeds empathy every time I sneeze. Roberta claims he doesn't take her career seriously because he wants her to have a baby. Of course, he's so sensitive, he'd probably end up breast-feeding the kid himself. I'd get rid of Berta in a minute if she wasn't so pathetic."

I'd nodded in agreement, but I hadn't seen anything especially pathetic about Roberta.

Sharon's house was a grand old Victorian summer cottage with a turret, a wide wraparound porch, and elaborate little brackets and gingerbread on every corner. It was at the top of a hill on a quiet one-way street in one of the better neighborhoods in Cambridge. All the houses around it had recently been spruced up in some drastic way, painted in elaborate San Francisco style or divided and converted to condos. Hers was the peeling gray wreck gentrification had forgotten. Sharon took care of the place in big expensive projects: a lawn service came twice a season to cut back the trees and hack through the weeds, a window-washing service blasted the grime off the huge windows every couple of years, a general contractor cleaned out the gutters annually. The small details of regular maintenance were left undone. Pine trees, rhododendrons, forsythia, and lilac bushes had all but taken over the porch and the windows on the first floor.

The inside of the house, too, was showing signs of wear, specifically the wear of all those housemates moving in and out over the years. Paint was chipped from around the doorframes, and there were deep nicks in the walls made by bed frames and bureaus and bookcases as they were carried up and down stairs. Five of the balusters supporting the staircase railing had been knocked out.

The living room, where we were sitting discussing Ryan, was dimly lit by two tiny wall lamps on either side of the mantelpiece and by the flickering television. Sharon had been smoking heavily, and a blue haze hung in the air above our heads. Most of the rooms in the vast house had grown dusty from lack of use. Sharon claimed she preferred not to clutter the place with furniture, so people could dance when she threw parties. In fact, she rarely entertained, and when she did, the events usually ended early and abruptly after she wandered off to bed unannounced, leaving the guests to depart in confusion.

I was telling Sharon about the dinner during the commercial breaks of *Jeopardy.* Sharon, like Ryan, was an avid watcher, a fanatic, even. I was fairly certain she was intellectually capable of achieving almost anything she set her mind to, but she seemed to have only one clear ambition: to appear as a guest on the show. She claimed she'd never be allowed on because she was informed enough to send the network into bankruptcy. She did know the answers (or the questions, or whatever the silly format demanded) to almost everything. She'd rant at the contestants and then, as soon as a commercial came on, hit the mute button on her remote and engage in conversations with me as if there'd been no interruptions.

"What did the sharks say when you were driving them home?" she asked.

"Who knows? They were fighting, one in the back seat, one in the front. I couldn't make out the content."

"Probably just as well. Poor Ryan. Those battles must drive him crazy."

"I guess. Although he's used to them by now. I tried to call Tony and confess that I'd let Vivian out of the bag, but he doesn't seem to be around. Maybe he's moved in with her."

"Unlikely."

She clicked on the volume of the TV and grew increasingly agitated as some poor soul answered everything incorrectly. "Idiot," she mumbled. "Did you hear that, Patrick? 'Where is Mozambique?' Ha! Where's your brain? Please." The idiot in question was a delightful little nubbin of a human being with a Fu Manchu mustache and, apparently, the intelligence of an Easter egg. He kept leaping on his buzzer even though he didn't seem to have a clue about the answers. Sharon sat up on the sofa, stubbed out her cigarette, and tossed back her hair. "If I could only get on this show, I could retire. I'd move to Oregon, grow dope, and watch the rest of the world implode. Mozambique! What kind of a world are we living in? And did you catch that other genius? 'Who are Leopold and Loeb?' Try Lerner and Loewe, moron. And she's a teacher, Patrick. Did you catch that? She thinks Leopold and Loeb wrote the score to *Camelot.* That's priceless, absolutely priceless."

"Unbelievable," I said, shaking my head. My guess would have been Rodgers and Hammerstein, a fact I didn't reveal.

I settled back and watched the show in guarded silence. For as long as I'd known her, Sharon's background had been a bit of a mystery to me. What I knew for certain was that she'd grown up in Los Angeles and gone to school at Radcliffe. Her mother was an elementary school teacher and her father taught history at UCLA. She claimed that she'd decided to sever ties with them close to twenty years earlier, right after she graduated from college, because she was sick of being held back by their pretensions. Other times she hinted that they had cut ties with her because they considered her life an embarrassment. When we were living together, she did get infrequent calls from California, and more than once I'd heard her weeping in her bedroom afterward. She had an older brother, whom she rarely mentioned. She usually received a Christmas package from "The Driscolls" in Fort Lauderdale, her brother and his family, I assume. Over the years, I'd heard veiled hints of alcoholism, tax evasion, and darker family secrets, but it was impossible to pin her down on facts; if pressed, she'd simply state that she didn't like to talk about any of it and shove the conversation in another direction. Whatever the truth, she obviously clung to many of her parents' expectations and standards, even if she applied them to TV game shows. I suspect she liked to watch the program just to prove to herself that she was more informed than the majority of the contestants. Maybe that was the only reason anyone watched it. If I'd admitted that I didn't know the correct response to the last question, she would have generously forgiven me, but only because we were friends.

Sharon was always loyal to her friends, even when they disappointed her.

"Now listen," she said at the next commercial break, "Tony is one thing, but Ryan is the one who concerns me. What are you planning to do for him?"

"For Ryan?"

"He's being eaten alive by sharks, Patrick. Something has to be done."

"I'm not ready to take on Ryan."

She pulled her knees in toward her chest and wrapped her arms around her legs. It was a surprisingly agile and childlike gesture. "I think I should meet Ryan," she said.

"Oh?"

"I've seen the rest of the circus; I might as well meet him. I like the sound of him. I can't stand to see good people treated the way he's being treated. Someone's got to help him out of the dungeon."

"He's not your type, Sharon, I promise."

"That wasn't what I was thinking. But I know lots of women who'd love to meet a gentle puppy like your brother."

"Ryan doesn't need a dog trainer."

Taking responsibility for introducing Sharon to Ryan sent chills down my spine. I could picture my brother collapsed in fits of nervous laughter, listening to her conversation. Sharon was exactly the sort of person who'd intimidate him into a panic. She was too open and confrontational. I could hear her pummeling him with embarrassing questions about his marriage and his sex life with Elaine. Besides, I was convinced that Ryan needed to hook himself up with someone who'd allow him to take care of her. Even Stacy, his four-year-old daughter, had started to mother him.

I couldn't think of a way to say all that without risking an insult. Sharon pulled a calendar out from under the sofa, and we set a date for dinner at my place. With luck, she and Arthur would be so locked in argument, she wouldn't have time to take on my brother.

When *Jeopardy* was over, Sharon led me into the kitchen and threw together one of her famous stews. She tossed almost everything that was in the refrigerator and half of what was on the shelves into an enormous pot, dumped in spices and hot peppers, stirred, and heated. She was wearing a navy-blue Laura Ashley jumper over a black peasant blouse she'd bought on a trip to Greece. The jumper had been given to her by a client who'd lost twenty pounds and could no longer wear it. The blouse had unmanageably wide sleeves with tassels on the cuffs, which kept falling into the stew as she tasted. In twenty minutes, she was serving up steaming portions of the stuff in deep mismatched bowls. These stews were among the most improbably delicious things I'd ever tasted. I'd tried making one or two myself, but the efforts always failed. Such subtleties as the sleeves probably made the difference.

"It's great, isn't it?" she asked, watching me eat a spoonful.

"Delicious."

"Of course it is. I'm a great cook. Great cooks make great meals, that's what they do." Sharon considered false modesty an insult and a waste of time. "I should open a restaurant. I could retire from the travel business, move to Maine, and open a nice little restaurant. People would kill for food this good." She tasted a spoonful and shook her hands. "God, that's fantastic. Where do you think I learned to cook like this? By the way, I give Roberta ten minutes, tops, before she's down here sniffing."

"Does she ever cook?"

"She lives on caffeine. That and the scraps she nibbles all day long. She stirs peanut butter and seeds and I shudder to think what else in little cups and squirrels them off to her bedroom." Sharon actually did shudder. "Every time I boil water she promenades down. Ben did all the cooking. Cleaning, too, from the looks of her room."

"If you want my opinion," I said, "I think you should ask her to leave. You've kicked people out of here before."

"The house is too big. I hate the thought of one single person using up so much housing space." She refilled her bowl from the bubbling caldron and ate leaning against the stove. "I never used to think about it, but lately I've been getting lonely here. Too many empty rooms all around me."

This second admission of loneliness in less than two hours was unprecedented. "Still, it might be better without some horror like Roberta," I said.

"Maybe. Next time I'll try to get some rich housewife from Wellesley to move in. The type who's looking for a little bohemian garret away from her husband and ends up having Bloomingdale's redecorate the place for her before she moves in. That way I'll be left with something when she goes back to the old man." She spooned out more stew for me and set the bowl on the table. "Tell me if you want me to bring anything to this dinner with Ryan. The last time I was over your place, I had to stop for pizza on the way home. I think you served Jell-O."

"Impossible."

Roberta clomped into the kitchen and rinsed out her thermos. She made a great show of scrubbing and drying it before she went to the stove and sniffed. "Fantastic."

Sharon frowned at me. "Help yourself, Berta. There's plenty."

"I'll have a taste," she said. She filled something the size of a demitasse and sipped delicately. "Fantastic. But you can tell Sharon's a good cook by the way she looks. Robust, healthy. God, I wish I could let myself go the way you do. So what's the discussion down here?"

"My brothers," I said. "One's getting married and one isn't."

"Brothers. I happen to know a lot about brothers. My brother is the one who introduced me to Ben. Can you believe it? They were college roommates. This from my own flesh and blood."

Sharon shook her head wearily. "I've heard this, Roberta. In fact, I'd guess I've heard it three times."

" 'Michael,' I said to him, 'I am not interested in meeting some roommate of yours.' Next thing you know, I've been married ten years. Ten years! You want to hear a synopsis of the ten years of my marriage, Patrick?"

"He doesn't have time," Sharon said. Roberta merely hugged her, as if she, Sharon, had been joking.

"We met," she said, her arms around Sharon, rocking her from side to side, "fell in love, moved in together, got married, got to know each other, got sick of each other, and fell out of love. As for the next nine years, they're a blur."

It wasn't until after dinner, when it was late and the house was turning cold and Sharon was getting bored and restless and—I knew the signs—eager for me to leave, that I mentioned, in as casual a way as I could manage, that I was going to New York that weekend. It took a fair amount of throat-clearing before I got the words out. Sharon gave me one of her frowning looks of dismay, and I quickly told her that I was planning to fly under the name S. Driscoll so she could get the points on her frequent flier account.

"I accept," she told me, "but that doesn't mean I approve. I still think you're making a mistake."

"Approve?" I said, as if the thought had never crossed my mind. "What makes you think I'm looking for approval? I'm just letting you know in case you need to get in touch with me."

"I'll keep it in mind. Anyway, I'm going to bed. You can stay as late as you like. Just leave quietly."

Part
3

Fifteen

}

In the days before I left for New York, I called Tony repeatedly, but he was never at home. His answering machine had an impersonal recording of a computerized voice, something that had come with the tape. "I am sorry," it announced, "there is no one to answer your call at this time. At the sound of the tone, please speak loudly and clearly." I'd never had the courage to respond. Although I was annoyed he'd told Rita about the house, I was a lot more concerned about my own, greater indiscretion, and I figured I should get a confession out of the way as quickly as possible.

When I called Ryan to invite him to dinner, I asked if he had any news of Tony's whereabouts. "Your parents seem to think he's in Miami on business," he said. "Tony's got all the luck. I'd give anything to spend a few days in Miami."

"Don't waste your envy," I told him. "It used to be nice, but now it's close to a hundred degrees every day, and it hasn't rained for at least a decade. By the year 2000, the city will be uninhabitable."

"Go on, Patrick. Don't you remember Jackie Gleason used to call it the Sun and Fun Capital of the World?" Jackie Gleason and Jimmy Piersall, the Red Sox player whose father drove him to a nervous breakdown, were Ryan's childhood heroes. "Between you and me,

Pat, I hope you get Tony before your parents do. He should at least be warned the lovebirds know about this other gal."

"Vivian," I reminded him.

"No names, please. It seems more loyal to Loreen if I think of this new one as 'the other woman.' Not that I'm thinking of her very much."

Ryan was enthusiastic about the dinner. He laughed uproariously when I asked him if he could make a particular night, as if the idea that he might have other plans was absurd. Most of Ryan's friends were either dour, alcoholic bachelors he knew from high school days (many of whom still lived with their parents) or married couples he and Elaine had met at childbirth classes. Elaine socialized with the latter, and even Ryan found the former too depressing to spend time with. He spent his evenings in the basement, watching game shows and sporting events on cable TV. He was always about to join the YMCA, or "one of those goddamned gyms," but he never did.

"Promise me one thing," Ryan said. "Just promise me you're not trying to fix me up with this Sharon. I've heard too many stories already, and the last thing I need right now is some kind of match-making deal to complicate my life."

"Ryan, you know there isn't much I can say with honesty, but I can honestly say I am not trying to fix you up with Sharon."

"Well, that's a relief. Or a disappointment. Something, anyway."

The Friday I was to leave to visit Jeffrey, the rattling of the bedroom windows woke me. I got up from my air mattress, lifted the venetian blind, and saw a threatening sky. It was my favorite kind of late-March weather—bleak. I even like the sound of the word "bleak"; it's so reassuringly harsh. There was a chill in the room, which made me hope it might even be a few degrees below the normal high temperature, which for that particular date was 46 degrees in Boston, 48 in New York.

I was planning to leave on the Pan Am shuttle right after work. The Trump would have been marginally more convenient, and they were giving away pens on each flight, but I didn't want to risk flying on a morally bankrupt airline. I'd packed my knapsack the night before. All I had to do was take a shower, get dressed, and sneak out. On the weekends I went to New York, I always tried to leave the apartment long before Arthur got up, to reduce my feelings of guilt, feelings Arthur might easily have exacerbated by following me from room to room, making sure I'd packed a toothbrush, a towel, and clean underwear. Arthur could play me like a pinball machine. Whenever he sensed I was drifting, he'd either turn mercilessly kind or do something Arthurishly inept, like accidentally sticking his finger in the socket as he changed a light bulb or starting a fire while making toast.

Before leaving the house, I went to the kitchen table and wrote a sentimental mash note on the back of a shopping list, telling him how much I loved him and was going to miss him. I always missed him when I went off to betray him, and I never thought of him as fondly as I did when I was on the shuttle heading south. I taped the note to the mirror in the bathroom, knowing he wouldn't find it for at least an hour after he got up. Arthur used mirrors to shave and to make sure his tie was on straight, and that was that. Vanity, thy name is not Arthur. The first thing I usually did after stumbling out of bed was check the mirror to make sure I was still alive and to assess the damages of another sleepless night.

Since I had almost two hours to kill before work (meaning I was due at the office in an hour), I took the subway to Porter Square for one of my dreary triweekly workouts.

I belonged to an absurdly flashy health club that was a kind of discotheque and fitness palace combined. Virtually every wall was covered with mirrors, and there were so many high-tech laser lights and flashing chrome exercise machines, I was sometimes tempted to wear dark glasses. Most of the members were perfectly pumped and toned, but where they got their exercise was anyone's guess. The majority of the people I observed used the place for professional networking and displaying their million-dollar leotards and sneakers. I'd been going there for almost six years now, since the very week, in fact, that I moved in with Arthur, but I'd never felt I belonged. More often than not, I felt like the only black-and-white weakling in the middle of a Technicolor gladiator epic.

There was practically no one at the gym that morning, which gave it a little of the morning-after feel of an empty nightclub. I sat on the sparkling red-and-blue benches, wearily pushing and lifting. I finished off my workout with three bracing minutes on an exercise bike with a computerized control panel that did everything but tell you your red blood cell count and your fortune.

I left feeling more deflated than pumped up. It had been a complete waste of time, and there wasn't even anyone in the shower interesting enough to compensate for the risk of athlete's foot. In six years of working out, I hadn't noticed any significant change in my body. What really discouraged me, though, was realizing that in the course of those six years of working out—and living with Arthur— I'd reached the age where absolutely no change in my body might be considered an accomplishment. At thirty-one, I'd begun fighting against the tide.

It was raining lightly when I got outside. I put up my black umbrella and walked slowly down Mass Ave toward Harvard Square, window-shopping in all the hilariously useless boutiques that had recently moved into that part of Cambridge. If I ever wanted a six-thousand-dollar quilt hand-sewn by a ninety-seven-year-old Amish grandmother, I'd know where to go. The whole of Cambridge was slowly but surely being turned into a theme park.

I came to a dead stop in front of a florist shop with a sign in the window that read: ONLY FIFTEEN DAYS LEFT. I peered through the glass. There were no indications that the place was going out of business, they weren't running a time-limited sale, and it wasn't fifteen days from any holiday I'd ever heard of. It could only be a warning of imminent doom. I'd been in the shop several times; the owner was a bearded prima donna who was unfailingly condescending to his customers, as if they couldn't possibly appreciate plants and flowers as much as he did. He was at the counter now, pruning a ficus tree, with a cigarette hanging out of his mouth. It was unlikely he'd have inside information about the end of the world, but you can never be sure. I headed down the street, contemplating the final days of human existence in such a thoroughly pessimistic mood that I decided to walk straight to work, thus managing to get to the office almost exactly on time.

Fredrick was just setting up shop at the reception desk, organizing Xerox copies of Charlotte Brontë's juvenilia and unloading a bag of brioches. He had on a bright-orange sport jacket and a T-shirt emblazoned with the words NO ONE KNOWS I'M A LESBIAN. He looked at his watch, a Rolex given to him by his priest, and lazily said, "A miracle. He's on time."

"Not so unusual. I go through periods of competence every once in a while."

"Well, here's a challenge for you." He handed me a message slip. "Mr. Whisper. Sounded like he was calling from a phone booth in the subway. I couldn't make out most of it, but it had something to do with his hotel reservations in Bermuda."

"That again," I said and crumpled up the paper.

*   *   *

As the day wore on, I found myself with a nagging desire to get all my work in order, just so things would be settled on the day of reckoning, fifteen days thence. While doing this, I made the horrifying discovery that Professor Fields's reservations were in even worse shape than I'd imagined. The airline had canceled Fields and niece Zayna from their flight to Bermuda because I hadn't called in their ticket numbers the week before. It was exactly the kind of detail that was always getting me in trouble. In fact, I was so thoroughly negligent about the trip, I hadn't bothered to issue the tickets at all. Now Fields had no hotel and no flight reservations. I called the airline and was told that the plane was so overbooked as it was, I shouldn't pin any hopes on the wait list. In a similar situation, I decided, Sharon would secretly engineer the breakup of the relationship between Fields and Zayna before the departure date, thereby eliminating the whole reason for the trip. But that would have taken more time than I was willing to devote to it. When I did mention the dilemma to Sharon, she just shrugged and said, "Fake ticket, Patrick. What's the big deal? People at the gate are so distracted, you could hand them a tea bag and they'd let you on."

I knew she was being particularly dismissive because she didn't approve of my visit to New York. She saw my sexual dalliance with Jeffrey as a way of letting off steam, and she'd have preferred that I take her advice, let my frustration boil over, and leave Arthur.

I had serious doubts myself about my relationship with Jeffrey, but I wasn't able to give it up. The two of us had been friends for twelve years, the bond between us being a similar lack of self-esteem. We'd picked each other out as kindred spirits when we were freshmen in college. Ours was a happily celibate romance that consisted primarily of each telling the other how much better he was than he thought.

Around the time I got involved with Arthur, Jeffrey hooked up with a ridiculous person named Kyle Thurman, an aspiring actor. Kyle was not without talent, but I was fairly certain he was too much of a narcissist to appreciate Jeffrey. I myself was narcissistic enough to secretly believe that, given the timing of the relationship, Jeffrey had latched onto Kyle in reaction to my entanglement with Arthur. I was against Kyle from the start—among other things, he was infuriatingly indolent in the way that handsome men so often are—but I had just enough restraint to hold my tongue. My friendship with Jeffrey dimmed during the years of his love affair. The strain of pretending to like a friend's lover is enough to kill any friendship. We saw each other less and less and eventually lost touch completely for more than a year. Then, two years earlier, I got a tearful call. Kyle had moved out. I was surprised he was capable of such decent behavior, but Jeffrey was devastated. I went to New York to console him, thrilled that at last I had the perfect opportunity to tell him exactly what I'd thought of his lover all along. That took a couple of hours, and then I got around to one of those standard ego-boosting talks, the one about how handsome and sexy and bright and appealing he was and how Kyle didn't know how lucky he'd been for three years.

And then, just to prove I meant what I'd said, I tore his clothes off.

We spent the rest of the weekend making up for lost time. He told me his sex life with Kyle had been largely a triumph of style over substance, and I confessed that if my life with Arthur were on videotape, I'd fast-forward through the sex scenes. In a funny way, nothing much seemed to change in our friendship, and we never really discussed the new turn our relationship had taken. I suppose this betrayal of Arthur was deeper than the emotionless, often anonymous, flings I'd had from time to time in the past, but I rationalized by telling myself that having this New York escape was what made it so easy for me to stay with Arthur, so everyone benefited in the end.

My day at the travel agency was going disastrously, and I decided to do my clients and myself a favor and leave early. It was pouring down rain by the time I left; all the drains on the dirty Cambridge streets were clogged, and water was washing up over the sidewalks. I caught a cab to the airport. The rain was driving against the windshield so forcefully, the driver didn't even bother to turn on the wipers. I always worry about air safety when I board a plane, but never so much as when I was about to visit Jeffrey.

I took a seat by one of the huge plate-glass windows in the airport lounge and watched the mechanics in their orange slickers, messing with the plane. They were laughing, some doubled over as if they'd just played a riotous practical joke, like leaving a gasket off one of the engines.

The man sitting next to me was deeply engrossed in a paperback but was biting the skin around his thumbnail, obviously a nervous wreck. He was one of those hip young executives with a leather backpack and an expensive haircut. He caught me looking at him and smiled anxiously. "Lousy weather for flying, isn't it?"

"It's not so bad," I said calmly. "We'll be above this storm in a few minutes." I love talking people out of their irrational fears, especially when they're fears I share. I launched into a lengthy discussion of airline safety records, crash statistics, and weather reports, the kinds of facts and figures only a true neurotic who thought he could influence fate with acts of memory would bother to learn. My companion, however, seemed marginally reassured; at least he stopped biting his thumb. He had a severe, elongated face shaped almost like the sole of a shoe.

"Reading anything good?" I asked, pointing to his book.

"Great," he said. "John O'Hara. Have you read him?"

"I practically live on him. Which is this?"

He held up a copy of *Appointment in Samarra*.

I jumped out of my seat and ran to the nearest phone.

"Sweetheart," Arthur said. "Shouldn't you be heading off to the airport soon?"

"I'm *at* the airport," I said. "The ceiling was leaking onto my computer, so I was forced to leave the office early. Listen, Arthur, I just wanted to apologize."

"For what?"

"I was supposed to do the shopping this week, and I forgot all about it. I'm just too keyed up about Tony and that whole situation. There's no orange juice at home, and there's no bread, and I'm pretty sure the milk has gone bad."

"Aw, well, it's sweet of you to warn me. I'll pick some up on my way home tonight."

"I know, I know, but you don't understand. The point is, I was supposed to do the shopping and I didn't. I let you down. I had a job to do and I didn't do it. You would have done it. You wouldn't leave me in the house for a weekend with no food. I just don't deserve you, Arthur. I never have."

"Calm down, will you? We're talking about a loaf of bread here."

Of course that wasn't what I was talking about, but fortunately, Arthur didn't know it. "And I still haven't filled out that mortgage application."

"You can do it when you get home."

"And you slept so late this morning I didn't get a chance to ask you if you have plans for the weekend."

"I'm going to the movies tomorrow night with Beatrice and Mitchell. They've taken pity on me and are going to make dinner, too."

"Beatrice probably thinks I'm a jerk." Suddenly, it mattered to me very much what Arthur's ex-wife thought of me.

"She likes you, Patrick. Why would she think you're a jerk?"

For one thing, she was uncannily perspicacious. It was Beatrice, for example, who'd informed Arthur that he was gay. "Never mind, Arty. Any other plans?"

"Reading, laundry, the Sunday papers. Gilbert and Sullivan. I think I'll listen to *Pinafore* this week. That has that gorgeous aria 'Sorry her lot who loves too well.' The one you love so much."

I could picture him padding around the house in his robe and slippers, reading Dickens, planning more good deeds, while I flung Jeffrey around his living room. "Oh, Arthur," I said, "it sounds so lonely. Why don't you call someone tonight and make plans?"

"I'm looking forward to a quiet weekend. What flight are you taking?"

"The five-thirty. If it crashes, claim my body before my parents get to it."

"There isn't going to be any crash. I'm sorry to disappoint you. Just have a good time. Say hello to Jeffrey for me."

"I will."

"I'll see you Sunday, sweetheart."

"Bye." My throat was constricting. "I love you, Arthur," I said.

"What was that?"

"I said I love you."

"You're slurring your words, Patrick. I can't understand a thing you're saying. Speak up."

"Never mind. Just have a good weekend."

I hung up the phone and headed back to my seat. I'd go to Barney's and buy him an expensive sweater, then head over to the Strand to see if they had a particularly nice edition of *The Seven Storey Mountain*.

Jeffrey's self-image was so low, he'd entered college with the intention of going on to med school and becoming a surgeon. But painting was the only thing he showed any interest in when I first met him, and I like to compliment myself by claiming that I was the one who convinced him to drop out of premed in his junior year. True, he ended up with one of those liberal arts degrees that are about as useful as a humidifier in New Orleans, but he was at least doing what he loved. He worked on huge canvases, brushing on layer after layer of paint so the finished product was a densely textured swamp of color. His paintings were strangely beautiful and, from the bits of information he let slip, had drawn attention from a few galleries. He lived in a vast, two-bedroom apartment at Broadway and 103rd Street, a place he'd inherited from a throng of disappearing roommates. The name on the lease was Tyson Trill. Not one person who'd lived there in the twelve years Jeffrey had been in residence had ever met Tyson Trill, although there were elaborate, fanciful stories abounding and a very small navy-blue blazer in the hall closet, said to belong to the tiny mystery tenant. Like everyone else I knew in New York who lived in a sunny two-bedroom apartment, Jeffrey paid under five hundred dollars.

He'd always been a molelike person, reclusive and quiet, but the threat of AIDS and then the disappearance of Kyle had driven him even deeper into his hermetic existence. But Jeffrey's agoraphobia suited him. He had his painting, his money-making career as a medical illustrator. He read any book written before the First World War and had a huge collection of used jazz records, scattered throughout his apartment in some crazy order that only he could decipher. Although I wasn't in love with Jeffrey—perhaps because I wasn't in love with Jeffrey—I couldn't get enough of his scrawny body.

Sixteen

〜

It was raining hard when we landed, and I decided to go to hell with myself and splurge on a cab into town. But at Ninety-sixth Street I was overcome by a fit of parsimoniousness and had the driver pull over. I saved about fifty cents, and by the time I got to Jeffrey's block, I was drenched. I let myself into the building, took the elevator to the third floor, and entered his apartment as quietly as possible. I stood in the narrow hallway by the front door, shook the water out of my hair, and took off all my clothes. Then, thinking better of it, I put on my T-shirt. I made my way through the cluttered living room, stepping over piles of records, and stood to the side of his open bedroom door. I could hear him opening and closing drawers. "Guess who?" I called out and stepped into the doorway.

Kyle was sitting on the floor, rummaging through the bottom drawer of Jeffrey's bureau. He looked up at me for one disinterested second and then went back to what he was doing.

"Patrick, isn't it?" he asked blandly.

"Yes," I said, "it is. Hi. How are you?"

"Oh, pretty swell."

Jeffrey came up behind me, holding a kettle. "Patrick," he said, "you're early. And practically nude."

"The rain. I got wet, and I had to take my clothes off."

"Apparently," Kyle said.

"Well, this is a coincidence," Jeffrey said. He held up the kettle. "I'm just making coffee."

"Milk, no sugar, in mine," Kyle said. "And don't make the coffee too strong. You always make it too strong. I'm on stage for ninety minutes tonight, and it won't do if I piss down my leg."

"I'll do my best. Patrick?"

"No milk, lots and lots of sugar, please."

"Well, that should be easy enough. You two remember each other, don't you?"

Kyle grinned without looking up, and I mumbled something about Kyle being unforgettable.

"Oh, and there's a robe in the closet," Jeffrey said. "It's blue, hanging on the back of the door."

I knew the robe well; I'd worn it at some point on almost every one of my recent visits.

"I'm glad to see you're still getting some use of that," Kyle said. "I gave it to you for your birthday four years ago. I'm happy you didn't throw it away."

"Throw it away?" Jeffrey laughed as if we were discussing using a Van Gogh for dart practice.

Jeffrey and Kyle took seats side by side on the sofa in the living room, a stack of records and magazines between them. I sat facing them in a bentwood rocker that Kyle had given Jeffrey once upon a time. The coffee was absurdly weak, infuriatingly so. There's nothing I like more than strong, sweet coffee heated to just below the boiling point. When I began seeing Jeffrey on a regular basis, I taught him my secret method for brewing coffee, a process that involves paper towels, jelly jars, ice cubes, and eggshells. Arthur had never been able to get it right, but Jeffrey had caught on immediately. It was discouraging to think that he'd give it up so quickly, just for the sake of pleasing Kyle.

The whole setup felt uncomfortably like times when I'd visited the happy couple in New York a few years back. Kyle was relating some story about a repertory company he had recently joined, while Jeffrey stared off into space with an entirely unreadable expression. I suppose he didn't want to offend Kyle or me by acknowledging the presence of either of us. One of his paintings was hanging over the sofa, a broad field of grays and reds. The two of them fit under it perfectly.

Jeffrey's legs were splayed out in front of him. He was wearing a pair of ratty, paint-splattered sneakers, the closest he came to arty affectation, and a soiled blue sweatshirt. He liked to sit slumped down in chairs and sofas, but this position looked painful.

"Straighten up, Jeff," I said. "You're going to ruin your back."

He looked up at me, slightly alarmed, I thought, by the intimacy of the scolding.

Jeffrey had a narrow face with large, crooked features and wonderfully fat lips. He had a headful of dark, tangled hair, which he cut himself into an uneven, caveman mop. I loved his shaggy, sloppy looks and the casually neglectful way he presented himself.

Kyle was another story. I hadn't seen him in at least two years, and I had to admit he was a lot more memorable-looking than I'd remembered. He was solid and tall, and his attractively dark face was all angles and shadowy little hollows. Age had added character to his eyes in the form of crow's-feet and faint dark circles. A decade of drug addiction or alcoholism, and he'd have a wonderfully expressive face.

I kept wrapping the robe around my legs more modestly, not that it really mattered much at that point, trying to listen to Kyle. I wished I could snap my fingers, disappear into a hole in the floor, and wind up back in Cambridge, where I belonged, filling out my mortgage application and being frustrated with Arthur.

Kyle's mouth finally stopped moving, and since it was obvious Jeffrey's wasn't about to kick into motion, I hesitantly took a turn. "So, Kyle," I said, "what plays are you doing with the new company?"

"None you've heard of," he said. The tone implied the fault was all mine.

"You're probably right." I sighed. Although I wouldn't admit it to my best friend, I've never seen a play I've enjoyed quite so energetically as I enjoy even those movies I don't much like.

"Anyway," he said, "it's Dennis now."

"Excuse me?"

He looked out the window. "My name is now Dennis."

I turned to Jeffrey for help, but he only shrugged. Kyle picked an album cover off the sofa and whacked him on the head with it. "Don't give that look, Jeff. I'm not embarrassed about it anymore. It's just a fact." He turned to me. "My agent and I decided 'Kyle Thurman' was associated with some questionable things I did early on that I'd rather forget about. So, beginning with this new company, I'm Dennis Stone. Anyway, the 'Kyle Thurman' sounded too invented."

"Interesting," I said. "Your real name sounded too invented, so you had to invent a name to sound real. Life is ironic."

Kyle gave me one of those distressed looks, the kind I reserve for people who tell you, an hour into conversation, that they believe in flying saucers.

Jeffrey perked up. "Oh, Kyle isn't his real name. It's Sandy. Sandy Simon, isn't it?"

"Something like that," Kyle said. He looked at his watch, stood up, and brushed the front of his pants. I'd seen Kyle act several times, and he was quite convincing on stage. Once, in a barely coherent production of *Street Scene* performed in a church basement in Brooklyn Heights, he'd moved me close to tears. In real life, however, all his actions looked overrehearsed and poorly blocked. "It was good meeting you again, Patrick."

He extended his hand, and I rose to shake it.

"Still living with the lawyer?" he asked.

"Arthur. Yes, I am. If you want to call it living."

He turned away as if I'd said something embarrassing, and I had one of those horrible moments of seeing myself through someone else's eyes. "We're buying a house together," I added, suddenly wanting his approval. "Dennis."

"Remember that time we all went out to dinner after my show? He told me he liked my performance, and for some reason, it struck me as the only sincere thing I'd heard all night. It stayed with me for hours."

Kyle put on a long, baggy raincoat and casually draped a scarf around his neck. He pulled on a woolen cap. "Arthur's a real person. Just like Jeff." He looked toward the lump on the sofa. "You and I can spot real people, Patrick. It's a talent. Tell him I said hello, although he probably doesn't remember me." He walked down the hall, stepping over the pile of my wet clothes. At the door, his hand on the knob, he turned and said, "Have fun, boys," and walked out.

It was a stagy exit, but it wasn't a bad one.

Jeffrey and I sat in the living room in silence. The window was open a crack, and the room was filled with the sound of cars and buses hissing through the rain as they sped down Broadway. Jeffrey had his feet crossed at the ankles and his arms folded across his chest. His head was thrown back, and he was looking up at the wall behind him.

"What do you think of this painting?" he asked, pointing his chin to the canvas above.

"I've always liked it." I never knew how to discuss Jeffrey's work, which seemed to me both beautiful and cheerless.

"Someone's interested in buying it."

"Don't cheat yourself. You're likely to, you know."

"It isn't as if I have buyers lining up."

Jeffrey's passivity about his painting was based on either his doubts regarding his own talent or his belief that his work was so sublime he could afford to sit back and wait for the world to come to him.

The name had to come up sooner or later, so I ventured forth. "Kyle looks good," I said cautiously, keeping my eyes on the canvas.

Jeffrey sat up. "Do you think so? I thought he looked exhausted."

Indolence notwithstanding, Kyle could swim the East River, run a marathon, sit through a nonstop performance of the entire *Ring* cycle, and still be ready to pose for a publicity shot if the call came. One of the more irritating aspects of Jeffrey's relationship with Kyle was his insistence upon viewing Kyle as a lost, pathetic lamb who needed to be taken care of. "So you two have been seeing each other again?" I asked, even though the question had been answered already.

"Strangest thing, Patrick. He came by one night a few weeks ago. I hadn't heard from him in months. It was about two A.M. He let himself in. I didn't know he still had a key. He was upset about the name business, and he didn't have anyone to talk to. You can't blame him, really."

I could, but now was not the time.

"So we stayed up all night and talked. Do you and Arthur ever do that?" he asked, staring off into space. "Sit down and bare your souls to each other, tell the absolute truth?"

"The absolute truth?" I asked. "What's that?"

"The truth, Pat, about your relationship, the way you feel about each other, what you think about him when he isn't around."

"God, no," I said, horrified at the thought. For one thing, telling Arthur the absolute truth about the way I thought of him seemed unnecessarily cruel. Jeffrey was beginning to sound a little too dreamy for my tastes. If he was turning spiritual, I was being pushed

Seventeen

It rained the rest of the night and most of Saturday. Jeffrey and I stayed in his apartment, reading and listening to noisy Afro-Cuban jazz. I was more in the mood for one of Tony's New Age CDs, Deep Soup or Seadreamscapes, that tinkling, melancholy sound like something you might listen to in a bomb shelter, waiting in peaceful hopelessness for the end of the world.

I suppose I must have been upset that Jeffrey and Kyle were getting together again, but I spent almost the entire weekend thinking about Arthur and not about Jeffrey at all. I was dreading the thought of going back to Boston knowing that my weekend visits to New York were a thing of the past. It was easy for Jeffrey to talk about turning over new leaves when he and Kyle hadn't seen each other for almost two years, but it was a little late in the afternoon for Arthur and me to attempt some kind of about-face. Not to mention that Arthur was unwilling to admit that there were any problems to begin with. When he'd come home and excitedly announced that our offer on the yellow house had been accepted, I began to get extremely apprehensive, as if I'd made some move I couldn't back out of. I was so desperate to talk the matter over with someone, I'd even thought of confiding in Tony. Fortunately, he had been out of touch, so I was able to keep my anxiety bottled up. The only hope I had left now was that, assuming I sent in the mortgage application, the bank would turn us down.

By Sunday morning the rain had cleared. I woke up in Jeffrey's narrow bed, far away from him, and listened to cans and paper blowing down the sidewalk and against the buildings three stories below. I love the sound of trash blowing along the street in New York. There's something intimate and soothing about it, the Manhattan equivalent of chirping birds. I peered out the dirty window beside his bed. The sun was flickering in and out of lofty cirrus clouds, and the sky was a sharp blue. I slipped out of bed, put on my jeans, a striped dress shirt, a pair of Jeffrey's paint-splattered sneakers, and a black sport coat, and quietly left the apartment.

The air felt improbably fresh and sweet, as if all that poisonous acid rain had washed the sky clean. Tilting my face to the sun, I headed south on Broadway, with the dusty, warm wind blowing my jacket open. I put on round sunglasses, a pair of Arthur's, which I'd swiped from him for the weekend, the very pair he'd been wearing the day we met.

I love the quiet, day-after-the-bomb atmosphere of New York early on Sunday mornings. There was a young couple kissing under the marquee at the Metro theater, newspapers and plastic bags blowing around their feet. Taxis sped past. I imagined that each was carrying an exhausted lone rider heading home after a night-long tryst. One of my most treasured fantasies of romantic love was getting into a taxi and speeding away from my beloved.

I began to feel swamped with melancholy as I walked along. Dust blew into my eye, and I stopped under the awning of a bagel shop, took off Arthur's sunglasses, and tried to dislodge it. Tears would have done the job nicely, but that physiological phenomenon was such a rare occurrence with me, I might just as well have been waiting for it to snow.

As I continued walking down Broadway, I engaged in one of my favorite mind-filling activities: I pretended I was on the Oprah Winfrey show. Getting on a talk show is one of the great ambitions of American life, right up there with giving an Academy Award acceptance speech and being Jackie Onassis. In this case, the topic of the day was Returning to a Monogamous Relationship After Breaking Off a Clandestine Affair.

I was telling Oprah that, yes, the affair had been exciting for a while, I did enjoy it. But then I realized I just couldn't handle the deception. All the lies were making me feel like a worthless human being. I couldn't reveal the most intimate facts of my life to the person I really cared most about, who, as it turned out, was the person I'd spent the past two years deceiving. So I broke off the affair, told my lover we couldn't go on anymore. And I'd written a best-selling self-help book entitled *Realignments,* and now, in addition to being deliriously happy, I was rich. Life was one big Hallelujah Chorus.

By the time I got through taking questions from the audience and listening to the other numskulls on the panel, I was practically to Times Square. The sun was shining brightly but without much heat, and I decided to walk to my favorite Manhattan hotel and treat myself to a ride in one of their glass elevators. It was a free thrill I'd come upon when I was looking for a bathroom in Times Square a few years earlier. I'd gone to ride the elevators at least half a dozen times since, and often passed along the sightseeing tip to customers at Only Connect. Bored with Oprah and feeling otherwise inspired, I switched the channel and hopped onto the panel of the Donahue show, where the topic was Fun in New York on Five Dollars a Day.

The hotel was one of those sleek cement-and-glass monstrosities that were going to make a spectacular implosion in about a decade. Starting on street level, there were five floors of vast, empty lobbies, designed, I suppose, so the house detectives could screen out the real deadbeats before they got to the verdant restaurants and lounges on the main floor and opened fire into the crowds. The whole hotel revolved around the dizzying valley of an atrium, that marvelous architectural invention, currently as ubiquitous in hotels as beds. This atrium was, to be fair, quite spectacular, soaring up fifty stories, with full-sized trees growing in the lobby and ivy plants trailing down from the upper reaches. Soon we'd all be living in these climate-controlled domes, where weather and fresh air were entirely beside the point.

There were few people milling around the street entrance and no line at the bank of elevators. I stepped into an elevator and punched the button for the top. The little cubicle lurched upward through several floors, and then the main lobby and the restaurants and all those potted trees were beneath me. The overdressed guests and the bellhops pushing clothes racks and the waiters bustling about with trays on their shoulders grew smaller, a colony of tiny, scurrying people, moving about meaninglessly. I pressed my body flat against the glass wall, daring it not to do its job and send me flying through space.

At the top floor, the elevator stopped. Instead of rocketing immediately back to the lobby, as I usually did, I decided to get out.

The carpeted hallways were quiet, with the muted, buzzing sounds of heating systems and distant vacuum cleaners. I leaned out over the railing as far as I could, trying to see the restaurant below, but the place had been suicide-proofed, and the view straight down was limited.

At the far end of the hallway was an immense round window that looked out to a maze of building tops and scraps of blue sky. There was a row of backless leather seats in front of it, from which you could safely watch the murders and muggings on the streets below. A man and a woman were seated there now, sunken into the leather cushions, kissing passionately. I stood back from them at a safe distance, partially hidden by a concrete pillar. The man was in his shirtsleeves, and the woman had on a long raincoat; there was a single suitcase at their feet. It must have been she who was leaving, while he stayed on. Perhaps they'd met that weekend and she was returning to her husband. I could make out only their silhouettes against the bright sunlight streaming in the window. Quietly, I stepped in closer. I usually hate being enlisted as an audience for strangers' lovemaking or public displays of rage, but I was transfixed by the sight of these two, so oblivious to their surroundings and that window right in front of them.

And then some shadow passed over me, and I leaned against the pillar, weakened by longing and by the realization that there wasn't anyone in my life now—there never had been anyone in my life—to drag up to the top of this hotel and clutch at passionately in the quiet hallways. I came only for the view and the fleeting thrill of the nausea the elevators produced. I was so completely undone by this thought, I slid my back down the column until I was squatting on the floor. I envied these two desperately and wanted to run away, but I couldn't even avert my eyes.

After a time—I wasn't sure how long exactly—the woman stood and adjusted her coat. She had thick, dark curls, and she flung them off her face with a toss of her head. The man, his back to me, was slumped in the seat, with his head in his hands. "You'll be back in a week," the woman said, wiping at her eyes. "Only seven days."

And then she looked over at me, startled, perhaps, by my ridiculous posture. Her lover turned to follow her gaze.

He shaded his eyes. "Patrick?" he asked. "Is that you?"

Vivian was catching a plane back to Chicago, an eleven o'clock flight, and she was already running late. Tony had to stay on in the city for another week to finish up a job. This was the hotel where they'd met eight months earlier, in an elevator as they both were headed for this very spot. Didn't I remember that I had told Tony about the view from this window? They'd both been staying at the hotel that week, but if it hadn't been for my travel advice, they might never have met.

The three of us were standing in front of the low leather seats. They had their arms around each other's waist and were leaning shoulder to shoulder. Tony was talking in a quiet, hushed tone that I'd never heard him use before.

Vivian was older than my brother and slightly taller; she had an air of dignity about her that made me think she was more worldly and—despite his bravado—self-assured than Tony. She had all that glamorous, curly dark hair and those fashionable puffy lips, but she was hardly the beauty-queen type that Tony usually went for. Her coat was rumpled and she had a network of fine lines encircling her mouth. There was something in the way she was looking at me, as if we were old friends or at least knew each other well, and in the way she was leaning against Tony, almost as if she were propping him up, that made me feel she was drawing me into an alliance with her, one in which we were both committed to protecting my younger brother from himself. She hadn't said much more than hello, but it seemed to me, as Tony babbled on nervously, that she and I were having a silent conversation, one in which she was sizing me up.

She interrupted Tony in the middle of his long-winded description of their walk across the Brooklyn Bridge. "I'd better get going," she said. "If there's any traffic, I'll miss my plane." She picked up her suitcase and carried it to the elevators.

I offered to look at her ticket to see if there was some way I could tinker with it so she could take a later flight.

"That's a great idea," Tony said. "Patrick knows every sleazy trick in the book. Show him the ticket, hon."

Vivian turned down the offer graciously. "I have to get back anyway. And you two should have some time alone to talk."

We got into the elevator and they stood facing me, with their backs to the glass wall, all that scenery wasted. As we descended, Vivian spoke to Tony in a soft voice, so quiet I could make out the whispering sounds but none of the words. Her curls were brushing against his face, and he reached out and gently held her hair back. The gesture was so intimate, I turned away.

Eighteen

}

"What is it?" Tony asked. "What is that brings two people together, gets them to the same spot at the same exact moment? How is it that Vivian and I each decided to go up to the top floor at exactly the right moment? Is it fate, luck? What the hell is it, Patrick?"

I shrugged and finished my drink.

At Tony's insistence, we'd gone back to his hotel room and he'd mixed a couple of Bloody Marys. I'd gulped mine as if it were a good strong cup of coffee. The drink was basically a tumblerful of vodka and ice, with a splash of tomato juice thrown in as an afterthought to legitimize drinking it at such an early hour. The alcohol had wasted no time in knocking off a substantial number of brain cells, and I was feeling pleasantly dazed and disoriented, happy to be in the secure confines of the hotel. I was sitting on the top of the desk, between a pile of damp towels and a silver bucket. There was an empty champagne bottle in the bucket, floating in a pool of melted ice. The sheets on the lake-sized bed were tangled into knots, and the pillows were scattered about the gray room as if my brother and Vivian had been playfully tossing them at each other before she departed. Tony was at the window, looking out with his arms spread against the glass. The sight of all that blue sky in the background made me feel as if we were in the stateroom of some elegant airship.

On the elevator up from the lobby, I'd had a chance to look at Tony more closely and assess the toll exacted by his stressful bout with love. He'd aged noticeably since the last time we'd been together, more than a year earlier. He'd always had a narrow face, but now his cheeks had sunken in so that his mouth seemed to protrude in an almost simian way. There were dark circles under his limpid brown eyes, and his hair was greasy and, for him, unusually long around the ears. At age seventeen, Tony had begun going to a barber once a week to have his hair trimmed. He was the only man of my generation I knew of who indulged in this ritual. He was one of the most impeccably groomed and manicured people I'd ever met. His face was always so scrubbed and shiny, I sometimes wondered if he didn't go for professional facials. This fanatical personal hygiene routine was obviously part of his campaign to take rigid control of his life, make the most of what he had, and attempt to get as far from O'Neil's Men's Shop as he could. Ironically, everything he did made his physical resemblance to my father more striking.

It was almost a relief to see him looking a bit disheveled, the antiseptic cleanliness of his face replaced by a kind of dissipated sensuality. His lips were fuller and redder, as if they'd been rubbed raw from kissing Vivian too passionately.

"You want to hear the scariest thing?" he asked, his back still to me. "As I was leaving my room to go up there to that window the morning Vivian and I met, I thought: Maybe I should call Loreen first. Then I decided to wait. If I had called her, I never would have met Vivian. Maybe we'd all be better off."

"Speaking of calling Loreen . . ."

"I haven't in almost two weeks. I'm a coward, Patrick."

I was feeling rather cowardly myself. I'd tried to bring up the topic of the dinner conversation with our parents but had stalled midsentence each time. "Is there any more vodka?" I asked.

"For someone who didn't want any booze, you downed that pretty quick."

He took my glass and went to the bar he'd set up at the sink in the bathroom. He had on a dark-green shirt with black stripes and a pair of baggy khakis. It was the first time in a while I'd seen him in anything other than a conservative, freshly pressed suit. But this casual outfit didn't hang on him quite right. He had the sleeves of the shirt rolled up over his wrists and the top buttons undone, but he still looked like a spy trying too hard to blend in with the rest of the crowd.

"What are you doing in New York anyway?" he asked.

"Nothing too exciting."

"Business?"

I was about to toss off the whole subject with a noncommittal yes, but I was suddenly overcome with a longing to tell him about Jeffrey, partially because I couldn't stand having him believe my relationship with Arthur was so cozy and partially because I didn't want him to think he had the exclusive rights to infidelity. "I was visiting a friend," I said, as ambiguously as possible.

He looked over his shoulder at me as he unscrewed the cap on the vodka bottle. "A friend?"

"Something like that. You and I probably have a lot more in common than you'd like to think."

"You're probably right," he said. "Tell me about . . . him, I suppose, isn't it?"

I began a rambling, incoherent description of my flight to New York two days earlier. When I got to the point of actually mentioning Jeffrey, loyalty to Arthur took over. "Look," I said, "let's not get into it. It's too complicated, and besides, it doesn't make any difference."

"Not to me, but I can think of at least one person it might make a difference to. Especially if you and Arthur are buying a house together. You're not backing out of that, are you?" He handed me my drink.

"I doubt it," I said. "I have to live somewhere."

"Good. Just plain, simple settling down with someone looks awfully good to me right now. And I might as well tell you, Pat, I slipped up and mentioned the house when I was talking with your mother. I wanted to have something hopeful to say to her, and that was the first thing that sprang to mind. They would have found out sooner or later."

"Don't bother getting defensive, Tony. I know all about it, and I'm in no position to complain. I wouldn't think of complaining and jeopardizing our beautiful new friendship."

The words sounded a good deal more harsh and sarcastic than I'd intended, but I didn't know how to take them back.

"Don't make jokes," Tony said. "It means a lot to me. I haven't always been a good friend to you when you needed one. Vivian pointed that out to me. So I especially appreciate all the help you've been."

His voice was so quietly, even grimly sincere, it seemed like as good a time as any to start confessing my own slips.

"I'm afraid I might have been more help than you bargained for. The fact is, I told your parents about Vivian."

Tony took a seat in the chair by the window and calmly put his glass on the floor.

"It was an accident," I said. "At least I think it was an accident. Anyway, I don't know, but I told them."

"You told them about Vivian," he said, as if he was trying to understand what the words meant. He pushed the sleeves of his shirt up almost to his biceps. "What did they do?"

"The usual. They blamed each other and started fighting."

He shook his head and took a long drink of his Bloody Mary. "Have you ever heard of anything sadder in your life than those two?"

"You're not angry?"

He shrugged it off as if it was of little importance. "In some ways I suppose it's easier than me telling them myself. Your father must be going nuts. Taking it out on her, I'll bet."

"Probably."

"She's taking it out on him."

"Probably."

"What a life. As if I don't have enough on my mind, I have to worry about them, too. I thought moving out to Chicago would help. I guess I should have kept going. Hawaii, maybe. Let's face it, Patrick: I don't know what I'm doing anymore. I'm not saying I'd change anything, but Vivian's turned my life upside down. She's either the best thing that ever happened to me or the worst."

"She seems nice," I said, a comment so hopelessly bland, Tony merely frowned.

"I've even started to question my job. I'm down here for two weeks trying to eliminate half the staff of an insurance company out in Queens. I spent three days in one office going over some lady's job with her, trying to figure out what the fuck it is she's been doing forty hours a week every week for the past twenty years. 'Writing reports,' she tells me. It turns out she's been writing a meaningless daily report on an insignificant procedural detail and mailing it off to a person at the home office in Detroit who's been dead since 1967. Finding that kind of dead wood and getting rid of her usually makes my day. Like cleaning the grout in the bathroom. But this time I couldn't do it. She's two years away from retirement. I let the poor slob slide by. 'Keep up the good work,' I told her. I must be going soft."

He looked down and felt his stomach, possibly to see how soft he was getting. I wanted to say something reassuring, but I was pretty sure he wasn't really looking for comfort. Part of what was good about his relationship with Vivian was that it was making him squirm. He just had to have faith it would come out all right in the end.

We sat in silence, and I watched the clouds drift across the clear sky in the window behind him and played with the empty champagne bottle.

"You know," Tony finally said, "I wish Ryan was here. Do you get to see much of him?"

I told him I'd invited Ryan to dinner, although I didn't mention Sharon, since Tony had always taken a grim view of her.

"If Ryan was here, we'd do some tourist crap like go to the Statue of Liberty or take a Circle Line cruise around Manhattan. It might be fun."

I reminded him that Ryan was prone to motion sickness.

"That's not true," he said. "That wife of his put the idea in his head because she didn't want him going out fishing with that friend of his that has the boat, the retarded one. Ryan always had the strongest stomach of the bunch of us. He should have been a nurse. Either that or a cook in some place like a nursing home or a hospital for hopelessly deformed children. He's always happiest taking care of people. Remember the diet?"

"The diet" was one of the more memorable events of our childhood, although we rarely spoke about it.

When I was about eight, my father began suffering the ill health that was to plague him ever since. He came home from a series of hospital tests and announced that he had high blood pressure. "The doctor told me it's probably your cooking that's killing me," he said to Rita.

My mother was doubtful. "That's the stupidest thing I've ever heard," she said.

He tossed a piece of paper at her that outlined a complicated program of dietary rules. "I have to follow this," he said, "assuming I want to live."

For the next few weeks, religiously, he kept to a regimen of salt- and fat-restricted meals, which my mother grudgingly cooked for him. His diet became the sole topic of his conversation. Everyone who came into the store was treated to a detailed description of his daily intake and the willpower he was exerting in following his doctor's orders. Congratulations rolled in, and he began to enjoy a certain self-righteous martyrdom.

I suppose it was the praise that finally set Rita off and made her go on the same diet. To do him one better, she decided to limit her intake even more. It became a kind of contest between them to see who could be the purest and eat the least. They both began to lose weight; after two weeks they were gaunt. The dinner table conversation grew unbearably tense, my father smoking and my mother drinking cup after cup of black coffee, each proclaiming an absence of hunger and no interest in food. The meals my mother prepared for the rest of us grew increasingly Spartan, until we were practically living on Pepsi and saltines.

Then late one afternoon, I came home and the whole house smelled of roasting meat. Ryan, who was about thirteen, was standing in the kitchen, tearing up lettuce and whistling. That night he brought an immense pot roast to the table and carved thick slabs for himself and Tony and me, and we ate voraciously. My mother burst into tears and started to mumble incoherent apologies. Both she and my father broke their fast. "The diet" was never mentioned by either one of them again. Ryan's pot roast was such a success, he cooked the family meals regularly until he married.

Tony looked out the hotel window mournfully. "When you come down to it, we owe Ryan a lot. He was always taking care of us when we were kids. Now his life has turned to shit, down in the cellar."

"And getting worse," I said. "His wife wants a divorce."

"That's good news! I never liked that little bitch. Who'd guess that someone that short could be that pushy?"

"That isn't the point. Ryan loves her. He's all broken up about this. It's not as if he's out meeting new people all the time."

"I just had a crazy thought, Patrick. You don't think he and Loreen . . ."

"Do yourself a favor and don't finish that sentence."

"You're right; that would be too much to hope for. Now that you've met Vivian, Pat, now that you've met her, do you blame me?"

"But, Tony," I said, "I never did."

Part
4

Nineteen

⟩

As soon as I returned to Cam-
bridge, Arthur began reminding me, in a number of subtle ways,
about the mortgage. I kept finding loan application forms, ads for
mortgage companies, Arthur's bankbook, or the real estate section of
the newspaper on the kitchen counter, on the floor of the bathroom,
on top of the stereo, and in other places where ordinarily he didn't
leave things. It wasn't Arthur's way to make direct demands.

I was feeling virtuous that my days of fooling around with Jeffrey
were at an end, so I didn't see any need to rush. Every day, I carried
the papers to work in my knapsack, but each time I took them out,
to read through the fine print, I'd develop such a severe case of
eyestrain, I had to put them aside.

Then one night at the beginning of the second week in April, I
came home from the gym while Arthur was out for his evening walk.
I rarely had the place to myself at that hour, and I tossed my body
onto the sofa, drinking in the luxury of being temporarily alone.
Very quickly, however, I made the mistake of using my solitude to
wander around the apartment, following a trail of clues Arthur had
left behind and trying to piece together his evening. A roasting pan
was soaking in the kitchen sink, filled with soapy water and grease,
and on the counter was a plate of chicken, broccoli, carrots, and
mashed potatoes, all set for me to pop in the oven and reheat. On top

of the desk in the living room was a stack of envelopes and an open checkbook. He'd obviously spent a substantial amount of time writing checks to worthy causes and paying off bills, some of them mine. There was a pile of literature from Amnesty International on the arm of the sofa and a copy of *The Magic Mountain* spread open on the floor, with corrections of the translation he'd penciled into the margins years earlier.

Beside this tome was a pad of legal paper, on which Arthur had sketched a floor plan of the yellow house. In each of the rooms, he indicated where various pieces of furniture would go—brown sofa, red chair, glass-fronted bookcase. The smallest of the three bedrooms he'd designated as "P.'s Place." This box he'd crowded with amusing little drawings of crucifixes, candles, and stick figures with halos over their heads. Everything was roughly sketched, but he'd clearly spent a lot of time decorating the room that was to be my study.

I might have been able to ignore the indications of Arthur's goodwill, kindness, generosity, intelligence, and optimism scattered all over the apartment—the chicken dinner, the charitable contributions, the reading material on the plight of the exploited multitudes, the improved Thomas Mann—but I couldn't get past that lovingly drawn depiction of my room, with all its tacky religious paraphernalia. It struck me as so unthinkably tender, I collapsed back onto the sofa and spent the next hour reliving the day Arthur and I had met, exactly the kind of fond, maudlin ruminating I usually manage to avoid. The miserable result was that by the time Arthur came home from his walk, I was sitting at the Formica table in the kitchen humming "When first my old, old love I knew" from *Trial by Jury* and filling out the mortgage application.

Arthur and I had met six years earlier at a cookout, late in the afternoon on a hot Sunday at the end of June.

I spent the week before that fateful cookout shut up in my room in the turret on the top floor of Sharon's house, nursing a mean case of poison ivy. I have no idea where I got it—I'd never had it before and haven't had it since—but after the last day of school that year, I broke out in a shockingly ugly rash that covered my body from my hairline to my ankles. I was so miserably uncomfortable, and so embarrassed about my appearance, that I took to my bed for six days, moving only enough to turn the pages of a nine-hundred-page novel I was reading about sex in suburbia. Sharon initially indulged me by carrying her TV and video machine up to my bedroom and bringing home tapes after work. But by the Sunday of the cookout, she was disgusted with my malingering. Her theory was that my poison ivy was psychosomatically induced—a manifestation of my doubts about teaching, a physical collapse to celebrate the end of classes.

She was possibly right, but school was only part of the problem. I was also recovering from a period of foolish romantic entanglements that were typical of the kinds of relationships I kept falling into in my early twenties.

I had only one serious lover before Arthur. He was Warren, a generous, opinionated bully I met shortly after moving to Boston. He designed computer programs for a living, but it soon became apparent to me that he was, at heart, a frustrated psychiatrist. The sentence he uttered most often in the endless year we were involved was: "Sure that's what you *said*, Patrick; now let me tell you what you *meant*." I was foolish and narcissistic enough to always listen to his interpretations and believe them. Worse still, I was flattered by his frantic jealousy. My only defense is that I was young. It took me several years of my own romantic betrayals to figure out that jealous accusations of infidelity are most often thinly veiled confessions of the same. Warren was a short man, so aggressively homely he was attractive. I don't know how to describe his face except to say that it looked as if someone had stuck a lot of mismatched features onto a yam, glued a clump of hair on top, thrown his hands up in disgust, and said, "Ah, to hell with it; it'll have to do." But what he lacked in beauty, Warren made up for in swaggering, self-assured sexual energy, which I, and an astonishing number of other fools, found irresistible.

Warren and I had one of those embattled relationships that inexperienced twenty-two-year-olds, jaded forty-year-olds, and, for all I know, computer programmers of any age are likely to mistake for true love. It consisted mainly of a lot of angry phone calls, shouting and name-calling sessions, biweekly breakups followed by thrilling reconciliations. We had no shared interests—for an entire year I avoided asking what a data base was, for fear he'd tell me—except a fondness for arguing.

Still, when Warren decided to be charming, it was easy to forget he was ever anything else, and the relationship might have gone on for some time if he hadn't moved to Texas, a state with a climate I could never tolerate.

After Warren, I began a series of brief, depressing involvements with people I didn't really know and wasn't all that fond of. These usually dragged through a month or two of tense, quiet dinners, long, boring walks, and unhappy mornings waking up beside someone I might or might not ever see again, depending on whether one or the other of us found something better to do before the upcoming Saturday night.

The last of these entanglements was a three-month-long parody of romantic love with a nonentity whose name I could never remember. This meaningful relationship ended when I phoned him one night, got a busy signal, and decided he wasn't worth the effort of redialing. The feeling was obviously mutual, as I never heard from him again. I'd been more remorseful about setting mousetraps than I was about ending it with what's-his-name, but I was nearly overwhelmed by the pointlessness of the whole three months I wasted on him. It made me realize how desperate I was for the illusion of love.

A few weeks later, I developed poison ivy and went on strike.

On the Sunday of the cookout, Sharon threatened that if I didn't get out of bed and go with her, she'd take back her TV. So I smeared a layer of calamine lotion, put on long pants and a T-shirt, and went off.

The cookout was in Cambridgeport, in the backyard of a married couple Sharon had recently sent trekking in Nepal. He was a corporate lawyer, and she had started a company that gave expensive seminars in "Writing" to illiterate businessmen. They were the usual Cambridge success story: a couple of ex-radicals who had grown tired of pounding the pavements in peasant blouses and love beads and had plunged into the world of capital gains and designer shower curtains with stunning enthusiasm.

When I was growing up, Cambridge was a city filled with smoky coffeehouses, folksingers, revival movie theaters, and cheap rooming houses where hippies slept dormitory-style on mattresses on the floor. Every disparaging comment about the place I ever heard from my parents only strengthened my determination to live there. But by the time I did, things had changed. The rooming houses were replaced with hundred-dollar-a-night hotels, and the folksingers were either cleaned up and recording for a major label or dressed in suits and selling software in the suburbs. As for the hippies, most of them were standing around that landscaped backyard, sipping Campari.

"I think I'll sit out in the car," I told Sharon. We walked through the gate and were immediately crushed by a mob of people carrying infants in expensive papoose packs. Outdoor speakers were blasting reggae (the only safe choice for all-white, politically correct gatherings), and there was a table set up against the back fence, with bowls of guacamole and other highly spiced foods from a variety of hot third world countries.

"You don't think *I* belong here, do you?" Sharon asked. She lit a cigarette and blew the smoke in the direction of a baby. "Just mingle for half an hour and then we'll leave, I promise."

She was ushered off by someone who wanted to tell her about his thrilling trip to Ecuador, and I knew we were in for the long haul. I went to sit in a folding chair set in the shade of a hedge of rosebushes. If I hadn't already been convinced that my appearance was frightening, the treatment I received at the party would have done the trick. Kids kept coming up to me and staring with their mouths open, until their parents rushed over and carried them off.

From my shady seat, I had a clear view of the gate leading from the street to the yard. I was keeping count of the number of babies being hauled in, a sure sign of the population crisis. Then I noticed Arthur, or rather a tall, balding man with strikingly large ears, wearing a peculiar pair of sunglasses with tiny round lenses. Unlike the dozen or so people who'd come in in the time I'd been watching, he had a great deal of difficulty opening the gate, a fact I found especially odd since all the task required was a simple push. When he finally stumbled in, he looked around in confusion, as if he didn't know anyone there or had expected to find a lawn sale. Wearing a pair of baggy khaki shorts that came down below his knees and a long-sleeved white shirt, he was standing with a slight stoop, almost as if he was apologizing for his height. There was something in his posture and perplexed expression that gave him a comical appearance I liked immediately.

A woman followed him into the yard, spoke to him briefly, handed over the baby she was carrying, and went into the crowd, calling out boisterous hellos. Arthur began to bounce the baby in his arms as he made his way over to the empty seat beside me. He sat down, cooing and clucking.

"Sweet, isn't he?" he asked, smiling at me.

The baby, who was about seven months old, had a beautifully delicate face but was wearing a bored, detached expression, as if he might have preferred to be at home reading Henry James. He was dressed in a pink bonnet trimmed in white lace, a rose sundress, and frilly white ankle socks. "What's his name?" The "his" stuck in my throat.

"Robin," Arthur cooed. "Isn't that right? Isn't your name Robin?"

This was a baby headed for a gender crisis if ever I'd seen one: girl's clothes and an androgynous name. I could imagine the way they'd decorated his bedroom. But Arthur was staring at him with such open adoration, I was touched. "My name's Arthur, by the way. Arthur Egger."

I introduced myself, and to my amazement, Arthur shifted the baby to his left shoulder and stuck out his hand. It seemed unnecessarily generous, considering my condition.

"I hate to ask you this," he said, "but would you mind holding little Robin here for a second. I have to take off these sunglasses. I don't like to wear sunglasses in the shade. Eyestrain."

I took Robin into my arms, and he gazed at me suspiciously, as if he was trying to figure out what, exactly, I was. Fortunately, he was too well behaved to complain. Arthur put his sunglasses into his shirt pocket and looked at me with his enormous, kind brown eyes. He had a bemused expression, a gentle so-what's-new look I'd later learn was as close as he ever came to flirting. I passed Robin back, and he said, "Boy, he's heavier than you'd think, isn't he? It's a good thing I saw my chiropractor this week."

"Back problems?" I asked. I like to discover the weaknesses in people I find appealing.

"Originally I was seeing him for neck problems. But now we're working on my back and knees. Lately, though, my ankles seem to be bothering me."

"Ah, well." A clear case of hypochondria if ever I'd heard one, and a pretty bad one, too. "Soon it'll be your toes, and then that should be the end of it, no?"

"He's making fun of us, Robin."

I was making fun of Arthur, but I'd have loved to take on Robin.

Arthur told me he'd just finished law school at Boston University and was supposed to be spending the summer studying for the bar exam. "But so far, all I've done is read Dickens. Have you read *Bleak House?*"

Hesitantly, I confessed I hadn't. I was relieved to see he wasn't put off by my ignorance. (While Arthur was fairly proud of his intelligence, he had an astonishing tolerance for stupidity in others.

Many of his friends were, like me, intellectual lightweights who gathered at his feet, entranced by the breadth of his knowledge and the scope of his reading.) He began discussing the book with such genuine fondness and unpretentious delight—almost as if the author and most of the characters were close friends—that I was enthralled. He made me feel I was a genius for not having read the novel; now I had all the pleasure of reading it for the first time still in front of me. When I told him I taught school, he became enthusiastic and complimentary, and suggested a number of books for my students. I was drawn to him, baby, wife, and all. He exuded some air of calm even as he shifted Robin from shoulder to shoulder, gurgled and made faces, and went without a pause from discussing Dickens and Jane Austen to talking incomprehensible baby babble. He was lightly flushed from the heat and looked completely self-confident in a shy, casual way I admired enormously.

Finally, Robin's mother came over and lifted him out of Arthur's arms. "Thanks for holding her," she said. "You don't know how much trouble you saved me. Imagine trying to work this crowd with a baby. She's an angel, isn't she?"

"She?" Arthur looked amazed. "I thought you said he."

"Dressed like this?" Robin had turned around in her mother's arms and was looking wistfully at Arthur, reaching out her pudgy hands.

"I guess I didn't notice," Arthur said. "I just liked holding him. Her."

When the woman had wandered off, Arthur explained that the mother, whom he'd never met before, had approached him and asked him to hold her baby for half an hour. He shrugged, modest but obviously pleased with himself. "She said I looked trustworthy."

"I suppose this is the kind of thing that happens to you all the time, people trusting you with their kids, their wallets, their secrets?"

"I wouldn't say all the time. But it happens." He smiled. "Wouldn't you trust me?"

I thought about it for a moment and decided he was one of the most trustworthy people I'd ever met. "I'm not sure what I have to trust you with," I said.

He looked at me oddly, as if he was surprised or perhaps distressed by my comment, one that I'd intended flirtatiously. It's relatively easy for me to flirt with people I assume to be disinterested, unavailable, or repulsed. I took his look as a sign that he was getting

bored with my company and decided to go on the offensive. I've
found it often helps to start insulting someone when he's obviously
wearying of you.

I asked him who in this dreary crowd he knew. The hosts were his
neighbors, he told me, and they'd invited him. But only out of pity
because his wife had recently divorced him.

I pointed out Sharon, who was holding court with a crowd of
laughing people on the far side of the lawn. She was standing in a
flower bed, crushing petunias beneath her sandals. I told him we
were housemates. "I'll introduce you," I said. "She knows lots of
people to fix you up with."

Arthur gave me another of his odd, questioning looks, as if he
wasn't quite sure what I meant, and then our conversation died. He
sat calmly, with his hands folded in his lap and a bemused look on his
face. It was just after six, that still, scorching time of the day when the
sun seems to blaze with a final show of intensity. The music had
stopped, and the crowd in the yard had begun to thin. The remaining
guests looked limp, despondent, resigned to the heat. I felt suddenly
relaxed, as if Arthur and I were set apart from the remains of the
crowd, floating in the cool shade of the rosebushes. I don't know
how long we sat in silence—probably no more than fifteen minutes—
but in that time, I felt a kind of brotherly intimacy with him. Then
there was a burst of wild laughter from inside the house. Two sunburned children in matching Day-Glo orange outfits ran across the
lawn, someone turned on the music again, and the spell was broken.
By the time Sharon came to announce she was ready to leave, I was
hesitant to go.

"In case you were wondering," I told him, "this is poison ivy. I
don't usually look like this."

He cocked his head to one side and smiled vaguely.

"This rash," I said, pointing. "It's poison ivy."

"I'm sorry to hear it. I guess I didn't really notice."

I should have taken all the things I liked about Arthur as warning
signs—his vagueness, his complete lack of interest in physical appear-
ances, his hypochondria. But what did I know? I was charmed by
him, by his calm and sincerity and some air of innocence I couldn't
quite pinpoint. One week later, I made dinner for Arthur and a
woman who'd briefly lived in Sharon's house following her divorce.
I thought the evening went remarkably well; the two of them left
together, and I was fairly certain I had a matchmaking career ahead of
me. When Arthur returned the invitation, I assumed Tina would be

there, tossing the salad. But it was just the two of us. After an awkward, silent dinner, he made an elaborately pained confession about the reason for his divorce and then knocked over a lamp as he made an awkward lunge in my direction.

The first time we were having sex, Arthur's phone rang. He apologized, got out of bed, and spent fifteen minutes earnestly answering questions from a telemarketing company about which brand of frozen vegetables he preferred. When he got back into bed, he seemed confused, as if he couldn't remember what we'd been doing.

I suppose neither one of us was ever passionately attracted to the other, which, at least at the beginning, didn't seem to matter so much. I liked Arthur. I liked him passionately. I admired him passionately. I had a passionate desire to please such a kind and admirable person. I suppose I must have figured that if I added it all up, the grand total would equal love.

The Peter Principle—the theory which contends that employees in a hierarchy are promoted until they're in a position in which they're incompetent—may or may not have validity in the business world, but it certainly applies to love relations. Arthur and I should have stayed in that patch of shade by the rosebushes forever, awkwardly flirting with each other and falling prey to misunderstandings and lost opportunities. Instead we moved on to dinner dates, sex, cohabitation, mutual dependency, with an inevitability that took on a life of its own.

Now we were negotiating buying a house together. Jeffrey was right: I did want a home, some safe and reliable shelter from heat and disease and the madness of the whole dying world. I suppose what I was most confused about was how much I was willing to pay for it.

Twenty

$\wr$

Sometime in that second week in April, the weather took a decided turn for the worse, and spring began to strangle the East Coast. We had a dose of unseasonable weather, which the TV meteorologists were euphemistically referring to as a "warming trend." I discovered that if I switched the stations at exactly the right moment, I could catch the weather report on all three local networks. One moronic weatherman outdid the next, smiling and rhapsodizing about what was clearly an environmental crisis. "Let's all get out there and enjoy the sun!" was the general attitude.

TV meteorologists have always struck me as a particularly insipid breed, with their apologies for each passing rain shower, even in the middle of a drought, and their apparent assumptions that everyone worships the sun, that big carcinogen in the sky. I called the TV stations to complain, but got surprisingly little response. One person I spoke with had the audacity to explain that normal temperatures are determined on the basis of thirty-year averages; once the greenhouse eighties were averaged in, our current heat wave would be nothing out of the ordinary. "In other words," he said cheerfully, "this is perfectly normal weather."

Arthur set up the furniture on the back porch, and we took to eating breakfast and dinner there on especially mild days. One Tuesday morning, we were sitting in the balmy breeze drinking coffee, going through our newspaper-scanning routine. I was summarizing a recent story about a wholesome, happily married, devoutly religious, outspokenly right-wing suburban minister who'd been arrested on child molestation charges. It was a pretty run-of-the-mill item, which I was forced to embellish with a few invented lurid details. I looked up at Arthur in the middle of a riff about sex in the sacristy and saw, in the bright morning sunlight, that the sparse hair around his temples and over his big ears was peppered with gray. I'd never noticed this before, and I was so shocked I dropped the paper. The graying was far from unattractive; if anything, it made for a particularly dashing effect. What stunned me was the realization that Arthur was visibly aging after all.

He had on the cotton sweater I'd bought him in New York after leaving Tony's hotel. (Because Jeffrey and I were calling it quits, my original plan to go to Barney's had seemed beyond the call of duty, and I'd stopped instead at a street vendor in Times Square and bought this "Ralph Lauren Original" for seven dollars.) It was a bright shade of blue, which seemed to be draining his complexion of color. On closer inspection of his face, it appeared that Arthur's chin might be sagging, too. I couldn't understand why I'd never seen these developments before. Even now, the hair and the chin looked to me more like disguises than actual physical changes.

He smiled at me with his wide, kind smile and cocked his head to the side inquiringly. Shaken, I picked up the newspaper and went on with my report. It wasn't until later in the day, when I was having lunch with Sharon, that I was stopped short by the realization that I, too, had obviously aged in the time I'd known him, had deteriorated physically and become more bitter and pessimistic as well. I realized that no one else would ever see that younger person, and if Arthur and I separated, I'd lose that part of myself forever.

When I mentioned all this to Sharon, she laughed. "You're missing a crucial point here," she said. "In fact, you're missing *the* crucial point."

"What's that?"

"You're unhappy! You aren't getting what you want out of this relationship, and that's what's killing your optimism and making you bitter. And frankly, it's probably what's speeding Arthur's aging process, too."

"I'm happy enough," I said. "At least I think so. I'm certainly as happy as anyone else in my family."

"I'll be the judge of that," Sharon said, "after I've met Ryan."

Arthur suggested that we have the dinner with Ryan and Sharon on the back porch, providing the mild weather held. I vetoed the idea. If Ryan caught a cold while having dinner at my apartment, my parents would never forgive me. As it was, they'd called several times to grill me with questions about what I intended to feed Ryan and why I'd invited him to my apartment all of a sudden when I hadn't done so for several years.

"He likes a nice healthy meal," Rita informed me. "He can't digest all that spicy food you live on. He's got enough problems without adding an ulcer to it."

"You don't get an ulcer from spicy food," my father said on the extension. "You get it from constant stress and anxiety, like if you live with someone who's always driving you up the wall."

"That poor slob is so upset about this divorce, he can't take much more. Why not give him a rain check? Have him over to see the new house. By then he'll be through with the divorce."

Since talking with Tony in New York, I'd been looking forward to seeing Ryan. I realized that I never spent any time with him and, in a certain way, I'd almost written him off as a hopeless case. The more I thought about it, the more likely it seemed that Sharon might be a good friend for him, encourage him to stand up for himself and, if nothing else, at least tell Elaine how he'd felt about her all the lost years of their separation.

"Why's that Sharon coming?" my father asked. "You're not trying to set something up, are you?"

"Oh, my God!" Rita cried. "Even Patrick isn't that heartless, Jimmy. Give the kid some credit for something."

It was unclear to me why they were so upset about the dinner until, at the end of one conversation, my father said, "I hope you're not planning to talk about Tony at this banquet."

"Tony?"

"Remember him? Your younger brother, the one who's getting married?"

"I suppose his name might come up."

"You see, Rita, I told you," my father said. "Didn't I tell you? That's what this whole thing is about. He's trying to get everyone lined up against Loreen."

"And I suppose that's my fault—is that what you're saying?"

"Well, you didn't try to stop it, did you? At least I had a man-to-man talk with Ryan and told him not to go."

"The last time I checked, Jimmy, it would have been impossible for me to have a man-to-man talk with anyone."

As usually happened when they were on a conference call, they began having their own private battle. Once I had the gist of their conversation, I hung up. It was unlikely they'd notice for a good five minutes, not until my father's strength had waned and the fight ground to a halt.

Tony had phoned twice since our meeting in New York, to report that my parents had made five calls to him in less than a week. But instead of hammering at him about Vivian, as Ryan and I had suspected they'd do, they were trying a different tactic. They were smothering him with daily praise for Loreen, how lovely and sweet and naive she was, how eagerly she was planning for this wedding, and how many thousands of dollars' worth of nonrefundable deposits she'd laid out thus far. The other woman had never been mentioned. Tony assured me that he'd steeled himself for an attack against Vivian, but he was totally unprepared for this assault. Every time he said Loreen's name, his voice dropped to a whisper, almost as if he felt he was causing her greater misery by discussing her.

"Can you imagine how desperate your parents must be to be going on like this?" he asked. "They're in this wedding up to their necks. Who knows what they'd do if I backed out of this."

"Have you talked with Loreen since you got back?" I'd asked.

"We talked: weather, movies, diets, and Sunday dinner. I told you," he said, "I'm a coward."

Twenty-one

The evening of the dinner turned out to be pleasantly cool. The heat of the previous days gave way to more comfortable temperatures, which I didn't trust; I was convinced the early hot spell was lurking in the clouds, waiting to swoop down again. I walked around in shorts and T-shirts even though I was freezing, and I ended up as disconcerted by the relatively seasonable weather as I had been by the heat wave.

With the memory of Ryan's famous pot roast fresh in mind, I wanted to serve my older brother something special. I can be quite a good cook if I try, but I tend to be distracted by options. In preparing a big meal, I usually buy too much food, start out determined to make one thing—a beef stew, let's say—and then decide midstream that I'll turn it into something else—a casserole, perhaps. A culinary freak results, one that only Arthur would find edible. I decided it was safest to make something with limited possibilities: sandwiches. I'm a masterful sandwich chef. There's only so much you can do between two pieces of bread. The real secret to making a perfect sandwich is to choose a thin and sloppy filling and serve it on slices of bread that are unevenly cut and not quite fresh. I'd concocted a recipe using roasted red peppers, smoked mozzarella cheese, and an anchovy-and-pine-nut spread, which I was fairly certain Ryan would like. And it wasn't very spicy.

Arthur was in charge of making a salad. Arthur cooks the way he drives; a little too cautiously and hesitantly. While I pounded the pine nuts with a mortar and pestle, he sat at the kitchen table chopping vegetables with the meticulous care you might use to perform eye surgery. He had on a short-sleeved shirt and a red tie, and he was breathlessly trying to sing "Love, unrequited, robs me of my sleep."

He held up a thin slice of cucumber. "Does this look about right, sweetheart?"

"It looks fine," I said.

"Are you sure? You barely glanced at it." He held it up to the light. "I think I should cut it thinner. I can tell you want me to."

"Thinner would be all right, too."

"Well, I don't know how you expect me to accomplish that, unless you give me a razor blade."

"Believe me, Arthur, if I had a razor blade, I wouldn't be standing here pounding anchovies—I'd be in the bathroom shaving around my jugular."

"Don't start getting critical, sweetheart. I asked a question, that's all."

I took out a sudden murderous impulse on the pine nuts, and Arthur began singing his patter song, cheerful once more. "You know," he said, "I don't understand why you didn't just tell Tony that your parents had lied to him in the beginning about the engagement. That might make him feel less responsible to them or at least angry."

Since I'd sent in my mortgage application, Arthur had been a lot more willing to discuss my brother's dilemma.

"To tell you the truth, I don't understand it, either," I said. "I suppose I must want to protect them."

He held up an absurdly large carrot. "Should I cut this in strips or in chunks or in those coin shapes?"

"Julienne it." I wasn't altogether sure what that meant, but it sounded complicated enough to keep him quiet for a while.

He went to the counter, got down a cookbook, and began leafing through it. As he scanned the glossary, he began recounting the story of one of his clients, a nineteen-year-old Salvadoran who was seeking political asylum in the U.S. If Arthur wasn't able to help him with asylum, the young man would be sent back home to face imprisonment or military service for a government he despised. The case involved the potential breakup of a marriage—mandatory in all the cases he told me about—and the additional heartbreaking detail that

Arthur, who spoke fluent Spanish, was the only person his client trusted enough to confide in. I listened for as long as I could and then, derailed by the sheer weight of his compassion, took the cookbook out of his hands. "We can do without the carrots," I said. "And I forgot to thank you for the flowers."

"You didn't like them."

"I loved them." Despite his doubts about Sharon, he'd brought home a handful of tinted carnations and baby's breath, which I'd stuck in an empty mayonnaise jar. Every time I caught sight of them in my peripheral vision, their ugliness broke my heart. I'd probably weep buckets when the hideous things finally flopped over dead.

Ryan arrived at the apartment in a state near nervous collapse. He handed me a bag filled with cans of the Australian ale he always drank. His hair was matted down around his ears, and his shirttails were sticking out of his pants, and he was sweating. "You're a wreck, Ryan. What's up?"

"It's awful, isn't it? I tried to get dressed up for this dinner, and look at me. Give me one of those beers, will you?"

"What happened?"

"I don't know how you live in this town, Patrick. I was driving through Harvard Square? I thought I was going to be attacked. All these hippies wandering around, crossing against the light. Hell on earth."

"Get off it," I said. "There haven't been any hippies in Harvard Square for at least fifteen years." As soon as the words were out of my mouth, I remembered Sharon's sandals.

We went into the living room, and Ryan flung himself onto the brown velvet sofa. The velocity of his fall made the springs give under him, and he fell back against the cushions and let out a muffled "Oof." "It's a good thing I don't have a bad back, or I'd start filing a lawsuit right now. Help me out of this contraption, will you?"

He settled into a chair, first arranging the antimacassar so his head hit the exact middle, and began to swill down his beer. "Anyway, I don't know if you call them hippies or skinheads or numskulls or what, but they all look like animals, and they were all swarming around the car, and I thought they were going to topple it over."

Ryan was performing the role of the suburban bumpkin for my sake, a role he was dressed for, in a pair of shiny gray pants and a color-coordinated, equally hideous sport jacket. He didn't like Cambridge much and had only visited me a few times in all the years I'd been living there.

"You sound exactly like your parents," I said, the A bomb in the arsenal of family insults. "And don't start talking about hippies in front of Sharon, or she might take offense."

"I love hippies, Pat. Hand me a joint, will you? When's she showing up?"

"Soon. But she has a policy of always being late."

Arthur walked in from the kitchen, and Ryan pushed himself out of his chair. Ryan was genuinely fond of Arthur—there were very few people Ryan wasn't genuinely fond of—but he tended to be a bit uneasy around him, perhaps because he was uneasy about our relationship. To compensate for his discomfort, Ryan went overboard with compliments and cheery goodwill gestures, which Arthur found wearying. Arthur's smile was a little too stiff now, and although he hadn't said as much to me, I knew he was dreading the entire evening.

"Look at this guy," Ryan said to me as he shook Arthur's hand. "White shirt, tie, real sharp. And tall. That's the one thing you can't fake in life, and God knows I've tried. You could eat beans off the top of my head, Arthur."

Arthur collapsed onto the sofa. "You're looking pretty snazzy there yourself, Ryan."

In light of Ryan's appearance, the compliment fell flat. There was a moment of prolonged silence, as if someone had farted loudly and no one wanted to acknowledge it. Ryan's face was more pasty and bloated than usual, his wrinkled shirt was unevenly buttoned, and his jacket didn't fit properly. To top it off, his upper lip was dotted with perspiration. He looked like a man who'd just held up a liquor store and made a getaway on foot.

"Don't mention my looks," Ryan finally said. "Looks have never been my strong point—right, Pat?"

"You've always had your charms."

"I'm happy to be alive, with the goings-on at the store and all this business with the marriage." He opened the bag of beer at his feet and tossed a can to Arthur. "Ever had this stuff? It's the only beer worth drinking."

"Patrick told me about your divorce," Arthur said. "I'm sorry to hear it."

I was standing at the window, pulling the dead leaves off the Swedish ivy plants. The only enjoyment I ever derive from houseplants is pulling off their dead leaves, an act that gives me the same satisfaction as peeling off layers of someone else's sunburned skin. Ryan looked over at me disapprovingly. I'd forgotten to tell Arthur not to mention the divorce. Unlike me, my older brother didn't believe in airing his dirty laundry in public. "Pat told you about that, did he? Well, I don't know what's going on with that, to tell you the truth. The whole thing's a mystery. When I said marriage, I meant the preparations for Tony's wedding."

"There must be a lot," Arthur said. "But the question is, who's going to be the bride, Loreen or Vivian?"

"Pat told you about that, too, did he? Well, who knows? I'll tell you the truth, Arthur: I'm trying to stay out of it as much as I can. I've got enough else to worry about. I guess you already know all about that. So what about this house you're buying?"

I headed to the kitchen to put Ryan's beer in the refrigerator and make sure the bread was getting stale. I could hear the strained tones of the conversation in the next room but none of the words. As I was slugging down a beer and giving the anchovies and pine nuts a few desultory whacks, Sharon called. She was at the office and was going to be held up even longer than she'd originally thought. She elaborated on her excuse in such detail, I knew she was lying. Sharon always skimmed over the minutiae of her actual daily life but paid close attention to the facts and figures of her fabrications.

"I wish you'd hurry," I said. "Ryan's been here for an hour and seven minutes already."

"Right. I'm hurrying."

The conversation in the living room went completely dead. Both Ryan and Arthur had massive throat-clearing fits, and then Ryan came into the kitchen to get another beer. He sat on the counter and watched me as I sliced the cheese. "If you're thinking of melting that, Pat, I'd try thinner slices."

"I'm sorry I told Arthur about the divorce," I said.

"Don't think about it. I guess Arthur's like one of the family anyway."

"Even so. I didn't want to get this dinner off to a bad start."

"Considering the guest of honor isn't here yet, we can pretend it hasn't started."

"Actually, Ryan, you're the guest of honor." I handed him a piece of cheese. "Repayment for a pot roast you made twenty-plus years ago. Something Tony reminded me of a couple of weeks ago."

"That guy's amazing. He remembers everything from childhood. It must mean he was happy."

"I thought you were the one with the happy childhood."

"Me? I was fat and miserable. Unless there's something I'm not remembering. You and Tony are talking all the time now?"

"I ran into him when I was in New York."

"No kidding? What were you doing down there?"

"Visiting," I said, and then waited a second too long before adding, "a friend."

Ryan glanced over his shoulder to see that Arthur wasn't standing behind me. "What are you talking about?" he whispered. "What's that tone of voice supposed to mean?"

"It's a long story. Anyway, I met Vivian."

He groaned at the mention of her name.

"I think Tony's in love."

"Good for him, Patrick. But what are you getting so involved in this for? If I were you, I'd begin my charity at home, with your 'friends' and everything." He went over to the bedroom door and looked in. "Too bad you have to leave this place. I forgot how nice it is to live aboveground. Somebody going swimming?"

I explained that I slept on the air mattress.

"You sleep on an air mattress on the floor next to the bed? What's going on around here, Patrick? What are you up to?"

Arthur walked into the kitchen, and Ryan quickly changed the subject, became his old jovial self again, and slugged down his ale. He took a seat at the kitchen table and started to talk in an overblown fashion about how happy he was for Arthur and me and how nicely our lives were turning out and how wonderful it was that we were about to buy a house. When he'd exhausted the topic, he told stories about his daughter in a sloppily sentimental tone. He wasn't drunk, but he was beginning to sound a little well oiled.

"So I'm talking to Stacy on the phone the other day, and she tells me I'm a big lout." He burst out in exaggerated laughter and shook his head. "That kid has an incredible vocabulary for someone four years old. I could barely talk at that age—remember, Pat? I guess you weren't born yet. I always forget I'm older. But will you tell me where a kid her age picks up a word like 'lout'?"

The obvious answer was that she got it from her mother. I hadn't dared to ask Ryan what would happen to Stacy when and if the divorce went through, but it must have been troubling him. Ryan lived for Stacy's weekly visits.

By eight o'clock, Sharon still hadn't shown up, and the three of us had moved back into the living room and were reduced to discussing movies none of us had seen.

"I've heard that new De Niro thing is good," Ryan said.

"Which De Niro?"

"Well, maybe I've got it wrong and it's Dustin Hoffman. Anyway, I can't remember the title or what it's about or who else is in it, but I definitely heard someone say it's a good picture."

"I think I heard that, too," Arthur said.

"And that new thing with what's-her-name is supposed to be bad."

"What's-her-name?"

"The one with the hair."

"I remember reading that, too," Arthur said.

When the bell rang, I jumped out of my seat and leapt for the door. Sharon stumbled into the apartment mumbling apologies, carrying a large white shopping bag. She had on her green poncho, and her hair was all caught up in a brightly colored knit hat she'd picked up in Jamaica. Although the light in the hallway was dim and I couldn't tell for sure, I thought I noticed a trace of lipstick around her mouth.

"It's about time," I whispered. "Ryan was getting ready to leave."

"I'm sorry, Patrick. I really am. It was unavoidable. I have to cut back on my work load."

She walked into the living room, leaving behind her a strong smell of something I couldn't quite place. I lingered in the hallway a moment longer, trying to figure it out, and then realized, with some dismay, that the smell was of ginger and garlic. In the living room, Sharon was standing near Ryan's chair, shaking his hand and rambling on about the business transaction that had held her up so long.

"He's going to L.A. tomorrow, but he has a phobia about airplanes and a list of airlines as long as your arm that he absolutely won't use. I spent about an hour explaining that Air New Zealand doesn't fly direct Boston to L.A. Then he tells me a half-dozen types of aircraft he won't board. I was with him for an hour and twenty-five minutes."

Obviously, she'd been at home, napping. She pulled off her cap, and her long hair cascaded down her back. Ryan remained standing, looking at her with kindly bemusement, his hands jammed into the back pockets of his pants.

"I like your sandals," he said. "So how's the guy getting to L.A.?"

"No idea. I convinced him he should be seeing a shrink. I mean, it doesn't take much to figure out that this plane aversion has something to do with his penis."

Ryan looked across at me. "Now, did you say 'penis,' Sharon?"

Clearly, this discussion had some potential, but Arthur intervened. "What's in the bag?" he asked.

"Promise me you won't get upset, Patrick?" She slipped her poncho off over her head and tossed it onto the sofa next to Arthur. "I was so late, I figured the least I could do was bring some food along. I hope everyone's in the mood for Chinese."

Sharon's generosity was legendary among her friends. It often happened that she'd show up at someone else's dinner party with the entire meal in tow. She did have good taste in Chinese food, but it seemed to me Sharon's compulsive gift-giving had more to do with her insecurities than with her generous spirit. Not to mention that my sandwiches were destined to be upstaged. I was about to object, when Ryan loudly proclaimed his devotion to Peking ravioli.

"You're in luck," Sharon said. "I've got three orders in here."

Arthur, whose left eye had developed a twitch, made a plea for my sandwiches, but Sharon merely frowned, a gesture as close to an apology as I was likely to get. "The things with the hard bread? Well, they'll keep. I mean, they're stale already, aren't they?"

"And Arthur made a salad." I was overwhelmed with affection for Arthur's perfect cucumber slices.

"Well, how about this?" Ryan asked. "We can have Arthur's salad with the Chinese food. And then you can wrap up the sandwiches, Pat, and we can all have them for lunch tomorrow. We could just spread newspapers out on the floor here and pass the containers around."

"Sounds good to me," Sharon said. "No offense, Arthur, but I can't get comfortable in this furniture."

She headed off into the kitchen to get plates, and Ryan sat back in his chair with a grin. "Not what you'd call a shrinking violet. Hey, Sharon!" he called out. "I brought some beer. It's in the big blue cans in the refrigerator. Help yourself." He started chuckling quietly. "As if anyone could stop her," he said to Arthur.

*   *   *

Later, when I thought back on the dinner, it seemed to me I should have been able to predict what happened. But obstinacy had prevented me from doing so, and it came as a surprise.

What did happen was that Ryan and Sharon took over the whole event: spread newspaper out on the worn carpet in the living room and sat on the floor across from each other, passing the cartons of take-out food back and forth, while Arthur and I leaned shoulder to shoulder on the sofa. We would have been a lot more comfortable sitting on the floor, but after listening to Ryan and Sharon's disparaging comments about the furniture, I felt a wave of loyalty to Arthur's family heirlooms and insisted we sit on one of them. The dinner party was divided into two neatly defined camps: the big, hungry people on the floor, noisily and ravenously slopping down sesame noodles and cashew chicken, and the hosts, dourly ensconced on the broken-down sofa. The seating arrangement contributed to the illusion that Ryan and Sharon had been brought together for a blind date. Given Ryan's admonishments about fixing him up, I worried over it at first; but he seemed to like Sharon almost immediately. Not that there were romantic sparks flying between the two, but they both appeared to be amused and happily entertained. They discussed *Jeopardy* for a good twenty minutes, then *Family Feud*, the Celtics, a variety of spectator-sports events, and Chinese restaurants. When Ryan tried to drag Arthur and me into the conversation, Sharon tossed us off, explaining to Ryan that the two of us knew nothing about TV, athletics, or food, a claim that I couldn't convincingly deny.

I felt coupled with Arthur in a way I hadn't experienced for a long time, and although it didn't displease me entirely, I had some fleeting envy for the two enthusiastic diners on the floor; they seemed to be having an infinitely better time than either Arthur or I.

Ryan managed to shift the conversation to the house Arthur and I were buying, by telling Sharon how delighted he and my parents were that Patrick was settling down into happy domesticity. All his comments were directed toward Sharon, but there was a sort of cautionary note in his voice, and it was clear the harangue was meant for my ears.

"I've seen the house," Sharon announced blandly.

"Is it as spectacular as Patrick says?" Ryan asked.

She shrugged. "A cellar, a roof, walls, and a few windows. If you call that spectacular, I guess it is."

Then, changing her tone completely, she gave an obsequious

speech about Arthur's work and the invaluable service his firm provided for thousands of people throughout the state, and about how she, despite the fact that she believed in going around the law whenever possible, supported his work without reservation. I was caught off guard by the flattery, since she usually took every opportunity to make digs at Arthur. Arthur was squirming long before she finished, and when she finally did come to the end of her rant, my sofa companion commenced in an equally sycophantic mode, telling her what a wonderful service she provided for people and how the value of budget-conscious travel should never be underestimated.

It was a little like watching two people fencing with each other while proclaiming undying devotion. Ryan beamed throughout, delighted to see everyone getting along so well.

When the food had been polished off—even the salad was devoured—Sharon stacked up the empty cartons, stretched her legs out in front of her on the floor, and squinted at Ryan. "I'm telling you right now," she said, "even though you probably don't want to hear it, that you never should have left that sales job with New Balance. Athletic shoes went over the top just about the time you got out. You should have come to me; I would have told you to stay."

"Actually, my wife told me the same thing."

"Ah, yes, the wife. Soon to be ex, I hear. We'll get to her."

I looked over at Ryan to try and gauge his reaction, but he was leaning back against a bookcase, his legs folded in a sloppy lotus position under him, and he seemed content, either from the beer or from MSG or from some stupefying combination of the two.

"So Patrick told you about that, too, did he? My marriage has been getting a lot of publicity."

"Not the marriage," Arthur said. "The divorce."

"I'm not supposed to know about the divorce?" Sharon asked.

Ryan shrugged, surprisingly unflustered. "I don't mind that you know; I'm just not dying to hear your opinion on the subject."

"I can live with that," Sharon said. "What else shouldn't we talk about? Tony and the parents, I suppose." She started to rummage through her huge straw bag, taking out an extra pair of sandals, a Boston phone directory, the ubiquitous battered book on time management, and a piece of rolled-up clothing that looked suspiciously like underwear. "I hope no one minds if I smoke." This clearly was not a question put before the board. "I'm so sick of this whole nonsmoking campaign, I could choke. You'd think that between AIDS, the environment, abortion, and John Sununu, people would find a better cause than making my life miserable every time I strike a match."

"Is it true smoking raises your cholesterol?" Ryan asked.

"I hope you're not thinking of taking it up," I said. Rita and Jim both smoked when I was growing up, and I still thought of it as a sophisticated and glamorous activity, even though it had nearly killed my father. I sometimes pilfered cigarettes from Sharon and surreptitiously smoked them on the back porch or in my tiny private room behind the kitchen.

"Cholesterol is another waste of time. Americans are obsessed with having enemies. No more cold war, so we have to replace the Russians with cholesterol as the focus of evil. Give up eggs and what, you're going to live forever? I'd happily hand over a couple of years of my life for a nice piece of fatty steak."

"Have you been to Hilltop Steakhouse?" Ryan asked.

"I practically live there. Except when I'm at home eating cold cereal." Sharon puffed out a train of perfect smoke rings. Ryan watched them, transfixed, and tried to cup one in his hands. "If I could get a job at an ad agency," she said, "I could quit travel and make a fortune. They always advertise cold cereal with pictures of families sitting around a breakfast table. My idea is to launch a campaign called 'Cold Comfort,' showing lonely single people sitting in front of a TV eating cereal out of a mixing bowl while they're watching *Jeopardy*."

"I could model for that one," Ryan said.

As soon as it was discovered that one of the negligent hosts had forgotten to buy dessert, Sharon insisted we go to an ice cream shop in Central Square, which, in her judgment, sold the best ice cream in the country. "And believe me," she said, "I've tried it all. I'll need a few minutes to clean out the back seat of my car, and we can leave."

Like me, Sharon was very proud of her driving and miserable anywhere in a car but behind the wheel.

"There's no point in driving," Arthur said. "It's only a ten-minute walk. At most."

"Walk?" Ryan couldn't have sounded more stunned if Arthur had proposed calling a helicopter.

"Don't worry," Sharon said. "They can walk; we'll drive. That way I can leave the back seat as is."

*   *   *

The front seat, as it turned out, wasn't quite usable, either, being the victim of failed recycling plans. Arthur and I stood on the sidewalk watching as Sharon and my brother heaved books and magazines and empty yogurt containers into the back. When there was enough room in the passenger seat for Ryan, Sharon pulled away from the curb, made a wide U-turn, and sped off down the street.

"There's a relief," Arthur said, watching them go. He took a woolen cap out of his pocket and pulled it down over the tops of his impressive ears. Then he reached over and turned up the collar on my sport jacket. "Don't want you to catch cold," he said.

I turned my collar down and said I thought the dinner had gone well, reminding him that the last time Sharon had come she'd launched a full attack against Gilbert and Sullivan.

It was chilly now, but the passing warm spell had forced open the buds on all the trees. Forsythia bushes and magnolias were in bloom, and the streetlights shone down through a thin shade of new leaves. We walked along in silence, and Arthur put his arm around my shoulder fraternally.

Sharon's car was parked at the door to the ice cream shop, directly in front of a fire hydrant. Her Honda was impounded by the police at least once a month for parking violations. She claimed she liked to gamble with illegal parking spaces, but gamble seemed an optimistic way of looking at it, considering the number of tickets she accrued daily. She and Ryan were standing at the end of a long line that snaked its way around the store. The cigarette in Sharon's mouth bobbed up and down as she spoke, and Arthur and I, walking in, heard someone ahead of her in line complaining about the smoke.

"Here we go," Arthur said. "I hope she knows it's illegal to smoke in a public building in Cambridge."

"Better not mention it," I said.

Of course Sharon ignored the complaints. She greeted us loudly and went back to a discussion of the airline industry with Ryan. My brother had his hands jammed into the back pockets of his pants, and although he was listening to Sharon and nodding his head, his eyes were scanning the line as if he expected an angry mob to start rioting. Eventually a tall woman in a beaded shawl came over. "I guess you can't read the signs plastered all over every wall that say No Smoking, is that it?"

"Signs?" Sharon asked, looking around.

"You're right," Ryan told the woman. "You could be a little more polite about the way you say it, but you are right." Then he gently took the cigarette from Sharon and rolled it between his fingers until the lit coal fell off the end. He put the butt in his shirt pocket and patted it. "We'll save this for later," he said. "Now what were you saying, Sharon?"

I'd never seen anyone save Sharon from herself with such tender efficiency.

Twenty-two

﹖

There were several standard types of clients who called Only Connect throughout the year, looking for predictable vacations. Fredrick had given them shorthand labels so the agents would know what they were getting before he put the calls through. The most common in New England from November until late March, and in many ways the easiest to satisfy, was the "Warm and Cheap." The Warm and Cheap caller announced himself by declaring that he didn't care where he was sent as long as it was hot, hot, hot, and didn't cost a fortune. The first person to figure a way to economically transport large groups of people to hell will make a billion dollars. Until then, Warm and Cheaps were remarkably eager to sign up for package tours to seedy hotels in the run-down capital cities of impoverished island nations. They almost never had a good time, but lack of air conditioning kept them sizzling and lack of consumer goods and decent restaurants ensured that they didn't spend much money. And after all, someone has to stay in Santo Domingo. The ones who seemed hesitant about leaving the U.S. could be shipped off to a sleazy motel in Fort Lauderdale or a Quality Inn in a drought-stricken region of California.

The "Joy of Sex" callers were looking for "a quiet, lush spot where me and my girlfriend can take a vacation." In winter, I usually sent these folks to Aspen, a spot that's neither quiet nor lush but gives the couple the aphrodisiacal illusion that they are, or at least might run into, Don Johnson and Melanie Griffith.

There was the "Whole Catastrophe" ("We're thinking of taking the family to Disney this July"), the "Banana Republic" ("Could you recommend a completely unspoiled spot, preferably where they speak English and have a nice hotel with a gambling casino?"), and the "Achille Lauro Affair" (anyone inquiring about a cruise). As the calls came into the switchboard, Fredrick would laconically buzz the various agents to try and find a taker. "I've got a Joy of Sex on line four, Patrick. If you take this one, I won't send you a Whole Catastrophe until Thursday. A deal?"

Sometime in early April, I developed a specialty with the "Party's Over" callers, a type that, in the end, had very little to do with travel. A Party's Over call usually involved a distressed-sounding individual, not necessarily traveling alone, although that was most common. Typically, the call began: "I want to go away tomorrow if possible, by this weekend at the latest."

"Boy," I'd say, "it certainly sounds as if you're eager to get away."

"I certainly am."

"Well, we'll see what we can do. Did you have any particular destination in mind?"

"It doesn't matter where or how much it costs. The important thing is I have to leave immediately."

This urgency and lack of concern for destination and price were the giveaways. I'd start tapping at the computer keys to sound as if I was doing something and was properly distracted. Then I'd nonchalantly mention that it was tough to find seats with so little advance notice. Most often, the caller would announce that he himself had had little or no advance warning. Making sure I sounded only moderately interested, and banging on the computer even more loudly, I'd say something on the order of: "Not bad news, I hope."

No more prodding than that was ever needed. A juicy tale of adultery, betrayal, a drug-addicted offspring, a suicidal spouse, or, in the most pathetic instances, a dead pet would emerge. Once the customer got going, it was easy to ask a lot of probing questions, since what he was really calling for was to tell his side of the story to some anonymous listener. After a while, I'd suggest several preposterous holiday destinations to which it was easy to find last-minute seats: Dubai, Blue Bell, Pa., Monrovia. I'd slip in a few cautious reminders that the problem, whatever it was, would still exist upon return. "Think how much better you'd feel," I'd end up saying, "if you stayed home and cleaned out your closets and desk drawers and paid all your bills."

It was never too difficult to talk these people out of going away, since they hadn't really wanted to go anywhere in the first place. It gave me a great deal of satisfaction to know that I'd been of some assistance. At least I was saving them money. Fredrick was pleased because he'd found someone who would always take calls from the most depressed-sounding individuals, and I don't think Tim, my boss, had any idea how much business I was turning away. I didn't mention it to Sharon, either; she hated talking people out of going away, because it meant a lost opportunity to cheat the airlines.

During one of our late-night calls, Tony pointed out that what I was doing with these clients was trying to help them put off major moves. "You know, like getting married," he said.

"Or buying a house," it occurred to me.

"Exactly. But you're happy about that, aren't you?"

"Delighted. Except I keep having these dreams that I'm moving to Australia. I'm sitting on a plane by myself, with one suitcase in my lap, and just as the plane lifts off the ground and they pull in the landing gear, it crashes into a tall building. And the building's always bright yellow, like the house." I'd had the dream three times since sending in the mortgage application forms and had woken up in a cold sweat each time.

"Heavy. You better get to a psychiatrist fast, before you make out any more checks. See if you can get some answers for me, too. Vivian thinks I should see a therapist, someone to help me out with my mess."

"Maybe it's not a bad idea." He was into opera; analysis was the next logical step.

"Come on, Patrick. I'm not the type. Anyway, I don't have the time to sit there. I wish I could describe the whole situation to somebody, show them some pictures or something, and have them go do it for me, like those people who do your Christmas shopping."

"I hear it doesn't work that way."

"Probably not. What's this about you trying to set Ryan up with that Sharon friend of yours?"

"They both happened to show up at my place for dinner on the same night, nothing more than that."

"That's not the news I got. Somehow I can't picture Ryan going out with her. I mean, someone who walks around in January in sandals and a sunbonnet obviously isn't operating on the same wavelength as the rest of the human race. Hey, I've got a great idea: if you're so eager to talk people out of taking trips, how about convincing Loreen to cancel the honeymoon?"

Whatever the subconscious reasons for the delight I was taking in helping the insulted and injured dig in their heels, it was the first time I'd felt I was doing anything worthwhile at the agency, and it made me happy.

A few days after the dinner with Ryan and Sharon, Fredrick rang my intercom and told me there was a woman at the front desk to see me.

"Did she give you her name?" I asked, trying to imagine what dreaded customer it might be.

"No," he said quietly. "I can't tell, but from the appearance, I'd guess it's either a Joy of Sex or a Party's Over. Tall, gorgeous, tons of hair. You'll see in a minute."

"Not Professor Fields?"

"No. Not even in another life. I'm sending her back."

A few seconds later, there was a knock on the open door to my office, so soft the customer must have been using her fingertips and not her knuckles. I barked out what I hoped was an intimidating "Come in," and Loreen Davis stuck her head into the doorway. There was a hesitant smile trembling on her lips, and in her low, self-effacing voice, she said, "I hope this isn't a bad time?"

I experienced a sort of anatomical landslide, in which my jaw, my shoulders, my chest, and my stomach all dropped at once. "Loreen," I said, as cheerfully as I could manage. "What a surprise! Come in."

She walked into the office with a dainty, halting step, as if she wanted to make sure her feet made no sound. Politely, she kept her eyes straight ahead, although I could see a look of contained horror pass across her features as she took in the chaos of the office in her peripheral vision. Just that morning, Tim had loaded several old airline rate tariffs into the bookcase, and it had collapsed onto the floor. Loreen had on a knee-length white skirt, a scoop-necked white angora sweater, and a pair of white running shoes. She walked with absolutely perfect posture, as if she were on a runway in a modest one-piece bathing suit. My parents often bragged that Tony's bride-to-be was "a dead ringer for Miss America," significantly neglecting to mention a specific miss; what they were referring to was not a particular set of features or facial bone structure but a type of beauty and a certain air of delicate self-confidence. Today's beauty queen, tomorrow's alcoholic housewife.

I got up and embraced her. She was so thin, I felt as if my arms could easily circle her several times. Not thin in a sickly, anorexic way, but with a kind of meticulous, carefully and healthfully maintained resistance to fleshiness. I'd have bet even money her weight hadn't varied more than an ounce in several years. I never really had anything to say to Loreen, and I always felt brutish and crass in her soft presence, but there was a glimmer of independence lurking in her somewhere that I admired a great deal. Today, however, she had a downcast look, and I was reminded that for the past six weeks I'd been trying to convince my brother to break off his engagement with her.

"It really is wonderful to see you," I said. "Take a seat, if you dare." I pushed some books and papers onto the floor and dusted off the cushion. Given the time, she must have been up and about for several hours; it was incomprehensible to me how anyone could remain so spotlessly clean for even a few minutes.

"If this is a bad time, Patrick, let me know and we can make an appointment or whatever."

"No; this is as good a time as any. You look different somehow."

"You probably haven't seen me in my work clothes. We used to have to wear nurse's uniforms, but they've got more lenient. We have to wear white now, that's all."

She took a seat in front of my desk, carefully arranging her jacket on the back of the chair and pulling her skirt modestly over her knees. I had never seen her dressed for work at the diet center, but it wasn't only the outfit that was different. Her hair was lighter than I remembered, as if she'd had it frosted, and it was teased up fairly high in that frizzed-out, prime-time, soap-opera look. Her eyes were heavily made up, and her face seemed smooth and poreless, as though made of porcelain. There was something captivating in her appearance, a perfect blend of natural beauty and artifice. Her lips were covered with raspberry gloss and faintly outlined in some darker shade of red or in black. It must have taken hours to apply and years of practice.

"You do look lovely," I said.

She smiled and turned away. "I should have called, but I had a couple of cancellations, and I thought I'd drive in and take a chance."

Her small voice was made for apologies and tearful admissions of inadequacy. "I'm sure this must be your busiest time, everyone planning their spring vacations."

I mentioned the annual rush to Bermuda and college-week trips to Florida, trying to sound professional and knowing. "Is it a popular time . . . for diets?" Somehow I always felt I was insulting her by even mentioning her work.

"January and spring are the biggest times. In January everyone's full of New Year's resolutions, and in the spring they're getting ready for bathing suits. But I had cancellations this morning, so I had some free time. I guess I already mentioned that." There was a hotel index open on top of my desk, and Loreen was smoothing her hand across one of the pages, ironing out the wrinkles. "It's actually kind of sad," she went on. "Spring should be happy, everything coming alive. For people with weight problems, it causes a lot of stress, which just makes them eat more, which creates more stress, which means more binging. . . ." She sighed, looked up at me, and shrugged.

Spring, clearly, was not such a happy time for Loreen. It would have been the right moment to say something upbeat about the wedding, but I didn't dare. "Still," I said, "it must be satisfying to know you're helping people. Like a doctor or a psychiatrist."

"Oh, not really. Most of the people come back in a few months, heavier than they were when they started out. And even more depressed and desperate to lose weight as fast as they can, which means the chances are they'll gain back still more. And that increases their risk of heart attacks. It's a cycle."

"Sounds it."

"I don't know if Tony mentioned it, but I've been looking into physician's assistant programs. Something with more challenge."

I made an encouraging remark. Obviously she'd come in to discuss something other than her career, and I didn't know if it was shyness, uncertainty, or some rules of male-female communication I was unfamiliar with that prevented her from coming out with it. Everything in her perfect posture and averted eyes suggested anticipation. She reached up to her throat and started to finger her string of pearls—more likely fake pearls, if Tony had given them to her. Out of desperation, I began hitting the computer keys. I brought up the file on her trip and started telling her that everything was in order, which was the truth. But she didn't seem the least bit concerned about the plans and assured me that she hadn't come to check on them, as if doing so would have been an insult. This narrowed the chances that she was here for a simple business transaction, and I felt myself sinking into dread. She had the pearls looped around her fingers, and she was still looking off, just over my shoulder. I leaned in toward her and tried to make eye contact. "Was there something you wanted to change or cancel?" With horror, I realized I was speaking in a soft, hushed voice, unconsciously imitating hers.

She looked down at her hands and laughed. "I guess there's a lot I'd like to change."

I'd never heard even a single note of irony in her voice before, and I wasn't sure how I should respond. Gutlessly, I chose to ignore it. "Well, that's what I'm here for," I said.

Sharon strolled into the back of my office, frowned at the collapsed bookcase, and lit a cigarette. I had the feeling she was about to make some outrageous comment, and I tried to motion for her to leave. Fortunately, she'd never met Loreen. "Well, guess what?" she challenged me. After Loreen's soft voice, Sharon's sounded like a subway train. "I have a date with your brother tomorrow night," she shouted and walked out.

Loreen spun around in her seat, but Sharon was gone.

"That was my friend Sharon," I said. I forced out a particularly unconvincing laugh, but when Loreen turned back to me, there were tears in her eyes. "Loreen," I said, "she's talking about Ryan."

She shook her head and squeezed her eyes shut, and two perfectly formed tears rolled down the smooth surface of her cheeks. "Don't mind me, Patrick. I'm under a lot of pressure these days. All the wedding plans and everything."

This said, she hid her face in her hands, and her thin shoulders began to heave. I couldn't help but notice that all that blown-out hair didn't move an inch. It really is unfair that the status of victim is, on top of everything else, so damned unflattering to one's appearance. The intercom on my phone buzzed, but I ignored it. I reached out and took Loreen's bony wrist. I had to restrain myself from calling her "honey" when I asked if she was all right.

"I'm fine, I'm really fine. No kidding. I'm just under a lot of pressure."

"I can imagine. I'll get you some Kleenex."

"No, no. I have some right here." She reached into the pocket of the jacket she'd hung over the back of her chair, took out a single sheet of tissue, blotted the tears under her eyes delicately, and squeezed her nose. Then she folded the tissue as if it were a lawn napkin and dropped it into the wastebasket. "It contains aloe vera," she said. "I have sensitive skin."

The intercom had been buzzing insistently, and when it finally stopped, the room seemed silent. The Spanish restaurant next door had begun preparing lunch, and my cramped office was filled with a smell of garlic that was making me ravenously hungry. "Would you like to get some coffee?" I asked. "This isn't the most appealing place to talk, I know."

She looked at her watch and shook her head. "I don't have time. I knew I shouldn't have come. I was afraid I'd end up doing something like this." She lifted up her shoulders in a heroic fashion and picked what might have been a fleck of lint from the angora sweater. "Something's wrong, Patrick. I know it is. I'm not a genius, okay, but I'm not exactly a moron, like some people seem to think."

"Tony?" I asked, as if there was any question.

She nodded. "I haven't seen him since Christmas. He calls less than once a week. I leave messages on that stupid machine of his, but I don't hear back. I even get the feeling your father knows something. He's been calling me a lot lately, checking to see how I'm doing. I mean, it's nice, but I didn't know I was engaged to him. Oh, and I got this."

She pulled a postcard out of her purse and handed it to me. I quickly scanned the message on the back. "Can I read it?" I asked.

"Yeah. Read it and tell me if that sounds like something you send someone you're marrying in a couple of months."

" 'Reenie, Stuck in New York on business. Tied up around the clock. No time to think. Incredible views from this place, but New York's a nightmare. Glad you're not here—you'd hate it. Miss ya. XX, T.' "

On the front of the card was a picture of the infamous hotel in Times Square.

True, he'd at least had the decency to tell her he was glad she wasn't there, but all things considered, I was appalled by the line about the "incredible views." And he could at least have sent her a postcard of Grant's Tomb or Radio City Music Hall; anything but the hotel where he'd met his lover.

"Isn't that sweet, how he says he misses you," I tried. "Tony's usually so secretive about his feelings."

"Well, if he misses me so much, why doesn't he call?"

I was at a loss about what to do with my hands, so I started playing with the postcard. It accidentally flew out of my fingers and over my shoulder, landing on the windowsill.

"Just leave it there," Loreen said. "Maybe it'll blow out the window. If he's busy, he's busy, but he probably has time to get lunch, don't you think? It takes less time to pick up the phone than it does to write a postcard, even one with as little on it as this. And most of those fancy hotels even have phones in the bathroom. And he's not exactly broke. He could have taken the shuttle up for an evening."

"Yes, well . . ."

I heard her catch her breath, and then tears started to roll down her cheeks again, in a steady flow. This silent, spontaneous flood was almost more than I could bear, but she was staring at me with her eyes open wide, and I felt locked into her pained, innocent gaze. If only her face hadn't been so carefully made up, or there were a chocolate stain on her sweater, or one of her long magenta nails were chipped, the whole outburst might not have seemed quite as sad. But there was no chance for that. Even her tissue was perfect.

"There's nobody I can talk to about this. You know, I never said this to anyone before, but my parents don't exactly love Tony." She actually laughed. "Yeah, well, that's the understatement of the year. They haven't liked him from the start. So I can't talk to them, and I don't want to turn my friends against him, not before we're married. And anyway, I guess the real truth is I feel so ashamed."

"Ashamed?"

"I mean, have I done something wrong, Patrick?"

"What could you have done wrong?"

"Sometimes I think everyone thinks I'm the kind of person who can't deal with bad news, like I'm going to kill myself or something. Well, believe me, Patrick, that's not me."

I considered the options for a moment, swiveled my chair around, and looked out the tiny window behind my desk. "Loreen," I said, "the fact is . . . the fact is, I was in New York a couple of weekends ago and I bumped into Tony. I was walking down the street and I bumped into him. How's that for a chance encounter?"

I turned back and looked at her. Her eyes were wide with curiosity, and she'd stopped crying. She pulled another tissue out of her jacket pocket and dabbed at her eyes once again and gave a rearranging push to her mass of hair, as if she expected Tony to walk into the office and she wanted to be certain she looked her best. Something in these prettying gestures made my heart sink. She was laying her own heart open, putting her biggest flaw on display, the one that was destined to disrupt her life for an untold number of years, stunt her growth, and pull her down as reliably as the force of gravity.

Loreen Davis was in love with my younger brother.

I turned back toward the window. "He really looked like hell— overworked, exhausted. . . ."

Twenty-three

After Loreen had left the office, my mind wouldn't stick on anyone's idiotic vacation plans, no matter how hard I tried to concentrate.

I called Tony's number in Chicago, but it was the middle of the day and of course he wasn't home. I thought about leaving a nasty message on his machine, saying that Loreen had come into my office and I'd accidentally told her I'd met him in New York, just to keep him guessing and make him sweat. But despite Loreen's hopeful look of love when I mentioned Tony's name, I found I couldn't really get angry with my brother.

The only call I took that morning was a Whole Catastrophe, and after listening to the customer for ten minutes, I told her I'd love to make reservations for her family's trip, but Disney World was being shut down by the Environmental Protection Agency and fined billions for destroying precious swampland in the lovely state of Florida. After lunch I told Fredrick I had to have my wisdom teeth pulled and would be out for the rest of the afternoon. I biked home, leapt into my Yugo, and sped out to the suburbs.

My parents and Ryan were hanging over the cash register at the back of O'Neil's, squabbling so loudly they didn't hear me enter.

"If you'd let me show you how to do it," Ryan shouted, "I'd show you."

My father gave him a shove. "Keep your hands off it. You'll break it, and there goes the whole investment."

"Don't treat him like a child, Jimmy. It's possible he knows how to work it."

"What's going on?" I asked.

They all looked up together.

"A miracle," my father said, "just when we needed it."

"Don't tell me you got fired," Rita said.

"Fired?"

"Well, what else would you be doing here in the middle of the day?"

Ryan straightened up, grinning. He brushed a hank of hair off his forehead and hiked up his pants. "Did Sharon tell you we're going to a Celtics game tomorrow night?"

"As if Ryan isn't having enough problems right now, he needs to start going to basketball games with that woman. I didn't know they allowed bare feet in the Boston Garden."

"Sandals," I corrected.

"Bare feet, sandals. You can still see the toes, which is what I find so attractive. I don't suppose you know anything about cash registers, Patrick. They just delivered this one, and we can't figure out how to open it."

"Isn't there a manual? Didn't they tell you how to use the thing?" I was sometimes exasperated by their inability to deal with the modern world, possibly because I was so bad at it myself.

"Some baldy came in here this morning and spent two hours giving a lecture," my father said. "Your mother went into a coma after one minute, and I fell asleep after two. The machine does everything except what you want it to. Your mother's idea, by the way. What we need it for, I couldn't tell you."

"For the future, Jimmy. Maybe you've heard of the future, progress, advancement? Well, welcome to the eighties, dear, or the nineties, or whatever decade this is."

"So what are you doing out here anyway, Pat?" Ryan asked. "You want a beer? Take your jacket off and relax."

I turned down the beer and tossed my jacket onto the glass counter. The jacket was black linen, a little too stylish for me, but I'd found it on sale at a used-clothing store and bought it, rationalizing that I needed a new image. Seeing it on the counter, next to all those ugly ties and hideous polyester shirts that were my heritage, I felt embarrassed for wearing it into the store.

"I don't like the look on your face," Rita said. "Don't tell me you've got bad news."

"I'm going to try and be very rational," I said.

"Well, don't go out on a limb for our sakes, dear."

I looked over at my parents and my older brother, huddled around the new cash register. Ryan was randomly pecking at the keys on the register, and every time he hit one, it beeped, as if to say, "Keep your hands off." My father had on a strikingly ugly suit, and the collar of his shirt was hanging loose around his scrawny neck. What had been anger at their machinations all morning suddenly turned into uncertainty. But as I'd driven all that way and had already taken the afternoon off, I started in:

"You have to stop pushing this wedding. I told you Tony is in love with someone else. Loreen is a wreck, and she's going to get hurt. She's hurt already. I wouldn't be surprised if she had a nervous breakdown. She came to the agency today and asked me if something was wrong."

"What did you say?" my father asked.

"I told her everything was fine, that Tony was overworked. I lied, in other words."

"At least you did *some*thing right," my father said. "It sounds true enough to me. Tony *is* overworked. And Loreen was at the house two weeks ago, and she looked fine. Did any of the rest of you think Loreen looked like she was ready for the nuthouse?"

"It's this thing that's going to send *me* to the mental hospital," Ryan said. "It beeps every time I hit a button."

"And furthermore," my father said, "as far as I know, Tony hasn't asked anyone to cancel any wedding plans. So, in other words, the groom is going through with the marriage, the bride is going through with the marriage, and so are the best man and the maid of honor, her parents, your mother and me, assuming we both live, the ushers, the bridesmaids, the priest, the altar boys, the photographer, the band, and the chump who's serving the roast beef at the reception."

"I told you they were serving chicken," my mother said. "I talk and talk and talk, and he never listens to a word I say. I don't know why I bother; he never was a listener."

Ryan looked perplexed by this irrelevant outburst, but my father merely ignored it and went on. "So everyone is going through with the damned thing except Patrick. And excuse me for saying so, Pat, but if it comes to that, your presence is not one hundred percent essential to the event."

"So you don't care that Tony is marrying someone he isn't really in love with?" I asked.

"He's marrying someone he got engaged to," my father said. "Beyond that, I really wouldn't know."

Quietly, my mother said, "And let's hope, Patrick, for everyone's sake, that you don't know anything beyond that, either." She pulled her half-glasses out of the breast pocket of her sport jacket, adjusted them on the tip of her nose, and peered down at the cash register. The tone of distress in her voice silenced me.

My father was scrutinizing me closely. He had a pen between his fingers, which he was holding as if it were a cigarette, unconsciously revealing his constant longing for his old habit. "What are you doing out of work in the middle of the day?" he asked me. "Don't forget they're damned nice to you at that job."

My older brother leapt to my defense. "Don't make it sound like they're doing him a favor by keeping him on. They pay him a so-so salary, and he works hard despite what he tells you."

"Oh, really?" my father asked. "And I suppose you heard all this from that Sharon?"

"Among other things."

The door opened, and a tall woman in a long green coat entered the store. She stood at the front, looking around uncertainly, and for a fleeting moment I saw the catastrophic mess of the place through her eyes. Surely my parents could be keeping things a little neater and running them more efficiently. It hadn't mattered so much years earlier, but now people were more accustomed to the sterile organization of shopping malls and franchises.

"Is she on stilts," my father asked, "or is that an optical illusion?"

"She's not that tall, Jimmy. Go see if you can help her, Patrick, while we figure this thing out. If she wants to pay cash, tell her to go somewhere else."

The woman, who did tower over me, was looking for a suit for her husband, something he could wear to her nephew's wedding and then use for less formal events. I asked her a few relevant questions and then examined her own outfit carefully. In a suburban men's store, it's the taste of the wife or girlfriend that really counts; rarely will a man admit to having an opinion on what he's wearing, and even then the woman makes the final decision. Shopping is not a manly pursuit. I pushed through the racks as if I were looking for a particular item and finally pulled out a gray pin-striped suit in light wool. I didn't have a clue how long it had been in the store, but it was a smart, standard cut, reasonably priced, and if there were moth holes in it, at least they weren't immediately visible. The woman was dressed in a late-sixties, Republican-cloth-coat getup, so I pointed out the quality of the suit's material, its enduring, conservative lines, and the bargain price. If she'd spoken of her husband with any hint of sexual boasting ("His shoulders are so broad, I can't find anything to fit him"), I'd have brushed down the front of the pants to plant a subliminal message. With men, the trick was to act as bored and nonchalant as possible, take an "Aw, what the hell, make your wife happy and buy the frigging thing" attitude, and then knock ten dollars off the ticket price as an act of wholesome male bonding.

The woman seemed interested and asked if I could put the suit aside until she brought her husband in. I told her we could hold it for twenty-four hours, neglecting to mention that we'd probably been holding it for a decade. I hung the thing up behind the cash register and told Ryan to keep an eye out for the woman's return.

Rita said, " 'I'll be back with my husband' translates into: 'I wouldn't buy this rag if it was the last piece of clothing on the planet.' "

"I think she liked it."

"Well, you always were a good salesman, which is why I think you should come work for us, which also happens to be the most decent thing you could do. . . ."

She began to rattle off her standard speech about why I should come to work at the store, but there was a good deal more nervous chatter in it than conviction. I heard some of what she was saying, but not all. My dealings with the tall customer had left me feeling refreshed, almost as if I'd temporarily earned back some family position I hadn't had for years. My determination to say something helpful on my brother's behalf strengthened, until finally I cut Rita off.

"You have to stop pressuring Tony to get married," I said. "You're ruining his life and Loreen's as well." I stood back from the counter, and without really looking at anyone, told them about Loreen's visit, and how, if we were on the subject of decency, it was worth mentioning that setting up Loreen in a loveless marriage was not the decent thing to do. "What do you think their life together is going to be like?"

"I suppose you know?" my father asked.

"I don't know," I said, "but I can imagine." And then, aloud, I did try to imagine it, Tony waking up every morning next to someone he didn't love, growing resentful and hostile, thinking of the opportunity he'd missed and the love he'd wasted, all for the sake of fulfilling an obligation that he never should have had in the first place. And if they honestly believed Tony deserved the punishment, then what about Loreen? She was the innocent bystander here, blissfully walking into a trap that was going to keep her a prisoner for years.

"She'll go through with the wedding," I said, "even though she knows something's wrong, because she loves Tony, but every day she'll wake up, knowing something's missing from her life, that there's nothing but emptiness under all the emptiness. She'll be devoured by longing for something genuine, love or passion or a kiss that's a kiss, knowing all along she's never going to get it from her husband.

"They'll buy a house and have some kids, and she'll take up shopping or drinking or compulsive TV-watching, trying to fill in the gaps, knowing she's made a horrible mistake but getting less and less able to do anything about it, to break free, start all over." I felt as if something inside me had snapped, and I easily could have gone on this way for hours, describing the life of misery that I imagined for Tony and Loreen.

Eventually, of course, I had to stop to catch my breath, and when I did, I realized that my confused and misguided soliloquy had lasted too long already. I felt ridiculous, as if I'd been overheard talking in my sleep. Thinking that it was time to apologize or simply leave, I reached over to pick up my jacket and caught a glimpse of my mother. Her face was ashen, and her lips were trembling, and her eyes, peering out over the tops of her half-glasses, were filled with tears. She cried almost as infrequently as I did, and I hated to think that my outburst might have made her so unhappy. I turned away nervously.

As I was slipping on my jacket, I saw very suddenly and very plainly that I hadn't been talking about Tony and Loreen at all. The whole long, rambling speech had been a thinly veiled description of what I'd observed and imagined about my parents' marriage, about the misery of their lives together and the unhappiness of their day-to-day existence.

Ryan was staring at me with a hard, admonishing gaze, and my father was watching my mother very closely, waiting for the dam to burst.

I mumbled an apology, a hasty "I'm sorry," and my father said, "I should think you would be."

He walked over to my mother, and with more tenderness than I could remember ever hearing in his voice, he said, "I think the lecture is over, Rita. Let's go to that dump around the corner and get a late lunch." He draped a cardigan sweater over her shoulders. Rita took off her glasses, smoothed back the stiff contours of her hairdo, gathered up her purse, and headed down the center aisle of the store. My father hobbled after her, a wraithlike figure held together by keloids and covered up with a cheap suit.

Once the door had swung closed and dusty silence had settled over the store again, Ryan shook his head and said, "Would you mind telling me what that was all about?"

"I wish I knew."

"I don't know what you think your duty is here, but whatever it is, I'd say you went beyond the call of it."

"I'm sorry," I said. "I didn't even know what I was saying until I'd stopped."

"I guess that happens sometimes."

He was still playing with the cash register, tapping at the keys, apparently with more success now, as the thing had stopped beeping. There was a look of confidence on his face, and without turning away from his task, he told me he'd enjoyed the dinner.

"I'm glad you liked Sharon."

"She's a nice kid."

When, I wondered, was the last time someone had referred to Sharon as a kid? "Pretty," I said, testing him, "don't you think?"

"Pretty eyes. Not contact lenses, are they? I didn't think so; she doesn't seem like the type. I think I've almost got this wrapped up here." He hit a few more keys on the register and stood back as the cash drawer sprang open.

"Why didn't you do that earlier," I said, "if you knew how to open it?"

He shrugged and put on a blue windbreaker. "Gave your parents something to think about this morning. Let's close up shop for a few minutes. Three hours in this place, and your eyes start to cross."

The buildings in the center of town had either been abandoned, which added an air of desperation to the streets, or been given a budget face-lift with new bricks and larger windows, which was even more grim. It had been years since I'd walked these streets with Ryan, probably when we were in high school, and as I trudged along beside him, I felt an odd kind of regret about all the time that had passed with so little communication between us. Ryan was the first person in my family I'd told I was gay. He and I went for a drive after supper one night when I was home from college on vacation, and I mentioned it to him in a casual, offhand way. I suppose I chose to tell him first because I knew he wouldn't be upset, or at least wouldn't let on if he was. When he reacted with his typical kindness and his concern for nothing more than my happiness, I think I was a little disappointed. Perhaps I'd wanted to try out my defensive arguments on him. In any case, I never thanked him for being so understanding at a time when I needed him to be, and of course it was too late to do it now. Ryan often suffered from his abundance of kindness.

Aside from the martial arts studios, the only businesses flourishing in town were the twenty-four-hour convenience stores and the fast-food outlets, and the streets were filthy with refuse from these: Styrofoam cups and plastic bags and cellophane wrappers and all manner of garish, unnecessary cardboard and paper wrapping. We walked along in silence, until Ryan suggested we go into a fast-food restaurant and get some coffee. We took seats in a plastic booth and drank out of our Styrofoam cups, and Ryan said to me, "As your older brother, Patrick, I have a piece of advice for you: Stay out of this wedding. Mind your own business and look at your own life. I'm not so interested in all the details, but I think you should try to take a bit more charge of your own problems. Don't you think that would be a good idea?"

"The world is full of good ideas," I said. "That's what's so sad, Ryan."

Part
5

Twenty-four

~

Arthur and Beatrice met when they were in college, were married shortly after graduation, and might have stayed together for a lifetime of connubial bliss if it hadn't been for Beatrice's realization and immediate acceptance of the fact that her husband was a homosexual. Beatrice had abundant insight and boundless compassion and didn't flaunt either as a sign of her moral superiority. When she spelled it all out for Arthur, he was shocked, not that he had reason to be; sometime in graduate school, years before Beatrice's revelation, he'd begun wandering through the reeds at the Fenway, taking immensely long breaks in certain bathrooms at Lamont Library, and spending more than a few afternoons a week in a Boston movie house that was open twenty-four hours a day but advertised no film on the marquee. At the time, he felt about his covert sexual doings as a somnambulist might feel about his midnight strolls, and it never occurred to him that they might have some relation to the rest of his life. I think Arthur was relieved that Beatrice had figured him out for himself, although he seemed a little hurt that she actually wanted a divorce.

If Arthur and Beatrice were no longer in love with each other, they were at least melded together in that inexplicable way people often become so in bad early marriages. They spoke on the phone at least once a week, met for lunch twice a month, and frequently quoted each other in conversation. Arthur and I got together with Beatrice and her new husband several times a year, usually for dinner and an evening at Symphony Hall. Beatrice took a lot of interest in me, although I was sometimes concerned that she thought of me as Arthur's new wife, particularly when she passed along recipes and advice on nonpolluting cleansers. (Beatrice herself employed a variety of illegal aliens, referred to her by Arthur, to clean house and cook the family meals.) She and I rarely spent time together alone, but when we did, she had a bad habit of lecturing me about Arthur, as if to prove that no matter what, she knew more about him than I ever would.

I liked Beatrice. She knew her own faults and never hesitated to point them out. She had an acerbic, unsentimental way with Mitchell, her new husband, and Bradford, their genius five-year-old son, but left no doubt that she adored them both.

Two days after Arthur and I received official word that our mortgage had been approved, Beatrice invited us to her house for a celebratory glass of champagne. Beatrice was big on celebratory glasses of champagne, at least where Arthur was concerned, and Mitchell was a wine enthusiast. They lived about eight blocks from us. I was always happy to visit, partially because even a Philistine like me could appreciate that anything Mitchell poured from a bottle was of exceptional quality, and partially because we could see them without facing the dilemma of trying to decide which of us was going to drive the car.

Arthur dressed with care that night, as he usually did when he spent time with Beatrice and Mitchell, and reminded me that I might want to wear something other than dirty blue jeans. "After all," he said, "we are having champagne."

Arthur suffered from the divorced man's affliction of wanting his current significant other to look good in the eyes of his ex-wife.

Beatrice and Mitchell owned a large town house in mid-Cambridge, one of those bright, cheerful places with too many skylights and too few interior walls. It was light and airy and air-conditioned, but they should have bought a place that was better able to accommodate their extensive library. Arthur's bookish influence on his first wife was evident: she still owned all the books he'd given her in the course of their marriage and had chosen for a second husband a psychiatrist whose real passion was Victorian novels. She let us into the town house, enthusiastically congratulating us and blowing her nose. I don't think I'd ever once met Beatrice when she didn't have a head cold, possibly because she saw a lot of children in her therapy practice. "Are you thrilled about the house?" she asked me.

"Speechless," I said.

The full implications of securing a mortgage had not yet hit me. I wasn't entirely sure how I felt about it, but I did notice that I'd been walking around in a kind of daze since Arthur had made the happy announcement. His excitement left me even more ambivalent.

"The speechless stage will pass, believe me," Beatrice said. "You should have seen me before we bought this place. I was more nervous than when Arthur and I got divorced. Oh, Arthur, look at that tie. There's a stain right here." She started to rub at the spot and then tossed down the tie in disgust. "I keep telling you to take your things to the cleaner across from your office."

"I did, dear. That's where the spot came from. It was fine when I brought it in."

Arthur and Beatrice expressed their fondness for each other by trading gentle insults, almost as if they were an old married couple. She led us into the living room and, between sneezes, told Arthur she'd read the novel he'd suggested and had hated it. As a way of maintaining intimacy, each read every book the other recommended; but, possibly to keep a safe distance between them, they always disagreed volubly about the books' merits. Most surprising of all was that neither of them noticed the pattern.

Beatrice was taller than I and had dark hair cut in an outdated but functional wash-and-wear shag. To her credit, she was not the type for wasting time in front of a mirror with a blow dryer and a styling brush. Her nose was constantly red from her sneezing, and she always wore baggy cotton skirts, their pockets stuffed with tissues and men's handkerchiefs. Sharon told me that the one healthy fact of my relationship with Arthur was that Beatrice and I didn't look alike. Beatrice and Arthur, however, could have been siblings. They had similar square, solid frames, protuberant ears, and kind eyes.

Bradford was sitting on the living room floor, pulling books off the bottom shelf of the bookcase that took all of one of the few existing walls. Without looking up at us, he started to mumble some barely coherent comments about how we'd interrupted him in the middle of what he was doing.

As might be expected from two mental health professionals, Beatrice and Mitchell had produced a precocious, furiously neurotic child.

Beatrice looked at us and shrugged. "Bradford, how about leaving the books alone and saying hello to Arthur and Patrick?"

"I happen to be in the middle of something, Mom. As you can see?"

"He's arranging all of the books in the house according to height."

"According to color!" Bradford cried. "I'm arranging them all by color."

"By color," Beatrice corrected, blowing her nose. "Height was last week. Next I suppose it'll be weight."

When she left to get her husband, Arthur poked me in the arm and pointed to Bradford, grinning fondly. Arthur's ability to get along with children extended from this oddball all the way to Stacy, my miraculously normal niece. Arthur admired Bradford's intelligence; I was dumbfounded by his neuroses. His bedroom was as orderly as the Library of Congress, with toys lined up according to height and clothes neatly folded and grouped in matching colors.

To highlight his peculiar demeanor, Bradford had inherited his father's gigantic frame and bad eyesight. As difficult as it is to admit, there was something about this big, bespectacled, compulsively organizational child I found unnerving. No doubt he would grow into a handsome overachiever and discover the cures for cancer, AIDS, and the common cold, but if he ended up murdering student nurses, I for one wouldn't be shocked to read about it in the newspaper. Arthur always knew how to engage him in stimulating conversation. He tossed a pillow on the floor and took a seat beside Einstein.

"Would you be willing to reveal your system for arranging the colors?" Arthur asked.

"Yes; it's a very simple alphabetical arrangement. If you'll look on that bookshelf behind you, you'll see that the black ones are first, then the blue, then the green, the orange, the red, and the yellow. Those are the basic categories."

"Hey, Brad," I said, "what about the browns?"

"I'm putting the browns together on a bookshelf in the other room, off by themselves."

Obviously there was something of major scatological significance in this, and I was eager to pursue it. Arthur must have noticed my face lighting up and quickly asked Bradford about his kindergarten comrades.

*   *   *

Arthur's replacement was fifteen years older than Beatrice, gray-haired and bearded. He had the easy, sincere geniality of a man who was either completely at peace with himself and the world or was dipping into the Xanax jar too regularly. Based on the evidence at hand, I was certain it was the former. I'd never once seen him lose his patience with either his wife or his child, and he treated me with good-natured disregard that acknowledged we had little in common and would never be friends but still allowed for pleasant conversation over dinner. What I liked best about Mitchell was the slightly de-praved gleam in his eyes, an especially fascinating feature in a man obsessed with the life and work of Lewis Carroll.

The doctors came into the living room, she with a tray of glasses, he with a rotund bottle of champagne, both grinning joyously. Arthur stood, hands were shaken all around, and Beatrice dragged her son up from the floor as Mitchell expertly worked the cork out of the bottle. Bradford demanded a glass for himself, and his father poured him a token splash, though not enough, unfortunately, to stunt the kid's growth. Mitchell proposed an upbeat toast about the house, and we went through the embarrassing ritual of clinking glasses.

I drank, not quite convinced by my own participation. I appre-ciated Beatrice and Mitchell's generosity in being happy for us, but I found it a little overdone. Arthur put his arm around me and pulled me to him, and I nearly spilled my champagne down the front of my shirt. His show of affection was too sudden for my taste. We'd had words on the walk over from our apartment, and I was still angry. What had started out as a simple disagreement about the acoustical problems of the opera house in Sydney—a subject of enormous rel-evance to our lives—had become a fierce argument about Australian politics, something neither one of us knew or cared a thing about. I didn't need Mitchell's or Beatrice's degree to figure out that the whole fight was the result of sublimated something or other. My choice would have been to skip the champagne and keep arguing.

Arthur's displays of affection around Beatrice and Mitchell always made me uneasy anyway. I had a sneaking suspicion they were re-lated to the success of Beatrice's second marriage. Then, too, there was something about Arthur's displays of affection that made me uneasy in general. I always wanted to shrug them off, like a sweater that's comfortable but offers no warmth.

When Bradford, who was looking slightly tipsy and off balance, demanded food, Mitchell and Arthur went to the kitchen to feed him, and I was left standing in the middle of the living room floor with Beatrice. She scrutinized me closely for a minute, blew her nose, and pointed to a low, benchlike sofa jutting out into the middle of the room. "Let's sit down," she said. "If I have another sip of this I'll be on the floor. I shouldn't be drinking with this cold anyway. You know, my mother used to claim she loved champagne, couldn't get enough champagne. Whenever we went to anyone's house on holidays, she made a big show of telling everyone how much she loved champagne, as if she lived on it. It was very embarrassing. Half my childhood, my father could barely afford to feed us, and she'd be going on about champagne. There was something truly pathetic in it. Now tell me what's worrying you most about buying the house."

I drained off my glass, thinking how to answer, anticipating her lecture. As soon as I opened my mouth, she cut me off and said, "You're worried you're making a mistake? Isn't that it?"

"Well, I suppose there's—"

"And what worries you even more is that Arthur seems to have no worries at all."

"He doesn't really—"

"Oh, don't believe it for a minute, Patrick. That's just his way. He's a nervous wreck about the house, too. I know he is. I'm sorry, did I interrupt?"

"No, not at all, I was just—"

"Arthur's way is to pretend he's absolute about every move he makes and always above reproach. That's why he's always so nice to everyone. He doesn't want to give you anything to call him on or point a finger at. It's very cowardly of him and very clever. You have to confront him, ask him outright about his own doubts. Here," she said, "let me refill your glass."

"I'm not exactly—"

"What? Good at direct confrontation? I could have told you that. I'd guess you function better in the deceive-and-escape mode. Am I right?"

"You—"

"I'm sorry I'm talking so much, Patrick. You probably think it's unprofessional of me. Well, it is. But after all, this is a social call."

She pulled a rumpled handkerchief out of her pocket and blew her nose. I saw an opening in the conversation and tried to make use of it to change the subject. I was interested in hearing what she had to say, but there's something physically exhausting about having your sentences finished for you. I started to talk about the weather, the unseasonable warmth we'd been having that spring, how it was a sure sign of global disaster, hot air trapped in the atmosphere, building and building until all life was suffocated by it.

She waved the handkerchief at me dismissively and stuffed it back into her pocket. "We'll file that comment under 'interesting association.' You're probably uncomfortable I'm talking so much about Arthur. Well, what else am I supposed to do with twenty years' worth of observations? When's the closing on this house?"

"About six weeks."

"All right. So there's still time to be direct. Clear the air now. Get Arthur to talk about his own concerns, and you'll feel a lot better. What do you think of that?"

"I—"

She sprang to her feet. "Damn, they're coming back already. I thought Bradford was hungrier than that. Just remember, Patrick, anytime you want to talk, you can call me."

It began to drizzle lightly as we walked home. Arthur looked up into the dark sky. "Why didn't you tell me it was going to rain?" he asked. "I mean, you know the weather reports for every day for the next six months, sweetheart, and if you'd told me it was going to rain, I would have brought an umbrella and we'd both be dry instead of drenched. Life would be simpler."

Now was obviously a good time to start taking Beatrice's professional advice. "You know what I was just wondering, Arthur? I was just wondering if you were having any reservations about the two of us buying this house together."

He stopped under the branches of an old maple tree sprouting on the edge of the sidewalk and looked at me with amused incredulity. "If I'm not mistaken, sweetheart, my ex-wife would call that projection. You're the one having doubts, so you assume I must be. It's a classic example, in fact. I'll have to mention it to Beatrice next time we have lunch."

We started walking again, and I looked over at Arthur and watched the light rain sliding down his impressive forehead. He returned to the discussion of the Sydney opera house, a building at a much safer distance than the yellow house.

He was right; I did know it was supposed to rain that night, but

I'd forgotten about it when we left the apartment. Maybe I *was* projecting my own reservations onto him. I could never be sure with Arthur. As we walked along in the rain, I began to feel chilled.

A couple of years earlier, in what must have been a fit of despair, I went to Arthur and told him I thought we should go to a couples counselor. He was kneeling on the floor in front of the stereo, making an opera tape—a birthday present for me, as it later turned out. He gave me an annoyed look.

"Why would we want to do that, Patrick?"

I suppose I hadn't thought the whole thing through very much, and all I could come up with was an apologetic and far too mildly stated confession that I wasn't especially happy and that I had a feeling something in our relationship wasn't working.

"You don't see me unhappy, do you?" he'd said, as if I'd made some horrible accusation.

"I don't know," I said. "I suppose not."

"Well, all right then." He went on to explain, the vein in his forehead throbbing, that when one person in a relationship is unhappy and the other person isn't, then the person who is unhappy must be the one with the problems. Going to a couples counselor would make about as much sense as putting both legs in traction after breaking one ankle.

I knew there was a hole in his argument somewhere, but it sounded rational enough to make me drop the subject.

I set about trying to make myself happier. It was shortly after that that I started sleeping with Jeffrey. While it certainly wasn't a perfect solution, it did brighten up some of my days, and it was a lot cheaper than analysis.

Now, as we walked along, I wanted to stop under one of the dripping trees and simply confess outright that I was uncertain about buying the house. But I was afraid he'd talk me out of my doubts or turn them around somehow, and the rain was streaming down his monkish face and I felt miserable about not having remembered to bring an umbrella. I listened to something he was saying about the opera house and invented a statistic to refute his argument.

Twenty-five

~

At one in the morning, I was tossing back and forth on my rubber air mattress, so overcome with anxiety I was hoping the thing would explode. That might release some tension or stop Arthur's snoring, or maybe eject me through the ceiling and out into the night air.

Finally, I got up and went to my room behind the kitchen. I folded a huge stack of laundry, dusted a few of my plastic religious icons, lit some votive candles, flung myself onto the bed, and tried to read a long magazine article about the death of planet Earth. At one time, the room must have been a storage closet, for it was always cool and damp, and there was a faint odor of mildew, which I'd come to like. I had the bed wedged into the corner by the drafty window that looked out to the back of the house. Sometime after midnight, the light drizzle Arthur and I had been caught in turned to a more steady downpour, and I could hear water plopping onto the floor of the porch as it seeped through the cracks in the roof. I got through two nightmarish pages of the magazine piece but had to put it aside; I was too distracted and morose to follow its apocalyptic arguments.

The phone was sitting on the floor beside the bed, its push-button face making suggestions. In the past, I'd used the extension in my bedroom primarily to call Jeffrey, and now it was staring up at me, a reminder that I hadn't spoken to him in over a month. I dialed his number, let it ring once, and then hung up. With my luck, Sandy-KyleDennis would answer and know who it was even if I kept silent. Not that he would have cared especially, but only a lonely insomniac or a drunk would be calling an ex-boyfriend at one in the morning, and I wasn't ready for Kyle to slap either label on me.

I decided instead to call another lonely insomniac, Tony. I heard opera blasting in the background before I heard his hesitant "Hello," and I shouted at him to lower the volume. He dropped the phone and graciously turned off the music. At least Vivian had him housebroken.

"What were you listening to?" I asked.

"An opera. The tragic one."

"That narrows down the field."

"Something's going on with Vivian, Pat. The other night she had me listen to some opera about a bunch of nuns getting their heads chopped off, and last week when I was away on business she went to see a movie the two of us had made plans to see together. She hasn't said anything, but I can tell there's something wrong. We haven't had sex in almost two days."

Two days. I was on the verge of tears. "She's probably upset she hasn't been invited to the wedding yet. Why don't you just call Loreen and start the ball rolling, for Christ's sake?"

"I talked with her earlier tonight. I called her planning to say something, but I ended up talking as if nothing was wrong. The pathetic thing is, I think she bought it. Does that give you an idea of how sad this situation is? She didn't even mention that she'd been in to see you. I should have settled things and broken her heart months ago—before I knew how rotten it feels to have your heart broken. And do you want to hear something really horrifying?"

"I'm all ears."

"The only reason I called was because I was talking to your father tonight and he sounded so miserable when I mentioned Loreen's name, I felt I owed it to him to call my fiancée. Vivian's right: I should get to a shrink."

"I spent the night with two of them. I can give you their number if you want."

"Who's this, that ex-wife of Arthur's? I don't like the sound of her."

"You don't like the sound of anyone. She and her husband invited us over for champagne. Our mortgage came through."

"No kidding? I'm glad someone's life is going well."

I suddenly felt so offended by the comment, by his apparent need to think that everything was going well for me, I wanted to leap through the phone and strangle him. "My life is not going well!" I shouted.

"Take it easy, will you? How am I supposed to know your life isn't going well if you don't tell me about it?"

Perhaps it was the late hour or the quiet dark of the house, or maybe the closing date on the house was making me desperate and all my buried discontent was floating to the surface. Whatever it was, I started confessing my doubts about the house to Tony and then, much more alarmingly, some of my doubts about my relationship with Arthur.

My brother was so quiet on the other end of the line, I gratefully assumed he'd fallen asleep. Finally, he said, as if making a painful confession himself, "I might as well tell you right now, Patrick, and I hope you don't get pissed off: I never liked Arthur."

"Now you tell me! I thought Arthur was the one person you *did* like. For the past six years, all I've heard from you is how wonderful he is."

"Well, what did you expect? That's what you always say about somebody's wife or husband or whatever he is. I'm not saying he's a monster, but he thinks he knows everything, and you can't get him to tell you what he really thinks of people. I can't prove anything, so don't tell him I told you, but ever since you two came out here and I let him drive my car, it hasn't been running the same."

"I warned you about that."

"I know, but I had no idea he was as bad as you claimed. The minute I saw him pull out of the garage at two miles an hour, with the emergency flashers and the wipers on, I knew that relationship was burned meat loaf."

"Well, whatever it is, we're about to sign a thirty-year mortgage."

"Don't be an idiot, Patrick. If you don't want the house, don't buy it. It's that simple."

"Simple, sure. But it's already too far along to stop."

"A bullet through the head's the only thing that's final. And I don't care how much deposit money you'd lose; it still has to be better than losing the rest of your life and all the money you're going to pour into the dump. Between you and me, what kind of person would buy a yellow house?"

"I'm not sure that's the best way to judge character. Anyway, he's a good person, Tony."

"I don't doubt it. It's too bad everything he does drives you crazy, that's all. Love and pity, man, it's a bad combination."

There was something in the conversation that was beginning to sound familiar, although I couldn't quite put my finger on it. Whatever it was, talking with Tony about Arthur made me feel more calm and relieved than I'd felt in weeks. After we'd hung up, I went back to the magazine article about the end of the world and read it enthusiastically. The pessimistic account of the death of all recognizable forms of life on the planet had a soothing effect on me. Shadows from the votive candles were flickering across the ceiling, and the sound of the rain leaking through the porch roof was almost romantic. I began to get happily drowsy and pulled a heavy blanket over me. When Arthur had suggested I make this tiny room my own, we'd agreed that no matter how much time I spent there, I would always sleep in our bedroom. But tonight, perhaps encouraged by my talk with Tony, I let myself drop off in the candlelight and slept, without interruption, until morning.

Twenty-six

In my years at Only Connect, I developed several theories on the nature and psychology of travel, the central hypothesis of them being that happy individuals at peace with themselves do not travel. Or at least don't like to travel. Of all the great travelers in history, the overwhelming majority took to the roads to avoid extreme malaise and, nine times out of ten, some degree of sexual panic. Travel, as a vocation, has consistently attracted almost as many guilt-ridden cross-dressers, repressed homosexuals, and tormented pedophiles as the religious orders.

Of course a one-week trip to the Bahamas can't really be called travel, in the grand tradition, and in that sense, Only Connect was more a vacation factory than a travel agency. Unfortunately, most people don't like to vacation, either. Young professionals need something to brag about at cocktail parties, so they go on vacations. The majority would rather spend their time off at the movies. If it weren't for the demands of upward mobility, Only Connect would be out of business.

Most people are afraid to fly but ashamed to admit it because it's considered lower-class to distrust air travel. If Lindbergh had come from a family of sharecroppers, people would still be crossing the Atlantic in ocean liners. As for hotels, those nonplaces are intrinsically depressing and unwholesome. Paying outrageous sums for the privilege of staying in them and having your life dictated by a staff of desk clerks, bellhops, housekeepers, and waitrons is an exercise in self-degradation.

All of which made my new vocation of talking people out of going away so gratifying. It wasn't only the Party's Over desperadoes who could be set on the right path; with a few probing questions and the proper attitude, anyone could be convinced to do what he really wanted to do: stay at home. "So you and your wife want to go to a romantic island? Are you really trying to tell me the romance has gone out of your marriage? How long have you been feeling this way?" "You want a seat at the back of the plane? In other words, you're tormented by the fear that the plane is going to crash. Why not take a nice long drive to Hartford instead? Rio will be there ten years from now."

If, however, I'd wanted to talk Professor Fields out of his trip to Bermuda, I should have begun at the beginning. By mid-April it was too late to do anything but make a genuine effort to get him seats on the plane. Then, too, my attitude toward the man had taken an unexpected turn: during his last whispered call, sometime shortly after Arthur and I heard about the mortgage, I began to feel a twinge of empathy for him. He'd called to make more inquiries about the nonexistent hotel reservation and the decor of the nonexistent hotel room and the size of the nonexistent bed, and there was something in his hushed voice and his pathetic, suppressed excitement that touched me. Obviously he was trapped in a passionless marriage and was trying to make some breathing space for himself by taking this ill-fated trip with Zayna. Memorial Day weekend was probably the only thing he'd had to look forward to in years, discounting the occasional visit to a zoo. As for Zayna, if she wasn't genuinely in love with him, she was pursuing her academic goals to the best of her abilities, and I couldn't very well begrudge either motivation.

I called the sales representative of the airline in question and told him that because of an unforeseen and tragic series of events, I had bungled a reservation and a customer of mine had been canceled from a flight. I told him that Professor Fields—"practically the president of Harvard"—was on the wait list and pleaded with him to do something about finding two seats on the plane.

The sales rep and I had met at a couple of airline functions and hadn't exactly hit it off. Gary Bolton was a pathologically disingenuous windbag with the kind of pink, overscrubbed skin that's a sign of severe self-hatred. He tended to give me leering looks and make ridiculous comments. "You've got awfully big feet, Pat, for such a skinny runt"; that kind of charming thing. I hated to beg for favors, but I made the best of it by reminding myself there's always something to be said for practicing humility.

Bolton responded to my Fields plight with the saccharine concern that seemed to be the only requirement of his job. He clucked his tongue a lot and repeated "Isn't that a shame" so many times I thought I was listening to a tape loop. Finally, he said, "Well, hold on for a minute and I'll see if there's anything I can do for you. Not that there isn't a lot I'd *like* to do for you."

There was so little conviction or sincerity in his voice, I suspected he'd merely gone to the bathroom to scrub off another layer of epidermis. When he finally came back on the line, he was noisily chomping on something—peanut M&M's, from the sound. Obviously he'd been off at the candy machine. "That flight is so damned tight as it is, people are going to be sitting on each other's faces and laps and everywhere else."

"Is there a regulation against putting passengers in the cargo hold? I know they wouldn't mind, just for a couple of hours."

"You know, we wouldn't be having such a big problem here if you'd called in the ticket numbers when you were supposed to. Had your mind elsewhere, I bet."

"Believe me, Gar, I would have called them in if it hadn't been for the accident. But how can you predict these things? You're walking to work, a bus comes along, jumps the curb, and you wake up in a hospital bed." Since I knew he wouldn't go for any excuse, I figured I might as well make it truly implausible.

"A tragedy," he consoled. "But I'll tell you what I can do for you; I'll put your friends at the top of the wait list. That way, if anyone does cancel, they'll be the first on. And in the meantime, I'll book them on a triple connection through New York, Atlanta, and Detroit. Just be thankful you're such a cute kid, or I wouldn't be going so far out of my way."

"Cute kid" had lost its appeal as a compliment on my eighth birthday, but I wasn't in a position to complain. This at least sounded hopeful. I finished off the phone call renewed by my good deed and convinced that Professor Fields was lucky to have such a clever travel agent working on his behalf.

Twenty-seven

$\}$

By all accounts, Sharon and Ryan were in the middle of a blossoming friendship. Since the meal at my apartment, they'd gone to two Celtics games together and had several dinners at restaurants Sharon picked out from among her Boston favorites. They'd apparently established a routine of watching *Jeopardy* together at Sharon's house. Rita called to complain that Ryan was spending more time in Cambridge than at home.

Despite Tony's feelings about Sharon, he seemed delighted with the news. He told me our older brother was making repairs on the staircase leading up to Sharon's second floor, replacing balusters and plastering the holes in the walls. "He called me up to find out how to do it. It was kind of nice, Pat. I mean, I'm sure it looks like hell. He's great in the kitchen but not exactly a handyman. I hope I get some points from Sharon for giving instructions."

What I was most curious to find out was whether or not their get-togethers qualified as dates. Sharon wasn't giving out clues on that subject, and I thought it best to restrain myself from asking. I was secretly thrilled for both of them, no matter what the terms of their friendship, but something about the fact that it had begun weeks after Elaine asked for a divorce made me uneasy.

If they were dating, they'd already passed number three, the critical date, according to Sharon's philosophy. As for the fourth fuck, it was anyone's guess.

One Sunday afternoon late in April, Ryan, Sharon, and my niece showed up at my apartment unexpectedly. I hadn't seen or spoken with Ryan since our talk at the store a couple of weeks earlier, and as he walked in, with Stacy held proudly in his arms, it struck me that his appearance was slightly altered. It would be going overboard to say he was glowing, but it seemed to me his face was less waxen than usual. Perhaps he'd been in the sun or the wind. If it was from a tanning booth, the dating question was answered. Sharon was trailing behind, a cigarette dangling from her lips. She was carrying a pink, pretty doll with as much interest as if it were a rotten head of lettuce. I pointed to it and raised my eyebrows.

She shrugged. "Transitional object," she said. She had on a bulky belted gray cardigan and a pair of flared blue jeans that were almost short enough to qualify as pedal pushers, but she, too, looked different, more relaxed than usual.

Ryan was beaming at Stacy. He always beamed when he had his daughter in his charge. "You remember Uncle Patrick," he said. "Can you say his name?"

Stacy took her thumb out of her mouth, swatted her hand at me as if she were shooing a fly, then buried her face in Ryan's neck. "Aw, she's being shy," Ryan said.

Stacy was a bright, pretty child, with fat cheeks, adorably stubby legs, and her father's round blue eyes. She loved to dance and pretend she was playing a piano and singing. I was convinced she'd become a professional musician someday, maybe a cabaret performer with a devoted following of gay men. She was four years old and had a better articulated sense of style than either of her parents. On her last birthday, I'd bought her a punky black skirt and red-and-white sweater I thought she'd like. After she thanked me for the present, she asked if I'd kept the sales slip so she could exchange the outfit. "It's not really *me*," she'd said apologetically. Today she was wearing lacy white ankle socks, black patent-leather Mary Janes, and a frilly pink dress with blue ribbons hanging from the waistline.

Aside from occasional holidays, I'd spent very little time with Stacy, and I was desperately afraid she didn't like me much. She'd never been able to pronounce my name, even though she had an extensive vocabulary. I was stung by the slight, but I had to respect her for having strong opinions and sticking by them. Ryan told me she probably had a crush on me, his usual optimistic assessment of friction between any two people.

Stacy and Arthur had become great pals the few times they'd met. She squealed with delight when he came into the living room now. "Uncle Arthur," she pronounced flawlessly.

"My best friend!" he said. He began singing "Surrey with the Fringe on Top," and Stacy wriggled down from Ryan's arms and ran to him.

Sharon looked at me reproachfully. "At least it's not 'Hello, Dolly,' " I told her. "What brings you two here? Not that I'm complaining."

"Sharon's always asking about Stacy," Ryan answered, "so I thought I'd drag her into town and show her off."

"Then I remembered how I feel about kids," Sharon said.

"She's joking. She and Stacy are in love with each other."

I wondered if this meant he and Sharon were in love with each other.

"Anyway, it's an incredible day. Sunny, windy, warm. We thought we'd hang out at the river. There's a love-in going on down there."

"Love-in?" Arthur asked. He was walking around the living room with Stacy balanced on the toes of his shoes.

"Every time Ryan sees a group of people in Cambridge, he calls it a love-in," Sharon explained. "It's a beautiful day, and we decided to take a walk."

"So we thought we'd drive over here and see if you guys wanted to come. We're going to drive up to the Square and find a place to park near the river and then maybe drive out to the ocean."

"Where does the walk come in?" Arthur asked.

"We had to walk up three flights of stairs to get here," Ryan said. "Anyway, we'll probably have to get out of the car at some point and walk to buy pizza or fried clams."

Both Sharon and Ryan burst into laughter at this comment, and the idea of spending time with them suddenly appealed to me enormously. I looked over at Arthur to see if he was interested. "Unfortunately," he said, "I have to prepare some work for tomorrow. But you should go along and enjoy yourself."

"Even if it sounded like he didn't mean it," Sharon said, "he did give you permission to go, Patrick. Of course we could all learn from Arthur's example, working on Sunday. I really do admire that kind of dedication."

"If you were any more dedicated," Ryan told her, "you'd have to put a bed in your office. Did you know she's sometimes at that office twelve hours a day, Pat?"

"I hate to be the one to tell you, but she does have a bed in her office. A futon rolled up behind the desk." I didn't mention that she kept it there for her afternoon naps.

Stacy was miserable that Arthur wasn't coming along, but she accepted me as a consolation prize and let me carry her downstairs. She poked her fingers through my hair and asked if Arthur and I were married. "Certainly not," I said, mortified. "We're not even engaged. He's still available."

As Ryan had promised, the day was warm and windy, splendid late-April weather, the kind of gentle and breezy afternoon that can trick you into thinking all's right with the world—if you didn't happen to know it was about to come to a swift, fiery end. Ryan made a production of piling and strapping us all into his car, but after driving three blocks, we discovered that Memorial Drive was closed to traffic and we parked at the side of the road. Hordes of people were passing by on bicycles and roller skates, were jogging, hooked up to headphones—hopeful, happy people, dressed in bright, hopeful colors, exulting on a Sunday afternoon.

The wind was blowing across the river from the west, whipping up whitecaps on the surface of the water, and the sky was a deep shade of blue, heartbreaking for being so clean and so rare. Stacy and I were in the back of the car. She was trying to teach me a complicated counting game that was over my head. My attention drifted away from her, and for a fleeting moment I felt absolutely content and happy. Ryan had his arm draped across the back of Sharon's seat. He reached up and gave her hair a gentle tug as she blew smoke out the window.

"What do we do now?" he asked. "We can't drive."

This provoked an absurdly serious debate between the two on whether or not we should leave the car and actually walk to Harvard Square. I finally reminded them that it was less than a mile away.

"But Daddy has bad knees," Stacy informed me.

"That's right, honey, I do. And Sharon shouldn't walk too far because she smokes too much."

"I wish you hadn't said that, Ryan. Now we have to walk so I can prove my lung capacity."

"I meant it as a compliment, kiddo."

* * *

It took almost ten minutes for Ryan to unstrap Stacy from her car seat and dig a stroller, a bag of sweaters, two blankets, a box of cookies, and jug of apple juice from the trunk. Sharon and I watched from the sidewalk as Ryan handed the picnic items to Stacy and she loaded them into her stroller.

"I hope someone sees me pushing a baby carriage down Memorial Drive," Sharon said. "That would really confuse them. Especially if there's nothing in it but sweaters and apple juice."

Sharon and I walked along the river as Ryan played tag with Stacy ahead of us. The ribbons on Stacy's dress blew out behind her in the warm wind, and she ran with the jerky, halting steps of a wind-up toy. "Can you explain to me," Sharon said, "how it is that Ryan knows how to be such a good father and doesn't have a clue about how to be a son? Cute together, aren't they?"

"You and Ryan are kind of cute together, now that you mention it."

Sharon leaned against my shoulder and adjusted the straps of her sandals. "If there's one thing in life I've never wanted to be, it's 'cute.' "

"I meant it as a compliment, kiddo."

"Yeah? Try 'tough broad' next time."

I thought to make some gratuitously flattering comment, but it was impossible to get away with those kinds of palliatives with Sharon. She always made sure compliments blew up in your face. "I wonder what Elaine will think when Stacy tells her she spent the afternoon with a woman friend of her father's."

"I haven't met her," Sharon said. "You'd know better than I would. But to tell you the truth, Patrick, I'm not interested in hearing about her, so don't tell me."

"Does Ryan talk about her much?"

"No, of course not. He's much too polite to bore me with horror stories about his ex-wife. Or almost ex. The only time her name even comes up is when I mention it. I'm trying to convince him he should meet with her before he signs any papers."

We walked along in silence, watching the bicyclists and the skaters pass. Sharon took off her sweater and tossed it into the stroller. There was a green-and-white tent set up near the footbridge over the river, and the faint sounds of banjo music were blowing down to us on the wind, along with paper cups and empty soda cans. A crowd had gathered in front of the tent, lying on blankets on the grass. Ryan had Stacy in his arms now and was whispering into her ear. He turned around and pointed to the tent. "Love-in," he mouthed.

"Come on, Sharon," I said. "What do you really think of Ryan?"

She'd stopped and was bent over, lighting a cigarette, her hands cupped elaborately around her mouth. She raised her eyes as if there was something in my tone she found objectionable. She shook out the match and stood up. "You know how much tolerance I have for jerks, Patrick. None. I wouldn't be spending time with him if I didn't like him. I expected him to be sweet but boring. So he's a little of both, but not too much of either. And I like the kid a lot, too. She could do without some of that lace, but she's got a lot of potential."

We found a place on the grass near the tent, and Ryan spread a blanket, stretched out on his stomach, and fell asleep. Sharon was besieged by several groups of friends and clients, who, spotting her, had to introduce her to the people they were with. Sharon had the kind of strong personality and striking appearance people loved to show off to their friends, as if it was an accomplishment to be accepted into her inner circle. They'd come and sit by her, and she'd pummel them with questions about themselves until they'd wander off, grinning and pleased. "The real key to success in life," she'd once told me, "is to ask people questions about their lives until you're blue in the face. Start with 'How are you?' and keep going until they pass out with amazement at how fascinating they are." It also had the effect of never giving anyone the chance to ask her a thing about herself, a fact she never mentioned. She had Stacy in her lap, braiding her hair, and she introduced her to some people as her sister, to others as her illegitimate daughter, and to others still as her young friend. Her introductions of Ryan and me were equally capricious and farfetched. "Let 'em guess" was another in Sharon's endless list of mottoes to live by.

Ryan had on a pair of uncharacteristically tight blue jeans—faded and with a hole in one knee—and a long-sleeved blue T-shirt with a pocket over the right breast. The combination of tight pants and baggy shirt was more flattering than most of his outfits, and the blue of the T-shirt brought out a light in his eyes I'd never really noticed before. When he woke from his nap, I asked him where he'd got his outfit.

"Nice, isn't it? I got it at some dump Sharon took me to. Some place with a lot of skinheads milling around, buying rags."

"Used-clothing warehouse near MIT," Sharon translated. "I told him I wasn't going to a Celtics game with someone in a leisure suit. This is the right look for him."

"Except the pants are so tight I can hardly breathe," Ryan said. "They squeeze in the fat pretty well, though. Look at this." He grabbed at his stomach. "You'd never guess it was there, would you?"

"I told him he should take up smoking," Sharon said. "It's done wonders for my figure."

We stayed on the riverbank for hours, listening to the music and sopping up the warm, weak sunshine. Late in the afternoon, the sky began to grow milky with high clouds and the wind shifted and blew with a faint chill. We gathered up our blankets and sweaters. Ryan insisted we take a cab back to the car.

I helped them load everything into the trunk and strapped Stacy into her car seat and kissed her on the top of her head.

"I'll walk home from here," I said.

"Don't be stupid, Pat. We'll give you a lift."

"It's three blocks, Ryan. I'll make it."

I hated the thought of leaving them and going back to the apartment. I'd felt happy and even optimistic throughout the entire afternoon. Maybe they were in love with each other. Maybe optimism emerged from love, before love turned to bitterness and boredom. I stuck my hands in the pockets of my pants and headed down the street glumly.

Ryan's car sped past, and I saw Stacy waving out the back window. Then they screeched to a stop and backed up at about fifty miles an hour; obviously, Sharon was driving. Ryan had his head out the window. "Get in, Pat. We decided to drive up to Gloucester and get some fried clams at a place Sharon's always raving about."

I started to explain to them why I couldn't go along—Arthur, the house, cleaning.

"Just shut up and get in."

I ran around to the other side of the car and leapt into the back seat. Sharon stomped on the gas pedal, and we sped off.

Twenty-eight

O n the last day of April, a warm,
sunny Thursday less than a week after the outing with Sharon and my
brother, Fredrick buzzed my intercom and told me I had a call from
"a Jeffrey something-or-other."

I hadn't heard from Jeffrey in more than six weeks. I missed
him—often at first, intermittently as time went on. Since he'd gone
back with KyleSandyDennis, I'd worked hard at extinguishing the
longing I felt for him from time to time, mostly by reminding myself
that Jeffrey had done me a bad turn: for a year and a half I'd assumed
and worried that I was using him for sex, and then he went and
turned the tables on me.

I picked up on his line, determined not to give in to the excitement I felt at the mention of his name, and said, "Kyle did another
name change and left you again. Am I right?"

"What is this, Patrick? I don't even get a 'Hi, how are you?' "

"We've been friends for over a decade, Jeffrey. It's too late to
start wasting time on polite conversation."

"And you think I'd only call if I was in trouble. Has it occurred
to you I might be calling with some good news, or just to say hello?"

I told him I didn't consider anything impossible, but the good-
news option wasn't the first one to cross my mind.

"That *is* why I'm calling," he said. "Remember that painting over my sofa—I mentioned I might have a buyer the last time you were here? Well, I sold it. I thought I'd use some of the money to call my oldest friend. You can congratulate me now."

I did congratulate him, and enthusiastically, too. If there was anyone who needed a career boost, not to mention an extra fifteen hundred dollars, it was Jeffrey. It wasn't as if I wanted to carry a grudge against him, especially since it served me no useful purpose I could think of. The sound of his voice had melted away a substantial amount of my resentment, and as we talked on about the painting, I tried to come up with as many encouraging remarks as I could without going overboard.

"So," I said after a while, "Kyle's still Dennis, and you're happy in your happy home: is that it more or less?"

"We decided I should call him Sandy. I was always getting confused between Dennis and Kyle. Not that it matters much what I call him anymore."

"Oh?"

"I asked him to move out two weeks ago."

"You did?"

"I did."

"And did he?"

"It's my apartment, Patrick. Of course he did."

"I hope this doesn't mean you're getting assertive."

"Only in some areas." He recited a detailed list of all the petty annoyances and irritating personality quirks that had forced him to ask Kyle to move. But the list was a little too long, the annoyances too petty, and the sound of the speech a little too rehearsed. When he got down to mentioning that Kyle swept the kitchen floor six times a day and liked to eat English muffins in bed, as if these were serious character flaws, I knew Richard Burton had once again walked out on my friend. I listened a bit longer, agreeing wherever I could.

"I know exactly what you mean," I said. "I couldn't stand to live with someone whose toes are always cold. It's so inconsiderate. The least he could have done is wear socks to bed."

"You know, I suggested that, Pat. He acted as if it was an insult."

"You didn't have any choice. You're too good for him. You always were. Listen, didn't I tell you that the last time you two had a falling-out? You could have anyone you want, Jeffrey."

I didn't see anything pathetic in the fact that Kyle had walked out on Jeffrey a second time, but the fact that Jeffrey felt he had to cover it up—and for me, of all people—struck me as a bit sad. The sunlight slanting in the tiny window behind me had moved across my desk in the time we'd been on the phone and was now yellowing a newspaper lying on the floor. Jeffrey had been trying to talk himself into happiness over Kyle's departure for more than half an hour. I reminded him that if he spent all of his money from the painting on a single phone call to me, he'd end up hating me.

"I'd never hate you, Patrick. Talk to me for a few more minutes. You haven't told me anything about your life."

"I didn't want to depress you. What do you want to know?"

"Anything at all. You must have some news. For example, when do you think you might come down to New York for a visit?"

I suppose there's something hopeful in the ability of human beings to adapt to almost any situation with relative ease, but I was a little disappointed to find myself abandoning all pretense that I'd moved on in my life and telling Jeffrey I'd love to come and stay with him the next week.

When May began with a spell of suffocating, totally unseasonable heat and humidity, I decided to give in to the climatic changes and try to adapt. Years earlier, when snow was still a fact of life in the Northeast, Sharon had given me a pair of cross-country skis she'd found at a garage sale. Her theory was that if you stopped fighting against the weather extremes of New England, it was possible to enjoy them. I was never able to figure out the complicated system of waxing that would have made the skis of use to me, but the mere fact of having them hidden in the back of some closet in the basement made me look forward to every predicted blizzard with an eagerness I'd never felt before.

So during that first miserable week of May, I spent over a hundred dollars on a hammock for the back porch of the apartment. Any movie I'd seen set in a subtropical climate featured at least one happy individual prostrate in a hammock, sipping an iced alcoholic beverage, sweating like a beast, and smoking cigarettes. I hung it from the porch posts so it was suspended above the railing. If I rocked gently, I could swing out over the weed-choked backyard three stories below. It wasn't much more comfortable than any of the other furniture in the house, but I found all that air circulating around my body surprisingly reassuring. I would come home after work, climb cautiously into the thing, and induce a tropical torpor by reading *An Outcast of the Islands*, drinking canned piña coladas, smoking cigarettes I pilfered from Sharon, and listening to a tape of Stan Getz

playing bossa nova. Arthur was horrified by the precarious position-
ing of the hammock and told me he was delighted there was no
similarly dangerous place to hang it at "our house."

"Our house" came up in Arthur's conversation regularly. At best,
I changed the subject, and at the worst, I snapped at him, reminding
him that the place wasn't ours yet. Arthur had started to collect boxes
in preparation for the big move. He'd met with the current owners
twice. He was getting lessons from them on how to maintain the
garden and the flowering trees. I'd managed to come up with credible
excuses for missing both meetings. I couldn't face going out to the
house with Arthur, although I often bicycled there by myself and sat
on the sidewalk opposite, staring at the yellow walls, alternately
trying to imagine what it was going to be like living there and what
the neighborhood would look like if the house suddenly burst into
flames and was reduced to a pile of ashes.

I'd been sleeping in the back bedroom more frequently now and
discovered that my insomnia had virtually disappeared. I still went
through the charade of putting sheets on the air mattress every night
and crawling under the covers, but as soon as I heard Arthur snoring,
I crept out.

Arthur and I were having dinner on the back porch one night,
when I told him I was planning to go to New York the upcoming
weekend. I was in the hammock, swinging out over the railing with
a plate of sandwiches resting on my chest.

"I wish you'd stop that swinging, sweetheart, at least while I'm
eating. I'm getting a little seasick." He reached out and brought the
hammock to a stop. "You know, I was under the impression you and
Jeffrey had had a falling-out. You haven't visited in a while."

I told him that Jeffrey and Kyle had had a brief reprise of their old
relationship and that I hadn't felt like stepping into the middle of
their ardor. "You know what it's like to sleep in someone's guest
room and hear the hosts ripping down the curtains and knocking over
lamps while they're fucking."

This struck him as hilariously funny. "No one does that kind of
thing, sweetheart. I don't know where you get your ideas about
passion." He laughed and went back to his sandwich and his newspaper, and I started rocking the hammock again.

As the weekend approached, I found myself getting increasingly
anxious. I was excited at the prospect of ripping down Jeffrey's cur-

tains, but the idea of the trip itself—packing, flying, trekking into the city, and wandering back home—exhausted me. I'd had a similar reaction when I was standing in line to see *Lawrence of Arabia* for the eighth time and realized I just couldn't face another viewing of the film, masterpiece or not. It was one thing when having an affair with Jeffrey had simply been a matter of deceiving Arthur; now the stakes seemed higher, and I had a vague sense that I was deceiving myself somehow.

Out of desperation, I called Tony late one night, and after a lot of moronic chitchat about a trip to Paris I had no intention of taking, I told him about the latest turn of events in my love life. He listened with a surprising degree of interest and shocked me by asking for explicit details. When I was finished, he said, "You're wasting your time with this guy, Patrick."

"You're probably right," I said. I sighed and looked up from the brown velvet sofa at all the furniture in the living room, which was about to be packed up and carted off. "Which guy do you mean?"

"Both of them. Are you in love with the loser in New York?"

"No, I guess not."

"What about Arthur?"

"Well . . . that one's more complicated."

"Let's face it, Pat: you've got table scraps on one side and crumbs on the other."

"Which side is the table scraps?" Of the two options, that sounded the more promising.

"It doesn't matter. You're just trying to piece together a life, and it won't work out. A little bit of this and a little of that, but the whole mess is never going to add up to enough."

"You're sounding awfully sensible."

"The voice of experience. It's what I thought I could do with Loreen: have a half-assed marriage in Chicago, a couple of things going on the side, and everything would be fine. Then I fell in love and fucked up all my plans. Don't go to New York, Patrick. Isn't that the advice you'd give me?"

"I guess it is." The big puffy cushions on the sofa were beginning to flop down around my face. I rearranged them and thought about his advice. "And if I did suggest you stay home," I said, "would you listen to me?"

"Nah. I'd go to New York anyway."

Twenty-nine

I was plagued by Tony's advice for the next several days, possibly because I knew it was sound. I thought hard about whether or not I should visit Jeffrey. I thought about it when I was at the office, at home, at the movies, the gym, the grocery store, the dry cleaners, and strapping myself into my seat on the shuttle to New York.

As soon as I stepped out of the terminal at La Guardia, the overbaked, smoggy city air assaulted me, a reminder that I'd actually arrived. The sky was a sick shade of yellow, as if the whole of New York had come down with a mean case of hepatitis. I sat down on a bench in the sun, wondering if I should take a bus or a taxi into town or get on the next flight home. The seat was so hot it felt as if the plastic would stick to my ass when I got up, assuming I ever gathered enough energy to move again. All the weekends over the past year and a half I'd made this trip into the city piled up in front of me like an overwhelming heap of time wasted on distractions. I sat plastered against the bench, sweating and miserable, contemplating the picture Tony had painted of my life: crumbs on one side, table scraps on the other. Some smorgasbord!

When I finally pulled myself together, I walked back into the terminal and bought a ticket for the next flight to Boston. I called Jeffrey and told him I was at La Guardia.

"Right on time," he said. "When should I expect you?"

"Maybe in a few months, Jeff. I'm heading back to Boston."

"Back to Boston? What are you talking about, Patrick? Didn't you just arrive?"

"I did. But I shouldn't be here. I've got too much to take care of at home."

"Does this mean you're going to really try and settle down with Arthur once and for all?"

"Either that or leave him," I said.

It was still early evening when I got to the apartment. Arthur had told me he was going to dinner and a movie with Beatrice that night. I rummaged through the refrigerator to try and find something to eat, but all I came up with was a pint of chocolate-chocolate-chip ice cream, apparently a secret vice of Arthur's. The living room and the bedroom were both in a state of chaos, with Arthur's clothes and newspapers scattered around the floor and draped over the furniture. Perhaps on those weekends when I went to New York, Arthur spent all his time eating junk food and living in squalor. There was something reassuring about the thought.

I collapsed in a stupor in the hammock, rocking gently and sipping a canned daiquiri. The porch looked out to a kind of courtyard formed by the fenced-off yards of the houses surrounding ours. At certain times of day, the sounds from the apartments behind us were drawn out of the windows by breezes from the river and echoed loudly off the building walls. There was a couple living somewhere back there who existed in a state of constant warfare. I was never able to determine which building their voices came from, so the whole echoing courtyard took on, at certain times, the atmosphere of a battleground. That night they were fighting in their usual circle of drunken insults and accusations. "Because I know it's true," the woman shouted. "How can you deny it when I know it's true? Go ahead, just try to tell me I'm not right, go ahead." I imagined the two of them living isolated from the rest of the world, snug and cozy in their apartment, tearing each other to shreds. There was something in the naked passion of their exchanges that horrified and fascinated me. I listened for a while, then turned on my bossa nova tape and tried to read a futuristic novel about a world gone haywire.

And then, as the sun set behind the circle of buildings around me, and the tape played over the screaming of the couple, and all that heavy, polluted air pressed down on me, I was consumed by a wave of nostalgic reminiscence. I remembered a night years earlier, a similarly hot night although it was probably sometime in July. Arthur and I were just getting to know each other then, and we decided to spend the evening on a sightseeing cruise around Boston Harbor. There may have been dinner served on board, and there may have been a jazz band, but what I remembered most vividly was a brief moment when we went to the deserted bow of the boat to see the lights in the distance. The air had turned suddenly cool, and we put on sweatshirts and looked out at the hot city shimmering in the distance. As I lay sweltering in the hammock, I thought back to that time when the midsummer heat wave had been a passing spell of weather, not a harbinger of doom, and when standing on the bow of a boat with Arthur had filled me with calm optimism. I felt such an intense longing for a cool breeze to come circulating around my body now, I nearly burst into tears. I opened up my novel again and read for a few more minutes. Then my arm flopped down and the book fell from my grasp and over the side of the hammock and dropped three stories to the ground below.

I fell asleep.

When I woke, the sky had grown dark and the windows of the houses all around me were lit with pale yellow light. The tape had shut off. Crickets were chirping, and the air was filled with the faint murmur of television sets from all the open windows. I looked at my watch and discovered it was after ten; I'd been asleep for hours. I was groggy from having napped in the heat for too long. I was afraid I might topple over the rail and suffer the same fate as my book if I tried to get out of the hammock, so I lay there, trapped and sweating.

A light clicked on in the kitchen, and I heard Arthur say, "We've got beer and coffee, and I can make you some iced tea. Your choice, dear."

"Iced tea," Beatrice said. "I told Mitchell I'd be back before ten, but I suppose he and Brad will survive." She sneezed.

"Does Mitchell get jealous when you go out with me?"

"Don't be idiotic, Arthur. Mitchell is above jealousy, guilt, pettiness, all useless emotions. And certainly in this case . . ." I heard her walk across the kitchen floor and open the door to my bedroom. "I've always liked this little room. What does he do with all these statues?"

"He collects them. Catholic memorabilia. I call it the chapel." Arthur had never called my room "the chapel" in front of me. Perhaps he had secret, condescending nicknames for me, too.

Anyone in my position with a molecule of decency in his bones would have announced his presence immediately. Excluded from that category, I gripped the edges of the hammock and tried to prevent it from rocking. The light from the kitchen window spread out across the chipped porch floor just to the edge of the railing, and I felt safely hidden in shadows.

"So he's been sleeping in here?" Beatrice asked. She slammed the door shut.

"For a couple of weeks now."

"Well, that makes sense, given his concerns about buying the house. I must say, though, I wouldn't call it a good sign."

"I know, dear. Give me credit for being able to figure out some things on my own. Once we get into the new house, everything will fall in place. These reservations of his are just a passing fancy." Ice cubes rattled. "Tell me if this is too sweet."

The iced tea wasn't sweet enough. Beatrice wanted two more tablespoons of sugar. They debated sitting out on the porch, but fortunately, Beatrice had always considered the porch structurally unsound. I was getting the same kind of voyeuristic thrill out of listening to their conversation that I get from leafing through someone's bedside diary, but of course what I was really waiting for was more discussion of me. I had to suffer through a long, dry conversation about the film they'd just seen, including an analysis of the legal and psychological accuracy of the script. They moved on to a novel about divorce Beatrice had recommended and Arthur had hated. I was about to doze off again, when Beatrice posed one of her typically blunt questions, exactly the kind of thing I was waiting to hear. Why, she asked Arthur, was I always running off to New York? Did he think there was a chance I might be having an affair?

"I really couldn't tell you," Arthur said mildly.

"Please don't make it sound as if it isn't your business to know."

"I'm not so sure it is."

"Oh, Arthur." She sighed and ice rattled. "That comment is so *you*."

"Why is it that whenever you describe a particular behavior as being so *me*, you mean it as an insult?"

"Let's not change the subject. I'll lavish pity on you later, if you want it. You really don't care if Patrick is having an affair?"

"If he is having an affair, it doesn't look to me as if it's posing any threat to our relationship. If he wants to play around a little, and he watches out for himself, why should I care?"

If I'd known Arthur would take such a liberal view of things, I might have saved myself a good deal of sneaking around behind his back, not that I didn't enjoy it.

"Maybe I'm having an affair, too," Arthur added.

I was astonished to realize the possibility had never crossed my mind.

"Oh. Well. Are you?" The possibility had obviously never crossed Beatrice's mind, either.

"I flirt with someone at work. Stewart, the other homosexual at the office. Someone to have lunch with when you're unavailable. It's all very harmless."

"You're being too casual about this, Arthur. I don't believe anyone can be so casual about the infidelity of someone they claim to love."

If Arthur responded to her comment, I wasn't able to hear it. Perhaps he'd shrugged or made some gesture with his hand or perhaps he was thinking it over and sipping his tea. Whatever was going on in the kitchen, I felt as if I'd come across an entry in the diary I didn't want to read. I could guess what Beatrice's next question was going to be. I climbed out of the hammock as quietly as I could. "Well, Arthur," she said, as I crawled along the porch floor, "*do* you love Patrick?" Whatever the answer to that question was, I didn't want to hear it. I made it to the back staircase before Arthur had a chance to speak, and in less than a minute, I was out the door and on my bike.

The night was still hot, and a swampy smell was blowing up from the polluted river. I pedaled along the path by the water. The branches of the sycamore trees lining Memorial Drive were batting back and forth in the warm wind, and the flowers of the dogwood trees were shedding petals all over the sidewalk.

I locked my bike to a lamppost in front of Sharon's house and was about to make my way through the tangled bushes to the front door when I noticed a blue Chevy parked in the street. I peered in the window: Stacy's safety seat in the back and a couple of empty cans of Ryan's Australian ale. I looked up at the house, but the windows were so blocked from view by the overgrown bushes, I couldn't tell if there were any lights on. I got back on my bike and pedaled toward home.

Thirty

When I got to Only Connect Monday morning, Fredrick, our hedonist receptionist, was sitting at the front desk dressed in a conservative pin-striped suit, white shirt, and wing-tip shoes. He was eating a dry bagel in an uninspired, dubious sort of way and casually leafing through a computer magazine.

I would have been less shocked if he was sitting there naked, especially since he'd been decked out in an outfit resembling red silk pajamas the last time I'd seen him. I was eager to find out the meaning of this transformation, but Fredrick, who was a master at self-deprecation, was more sensitive to even a hint of an insult than anyone I'd met. As I stood at his desk leafing through my call-back slips, I casually mentioned that he looked nice and asked if he was growing a goatee.

"Not a goatee," he said. "A whole new life. I have an interview at the Harvard Business School this afternoon."

"A whole new life," I sighed. Nothing sounded more appealing or remote.

I'd left Sharon's on Friday night determined to go home and tell Arthur everything—about Jeffrey, about sleeping in the back bedroom, and most of all, about my intense desire to pilot a kamikaze flight over the yellow house. The confession should have been easy, especially since it now appeared he knew it all anyway. But as I was biking home along the river, I stopped to look back at the moon. It was a perfectly formed, bright crescent sliver hovering just above the tops of the sycamores. I was transfixed by the sight but ultimately distracted by the more earthly lure of a shadowy figure leaning against a nearby tree. One furtive thing led to another, and by the time I got home, Arthur was sound asleep. I studied his quiet, peaceful face and went back to my own room in defeat.

Late that Monday afternoon, Fredrick buzzed my intercom and told me that a Mrs. Arrow was on the phone for me. Whenever she called the office, my mother gave a name taken from the label of one of the cheap shirts in her counter at O'Neil's, because she was convinced I'd lose my job if I received too many personal calls.

She was phoning, she told me, to invite me to the house for dinner the following week. "Your father survived another year of deteriorating health, so Ryan's throwing a chicken in the oven and turning on the gas. I'm going to buy a cake, providing James isn't diagnosed with diabetes between now and then. I thought you and poor Arthur might like to join us."

"I can't answer for poor Arthur, but I suppose I should come."

"Don't sound so excited, dear; you might have a stroke."

"You don't have any suggestions for a present, do you?"

"I'm afraid not. Maybe his cardiologist could give you some ideas."

I found the comment a little stinging, even for Rita, and I began to wonder if she was still angry at me about the speech I'd delivered on the subject of Tony and Loreen's marriage. "You sound a little off," I said. "Are you all right?"

"Oh, I'm fine. I'm absolutely fine. What about you? Aren't you fine?"

"On top of the world."

"Good, I thought you would be." She paused, and I heard the new cash register beeping a protest to whatever she was doing to it. "It's that brother of yours," she finally said.

"Maybe we shouldn't talk about Tony."

"I'm talking about Ryan, the one person in the family we could rely on to be sweet and good-natured and kind and gentle. I don't know what's happened, but all of a sudden he has an answer for everything. I wouldn't dare contradict anything he says, half of which is totally off the wall. He even looks different. Frankly, dear, I blame you for introducing him to that woman."

"Sharon?"

"Unless there's another one I don't know about. I suppose he'll be moving in with her next. He practically lives there as it is. He spent Friday night there and almost didn't make it back in time to pick up Stacy on Saturday. And instead of bringing my granddaughter here to spend some time with your father and me, he took her right back to Cambridge. They went to your office to watch Sharon work and then went for a walk around a cemetery. In other words, what every four-year-old girl loves to do on a Saturday afternoon. Poor Elaine must have had a fit when she heard about it."

I was so thrilled by this news, I had an urge to slam down the phone and run to congratulate Sharon. But I didn't want her to think I was sitting around gossiping about her, even though she probably would have appreciated it. "I'm sure Ryan knows what he's doing," I said. "Don't forget he's an adult."

"Sure he's an adult, a married adult. He's going to lose visitation rights if he doesn't watch out. And this morning he announces he's taking a day off later in the week so he can go to Boston to have some kind of fancy haircut. Thirty-five years he's been getting his hair cut at that horrible place down the street, and all of a sudden he has to go into Boston to get a haircut. Just between you and me, there isn't enough hair there to worry about one way or the other." I was about to attempt a defense of my brother, when she inhaled sharply and said, in a voice softened by regret, "I suppose I should be happy for him, shouldn't I? Well, I know it doesn't sound it, Patrick, but I'm trying." She reminded me to be on time for the birthday dinner and hung up.

Later in the day, I went into Sharon's office to see for myself if her weekend with Ryan had made any visible changes. She was leaning back in her chair, with her bare feet up on her desk, talking on the phone and drinking some iced beverage from one of the most absurdly large plastic cups I'd ever seen.

No visible changes.

Her office was a vast octagonal room with long windows that looked out to the alley in front of the house. The floor and the desk were covered with brochures and tickets and travel guides and stacks of old newspapers. The man who came into the agency twice a week to clean refused to enter Sharon's office. She'd accused him of disarranging her filing system because he'd once made the mistake of emptying her wastebasket.

I sat down in front of her desk and picked up a copy of a letter she was writing to an airline. "Enclosed please find an unused ticket and death certificate for my client, Mr. B. Trembley. Please issue a full refund to his bereaved widow, B. Trembley. As the passenger died en route to the airport, it wasn't possible to cancel reservations." Et cetera.

This was a classic Sharon letter, a version of which I'd written many times in the years I was her assistant. Sooner or later, someone at the FAA was bound to catch on to the fact that her clients had an astonishingly high mortality rate. I put aside the letter and started to leaf through a tour guide to Bermuda, one with glossy pictures of the island, all pink beaches and flawless blue skies. Maybe all that pink and blue induced a regression to babyhood, which accounted for the island's popularity among heavy drinkers and honeymooners.

As I sat looking through the pictures, I began to catch some of what Sharon was saying. It sounded, unimaginably, as if she was telling her client that he was past the deadline for the cheapest airfare and there was nothing she could do for him. I sat up and took notice.

"I know I did it once," she said, "and the way I see it, you should be grateful I did. But I can't do it again and put my reputation on the line. Let's face it: if you'd called me on time, I wouldn't have to cheat and lie to get you a cheap fare. You realize you're asking me to cheat and lie so you can save a buck."

Her head was tilted back, and her hair was hanging down to the floor. She put her cup on her desk, looked over at me, and winked. "You're asking me that question? How would I know? Well, take a bus, if that's how you feel about it." There was a long pause, during which she held the phone away from her ear. "When you've thought it over, call me back and I'll accept an apology." Then she made an obscene hand gesture at the phone and hung up.

"Don't look surprised, Patrick. I'm calling it the new me. Haven't you heard I've changed my ways?"

"Of course not. I don't know if I can stand anyone else changing her ways today."

"Fredrick? Sad, isn't it. Business school. I'm sure his decision has something to do with sex. As for me, I'm tired of risking my job for the sake of a lot of jerks who don't even appreciate me. It's all part of the show for them. And believe me, sticking to the rules is going to be like having a whole new career. You know how I love challenges."

"How long has this been in effect?"

"Since this morning. Give me that letter you were just reading."
I passed her the Trembley refund request. She rolled it into a ball,
threw it in the wastebasket, and dumped some of her drink on it. "He
can die by his own hand."

She got up from behind her desk and, as if to prove to me how
serious she was about her resolve, began to poke through the stacks
of paper flung into the various corners of the room.

I swiveled around in my chair to follow the path of her cleaning
binge. "Do you mind me asking what brought this on?"

"A lot of things coming together at once. But Ryan was the
catalyst. I give him credit for that. He came in here with Stacy this
weekend to watch me work. I was talking to some clients about how
I could get them a package to Mexico for two hundred dollars—a
wild exaggeration to begin with—and right in the middle of going
through the yellow pages to find out where they could rent a wheel-
chair, I looked over at Ryan and I felt like a complete fool. I knew he
was right; all this work I do for people is a pathetic plea for acceptance. In the end, the clients don't care one way or the other and I've
taken all the risks, and I'd be much better off looking for acceptance
and love somewhere else." She tossed a bulging folder marked "Doctors' Stationery—Newton, Wellesley, and Needham" into the wastebasket.

"Ryan said all that?"

"Not exactly. But you know how sane he is. He just sat there
grinning in that sad way of his, and I could tell what was going
through his mind."

The extreme heat of the weekend had broken, but the day was still
warm. Inexplicably, Sharon was wearing a heavy sweater and a pair
of woolen slacks, and her face was beaded with sweat. How someone
who paid no attention to what she put on in the morning had so
effectively transformed Ryan's wardrobe was a mystery.

Her effort at going clean was a noble one, but the office was so
magnificently disorganized, it would probably take weeks to set
things right and throw out all the phony letters and bad tickets and
falsified hotel vouchers. After ten minutes of pushing papers, she sat
down on the edge of her desk and lit a cigarette. She tossed back her
long hair and pulled her feet under her.

"I almost stopped by your house on Friday night," I said. "I
happened to be in the neighborhood around midnight."

"Midnight? You should have come in," she said. "I had an all-night poker game. You can count poker as one of your brother's previously undiscovered talents. He won a hundred and forty dollars. I won five hundred and seventeen. Not one of my better nights."

"What time did the game break up?"

"Early morning. Ryan had to rush out to pick up Stacy. We went out to Watertown, and I took him to see your new house."

"I don't own it yet. Did he say anything about it?"

She shrugged. "He liked it. But he didn't make any rash comments. Too sane. Too sane to get involved, Patrick." She rummaged through her huge straw bag and passed me a strip of pictures. "Kind of cute, if you don't look at me," she said.

There were four pictures of Sharon, Ryan, and Stacy. The three of them were squeezed into a tiny photo booth, laughing and jockeying for position in front of the lens. Only in the final frame was there any sense of order. There, Stacy was sitting on Sharon's lap and Ryan had his arm around Sharon's shoulder. The three had calmed down considerably but were still smiling. Sharon was staring into the camera, her piercing, pretty eyes defiant. But it was Ryan who seemed to dominate the photo, with his broad grin and outstretched arms.

I got up to hand her the photos and instead found myself embracing her.

"Watch out for the cigarette," she said. "What's all this about?"

"Nothing," I told her. "I just like the picture, that's all."

Thirty-one

I'd been fairly certain Arthur would turn down the invitation to attend my father's birthday dinner, but to make absolutely sure, I told him my mother was cooking. Arthur once ate a meal Rita had cooked in a Crock-Pot and was sick for a week. The rest of us were fine. I think we'd grown used to her culinary eccentricities over the years, the way some pilgrims adapt to drinking water straight out of the Ganges. After she and my father had abandoned their crash diets and Ryan proved himself to be the real cook in the family, my mother became much more interested in kitchen appliances than food. Another insomniac, she stayed up watching television until 3:00 A.M. most nights, calling 800 numbers to buy the specially priced vegetable slicers and dicers, bread-baking machines, hamburger presses, sandwich makers, and the deadly Crock-Pots. The one familial courtesy that was extended without question or fail was never discussing her cooking.

Food poisoning or not, Arthur accepted the invitation and claimed he was looking forward to the occasion. "But why?" I asked. "You can't stand my family."

"I think that's unfair, Patrick. I've always found them amusing."

I wanted to tell him the circus was in town next week if he was so hot for entertainment. I wasn't eager for him to come along because

I knew my family would fall all over him, riddle him with compliments, and thank him for buying me a house.

What worried me was that Arthur knew that, too, and that was why he was insisting on going. Now that the closing on the house was less than two weeks away, he probably figured I needed one final push to get me to the lawyer's office.

That Sunday, Arthur dressed in one of his pin-striped suits and a navy-blue tie with chartreuse pigs printed on it. Beatrice had given it to him to replace the one the cleaner had ruined. The frivolous tie was definitely not his style, but in a strange way, it looked just right on him and drew attention, not to itself, but to the conservative lines of everything else he was wearing, the way a rhinestone earring can sometimes draw attention to a man's most masculine features. He did look imposing in his suit, tall and solid and, with his high forehead and throbbing vein, kind and intelligent, too. It was easy to see why he stood out in the presence of my short family and intimidated my parents and Ryan into fawning servitude.

I was standing in our bedroom, adjusting my collar in front of the mirror, when I caught sight of his reflection. He had the sleeves of his jacket hitched up and was playing with his cuff links. His face was tight with concentration. There was something in his look, in his big ears and his cleft chin and that Thomas Merton ring of hair encircling his head, that brought back a memory of another time in our relationship, when things had been much different and much simpler.

I went to him and patted the shoulders of his jacket and put my arms around him and mumbled something into his chest. He reached up and put his hands around my head. I pressed my body against his, made a grab at his behind, and, too late, realized I was barking up the wrong tree. Panic overtook me, and I tried to apply the brakes. I pretended I'd reached around him to straighten out his belt. But we weren't reading each other's signals. We fell onto the bed in a heap. I attempted to heave his body off mine, but all those hours in the gym hadn't paid off. I might as well have been trying to bench press a thousand pounds. And then my will to resist melted, and instinct, routine, and gravity took over, and it was like sliding downhill to the edge of a cliff. We fumbled with each other's clothes, underclothes, and bodies, and when, a few minutes later, the whole episode came to its inevitable conclusion, I felt as if the wind had been knocked out of me by the impact of desire and disappointment colliding head-on in the no-man's-land of our relationship, where love was a matter of fondness and passion had never existed.

Arthur got up from the bed and removed his shoes and socks. "Well, I feel better," he said and went to take a shower.

I still hadn't wrapped the present I'd bought for my father, so I had to relent and let Arthur drive to the suburbs while I sat in the passenger seat, fumbling with scissors and masking tape and the Sunday *Times*. Arthur had one of his Gilbert and Sullivan patter songs playing loudly, and he was whistling as we crawled along the highway.

"I still think your present is a little tasteless," he told me.

I'd been unable to come up with any ideas for a gift. My father had no hobbies or interests that I knew of, he considered all music noise, and his reading tastes were so broad it was impossible to buy him a book. Inspired by my mother's comment about the cardiologist, I'd wandered into a medical supply store and ended up buying him a pair of hospital pajamas, the kind that tie up the back.

"I'm not saying it's a fun present," I told Arthur, "but one of these days it'll come in handy, just watch."

"It's a hostile gesture, Patrick, considering his health problems."

I pondered this possibility for a moment and decided he was right. "I suppose I *am* angry at him. Sometimes I think he's faking all this sickness."

"How do you fake a kidney stone, sweetheart?"

"Well, I haven't worked all the bugs out of my theory yet."

"No one gives your father credit. I think there's a kind, sweet man hiding somewhere under the surface there." He looked over at me and smiled. He took one hand off the steering wheel cautiously and put it on my knee. "I enjoyed this afternoon," he said. "We should do it more often. Don't you think?"

I'd just finished wrapping the gift, and it looked remarkably ugly, covered in the front page of the newspaper. I kept turning it over in my hands, thinking that if Arthur and I had many more sexcapades like that afternoon's, I'd be the one using the hospital pajamas when I had my nervous breakdown. I probably hesitated too long before saying, obligingly, "Yes, I suppose we should."

My parents' house is a small ranch that was built at the height of the housing boom of the mid-fifties. As far as I can tell from photos, it was always a fairly ugly structure: lots of clashing horizontal and vertical siding panels, little stone walls that serve no purpose at all, wrought-iron decorations to draw attention to its architectural flaws, and, of course, a garage at least as big as the rest of the house. Over the years, my parents had put a new porch on the front, a "mud room" on the side, a porch off the mud room, and a deck off the porch. They'd blasted a hole in the side of the house and installed a massive and elaborately sectioned picture window. They'd cut down every tree in the yard, complaining that the trees attracted birds, and were contemplating having all the grass replaced with macadam. "I hate weeds," my father said. The crowning glory had been having the whole unsightly mess encased in red vinyl siding. The house was in a development of identical houses, each of which had, over the years, been made uglier in its own unique way and then landscaped into a surrealist fantasy.

But critical as I was of the houses, I think I still believed that these were the natural habitat of human beings and that everything else was merely an imitation.

Ryan let us in the front door and stood back, wiping his hands on a white towel he had tucked into his pants. "Look at this Arthur," he said to me. "Here's a man who knows how to dress. What an outfit!"

"See if you can get *him* to work at the store," my mother said, coming in from the kitchen. "He'd be a real asset. Oh, Arthur, that tie is absolutely stunning. Pigs! Tall people can get away with wearing anything. It's not fair. Let me see the label." She flipped up the tie. "Too expensive for our cheap customers. After all these years, it's a shame you haven't been able to influence Patrick's choice of clothes."

"I haven't been trying," Arthur said. He winked at me.

"Leave Patrick alone," Ryan said. "I think he looks great."

I thanked my older brother and returned the compliment. He was wearing an outfit similar to the one Sharon had picked out for him at the used-clothing store. The blue jeans were unripped but equally tight. He'd apparently gone to the expensive barber my mother had mentioned, and inexplicably, the new cut made him look as if he'd grown hair.

"You'd better take off your jacket," my mother said to Arthur. "We have to keep the heat on in here so Jimmy doesn't catch a cold and get carted off to the emergency ward before we serve the cake."

Arthur passed his jacket to Ryan, and my mother began to rhapsodize about the fit of his shirt.

She herself had on one of those fake-Adolfo red wool suits that became popular in the mid-eighties, probably based on the theory that anyone was bound to look better in them than Nancy Reagan did. In this case it was true, and I complimented her, even though she was paler than usual and clearly exhausted.

"I look like hell," she said. "Pardon the expression. Everyone's out in the family room, so we might as well join them."

"Everyone?" I asked as she led us through the kitchen.

"The birthday boy and Loreen."

"I didn't know Loreen was coming."

My mother stopped at the kitchen table and let out a long, weary sigh. "Oh, God. To tell you the truth, I didn't, either." She adjusted her red plastic headband nervously, pushing the stiff hair off her face. "Your father invited her. But let's try to have a nice dinner, shall we?"

"It certainly smells good," Arthur said.

Rita reached way up and patted his face gently. "Poor Arthur," she sighed, and then looked toward me.

The family room was a cramped box at the back of the house, with two small windows and a surprisingly low ceiling recently redone in swirled and sparkling plaster. The walls were covered with gruesome chocolate-colored paneling and the floor had dark-green wall-to-wall carpeting. The decor was "colonial style," which meant, in this case, not too much more than garish red slipcovers imprinted with eagles, and knotty-pine end tables.

To their credit, both my parents hated the look of the room and called it "the tomb" when company wasn't present. But they could never figure out exactly what made it so unattractive and were helpless to correct the problem. They'd always kept the television in the tomb and, as a consequence, had spent most of their married life sitting in the darkest, ugliest, and most claustrophobic room in the house.

My father and Loreen were seated on either end of the sofa, with their eyes glued to the TV set. Over the years, successive television sets had grown in size, and the present screen took up almost an entire wall. Loreen and my father were pressed against the cushions of the sofa as if they were trying to retreat from a stalking beast. My father had the remote control in hand and was zooming through the channels with the sound off. "Leave it up to Tony to have us install the cable," he said. "If it wasn't for Tony, the whole bunch of us would be living in the ice age."

My father never had a good word for Tony until Loreen was within earshot, and then, at a loss, he had to resort to these absurd compliments.

Loreen had on a beige dress with lace sewn primly into the collar, and she looked her most lovely and fragile, although perhaps a little thinner than when she'd come to my office. Her eyes were huge. I bent down to kiss her, and she turned her cheek up with cool detachment. "How are you?" I asked.

She didn't answer or say hello, just smiled vaguely and looked away. This cold shoulder was so uncharacteristic, I didn't realize quite what she'd done until a few minutes later.

My mother made Loreen scoot over so she was practically in my father's lap and then dropped herself onto the far end of the sofa. "You can put that present with the others, on top of the TV, Patrick. You and Arthur shouldn't have bothered."

I threw myself into a reclining lounger across from the sofa. "Happy birthday, Dad," I said.

"Don't take the most comfortable chair in the room," he said. "Arthur, don't let him get away with that. Doesn't Loreen look beautiful tonight? Have you ever seen a more beautiful complexion than this?" He held his fingers under her chin and tried to tilt her face up to the light. Loreen resisted. My father's shirt collar was sagging, his complexion was sallow, and next to him, Loreen did look as glowing and fresh as the face of a model on a box of soap powder.

"Happy birthday, Jim," Arthur said. He sat down in a black rocker with an eagle decal on the back. The chair was so tightly wedged into a corner, it might as well have been nailed to the floor. "You don't look a day older."

"More of Arthur's impeccable manners," Rita said.

My father frowned away the compliment and the insult and turned his attention back to Loreen. "Look at these pearls. They're something, aren't they. Tony gave her these."

"They're not real pearls," Loreen corrected. It was the first thing she'd said since Arthur and I had come in. She articulated each word carefully, and her voice had none of its usual soft apology. I looked over at my mother for explanation, but she was absorbed in drumming her fingers across her knees.

"No one wears real pearls, honey," my father said. "Everything's fake. I read in the paper the other day that some places, the thieves cut your head off with a chain saw to get your jewelry. Right on the street."

"Let's try to talk about something pleasant for a change," my mother said. This was clearly her theme for the evening.

Ryan appeared in the doorway from the kitchen with a tray of carefully arranged crackers and a bright-orange ball of cheese. "Poor Ryan," my mother said, "slaving in the kitchen night and day."

"Ryan's the cook and Tony's the handyman," my father said. "Remember the time Tony paneled the basement, Rita?"

"It's branded into my memory, dear. Right up there with Pearl Harbor and the day we got married. Where are the drinks, Ryan? Loreen's been waiting for the past hour. Thank God there aren't any alcoholics around here, or we'd all have the d.t.'s."

She looked at Loreen and laughed sweetly, as if she'd made a friendly compliment, but Loreen said nothing.

"I thought I'd wait for Patrick and Arthur to show up," said Ryan. "What will you guys have?"

Arthur stood. He looked absurdly, almost impossibly large, hunched over in the tiny room. "We can get our own," he said. "You don't have to wait on us, Ryan."

"Ryan loves to do this," my father said. "Make them one of those things Tony mixed for Loreen last Christmas. Wasn't that good, honey? What was that drink called?"

"The Pink Squirrels?" Ryan asked.

"I don't want a Pink Squirrel," I said. "And neither does Arthur." If I didn't make a stand now, he'd be offering us cream puffs next. "We'll have a couple of beers."

"Coming right up."

"Ryan looks a little different to me," Arthur said. "Has he been losing weight?"

"It's that new girlfriend of his," my father said. He'd turned his attention back to the TV and was flipping channels again.

"I didn't know he had a new girlfriend," Loreen said, the blue lights flickering across her face.

My mother leaned across Loreen and glared at my father. "Do you think we could stick with one channel, Jimmy? The flashing lights are about to give me a seizure. And she isn't a girlfriend, sweetie, she's just a friend of his."

"One he spends every night with," my father said.

Arthur picked up a copy of *Modern Maturity* from a stack by the rocker and began to leaf through it.

"Does anyone else find it a little close in here?" I asked. "Maybe we could open one of the windows."

The airless room had become stifling and seemed to be shrinking besides. If I leaned back in the recliner, my feet would have been resting on Loreen's lap and my head sticking out a window. I loosened my tie, but the suggestion of changing the air was turned down on the grounds that my father shouldn't be subjected to a draft.

"Let's discuss something happy for a change of pace," Rita said.

Newly bold Loreen, however, wasn't so easily put off. She was as heavily made up as she had been at the travel agency, but some of the natural color of her cheeks was seeping through her foundation. She pushed at her big hairdo defiantly, adjusted the fake pearls, and said, "I'd think Ryan's new girlfriend would be a happy thing to discuss. Is she coming to dinner tonight?"

"Let's hope not," my father said.

Loreen inched away from him and turned toward Arthur. "I haven't seen you in ages," she said. "It must be more than a year now. How have you been?"

"He's buying a house," my father said. "Didn't Tony tell you?"

"Tony?" she asked, as if he'd mentioned a stranger. "No, he didn't."

"Well, he is. And Patrick's chipping in for it, too. Everyone's settling down. It's what parents live for, hon. Now Rita and I can . . ."

His voice trailed off into silence.

"We'll have to have you over for dinner," Arthur said. "It's not a mansion, but I'm sure you'd like it. It's right next to a cemetery."

Ryan came in with the drinks and served them around the room. "We went to that cemetery the other day. Beautiful place. I don't much go for walking around on top of dead people, though."

"It's better than having dead people walk around on top of you," Loreen said.

Considering that Ryan lived in the basement, I found the comment a little sharp. Arthur looked over at me and raised his eyebrows. If anyone else had made the connection, they let it pass. Ryan took a seat on the floor by the TV and proposed a toast to my father's health, a proposal that was ignored. An advertisement for a diet milkshake came on the TV, my father cranked up the volume, and we all watched intently.

"Now, Reenie, honey," my father said, "what do you think of those things? From a professional standpoint, I mean. Any good?"

All eyes turned expectantly to Loreen. She shrugged and took a sip of her drink. "I don't know much about it. I think I mentioned to Patrick that I'm getting a little tired of the diet business. I'm planning to apply for a nursing program, possibly physician's assistant."

Arthur had been revived, either by the beer or by the mention of education, and he told Loreen he knew someone who was currently enrolled in a nursing program at Boston University. The two of them began chatting about the merits of various Boston-area schools, while my parents and Ryan and I looked on helplessly, with nothing to contribute. After a time, my father reminded Loreen that she should be looking into programs in Chicago, and my mother hastily suggested we get to the presents.

"Good idea," Ryan said. "I'm dying to see what you think of mine, James."

"Which one's yours, honey?" My father patted Loreen's knee. "I'll save the best for last."

"It's the shirt wrapped in the green foil." She laughed, a little drunkenly, and said, "Aw, shucks, there goes the surprise."

"That's all right, dear; he'll have forgotten by the time he gets to it. Why don't you open that one that looks like a rifle, Jimmy?"

"That's mine," Ryan told Arthur.

My father tore off the wrapping paper and pulled out an ebony walking stick with a brass handle in the shape of a duck's head.

"What a good idea," my mother said. "He needs a cane."

"I wouldn't call it a cane," Ryan said.

"I might not be in the best of health," my father said, "but I'm not so far gone I need a walker, Ryan."

Rita reached under the sofa and pulled out a paper bag. "Here, Jimmy. I meant to wrap it, but between one thing and the other, I didn't get the chance."

He opened the bag and took out a small plastic tub with a lid. "What is it?" he asked.

"It's for your pills!" Rita said. "You can keep them all organized in this. I got it at that health food store downtown. How that place stays open is beyond me. And talk about filthy! Everything in big dirty bins. I scrubbed my hands as soon as I got back to the store. You can arrange it any way you want. You can put a different pill in each section or all the pills for one day in each section."

"Patrick, yours must be the one wrapped in newspaper," my father said.

I tried to answer, but I was having trouble breathing. I could have sworn the walls were beginning to close in.

"Aren't those adorable," Rita said as my father unwrapped the pajamas. "Those are like the ones you wore when you had the gallstones out, Jimmy. You must have picked them, Arthur."

"Patrick got them on his own."

My father had the presents stacked up on the floor by his feet. "Where's the IV drip and the headstone?" he asked.

"I thought we were going to have a nice time tonight," my mother said. "Let's not ruin it."

Loreen's present was wrapped in shiny green paper with a gold felt ribbon tied around it. My father held up the package for inspection. "Isn't this beautiful? Look at this wrapping job. I hope Tony paid for half of it," my father said.

"No, he didn't," Loreen said.

My father was unwrapping the present as if he'd been trained by a bomb squad. When he finally opened the box, he held it out at arms' length, awestruck. "Oh, my God, will you look at that. That is really beautiful. Look at that, will you? Of course, it'll probably look like hell on me. Everything does. A shirt like this shirt needs someone with broad shoulders to fill it out, someone like Tony."

"Does he have broad shoulders?" Loreen asked. "It's been so long since I've seen him, I can't really remember."

"How long has it been?" Ryan asked innocently.

"Ryan," my mother said, "let's try to focus on the positive."

"That again," my father said. "You should have given out sedatives at the door."

Loreen wiped at the front of her dress as if she'd spilled her drink on it and began to laugh. "You could have put them in the pill container," she said. She threw her head back and let out a highpitched shriek of laughter. My mother joined in in the false way of someone laughing at a joke she doesn't understand.

Arthur had his hands clamped on the arms of his chair, trying to get the rocker to rock. My mother's accompaniment to Loreen's hysterics gradually faded, and she looked over at my father. He shrugged and turned on the TV volume once again. Ryan lifted himself up from the floor and announced dinner in ten minutes, and I hastily followed him into the kitchen.

"Should we offer her a drink of water?" I asked.

He held a finger to his lips to silence me and listened. "I think she's calming down," he said quietly. "What brought that on?"

"She knows something's up."

"The poor kid. Hey, Pat, are you all right?"

I was hanging on the edge of the counter, trying to establish normal breathing after nearly passing out in the tomb. "I'll be fine in a minute. What happened to the oxygen out there?"

Ryan handed me a can of beer. He went to the oven and lifted out a roasting pan with three chickens in it. "Look at this," he said proudly. "Perfectly done. I should open up a restaurant. I should get out of that store and open up a nice little restaurant down the Cape someplace. I think I could be happy doing something like that." He stopped and looked at me. "Did you hear that? Did you hear what I just said? I'm beginning to talk like Sharon, aren't I?"

"Speaking of Sharon . . ."

"Let's speak of Sharon, Pat. She's my favorite topic of conversation these days. You know, introducing the two of us was one of the best things you ever did for me. Did I thank you for that?"

"It has nothing to do with me. I think you've been a good influence on her. She's mending her ways at the office."

He looked up from the chickens, beaming. "You think so? She says she's going to stop cheating and risking her neck for those clients. She says I convinced her, but the funny thing is, I didn't really say anything to her."

He took the dripping chickens out of the pan and placed them on a blue-and-white platter and started to arrange orange slices and watercress around them in a floral pattern. "Have you talked with her today?" he asked.

"No. I expected her to be here."

He was grinning. Very quietly, he closed the door to the tomb. I had an insane, fleeting notion he was going to tell me he and Sharon were getting married.

He told me that at Sharon's suggestion, he'd contacted his old boss at New Balance and, after getting his fancy haircut, had gone in to talk with him about the possibility of being rehired. He was so pleased with himself as he reported this, he practically dumped the chickens on the floor. Nothing was settled yet, but he was feeling hopeful. "And that's only the beginning, Pat." He was done with the orange slices and was arranging a ring of roasted potatoes around the edge of the blue platter, looking very much as if he were going to burst from excitement. "I called Elaine last night," he finally said.

"Elaine?"

"I had a calm conversation with her for the first time in years. We're going to get together next week and talk."

"What do you mean, talk? Don't you talk every time you pick up Stacy?"

"Sure. 'Hi, how are you?' That kind of thing. But next week the two of us are going out to a nice restaurant to have a rational conversation. I've got a lot to get off my chest. It's what you suggested back in March." He tilted the finished platter toward me and swept his hand over his work. "Almost looks good enough to eat, doesn't it?"

"But what about Sharon?" I asked.

"I'm telling you, Patrick, if it hadn't been for her, I wouldn't have even dared suggest it. She was delighted. And you know what? I think Elaine sounded happy about it, too. Well, almost happy. We'll wait and see."

Ryan was grinning, pleased with himself, pleased with his chicken, his potatoes, Sharon, and even me. I tried to work up some anger toward him, but there was a look of such innocent happiness on his face, I couldn't. It wasn't in his nature to hurt anyone. He probably believed Sharon was delighted with the news. I congratulated him and helped him carry the plates of perfectly presented food into the dining room.

Loreen was immeasurably calmer after her fit of hilarity. The half-bottle of wine she finished off might have helped. She and Arthur continued their discussion of graduate schools, and it was clear from the way Arthur was looking at me across the table that Loreen was impressively informed and displaying a good deal more intelligence than he'd given her credit for.

But if anyone had had any doubts about Loreen's intelligence, they were dispelled shortly after Ryan brought the cake in from the kitchen, with seven candles glowing. All the lights were off in the dining room, and Loreen and Arthur made a discordant attempt at singing "Happy Birthday." When no one had joined in by the second line, their voices faded to mumbles.

Ryan set the cake in front of my father. "Make a wish, James, and blow out the candles."

"With my emphysema, that's the last thing I need. You do it, Reenie, honey. Make a wish that you get all the presents you want at the shower. It won't be long now."

Loreen laughed and lifted her glass. "Didn't I tell you?" she asked. "I guess I must have forgotten. I've decided to postpone the shower."

Arthur turned to me, without expression.

"Postpone?" my father asked.

"Yeah, delay, put off. Postpone."

My father looked over to my mother, but she was staring off into space blankly.

"It's an inconvenient time for a couple of my girlfriends," Loreen said, "so I thought we might just put it off for a bit. And, you know, I'm waiting to hear from Tony."

Then she leaned across the table and blew out the candles in a single breath.

Part
6

Thirty-two

"I'm not going to hound you about this, Patrick, but please don't get sympathetic. No sympathy and no anger on my behalf. I'd be a lot happier if you told me I'd been a fool all along and left it at that."

Sharon and I were in the alley behind the travel agency, picking through a barrel of trash. Over the weekend, Sharon had spent hours cleaning out her files and had inadvertently thrown away a ticket to Brazil she'd written months earlier and at a significantly reduced fare. If she issued another one now, or applied for a lost-ticket refund, the airline would very probably catch on to what she'd done. So far we hadn't turned up anything promising, although we'd gone through most of the barrels already.

I'd told Sharon, as soon as I got into the office that morning, that Ryan had informed me about his intended meeting with Elaine. She'd immediately dragged me out into the alley. Even though I was brimming over with sympathy, I knew better than to offer my condolences.

"I hope you don't mind if I at least say I'm surprised," I said now. "It doesn't seem like the kind of thing Ryan would do."

"What? Go back to his wife?" She pulled an envelope out of a trash bag and looked at it hopefully. "That's exactly the kind of thing Ryan would do. I guess I was just too stupid to see it coming. I underestimated his craving for predictability. That's the problem with getting tangled in a relationship. If that's what it was. Or falling in love, for that matter. Not that I did. You can never tell what's going on in the other fool's head."

She took her Luckies out of the pocket of her skirt, shook one out for herself, and passed the pack to me. I declined the offer. "Oh, go on, Patrick. I know you steal them from me sometimes. You don't believe I'd think less of you for smoking, do you? Or for trying to keep it secret. You'd be amazed at how many secret vices I have."

She lit my cigarette and sat on a milk crate, with her feet up on a pile of newspapers.

"What I meant about Ryan," I said, "is I'm surprised he spent so much time with you if he had her in the back of his mind all along."

"You can't even blame him for that. We never did sleep together, you know. We played poker, watched TV. We got cuddly on the sofa a few times. A couple of hugs and kisses. Not exactly the kind of thing I'm used to. My approach is usually more direct. I must be getting old. I made the mistake of letting him take the initiative. Look, Patrick, I'm not stupid, you know. It isn't as if I had any illusions about your brother, but I did think something was going on between us. I suppose he thought we were just good friends. So there's the problem. I was living in one fantasy, and he was living in another. The only time love works is when two people are deceiving themselves in the exact same way."

"We still don't know what Elaine is going to say."

"Irrelevant. Getting Ryan on the rebound was one thing, but I have to draw a line somewhere."

She had a coughing fit, looked at her cigarette with disgust, and threw it to the ground. I was beginning to get pleasantly dizzy from mine, a feeling intensified by the early-morning humidity and the stench of trash from all the barrels heaped up around us. "We're never going to find that ticket," I said.

"You see what happens? You try to change your life, and you end up in an alley, fighting the rats for the last remaining shreds of your old self. Believe me, I'll find the ticket."

"What if you created a monster," I said, "and Ryan turns out to be a pig like Tony and me after all?"

"Ryan's not a pig, and neither are you. I'll withhold judgment on Tony. I just hate being everyone's best friend. Christ, with my luck, they'll do me the honor of naming me godmother of their next kid. There's a depressing thought." She wrapped her arms around her waist and shuddered. "You know, I'm not such a fool, Patrick. It's just that I enjoyed spending time with him. Who'd have guessed he'd be one of the few men I've met who didn't want to be mothered by me. Then again, it probably wouldn't have worked out in bed."

"No," I said, "probably not."

"What are you talking about? Ryan's a sensualist. And believe me, there's nothing better than a sensualist who's been locked up in a basement for three years. A volcano waiting to erupt."

Of all the possible ways I could think of to describe Ryan, sexual volcano was not one. However, I usually trusted Sharon's instincts. She leaned over her legs and clasped her hands under her knees. Her hair fell over her shoulders and around her face. She looked like a little girl not chosen for a softball team, alone in a corner of the playground.

"The worst of it is that all my friends will shower me with sympathy even though they'll secretly be thrilled." She pushed herself to her feet, kicked over the milk crate she'd been sitting on, and began to poke through another trash barrel. "They're all in some kind of relationship, and there isn't a happy couple among them. But they come and visit me and we sit around and talk and they look at the big empty house and as they're driving home beside the person they've committed their life to and would like to have assassinated, they think: Well, at least I've got *some*one. I'm the perfect friend, Patrick. I talk and act like I'm on top of the world, so you don't have to take care of me, but one look at me and you get to feel superior. Don't think I don't know it. Am I making you uncomfortable?"

"Just a little. Maybe it's the cigarette. What about Roberta—is she onto any of this?"

"Oh, sure. Somehow or other she figured it all out. She told me I was lucky it didn't work out. I got so pissed off I told her she had to move."

"There's a positive step."

"We'll see if she actually goes or not. What about you? Have you started packing yet?"

I looked over at her mournfully but didn't say a word.

The closing was less than a week away, and Arthur had stacked the living room with boxes and packing materials. I found the sight so depressing, I avoided that end of the house altogether. The most I'd been able to do was fold a couple of shirts.

I'd pretty much given up on sleep. After the birthday dinner, I'd gone out on my bike around 2:00 A.M. and spent much of the rest of the night riding along the river in the cool dark, down past MIT to the Museum of Science, across the bridge into Boston, along the shadowy Esplanade, and out to Watertown and Newton. I was beginning to find the late-night hours more appealing than the day, cooler and softer and free from the deadly glare of the sun.

Loreen's announcement had shaken me. I realized that for months I'd been languishing in fantasies of ways to help Tony disentangle himself from his engagement, while he was taking no action at all. Then, from the least expected quarter, he'd been saved. He was getting out of the marriage and could look forward to a happy lifetime of servitude to Vivian.

Now that his problem was solved, I saw much more clearly that by spending so much energy thinking about my brother's dilemma, I'd missed the chance to resolve my own, and I was stuck.

When, after an hour of picking through the trash, I found the discarded ticket to Brazil, I was tempted to stick it in my back pocket and use it myself.

Thirty-three

Compared with most of my other troubles, my problems at Only Connect were so specific and concrete, I found them almost comforting. I still hadn't heard a word from the airline sales representative about Professor Fields's reservations, but I did manage to find zoologist and niece a suitable room at an outrageously expensive hotel right on the beach. The fact that it wasn't the hotel we'd been discussing for months was irrelevant. Most of the hotels in Bermuda are so similar in appearance and in name—Pink Sands Beach Club, Beach Club of Pink Sands, Pink Club at Sandy Beach, Sandy Club at Pink Beach—he wouldn't know the difference. There was some comfort in knowing, too, that the date of his departure would arrive, he'd go out to the airport and get on the plane or be turned away, and that would be the end of that—with the possible complication that he might try to have me fired if he didn't get on.

For a solid week, Fields had been calling me several times a day, obviously in a last-minute panic. I'd told Fredrick to inform him I was in meetings, no matter when or how many times he phoned.

"But he sounds frantic," he told me. "And believe me, I know what it's like to be frantic. He's even started speaking in a normal tone of voice."

"That *is* bad news. I'll get to him next week, I promise."

Ordinarily I would have gone into conference with Sharon about a final-hour solution, but she had worries of her own.

On the Tuesday after the birthday dinner, just four days away from Fields's departure date, I broke down and called Gary Bolton to try and pressure him to clear two seats. It was early in the morning—one of the nastiest side effects of my recent bout of severe insomnia was that I'd begun to show up at the office on time—and he was eating, as he had been last time we spoke. Grape-Nuts, from the sound of it. I thought there was something particularly disturbing about the fact that Gary seemed to eat only crunchy food, as if he were used to gnawing bones and chewing glass.

"I've been feeling a little out of touch lately," I told him, "and I thought I'd just check in and see how things are going. I was afraid you'd forgotten me."

"Not very likely," he said blandly. "You redheads are a rare bunch." Then he started choking on whatever it was he was eating. "Tell me this," he said between coughs. "What would you give me for a couple of seats to Bermuda on Memorial Day weekend?"

"Whatever money can buy."

"Not the answer I was hoping for, but I suppose everything has its price." He posed a few more leering questions, none of which I responded to. "You're no fun, Patrick. Cute kid, but no fun at all. I might as well tell you anyway. I got your friends their seats on that plane. I'd hate to tell you what I had to do to get them, but I'd love to demonstrate sometime."

Since rolling out of bed that morning, I'd had a headache, a low-grade crusher that was making a joke of my already laughable mental acuity—but at the sound of his words it dispersed, the way a heat wave can vanish in a matter of seconds with a blast of blessed Canadian air. Why, I wondered, had I been so critical of a man as kind and generous as good old Gary? I really was much too hard on people, and sooner or later I was going to have to do something about it. I thanked him so profusely, I was afraid I'd start hyperventilating. We chatted a few more minutes, going over old times, and I accepted a dinner invitation for two weeks thence. I'd wait until Fields was back from Bermuda, then call Gary and tell him I'd been hit by another bus.

Excited by the news, I was tempted to go against order, throw Fields's caution to the winds, and call his office. Instead I ran in and told Sharon my good news. She was combing her hair by the window, surrounded by a cloud of murky sunlight and cigarette smoke.

"I told you something would work out," she said. "Something always works out in this business. The travel industry is too insignificant for real tragedy. Although I suppose it's still possible the plane could crash at takeoff, the most fitting end."

When I got home from work that night, Arthur was knee-deep in crumpled newspapers, bubble wrap, and empty cartons. I fell onto the sofa, panic-stricken by the sight of him. A few days earlier, I'd told him the closing date of the house was inconvenient and asked if we could have it postponed.

"This isn't a wedding shower," he'd said, and I quickly dropped the subject.

I told him I'd solved one of my biggest problems at work that day. "And right at the last possible second," I said, "just the way I like it. It makes me feel so hopeful."

He was wrapping a lamp in layers of newspapers. "Hopeful about what?" he asked.

I thought about it for a minute and realized that what I meant was hopeful that something would happen to stall or cancel the purchase of the house. But he was sitting on the floor in front of me with his head bent down, and the overhead light was bouncing off his bald pate, and I couldn't bring myself to mention it.

"Perhaps you should try solving some of your problems at home," Arthur suggested. "I don't know how you think you're going to get all your packing done in time." He looked up at me and smiled. "You won't believe how much better you'll feel once it's done, sweetheart. Trust me."

Thirty-four

I waited for Fields to call again, but he stubbornly refused. Two days later, he showed up at Only Connect in person, and I welcomed him into my office with such a firm handshake and sincere grin that he shrank back from me as if I were about to rip off his clothes and knock him to the floor.

"I'm sorry I've missed so many of your calls," I said, offering him a seat. "This office has been a lunatic asylum. The receptionist had a nervous breakdown, and messages haven't been getting through. Harvard grad, high-strung, what can you do?"

He had on a dark tweed sport coat, with suede patches on the elbows, and a pair of baggy khaki pants. A good dry cleaner would have done cartwheels at the sight of his outfit. Whatever the drawbacks of lifelong tenure, you can't accuse the system of encouraging vanity. But there was something endearingly eccentric in his disheveled appearance, now that I looked at it in a certain light. It wasn't entirely out of the question that Zayna might have some real feelings for him.

I told him I hoped he and his niece were all packed and ready to go. "Tomorrow's the big day," I said.

He stared at my cheerfulness suspiciously. "Hot in here," he mumbled and took off his jacket. There was a grease stain in the shape of Cape Cod near the collar of his shirt, and a pen had leaked green ink all over the pocket. He loosened his tie and crossed his bony legs at the knees.

"Everything," I practically shouted, "is ready: the plane, the hotel. All in order and waiting for you. A good feeling, isn't it?"

He looked confused. "Wasn't this confirmed months ago?"

"Certainly," I said. "But I always get excited when someone's trip is coming up. Vicarious pleasure, one of the real advantages of this job. All the excitement of travel without having to leave your pets and your houseplants behind."

"I'm happy to hear someone likes his job," he said. "I do hope I'm not about to cause too many problems for you, Patrick." He tilted his head up and scratched his beard. I realized then, with some concern, that his voice had been perfectly audible since he walked into the office.

"A change in plans?"

"I'm afraid so. Zayna, as it turns out, won't be able to go to Bermuda with me. Something came up in her family. I'm afraid I'll have to cancel the whole trip. I know how much work you've done on this, Patrick, and I'm sorry you've gone to all this trouble for . . . I suppose the word is 'nothing.' "

I felt as if I'd sprung a leak and all my high spirits were hissing out. "It's no trouble at all. Cancellations are the easiest part of my job."

"I'm sorry to be telling you this at the eleventh hour, but I myself only found out last week. I have been trying to get in touch with you. Quite a shock to all of us, frankly."

"Kids," I said. "What can you do?"

He looked up at me with a hurt expression, and I regretted the comment. He had the unmistakable long face and sagging jowls of a man who's been dismissed by a lover. No matter what a person's age, his facial muscles go temporarily slack upon being dumped by a significant—or even insignificant—other. But what had he meant by "a shock to all of us"? Who was the us? Zayna had fallen for her Russian professor, or the man who sold jewelry outside the entrance to the subway, or maybe her roommate; her parents had found out about the affair and were forcing her to press sexual harassment charges; Fields had given her his American Express card and she'd run up a ten-thousand-dollar bill at The Gap and threatened black-mail if he made her return all those T-shirts.

"I don't know if it's appropriate to offer some sort of compensation for your time and effort," he said, "but if there's a standard fee, I hope you'll send a bill." He paused. "To my office."

Mrs. Fields was obviously still in the dark.

"Don't worry about it," I said. "This goes with the territory." The territory was my kind of job and his kind of love affair. I had his folder on top of my desk, and I leafed through the careful notes I'd made on the trip: dates the plane reservations had been accidentally canceled, desperate calls to Gary Bolton, fax messages to hotels in Bermuda. Stapled to the very back of the folder was a slip from the inn I'd reserved for the weekend trip with his wife. "Will you still be using your other reservations?" I asked.

"Other reservations?"

"At the inn? Outside Boston? With Mrs. Fields?"

"Oh, those," he said. "No, I don't think we'll bother with that trip, either. More trouble for you, I'm afraid. I don't suppose it's possible to get back my deposit?"

Since I'd forgotten to call in his credit card number in the first place, the deposit was hardly an issue. "Their policy is to keep the money, but I might be able to pull a few strings. I can't guarantee, but I suspect we'll work something out."

He stood up slowly and put on his jacket. "It's been a pleasure doing business with you," he said. "Perhaps sometime in the future I'll be making more definite plans."

He stuck out his hand, and I shook it, reminded of the last time I'd gone fishing and had pulled a cold, squirming mackerel off the end of the line.

I wanted to make a gesture toward him, offer some condolence, tell him he was probably better off without his undergrad girlfriend. I held on to his hand for a second longer than custom allowed, and he slid it from my grasp. Pretend you're on the Donahue show, I wanted to tell him. Pretend you're telling millions of people how you've triumphed over this compulsion to seduce your students, how much better you feel now than you have in months. Don't forget how much you love your wife, the strength of your marriage all these years. And then there's your best-selling self-help book, *Coed Codependence.*

But there was nothing I could say. He knew I didn't believe the niece story, but I was locked into it, one of the pitfalls of making a commitment to a lie.

The frayed sleeves of his jacket didn't quite cover his hairy wrists.

He gave them a little tug and slumped out. I looked at the folder on my desk, struck by the sudden silence of the office and the faint smell of pipe tobacco he'd left behind. I'd been unfair to him all along. He'd come in for the first time on a Friday afternoon when I was trying to get out to catch an early shuttle to New York to see Jeffrey. He'd begun to grate on my nerves as soon as I found out what he was up to, which, given what I myself was up to, should have made us great pals. If I'd been able to predict this tragic ending, I'd happily have booked everything and on time.

I should have called Gary Bolton to cancel the reservations, but I couldn't bring myself to do it. Maybe Zayna would have a change of heart at the last minute.

Thirty-five

It's often happened to me that in a series of depressing and disorienting situations, the one of least significance hits the hardest. And so I fell into a stupor from which I couldn't seem to rouse myself, as if the breakup of Fields's relationship with Zayna and the cancellation of his trip was likely to undermine the shaky foundation of my life. For much of the rest of the day, I remained inert, staring at green lights on my computer screen and paying no attention to the buzzing of my intercom.

Sharon wasn't in much better shape. Ryan had had his dinner with Elaine the night before, and Sharon was at a dead halt, pulled on one side by her desire to call him and find out how it had gone and on the other by her determination to write him off altogether. She and I arranged to spend the evening watching television at her house. She intended to work late but promised she'd show up before nine.

Cambridge was in full spring bloom now, fragrant with dying lilacs and wisteria and mock-orange blossoms. As I left the travel agency that day, the air was sweet and mild, and the windows of the office building across the alley were glowing in the afternoon light. I biked along the one-way streets behind Harvard Square, trying to absorb some of the brilliance of the sunset, letting the breeze blow my hair back. This was the way spring used to be, I thought, and then realized that, at least for today, this was the way spring was. Of course Sharon wasn't even remotely sentimental about flowers, but something in the fragrance of the air made me want to buy her a bouquet. I turned onto Mass Ave and headed for the florist shop near my gym.

The sign announcing 15 Days Left was still taped to the window of the place. Two months had passed since I'd first seen it that rainy morning I was heading to New York, and time had disarmed its ominous message. I cupped my hands against the glass and peered through the pane. The owner was behind the counter, smoking and taking snips at a bonsai with pruning shears. He shook his head to indicate he was closed, and I waved back, pretending I didn't understand. He opened the door, flicked his cigarette butt across the sidewalk and into the gutter. "I'm closed," he said.

"I wanted a bunch of irises," I said. It's amazing how effective feigned stupidity can be at the right moments, and how effective genuine stupidity is all the time.

"Right, but I just closed up shop. Maybe you heard me say that?"

He started to head back into the shop, and curiosity got the best of me. "I've been wondering about this sign for a while now," I said.

He folded his arms across his chest and leaned into the doorway, his weight on one foot. "Which sign?"

"The one that says 'Fifteen Days Left.' Fifteen days until what?"

He shrugged. "Whatever you want. I put it up for a sale I had six months ago and forgot about it. Then I figured it's always fifteen days from something, right? Somebody's birthday, anniversary, funeral."

"I thought you were predicting the end of the world."

"That'd be convenient, given my financial situation." He had very round eyes, too blue not to be contact lenses but attractive even so. "Nice bike," he said, nodding toward my rusting three-speed.

I could tell from the condescending tone in his voice that he wanted to think I was younger than I am. He himself was probably in his mid-forties. He had the lined face of a man who's spent too much time sitting in the sun at Key West and Provincetown, and he was going gray around the temples. There was something in his Marlboro Man look that was a little overdone—considering the weather and his job, he didn't really need the flannel shirt and the cowboy boots—but I liked the way he had his arms folded and his

head tilted back. He obviously thought I was so desperate for attention I'd be flattered by the insult to my bicycle, and I was disappointed to realize I was.

"It's not pretty," I said, slapping the handlebars, "but it works."

"I'll bet. What's your name?"

Kyle, I told him.

"Harvard student?" he asked.

I nodded. For reasons I've never understood, the words Harvard
University are the most powerful aphrodisiac in Cambridge. "Soph-
omore," I said, and then, realizing the best fantasies have at least a
shred of credibility, amended it to "Graduate student."

He told me he thought he had some irises in the back of the shop.
"Lock your bike up," he said, "and come in."

"Crumbs," I heard my brother saying as I followed the florist
into his back room. He sprawled out on a beaten-down sofa and
kicked off his boots. "Table scraps and crumbs, Patrick."

I left the store half an hour later, without the irises, and by the
time I'd biked to Sharon's house, I couldn't quite remember what the
florist's face had looked like.

Sharon had a policy against locking her doors. Locks were a
complete waste of time and effort, she theorized. She didn't want to
burden herself with carrying around a ring of keys and worrying
about whether or not she'd secured the doors. Half the time, she
claimed, she'd probably lock herself out. Her house was designed for
breaking and entering, with a huge number of windows surrounded
by trees, hatches into the basement, and trellises to climb to the roof.
The idea that bolting a couple of doors would prevent anyone from
getting in was laughable to her. "Do you think they'd try to get in the
front door?" she'd ask. When we were housemates, I'd found the
open-door policy a bit unnerving, but liberating. She'd stuck by her
rule for ten years and, perhaps through luck or perhaps through the
sheer weight of her determination, never had a problem.

Her yard was spectacularly overgrown now. All the trees were in
full leaf, and from the street, a good portion of the house was hidden
by the foliage. I locked my bike to her fence and made my way down
the leafy path to the side door. The forsythia bushes had finished
flowering already and were a mad tangle of green branches, spilling
out over the walk. The flowers on the lilac bushes beside the door

were nearly dead, although they still exuded a faint, sweet perfume as I brushed past.

I went in the back door to a tiny entry hall, a monument to Sharon's good intentions; there were stacks of bundled newspapers, dozens of bags of returnable bottles, cartons filled with plastic yogurt and cottage cheese containers. It was all prepared for the recycling center, but the effort would ultimately fail. There was too much piled up; soon Sharon would be overwhelmed and, in a fit of impatience, drag it to the sidewalk for the garbage collector. I called out to see if Roberta was at home, but there was no answer. The sunlight that filtered through the shade of the trees was fading quickly. I love the melancholy of deserted houses and empty, unfurnished rooms. I climbed the staircase to the second floor, checking out the repair job Ryan had done on the balusters and the plaster. It was an improvement but still unfinished, and the way things stood now, it probably never would be finished.

I pushed open the door to Sharon's room, a disaster area: sweaters and papers and money and jewelry scattered about, the bureau drawers all oozing clothes, an ironing board set up in one corner, an ancient TV in the other. The only bit of decorative furnishing that hadn't been buried under the mess was a tiny lamp on the table beside her bed. The base was cut glass, and the shade was a dainty skirt of stiff lace. Clearly it was from an earlier stage of her life, and it looked so incongruous, it was almost comical.

I climbed the narrow staircase to the top floor and entered the room in the turret where I'd lived when Sharon and I were housemates. Now that the trees were in bloom, the windows were all shaded, and the house could have been hidden in some deep woods. No one had lived in the room since I'd moved out, and Sharon had converted it to storage space. There was a stack of mattresses leaning against the wall, a discarded window fan, old Monopoly and Scrabble games, their boxes held together with elastic bands, and a pile of electric blankets and old quilts. I opened a window. A cool breeze blew into the room, stirring the stale air. I took down one of the mattresses and stretched out on it, staring through the window at the tops of the trees.

If I was going to make a drastic break with routine and be honest with myself, I'd have to admit that even though I didn't know the florist's name and he certainly didn't know mine, even though I hadn't really looked at him closely enough to positively identify him

264 • Stephen McCauley

unless he was standing behind his counter dressed in his flannel shirt, I wasn't looking for irises when I followed him into the back room of his shop. I wasn't looking for the cigarettes he offered, either. I wasn't even looking for the twenty minutes' worth of fumbling around we did on the dilapidated sofa behind the refrigerator case. I was looking for someone to drag up to the top floor of a hotel in New York and make passionate love to on a low leather sofa in front of a window with a view of the whole decaying city. I was looking for someone to shake up my plans, disrupt my life, and help me burn all my bridges. I suppose I'd have to admit I was looking for love.

I didn't even end up with irises.

I put my hands behind my head and drifted off.

I woke to the sound of a man singing "Cry Me a River," wildly off key, put the mattress back against the wall, closed the window, and stumbled downstairs.

Ryan was standing at the kitchen counter, unloading boxes of Chinese food from a shopping bag. He looked over at me, and his grin spread out across his face. "I thought that was your bike out front," he said. "Where were you?"

"Upstairs. Meditating."

"Great, great. Not with Roberta, I hope." He laughed uproariously, pleased with his own joke. He had on a pair of khaki pants and a navy-blue cotton sweater, subdued, flattering, and spotless.

"I can't get over your wardrobe," I said. "You look like a new man."

"Yeah, sure. And I'm twenty-one, too."

I slumped down into a chair at the kitchen table. "What are you doing here?"

"I had some news I wanted to tell Sharon. I almost called, but then I thought I'd just drop by and bring some dinner. Great having a friend who doesn't lock her doors, isn't it? I would have bought more food if I knew you'd be here."

There were six large, steaming cartons along the counter, enough food to feed at least five. He folded up the shopping bag and tossed it into the entryway with Sharon's good intentions. "She's never going to have that stuff recycled," he told me. "She'd need a forklift to get it all out of here. She kills me."

"You say that as if she were a stand-up comic. Is that the way you think of her?"

"I meant it as a compliment. Let me get you a beer."

He took a can of his Australian ale out of the refrigerator and sat down at the table across from me. "She's only got one can left," he said, "so we'll have to share it. I should have brought some along. Here, this'll calm you down."

It was after eight, and the sun had set. A chill was settling over the house. Ryan switched on the light over the table, but the dim bulb seemed to make the room darker. "I'm going to come through this house one of these days," he said, "and change every goddamned light bulb. It's like a crypt in here."

"When?"

"When what?"

"When are you going to come in here and change all the light bulbs?"

"One of these days, Pat. Like I just said."

He was looking at me suspiciously, his eyes narrowed. I wanted to lash out at him, slap some sense into his gentle face, but it seemed out of the question. The whole point of introducing him to Sharon had been to snap him out of his depression. If Sharon wasn't blaming him for running back to Elaine, it wasn't my place to do it. We sat in the dark kitchen, passing the beer back and forth, and I held my tongue until the desire to say something wounding had faded.

"So what's the big news?" I asked. "You seem pretty jolly."

"I had dinner with Elaine last night. We resolved a few things, Pat. And if you want to find out what, you'll have to wait until Sharon gets here. But I'm feeling pretty good about it, I'll tell you that much."

"Will she feel pretty good about it?"

"Sharon? I don't see why she wouldn't," he said. "Come in the living room with me. I want to make sure she has the video machine set to tape *Jeopardy*. She pretends she's on top of everything, but half the time she doesn't know what the hell she's doing. All those *Jeopardy* tapes she claims to have are about seventy-five percent static. Did you see the stuff I fixed on the staircase?"

"I saw it," I said. "But what's she supposed to do now?"

"Now? Well, now it's fixed, Pat, so she doesn't have to do anything. That's the whole point."

When Sharon arrived home, she burst into the kitchen shouting about a client she'd just spent two hours with, a "weak sister" she'd agreed to help by thinking up a scheme to get her to Tokyo for under four hundred dollars. As soon as Ryan came in from the living room, she brought her rant to an abrupt halt, dropped her enormous straw bag onto the kitchen table and herself into a chair.

"What are you doing here?" she asked. She reached into her bag and pulled out her cigarettes.

"I came to say hello." He put his hands on her shoulders and started kneading. "From the sounds of it, kiddo, I'd say you didn't stick with your business resolve for long."

"Yeah, well. She was desperate. What can I tell you? Did you bring the food, Patrick?"

"I brought the food," Ryan said. "The uninvited guest always brings the food."

It sounded like a piece of advice from Sharon's rules of order. She pulled a flake of tobacco from her tongue. "I don't suppose you remembered extra hoisin sauce."

"Would I dare show up here without it? See what I've learned from your friend, Pat?"

Invited guest though I was, I was beginning to feel increasingly uncomfortable and was trying to think of some way to tell them I had to leave without making it obvious I meant: so you two can have it out. Sharon had her feet up on a chair, and I was trapped behind the table.

"All right, Ryan," she said, "let's hear the rest of what you learned from Patrick's friend. What happened at this famous dinner last night?"

It wasn't a question so much as a challenge, and Ryan's innocent grin quivered and then expired. He went to the shelf over the counter and took down three ceramic bowls and a handful of chopsticks.

"Maybe we should eat first."

"I'm not the least bit hungry," Sharon said. "I am, however, dying to hear what happened at this dinner with Eileen."

"Elaine." Ryan's voice was as shaky as his smile had been. "If you're so interested, why are you asking like that?"

"Oh, I don't know, Ryan." Sharon had on a wooden bracelet, which she shook to her elbow. She stomped out her cigarette in one of the ceramic bowls. "Maybe I'm just a little bit pissed off, that's all."

"Well, maybe you should tell me why."

"Well, maybe I should just get going," I said. "I have some heavy packing to do tonight, and it's been a long day."

Sharon kept her feet up on the chair and gave me a look that was at once so pleading and so cold, I didn't dare move. Her head was encircled by a cloud of smoke, and in the dim light from the overhead lamp, her exhausted eyes belied the fierceness in her voice. "Maybe, Ryan," she said, "I'm a little bit pissed off because I'm sick and tired of being everyone's goddamned best fucking friend. Best friend and confidante and earth mother and mother superior. I suppose you're going to make me godmother of your next kid, too—is that what you came all the way in here to tell me?"

Ryan was standing at the counter, thoroughly confused. "What kid?"

"Or maybe you were planning to wait a little bit for the next one? Give me a beer, will you?"

"Patrick and I drank the last one. And you don't drink."

"I thought I might take it up. I figured I needed to boost my caloric intake."

"Eileen and I aren't planning to have another baby," Ryan said, "and Elaine and I aren't, either."

"Too bad. I love kids."

"We're getting divorced," he said. "She wants to remarry as soon as it goes through. We worked it all out over dinner last night, very civilized. Good food, too."

"Congratulations," I said. I tried to sound enthusiastic, but the news was hopelessly anticlimactic now.

"Congratulations," Sharon said. "Congratulations to the bride and the groom and the ex-husband." She slapped her palm down on the table. "I'd really like to stay up all night and tell you how sorry I am your wife found another man, but I'm exhausted and I'm going to bed. Call me in a couple of weeks, and maybe I'll be able to offer a little more sympathy. Sorry the evening didn't work out as planned, Patrick."

She pushed her chair back, gathered up her cigarettes, her straw bag, a bottle of spring water, and a roll of paper towels, and headed upstairs.

I expected Ryan to be cowering in a corner, but he was stomping around the kitchen. He washed the bowl Sharon had used as an ashtray, put away the chopsticks, and loaded all the cartons of food back into a shopping bag. "Here, take this," he said, handing me the bag. Then he took out one container and put it into the refrigerator, mumbling something about breakfast.

"If she's tired, she's tired," he said, "but she doesn't have to be so rude about it. Let me give you a ride home, Pat. I don't like the idea of you biking around the city at this hour. As your big brother, I'm supposed to help you use common sense every once in a while. We can load the bike into the trunk."

Before we walked out the front door, Ryan went to the foot of the staircase and called up, "I taped *Jeopardy* for you. It's in the machine and all rewound. Did you hear me?"

There was no answer from above. "Fine," he said. "Good for her," and we left.

Thirty-six

"I don't get it," he said. He was driving through the traffic in Harvard Square, blowing his horn at the inconsiderate pedestrians. "Is there something I'm missing here? I mean, I come in in a good mood, dinner in hand, tape her favorite show . . ."

"I think there's something you're missing here," I said. "Sharon is very fond of you, Ryan."

"If that's any example of her fondness, thank Christ I'm not on her bad side. Which way do we turn now?"

"Just keep taking lefts, and we'll get there." I'd talked him into driving past the yellow house so I could get my nightly glimpse of the place. I wanted to burn an image of the exterior into my brain; that way I'd have a realistic picture of what it looked like once I was trapped inside. "Anyway, the point is, she's very fond of you."

"You just said that."

"Hasn't it crossed your mind that maybe she has a crush on you? You've spent an awful lot of time together these past couple of months."

He pulled up to a red light and braked hard and looked over at me with a pleased, incredulous grin. "A crush? I didn't know we were back in junior high."

"Well, maybe you're not far off. But the point is, you mean

something to her, and you can't expect her to be thrilled when she spends two months making you feel good about yourself so you can go running back to Elaine."

"Patrick, for someone who's known Sharon as long as you have, you really don't know her at all. I've heard about some of the guys she's been with. If there's one thing I'm not, it's her type."

"Of course you're not her type. Maybe you noticed that nothing's worked out with her type. That's why she's so stuck on you. You're a decent person, Ryan. And I happen to know Sharon thinks of you as a sexual volcano."

"Volcano! If I'm a volcano, I give new meaning to the term 'inactive.' "

We'd turned off the main street and were winding our way past the cemetery buildings to the sheltered neighborhood with the yellow house. As we went over the railroad tracks, the beams from the car's headlights bounced into the trees. Ryan was nervously concentrating on the road, but he was smiling.

He pulled over to the side of the street and killed the engine. Every light was on in the house, and I could see the owners scurrying from room to room, obviously packing up for the big move. Arthur had met with them a couple of times, but I knew nothing about them. I had no idea why they were selling the house or where they were moving—they could have been bankrupt, for all I knew—but watching them racing around, taking down pictures and books, I envied them and what I imagined was their upcoming freedom.

"They're tearing the place apart," Ryan said. "You'd better get in there and stop them."

"Don't change the subject," I said. "How do you feel about Sharon anyway?"

"I've only known her about a month and a half. You know as well as I do I like her. She's changed my life, I suppose. All you have to do is look at me to see that."

"But what about romance? Are you telling me you don't have any romantic feelings for her?"

"Patrick, I have romantic feelings for Cybill Shepherd, too. What good does it do me? And you know, I didn't go running back to Elaine, like you accused me of doing. I didn't go out to dinner with her thinking we were going to work everything out. Maybe before I met Sharon, I would have, just because I'd been locked up in that basement for so long I didn't know there was anything else out there for me. But I still had to check things out, talk things over with her.

So maybe secretly I thought she'd fall all over me again, but right when we sat down and started talking, I knew that wasn't what I wanted. It's not as if Sharon gave me a chance to say any of this. She went off like a gun the minute she walked in the door." He lifted his arm and rotated his wrist, trying to catch the light from the street-lamp in his watch. "I can't see a thing. It's bad enough I'm losing my hair, but now my eyesight, too. What time is it anyway?"

I told him it was almost nine-thirty.

"I guess he should be here soon. Poor Tony; I don't envy him."

I reminded him things had worked out for poor Tony. "And what do you mean, he should be here soon?"

"His flight. It's due in sometime around ten."

I looked over at him in the street light. He was still wearing his sweet, kindly expression, a mild, dumbfounded smile on his face. I supposed he was contemplating the volcano issue, but it was hard to tell. Maybe the events of the past two months had driven him mad.

"Tony is coming to Boston?" I asked.

"You didn't know that? I thought you were on to everything, Pat. If it's all right with you, I'd just as soon leave. You're going to be looking at this place for the rest of your life, so I don't see why you have to sit here now."

It took a few more minutes to coax the details out of him. According to his information, my father had called Tony the night of his birthday and spent an hour and a half talking to him. He'd convinced Tony to come east and discuss the wedding with Loreen, and he'd even offered to pay for the ticket. "I don't understand why Tony didn't tell you about this," he said. "Maybe he was embarrassed."

"Where's he staying?" I asked.

"He's staying with your parents. He's renting a car and driving in, and then he and Loreen are meeting tomorrow."

Lack of sleep and nourishment were beginning to have a wonderful hallucinogenic effect on me. I asked Ryan if I could take the wheel for the drive back to my apartment, and as soon as we'd switched seats, I gunned the engine and made a U-turn up over the lawn of the new house, nearly taking a few of the precious bushes.

"Headlights!" Ryan shouted.

I switched them on and put my foot to the floor and we roared down the potholed street and across the railroad tracks.

Ryan grabbed hold of the dashboard. "For Christ's sake, Patrick, slow down, will you? You're going to snap an axle. What's wrong with you?"

"Nothing's wrong with me, kiddo. Just sit back and enjoy the ride. And I'd like you to promise to do something for me, Ryan. A favor."

"Whatever it is, I'll do it, providing I live."

"In about two minutes, you'll be safely driving again. And what I'd like you to do is go back to Sharon's house and go up to her room and have a talk with her. You can just walk right in. One of the advantages of having a friend who doesn't lock her doors."

"Well, of course that's what I'm going to do. Why do you think I wanted to get away from that house back there?"

"And whatever opinion you happen to have about yourself, just remember: in Sharon's eyes, you're a volcano."

Thirty-seven

Although Tony never booked his reservations through my office, we'd discussed air travel enough for me to know he was accruing frequent flier mileage on a particular airline. Furthermore, he'd had a brief but hot and heavy affair with a stewardess within the past year and a half, and he took that airline every chance he got, hoping she might be working on his plane. My knowledge of airline schedules corroborated Ryan's prediction of Tony's arrival time. I had half an hour to get to the airport.

I pulled over at my street, yanked the bike out of Ryan's trunk, tossed it into the backyard, and jumped into my Yugo. There was so much adrenaline pumping through my system, I probably could have run out to the airport a lot quicker, but I didn't want to push my luck.

The night had turned murky and humid, as if the sky were saturated with moisture. As I sped down Memorial Drive, I opened all my windows and cranked up the volume on a heavy-metal radio station. The sky was filled with planes circling the city, locked into holding patterns, suspended above by the strange laws of aerodynamics, enemies of gravity and logic. At any given moment, there are more than a hundred thousand people in airplanes, cutting through the atmosphere miles above the surface of the planet, leaning back in their seats eating peanuts, watching movies, reading magazines, making love. A vast city scattered across the sky. My brother was up there, safely removed from all his troubles, out of reach of my parents, Loreen, and me.

I crossed the river and got onto the highway that wrapped around the city and entered the Callahan Tunnel, all in record time. The yellow and green lights of the tunnel flashed across the dark windshield. There was little traffic, and I pressed the accelerator to the floor, imagining that the damp tiled walls were collapsing behind me and I was escaping disaster by mere seconds.

Three people were in the lounge awaiting the arrival of the flight from Chicago: A tall woman with long, straight brown hair was leaning against a wall, with her arms folded tightly across her chest, and a fat man in a blue windbreaker and a baseball cap was gazing out the window, his back to me. The third person, sitting on the far side of the lounge, staring off into space and tapping the arm of her chair, was my mother. I approached her slowly from behind and put my hand on her shoulder.

She looked up and smiled. "News travels fast, doesn't it, dear? Tony promised your father he wouldn't mention to you that he was coming in tonight."

"Ryan told me."

"Ah, yes, the new and improved Ryan."

"Where's your husband?"

"I suspect he's at home, sleeping. Unless he has some secret life I don't know about, a possibility I wouldn't rule out."

I wasn't as shocked to discover her sitting there in that lounge— even though it had never crossed my mind that she might be there—as I was to see her alone. As far as I knew, she never drove anywhere by herself, and the fact that she'd driven all this way alone and late at night seemed almost heroic, in a twisted sort of way. She had on a navy-blue skirt and a light-blue sweater and a string of pink beads. Her hair was held in place by a purple plastic band that clashed peculiarly with her stiff orange hair. Alone, she looked particularly short and slight, and older, too. She'd put on a thick layer of face powder and bright-red lipstick, and her eyebrows were absurdly dark and heavy. This Kabuki makeup had gone out of style decades earlier, and I realized suddenly, as if it had never occurred to me before, that her life would have been very different if she'd had a daughter.

Her raincoat was folded on the seat beside her; she'd driven out here prepared for anything. She picked it up carefully, set it down in her lap, and motioned for me to sit.

"Do you think she's pretty?" she asked, watching the tall woman leaning against the wall.

The woman was rubbing her upper arms nervously and rocking back and forth on the balls of her feet. She looked troubled, possibly dazed. "She might have been," I said. "She might be again. But something's going on. In her present condition, I'd have to say no, not pretty."

"That's what I'd say. I've been watching her for the past half hour now, and I'd say she was pretty once upon a time. Whoever she's meeting on this plane, she has mixed feelings about him. She has something to reveal. I'd guess she's meeting her husband, who's been away on business for two weeks."

"And she's met someone else in the meantime," I suggested.

"You *would* think that, Patrick. Actually, that's what I thought, too. Although she doesn't look too happy about it. She could be pregnant by this other person. Not bad guesses for someone who never exercises her imagination, are they?"

"Not at all. You should get out more often. When's the plane due?"

"Not for another hour. They said there was fog in Chicago, which probably means the wings fell off." She adjusted the band in her hair and then lightly pushed at the skin around her cheekbones with her fingertips, as if she was trying to tighten it. "Excuse me for saying so, dear, but you don't look well. Were you just running?"

"It's been a long day. Actually, it feels like it's been three long days."

"I suppose the answer is obvious, but do you mind if I ask you what you're doing here?"

Sitting alone with her in the quiet lounge, I felt much less at odds with her. She seemed so small and defenseless, I wished there were something I could do to protect her. I figured the closest I could come would be to tell her the truth, and I did.

"In other words," she said, "you've come to head him off at the pass."

"You could put it that way. And you?"

"Head him off at the pass; what else? I wanted to see him before your father got to him."

She widened her eyes as she said this, as if she was trying to impress me with the significance of her words, but I wasn't sure what she'd meant.

"Oh, Patrick," she sighed. "And I count on you to understand everything." She paused, looked around, and then inclined her head toward me and nearly whispered, "I've come to tell Tony, before he sees your father, that as far as I'm concerned, and I'm only speaking for myself, as if I would dare speak for anyone else, that he should do exactly what he wants to do about this wedding—it's his life. Marry Loreen, don't marry Loreen, marry the lawyer in Chicago, move to Shanghai, join the priesthood. But if he does come right out and ask me for my opinion, I plan to tell him I'd rather walk to Los Angeles barefoot than see him marry someone he doesn't love."

I was dumbfounded by her speech and by the sudden shift in her opinion, and my face must have given it away. "You look like you need a drink," she said. She told me she'd seen a cocktail lounge on the way in and suggested we go there and kill some time. As we walked down the quiet hallway, she took my arm, a warm, conspiratorial gesture that was entirely unlike her.

The cocktail lounge was one of those excruciatingly dark and silent places designed to make nervous fliers feel as if they've entered a bunker where they can store up invulnerability for their flights. The only other customers were two men in business suits slumped over the bar, obviously plastered.

We went to the back and sat on either side of a low metal table with a candle in the middle and a little bowl with four greasy peanuts in it. My mother arranged herself in the chair carefully, as if she was settling in for a long time. She put her raincoat neatly on the empty seat beside her and folded her hands on her lap. She looked weary and stooped. As we'd walked along in the bright lights of the airport terminal, I'd noticed the gray roots of her hair pushing out the orange.

A waitress, emaciated and exhausted, tottered over on high heels. She put napkins in front of us and stood silently beside the table, waiting for our order. She had black rubber bangle bracelets on her right arm, halfway up to her elbow. "I think I'll have a Rob Roy," my mother said, eyeing her critically.

She rarely drank, and I was surprised at the ease with which she'd produced this order.

The waitress looked at me dully. "You?"

"The same," I said, "whatever it is."

"That outfit isn't good for her," my mother said, watching the waitress depart. "A miniskirt with those heels and those toothpick legs is definitely not what she should be wearing. Why do people insist on drawing attention to their worst features? Look at that Sharon—"

"It's probably a uniform," I interrupted. "What she needs is a whole new job."

"Yes, you do," she said.

"Let's not get started, Rita."

She looked away from me. "I didn't say that to be critical. I suppose you took it that way out of habit. That must be partially my fault. I was trying to be helpful."

We watched the waitress standing at the bar, playing with her bracelets and talking to the businessmen. She clicked over to us on her spike heels, the twin drinks sliding on her tray. "One for you," she said condescendingly, "and, let's see, one for you. Anything else, I'll be right over there."

I found the drink pleasantly sweet and strong, and the first sip sent a flush of blood to my face. I pulled my sweater over my head and rolled up the sleeves of my shirt. Rita picked up her glass, the napkin wrapped around the bottom, took a measured swallow, and sighed deeply again.

"You know," I said, "it might not be any of my business, but if you're in the mood to tell me why you changed your mind about Tony, I'd be willing to listen."

"I didn't change my mind. I've thought it was a mistake for him to marry Loreen since I heard about this other girl. Vivian, isn't that it? I just didn't have the courage to say it. You act one way all your life, and it's not so easy to turn things around all of a sudden. Believe me, I was thrilled when she made that announcement about the engagement at dinner the other night. When your father convinced Tony to come out here and talk with her, I figured I had to do something."

She looked over at the two drunks slumped on their barstools. Her eyes were shining from the alcohol. "Patrick," she said quietly, still looking away from me, "I was twenty-one when I married your father, a complete innocent. I didn't know a thing about life or love, any of it, and he knew less. I'm not proud to say we both made a big mistake, but in my heart I know we did. I'm not saying we don't love each other, because I wouldn't say that, even if I thought it was true, which I don't think.

"Anyway, it's a horrible thing to get close to sixty and look behind you and see a mountain of regrets piling up. It's enough to make even me think twice. I saw Tony's marriage as one more I was tossing on the heap, and I thought, admittedly at the last moment, that maybe, for once in my life, I could try to do something I actually might look back at with pride." She finished off her drink and wiped at her mouth delicately. "I could possibly stand another of those."

I called the waitress over and ordered another round of drinks, even though the first had made me bleary. We sat in silence, waiting for her to bring them, and when she did, I foolishly clinked my mother's glass, as if this were a cheerful celebration. I hated listening to her talk about her life like this, partially because I knew there wasn't anything I could do to help. I asked her if she'd ever thought about getting a divorce.

"Oh, only every day of my life," she said. "But I've always thought of it as something I might have done, never as something I might still do. The first time it crossed my mind, it already seemed too late."

The candle was burning down in the amber ball on the table between us. I picked it up and sloshed the melted wax against the sides of the glass. We sat in silence for a long time, listening to the drunks at the bar and to the faint, bland music in the background. Once or twice we passed some comment on the waitress, who'd taken a seat at a table near us and was picking at her fingernail polish.

"You know, maybe I shouldn't bring this up, but I can't keep my big mouth shut," she said. "I was very upset that day you came into the store and made your horrible speech about Tony and Loreen's marriage and how awful life was going to be for them."

"I know you were upset," I said. "I've been meaning to apologize for a long time now."

"It isn't a question of apologizing. It was obvious you weren't talking about the two of them, and it upset me, that's all. I hate thinking that you view your own life that way. Especially since you don't seem to be doing anything to change it."

If I'd been just a bit more drunk, I might have let myself slide off my seat and onto the floor. Since I practically grew up in a confessional booth, I was familiar with the elation that follows being absolved of sin. I was delighted to hear that she'd misinterpreted what I'd said that day in the store. I was so delighted, in fact, that I didn't give much more thought to the way she had interpreted my reckless speech. She had her head tilted over to one side and was unscrewing an earring.

"If you really believe that's what the future holds for you, you ought to do something about it now, while you still have the chance. Take it from one who knows a thing or two about mistakes, Patrick." She took out her earring and dropped it into the glass ashtray in the middle of the table.

Looking over at her as she wearily removed her other earring, I kept thinking about Fields's reservations to Bermuda. I could rewrite the tickets in her name, and she and my father could take them and go off on a second honeymoon tomorrow, make a new beginning for themselves. But as soon as I tried to find the words to suggest it to her, I knew it was a foolish notion and that they could no more do that than get a divorce.

"We should keep an eye on the time," she finally said. "With our luck, we'll probably miss him."

I checked my watch. We'd been sitting at the table for close to an hour, and Tony's flight was about to arrive. I finished off my drink quickly and paid the bill.

By the time we got to the lounge, the two people who'd been standing there earlier were lost in a small, noisy crowd. The plane had landed and was pulling up to the gate, its lights flashing. There must have been a downpour while we sat having cocktails, for the big window in front of us was streaked with rain.

"I guess we just made it," I said.

But Rita stopped walking and gripped my arm.

"What's the matter?" I asked.

"Turn around, Patrick."

"What do you mean, turn around?"

"Trust me: just turn around."

But old habits die hard, and I didn't trust her. I looked into the crowd of people in the waiting lounge and saw Loreen standing by the gate. She was wearing a long raincoat with a belt pinched in tight at her narrow waist; a plastic bonnet covered her big hairdo. "I don't understand," I said. "What's she doing here?"

"I suppose she must be heading him off at the pass," she said, "like the rest of us. She just happened to get here at the right time."

We turned around and left quickly.

Thirty-eight

I didn't realize it then, but much later it occurred to me that I must have been quite drunk by the time my mother and I walked out of the airport. Whatever a Rob Roy is, it packs a fairly solid alcohol-and-sugar punch. I hadn't eaten much of anything that day, and I hadn't slept more than a few hours in close to a week. My judgment was surely clouded, although I may be trying to make excuses for what I did.

Even if I was under the influence, I knew better than to speed and run the risk of being pulled over by a cop. I'd already racked up a couple of moving violations that year, and adding a drunk-driving charge to the offenses would have cost more than I could afford. I suppose spending a couple of weeks in jail would have solved some of my problems, but it wasn't what I had in mind. I drove carefully through the tunnel and then along Storrow Drive on the Boston side of the river. The sky was still full of planes circling overhead, but otherwise the city looked different to me. The buildings seemed less imposing and the lights less dramatic. I scanned the radio for a late-night jazz station but couldn't come up with anything. It was almost midnight, right around the time I'd first heard from Tony, almost three months before.

I didn't know what he was going to say to Loreen when he stepped off the plane, if he'd be shocked to see her or if he'd been the one to tell her to come pick him up. If my mother's suspicions were correct, he'd apologize for having been so distant, complain about his job, maybe confess sorrowfully to a case of the last-minute jitters, and then tell her he loved her and start the ball rolling once again.

It was all out of my hands, and as I cautiously navigated my way home to Cambridge, I wasn't even that interested in finding out what happened.

Back at the airport, I'd taken my mother's keys and walked up to the top floor of the parking garage to get her car for her. She was a good deal more steady on her feet than I was, but I was feeling unusually chivalrous. As I was driving the big, boxy car down the endless series of circular ramps, growing increasingly dizzy, I thought about her words to me back at the cocktail lounge. And it hit me then that she'd been right about what I'd said in the store that day: I hadn't been talking about Loreen and Tony at all, and I hadn't been talking about my parents. I'd been talking about myself, describing my own life and my pessimistic, unhappy fantasies of what the future was likely to hold if I kept on course. By the time I'd reached the ground floor of the garage, aided considerably by power brakes and steering, the past three months had fit together and I knew exactly what it was I had to do.

It was long past one o'clock when I entered the apartment. I was in that odd euphoric state that accompanies fasting, sleep deprivation, and natural disasters. I could have passed out on the floor of the hallway or started to repaint the exterior of the house. Arthur was in bed, snoring after what must have been a fierce night of packing. The boxes in the living room were stacked high, all carefully marked and labeled, taped and tied up with twine. The moving truck would be pulling up in front of the house in five days.

I went into the bedroom and sat on the edge of the king-sized mattress and looked down at Arthur. His face was lit up in the bands of pale light coming in through the blinds from either the moon or the streetlamp. He looked so calm and innocent, I felt miserable for ever having blamed him for any of my own disappointments.

I shifted my weight on the bed. He woke and looked at me through one eye. "Hello, sweetheart," he said thickly.

I bent down and kissed him on his lips. "Hello, sweetheart," I said.

"What time is it?"

"Late," I told him. "I didn't mean to wake you up."

"I'm glad you did. I was worried about you. I was very worried. Then I fell asleep. Where were you?"

"Dentist. You should go back to sleep."

He pulled the sheets around him more tightly and buried his head under a pillow. I curled up next to him, reached out, and pulled his body in toward mine. He made a quiet, contented groan. I wanted to stay like that for a long time, our bodies huddled together comfortably.

"I'm determined to make things better for both of us," I whispered to him.

"They're fine as they are," he mumbled.

"But they're going to be getting better, sweetheart. I'm suddenly turning optimistic."

When I got up to leave the room, he asked me where I was going.

"I have to pack," I told him.

"At this hour?"

"Better late than never."

Before I'd even shut the door behind me, I could hear him snoring softly.

I suppose I really did take the coward's way out, but I've always thought there was something courageous in risking the label of coward, so I was able to rationalize a certain amount of valor into my actions. I should have stayed and talked things over with him, helped him make arrangements, deal with paperwork and plans, but I was afraid that if I did, I'd start to doubt myself once again and go back on my resolve. I was convinced I was doing the right thing, even if I was going about it in the wrong way.

The following morning, long before Arthur was awake, I was sitting in the back seat of a taxi, heading out to Logan once again. I had one small suitcase at my feet, stuffed with a couple of black sport coats and some bathing suits and six tubes of sunscreen. The roads were virtually empty, and the morning was clear and windless. Good flying weather, assuming there was such a thing as good flying weather. I was so sure that what I was doing was the best thing for both of us, I didn't worry even for a moment about the plane bursting into flames at takeoff.

The night before, as I was driving home, I'd stopped in at Only Connect, made a few entries in my computer, erased Professor Fields's name from his ticket, and hastily filled in my own with a thick red pen. I wrote him a check and mailed it to his office, along with a note telling him I was sorry it hadn't worked out with Zayna. "Anyway," I wrote, "you'd hate Bermuda. No animals and too much sun."

As Sharon would have predicted, the gate agent scarcely looked at my ticket when I handed it to him. He wished me a good trip, a nice day, a happy life, and let me pass.

The plane was filled to capacity with happy honeymoon couples dressed in amazingly similar pastel outfits. They were all best friends before we'd reached cruising altitude. In a couple of years they could hold a reunion on a divorce junket to the Dominican Republic. I certainly didn't belong in their midst, but I felt so blessedly invisible, it hardly mattered. After I'd gorged myself on a plate of microwaved eggs and had a couple of glasses of champagne, I fell into a sound sleep and didn't wake up until a steward shook my shoulder and told me we'd landed ten minutes earlier.

If I'd known how much I was going to love Bermuda, I probably would have gone sooner. I spent ten days on the island, sealed in my deluxe room at the Pink Sands Beach Club (or the Sandy Club at Pink Beach or wherever I was), with the drapes drawn and the air conditioning on Ultra Cool. I ordered up books from the gift shop, alcoholic punch from the bar, and two huge meals a day from room service. I made great friends with the housekeeper after assuring her that she didn't need to bother changing my sheets every day. She and I played gin rummy, and she told me the gossip about all the other people staying on my floor, what kind of underwear they'd brought, and what they kept in the drawers of their night tables. When the sun went down, I would put on a sport jacket, move out to the balcony off my room, and sit in the balmy breeze, watching the lights of Hamilton across the harbor. I spent hours watching a closed-circuit television station that broadcast a propaganda loop about the culture, history, and astonishing beauty of Bermuda, and by the time I was ready to fly home, I almost believed I'd seen the island.

When I got back to Cambridge, Arthur had moved. Except for the small room at the back of the house and the Formica-top table in the kitchen, the entire apartment was empty. I looked through all of the deserted rooms to see if he'd left a note or a message of any kind for me, but the place was brilliantly clean, as if a whole crew had come in and scoured out all traces of Arthur's ten-year occupancy.

It must have been something about the sterile cleanliness of the place, with its meticulous finality, that set me off. I went into the back bedroom, curled up on my mattress, and burst into tears. I hadn't cried in such a long time, the novelty of the experience thrilled me. I lay there for well over an hour, trying to think of everything I could to make myself sob louder. When I was finally finished, I had a throbbing headache. I walked out to the empty living room and sat on the floor in a corner, waiting for another weeping spell to strike. But the more I looked around the empty room, the more I liked it. I'd never realized before quite how spacious it was. And without all the dusty antiques and overstuffed chairs, I discovered I was better able to breathe.

Part
...
7

Thirty-nine

$\lbrace$

My younger brother was married on a Saturday in mid-July when record-breaking heat was forecast and the radio was issuing warnings about the potential health hazards of outdoor activities such as jogging, walking, and inhaling. Just another pleasant summer afternoon in the brave new world. Since returning from Bermuda, I'd made a diligent and reasonably successful effort to give up listening to hourly weather reports and keeping an exact count of how many degrees above normal the temperature was at any given moment of the day. But the ferocity of this heat wave had made it to the front page of the newspaper, and I couldn't ignore it altogether. By eleven that morning, when the wedding party and the guests were gathering outside the church, the sky was a blank white dome, and everything under it seemed to be gasping and melting. The grass in front of the church was scorched brown, the trees were drooping, the air was soupy, and the macadam of the parking lot was soft and gummy underfoot.

"Watch yourself," I said as I helped Rita from the passenger seat of her air-conditioned car. "It's deadly out here."

She stepped into the furnace and calmly brushed down the wrinkles of her dress. "Did you think this was going to be a fun day, Patrick?"

"I suppose you'd prefer rain?" my father asked. He stepped out into the staggering heat, adjusted his tie, and looked up into the glare of the sun. "Well, maybe it is a little warm."

He was happily accepting responsibility for the events of the day and was determined to put everything in the best light.

The church itself was not air-conditioned, and despite the ceiling fans whirling on high, the relief from the sun offered by the stained-glass windows, and the slight breeze stirred up by one hundred over-dressed guests fanning themselves with prayer cards, two women grew faint during the service and had to be helped out by the ushers.

It came as a pleasant surprise that one of the stricken was not the mother of the groom. Then again, I suppose Rita must have had a lot more on her mind than the heat. She and my father sat side by side in the pew in front of me, and I heard them whispering to each other throughout the ceremony. He asked her for his eyeglasses, she asked him to repeat something the priest had said, he loudly accused her of making too much noise, and, in a harsh whisper, she claimed that he was disrupting the service.

The parents of the groom had chosen disturbingly similar outfits, light-blue suits and white shirts. My mother's outfit at least had a skirt to distinguish it from my father's, but she was wearing something around her neck that looked a lot like a man's tie. Sitting down, they were the same height, and from my vantage point, they could have been twins, or a crazed brother-and-sister team who'd lived too much of their adult lives under the same roof and blurred the lines of their identities.

I lost most of my consciousness after the first twenty minutes of the mass. The heat and the drone of the priest's voice and some overpowering atmosphere of collective boredom conspired against me. I heard an elderly relative breathing heavily behind me, possibly snoring, and then my brain shut down. It wasn't until Tony and Loreen were officially declared man and wife that I came to again. I saw my mother grab hold of my father's arm, as if to steady herself. Her body began to tremble, and she sobbed so loudly that a disconcerting silence fell over the gathered crowd for what was probably ten seconds but felt like an hour. Loreen's parents were across the center aisle from us, and they glanced over to see who was keening. Mrs. Davis recoiled when she spotted my mother. No one in our family knew exactly how much they did or didn't know about Loreen's bumpy ride to the altar, but neither of the bride's parents was going out of his or her way to be friendly. My father glared at them, put a protective arm around Rita's shoulder, and whispered something into her ear. She gave him a little shove, as if to push him away.

Sharon was sitting beside me, and she leaned over and whispered in my ear, "Look how cute! They're fighting!"

Of course I had no idea what my father had said, but I thought there was something tender and loving in his rejected attempt to console Rita. Maybe he was just feeling he could afford to be generous, since the wedding had turned out as he'd wanted. I hoped he hadn't been so tactless as to make some comment to my mother about their own wedding day.

Despite everything, Loreen did make a beautiful bride, all springy curls and satin skirts and lace sleeves. She was carrying a bouquet of pink and white roses. The flowers were wilting in the heat, making her look all the more lovely by comparison. Somehow or other, she seemed to have shut down her sweat glands for the morning. Perhaps she was wearing too much makeup for the garish, hot sunlight, but when it came to cosmetics, you had to trust Loreen. She knew what she was doing, and she had obviously prepared herself for the photographic record of the wedding, not the wedding itself. Years thence, no matter what happened in the course of her marriage, she'd look like a beauty queen in her photo album.

As man and wife walked down the aisle out of the church, Loreen held on to Tony's arm tightly, as if she'd just brought a sinner to God and was carrying her convert out into the light of day, her head high, her back straight. As she passed by my pew, she nodded and smiled, but it was impossible to tell if it was love or simple victory that was blazing in her eyes.

Tony wasn't faring quite as well. He had the fixed, frozen expression of a man in a mild state of shock. He could easily have been a passenger on a transatlantic flight who realizes, halfway to Paris, that he's left the oven on or the back door unlocked, forgotten to feed the goldfish or pick up the baby at the day care center. He'd lost more weight since I saw him at the hotel in New York, and he looked shriveled and deflated. But Tony was handsome, and the circles around his eyes made him appear hungry and desperately romantic. He had the kind of fierce and haunted face that would be irresistible in the soft light of a hotel cocktail lounge, and thirty years down the road, it would be indistinguishable from my father's.

As the happy couple passed, his eyes were so deep-set and far-away, it seemed possible he'd slipped off into a fantasy world where none of this was happening, where Vivian was holding on to his arm and a two-hundred-pound soprano was singing her deathbed aria before the curtain went down.

I might have known more about what was going through my brother's mind, but we were scarcely speaking to each other anymore. The evening I returned from Bermuda, Tony had made his final midnight call to me. It was early June then, one of those cool, humid nights in Cambridge when the air is salty and still. Earlier that evening I'd found a wicker chair on the street, and I was sitting in it, with a sheet wrapped around my body, when the phone rang. I was reading the newspaper, a task I was discovering took a lot more time without the help of Arthur.

"Where the hell have you been?" Tony asked. He sounded close to frantic. "I've been trying to get hold of you for over a week now."

"I was going to call you tonight," I said. "I decided to take a vacation. I went to Bermuda for a few days."

"Bermuda? What the hell was it, a honeymoon?"

"Not that exactly. Something like it, I suppose. What about you? What have you been up to?"

He seemed indignant that I didn't know, that I wasn't apprised of the latest developments in his life. "Haven't you been talking to your parents?" he asked.

"Not recently," I said.

"Well, why not? Don't you care what's going on with me?"

I did care, but I was fairly certain I knew.

He let out one of his mournful sighs and began tapping his tongue against the roof of his mouth, making peculiar little clicking noises. When he'd pulled himself together, he said, "I've been in Boston, Pat. I've been making the final plans for the wedding. Don't yell at me, okay? I know I'm taking the easy way out, but what can you do? Loreen and I are going to get married after all, and that's it, there's nothing else to say."

"You don't have to apologize to me, Tony. You had a choice to make, and you made it."

He started clicking his tongue again, and I realized he was probably trying to prevent himself from saying too much or even crying. "Your father called me the night she put off the goddamned shower. He talked to me for almost two hours. Fortunately, he was paying.

Two solid hours, can you believe it? Have you ever talked to him for more than a few minutes?"

"Not that I can remember. What's he like?"

"A sad case, Patrick. One of the loneliest people I've ever talked to, but not a bad guy, in the end. I don't remember half of what he told me, and frankly, I wouldn't care to repeat the half I do remember. All this stuff about his life, your mother. Basically, a two-hour rant about how unhappy he is, as if that's supposed to make me want to go ahead and marry Loreen."

It didn't seem to have occurred to him that my father's strategy had worked.

"Anyway, I listened and listened, and then I told him I couldn't stand to hear any more, that I was sorry for him but he'd obviously just made a lot of bad choices. Then he said, 'Well, maybe I did, but where would you be if I hadn't?' So what could I say to that, Pat? Where *would* we be? I figured I owed it to him."

"To marry Loreen?"

"No, but at least to go to Boston and talk to her. He paid for the plane ticket. That's where I made my mistake. I should have bought it myself.

"I didn't know what I was going to say to her until I saw her at the airport. I guess your father must have told her what time I was coming in. She was standing there waiting for me, and I swear I almost lost it as soon as I saw her. She had on a rain bonnet, one of those cheap things you get at K Mart. Clear plastic, with little blue dogs printed all over it. She always looks like she stepped out of a magazine, and that night she had to go wear that goddamned hat. I don't even think it was raining. Do you know the kind of hat I mean?"

"I have a pretty good idea. I think your mother used to wear one when we were kids."

"Really? I thought there was something familiar about it. Well, maybe that explains it. She looked exactly like your mother standing there. She looked so wounded standing there, I started to apologize. I didn't even know what I was doing. I told her everything, even about Vivian."

"You did?"

"Not all of it, but most of it. I didn't know what else to do. I wanted to make everything right for her."

I rifled through the stash of facile, hopeful comments I kept on hand, but not much seemed to make any sense. If he'd really wanted to set everything right, he'd obviously made precisely the wrong move. But the more I thought about it, the more convinced I was that he'd never intended to break off the engagement in the first place. His affair with Vivian was a passing flirtation with love, with freedom from all the bad choices my parents had made a generation earlier; but the pull back was too strong. I should have read all Tony's tough-guy talk and bravado as a smoke screen sooner, just as Ryan had undoubtedly done.

"Who knows, Tony?" I'd finally said, choosing the easy way out myself. "Maybe you really are in love with her."

"Maybe I am. Maybe I will be. Ryan says no one's in love when they get married."

Later in the conversation, he asked me if I'd moved into the house yet. I told him I wasn't moving after all, that Arthur had bought the place himself and I was staying on at the apartment until the building was sold and I was forced out.

"So that's it? Arthur's out of the picture?" he asked. "Just like that? God, it sounds sad, if you don't mind me saying so."

"I am sad," I told him, "but I can't really say I'm sorry."

He kept silent for a moment and then changed the subject. We made some inconsequential small talk, and a few minutes later he announced he was tired and had to get to bed. The one good thing about having decided to marry Loreen, he said, was that now he was getting some sleep. "Sometimes twelve hours a night," he added.

Over the next six weeks, our phone calls fell off. Tony called less frequently and then only during the day, when we were both at work. I left him a few messages, but he never returned my calls. When we did talk, he sounded more and more the way he had before he met Vivian and had a clear idea of who he was. He dropped his voice down about another octave and put some of the gravel back into it. He bragged to me about the branch office of an insurance company in Louisville he'd observed for two weeks and then shut down completely. "Bunch of lazy bums sitting around doing nothing all day, Pat. They're out now. One computer the size of a phone book replaced the entire crowd."

He berated me for booking flights on foreign airlines, told me my politics were unsound, insisted that my environmental concerns were ninety percent sentimentality. A few times he asked me how things were in my personal life and then warned me not to get too personal. Vivian had cut off all communication with him, and he told me he was getting over her. His life was beginning to fall back into place.

After all the talk over the last few months, I was losing him again. Perhaps he was angry at me for not helping him find a way out of his dilemma, or perhaps he was angry at me for finding a way out of my own, or maybe I simply knew more about his life than he now wanted me to know. Whatever it was, some door between us slammed shut, and I had the feeling it wouldn't open again, unless sometime in the future he wanted to discuss the possibility of divorce.

One evening in early July I called him to ask a question about the honeymoon. Late sunlight was slanting in through the living room windows. His hello was hesitant, and his voice was feeble, as if he'd just woken up. I could hear Puccini playing in the background, the volume loud. I felt as if I'd broken in on some private misery, and without saying hello, I hung up the phone as gently as I could. We hadn't spoken since.

We were barely out the doors of the church before Sharon was lighting up a cigarette. She'd been playing with a pack of Luckies for the last ten minutes of the ceremony. She shook out the match and tossed it to the ground. "Listen, Rita," she said, her hand on my mother's shoulder, "you have to keep reminding yourself that Tony made his own decision. He decided to go through with it, and he did. And there is a chance he actually might be happy. Who knows?"

"We'll keep it in mind," my father said. He was eyeing her cigarettes hungrily. When she offered him the pack, my mother said, "Oh, go ahead, Jimmy. You don't need my permission to dig your own grave."

Although Ryan and Sharon were not officially living together, Ryan did spend most of his time in Cambridge now. The night Tony had flown into Boston, Ryan went back to Sharon's house, as he said he would. I never heard the details of what transpired, but Ryan wasn't seen for three days, and when he surfaced again, he jump-started a new life for himself.

Within a week, Ryan invited my parents to Sharon's house for an elaborate meal he and Sharon had prepared. He announced then that he was leaving the store in the fall and going to work at New Balance. Sharon began telling my father how he could reorganize the business, sell the property, retire with a fortune, and take my mother on a round-the-world cruise. My father claimed he thought Sharon was insane ("All that hair's eating up her brain," he liked to say), but the two of them had struck up an odd kind of friendship. They shared cigarettes and insults, and for all the ways in which she challenged him, I think Sharon loved my father, saw a lot of herself in him.

Sharon wore leather sandals and a yellow sundress to the wedding. The dress barely made it down to the middle of her thighs. Her hair was pulled back off her face in a thick ponytail. I watched her looking across the scorched lawn of the church to where Ryan was being photographed with the bride and groom beside a statue of a minor saint. "Who'd have guessed Ryan would look so good in a tuxedo?" she said.

"You should have seen him when he got married," Rita said.

My father nudged her with his elbow, and she quickly amended her comment. "I guess we all looked better six years ago," she said.

When Mr. and Mrs. Davis came out of the church, holding hands, they gave my parents a nod and a perfunctory smile and moved on. Sharon looked at me and raised her eyebrows. "Your daughter looked great today," she called out. "Which one of you does she take after?"

They were forced to stop. Ignoring Sharon completely, they made a few comments about the weather to my parents. They kept their hands clasped tightly throughout the brief conversation, and when they walked off, my mother said, "They certainly weren't overly friendly."

"Unhappy people usually aren't," Sharon said. "No offense, Jim."

My mother watched them crossing the brown lawn. "They seem happy to me," she said wistfully.

The reception was held in a function room at the hotel near the shopping mall where I'd had dinner with my parents and Ryan months before. The room was one of those blank brown boxes with sliding accordion walls and absurdly decorative gold light fixtures. It was so sealed off from the outside world, it should have been depressing. But the fact that there were no windows came as a relief. The air conditioning was turned up high enough to cool down the city of Miami. Half the women draped sweaters over their shoulders as soon as the icy chill hit them.

I was seated at a table with a group of distant cousins and their spouses and their noisy kids. Most of them lived out in the suburbs, and despite the fact that I mentioned several times that I was a brother of the groom, few of them seemed to know who I was.

It was clear to me that the seating arrangement had been chosen so the only other single person in the room and I would be paired up. She was a former co-worker of Loreen's from the diet center, a short, round woman named Benny. She was silent throughout the meal, ate nothing, and drank so much wine, the waiter had a hard time keeping up with her. When the dancing began, she looked out at the floor for a few minutes, then turned to me and said, "Excuse me, Patrick. I think I have to go vomit."

I couldn't help but wonder whom she would have been teamed up with if Arthur and I were still together.

In that sealed-off room, immune to sunlight and weather, it was hard to tell what time of day it was. As the afternoon wore on, the smell of alcohol and perfume and coffee and flowers made me slightly dizzy. I began to feel I was floating off, far away from the crowds of laughing couples in their bright summer clothes. The band was starting to sound as if it were playing in a distant room.

At the head table, Loreen was leaning across Tony, talking to the maid of honor, Mr. and Mrs. Davis were holding a private conversation, and the photographer was desperately trying to get my parents to sit close enough together so he could get them both in the same picture. Ryan and Sharon were standing still on the dance floor. Ryan had his arms around Sharon's shoulders, talking to her and laughing. Her head was tilted back, and she was blowing smoke up to the ceiling.

I left my table and wandered out into the hotel lobby. The place was deserted, and the sunlight streaming through the tall windows was so bright after the darkness of the function room, I was nearly blinded. I headed for the men's room but was sidetracked by the sight of a bank of phone booths behind the reception desk. There's something about the claustrophobic privacy of phone booths I can't resist. I went into one and closed the door. A yellow light went on overhead, and a fan began to rattle. I inserted my money, dialed a number, let it ring once, and hung up.

When I got back from Bermuda, I kept planning to call Arthur, explain myself, apologize, try to save some trace of dignity, but I wasn't able to do it. I often rode my bicycle out past the yellow house, but only late at night, when I was certain Arthur would be sleeping soundly. The stalemate might have gone on indefinitely. Then we bumped into each other.

It was late on a warm night in the middle of June. Harvard Square was jammed with students and tourists, strolling arm in arm, listening to the street performers set up in the doorways of the closed shops. I was sitting on the steps of the Brattle theater, looking down at the crowds passing in the street. A young woman was on the sidewalk below, strumming a banjo and singing "La Vie en Rose." She had a string of Christmas tree lights wound through her hair. A cool breeze blew down the street. I looked up in the direction of the wind and saw Arthur standing at the edge of the crowd, eating an ice cream cone. He was staring at me, expressionless. It had been only about three weeks since I'd seen him last, but across the crowd, he looked to me like someone I'd known a very long time ago.

I climbed down off the steps and went to him and said hello.

"Hello, sweetheart," he said. "Nice night, isn't it? Out roaming around?"

I shrugged. "I suppose so. What about you?"

"I'm waiting for a friend to get out of the movie. Something I've already seen."

He told me he had half an hour to kill. We walked through the crowds and turned down toward the river. We sat on the edge of a fountain behind the Kennedy School. Arthur took off his shoes and socks and stuck his feet into the cool water.

"Arthur," I said, pointing to his feet, "that's so unlike you."

"Not at all," he said. "I hope you realize I'm a lot angrier with you than I'm letting on right now. The fact is, things are going reasonably well for me at the moment, so I'm in a generous mood. You'd be amazed how attractive you suddenly become to people as soon as they hear you've been left standing at the altar. You should try it sometime."

"The friend at the movies?" I asked.

"Someone I work with."

"Stewart," I said, remembering the name from his conversation with Beatrice.

"That's right. Are you still at the apartment?"

I nodded. "With any luck, the economy won't turn around for a while and the house won't sell."

"Enjoying all that space?"

I stuck my feet into the fountain beside his and admitted that I was.

"Lonely?" he asked.

"I suppose so." I'd left the apartment precisely because the newly spacious rooms seemed too empty. "Not you, I gather."

"No," he said, "not really. I know what I want, Patrick, so it's not as if I have to spend a lot of time by myself trying to figure out a plan for the future."

I could have asked him how things were going at the house, but I didn't want to bring up the subject. We sat at the fountain a little while longer, listening to the splashing of the water and the hum of traffic on Memorial Drive and the indistinct roar of a crowd on a playing field somewhere in the distance.

We walked back to the theater in silence. As I started to wander off, he put a hand on my shoulder and said, "I'm sure we'll be friends again sometime, Patrick, but let's not rush it, all right?"

Later that night, as I was biking along the path by the river, I saw him walking with his arm around a tall, gray-haired man. I couldn't make out their faces, and I'm certain they didn't see me, but as I sped past, I heard Arthur laughing.

Sitting in the phone booth in the lobby of the hotel, I longed to call him, perhaps because there really wasn't anyone I was closer to, no matter how distant we were now. But it was too soon to try and be friends. I missed him, but what I'd told Tony was true, too. I wasn't really sorry.

I left the phone booth and took the elevator to the top floor of the hotel. There was a swimming pool on the roof, enclosed under a high glass dome. The heat and the humidity and the intensity of the sunlight assaulted me as soon as I stepped into the bright greenhouse. I saw a bar at the far end of the pool, and I made my way there, crossing the slippery AstroTurf in my polished shoes. Two people were in the pool, a woman lying on a huge floating sponge and a man hanging on to the side, both inert, prostrate in the heat. I took off my jacket and put on a pair of sunglasses and ordered a glass of soda water.

Everything outside was baking under the sun: the housing and condo developments dotting the suburban landscape, the roads and cloverleafs, and the monolithic shopping mall across the highway, surrounded by the moat of the parking lot, with hundreds of cars shimmering in the sunlight, reflecting the glare back up into the white sky.

I'd had enough of the wedding, of the cake and the dancing couples and my poor forlorn brother. I couldn't face another minute of it. I stayed at the pool drinking water and staring out at the sweltering world, terrified and mesmerized by the sight of it, all that harsh glass and steel and the strangely delicate glistening of the heat waves.

Late in the day, the sun began to turn orange as it dropped lower on the horizon. I stared off into the distance, past the shopping mall and the tangle of roads, to the hills south of Boston. A bank of dark clouds seemed to be rolling in. Somewhere out there, it was raining.

By the time I walked out of the hotel, the breeze had picked up and clouds had dimmed some of the sun's glare. The flags in front of the hotel were snapping in the wind. If anything, the heat was more oppressive than ever as the humidity built; but a storm was definitely moving in, a bank of dark clouds bringing with them violence and electricity and the promise of relief.

The author would like to thank the following for their assistance: the Writers' Room at the Massachusetts Artists' Foundation, Dorset Colony House, the Ragdale Foundation, and George Hodgman.